Concerto in Dead Flat

**Center Point
Large Print**

**This Large Print Book carries the
Seal of Approval of N.A.V.H.**

ॐ श्री गणेशाय नमः

Concerto

in

Dead Flat

A Chris Klick Mystery

RIDLEY PEARSON

writing as

Wendell McCall

CENTER POINT PUBLISHING
THORNDIKE, MAINE • USA

BOLINDA PUBLISHING
MELBOURNE • AUSTRALIA

This Center Point Large Print edition is published in the year 2002 by arrangement with Baror International, Inc..

This Bolinda Large Print edition is published in the year 2002 by arrangement with Baror International, Inc.

The text of this Large Print edition is unabridged. In other aspects, this book may vary from the original edition. Printed in Thailand. Set in 16-point Times New Roman type by Bill Coskrey.

US ISBN 1-58547-157-7
BC ISBN 1-74030-547-7

Library of Congress Cataloging-in-Publication Data

McCall, Wendell.
    Concerto in dead flat / Ridley Pearson writing as Wendell McCall.--Center Point Large Print ed.
       p. cm.
    ISBN 1-58547-157-7 (lib. bdg. : alk. paper)
    1. Klick, Chris (Fictitious character)--Fiction. 2. Private investigators--England--Oxford--Fiction. 3. Americans--England--Fiction. 4. Conductors (Music)--Fiction. 5. Oxford (England)--Fiction. 6. Missing persons--Fiction. 7. Large type books. I. Title.

PS3566.E234 C66 2002
813'.54--dc21
                                                                2001032406

Australian Cataloguing-in-Publication is available from the National Library of Australia.

British Cataloguing-in-Publication is available from the British Library.

CHAPTER 1

P ut your lips together like this," she said. But my lips would never go together like that and we both knew it. Hers were a youthful pink. Pouty. The oversized, sensual lips of a French woman in her early twenties. Placed tightly together—as they were now—they resembled a budding red rose. When parted, they were the exploding morning flower, hungry for the heat of the sun.

My passport lay open on the bed. It showed a man approaching forty with sandy hair and strong features. A head shot, it didn't show my six foot four inches, or my two hundred and ten pounds; and in the cheap photo, my eyes looked more blue than the gray green they actually were. Nowhere did it mention that I was a self-employed, former professional musician who spent his time chasing down recording artists owed back royalties typically "mistakenly" misplaced by creative corporate accounts. On the plane over to Italy I had listed my visit as tourism, but this was in fact a small white lie. I was in Paris on business, and business wasn't looking so good.

Because of an acute lack of space in my Parisian hotel room—room 31, Hotel de Grande École—my tutor, Sylvie, had taken to the bed where she now sat cross-legged, her books and papers chaotically spread before her, her cotton skirt tossed over her ankles, her lips bunched tightly and pointing at me as if inviting a kiss. My mind was not fully on the French language as it should have been.

"It has been twenty years since I've done this," I reminded her. It felt like about that long since my last kiss as well.

"You can do it," she encouraged in her delightful French-scented English. "Think of all the money you are paying me."

That encouraged another try with my lips. Later, when I reviewed our conversation in my head, I realized how the content could have been so easily misunderstood, especially when muffled by a wall and overheard by the hotel guest occupying the room next door. It seems this hotel guest was out on her room's half-balcony during this brief exchange in my tutorial. Believing Sylvie and I were discussing sexual acts for hire, she had promptly complained to management. So the next morning there I was, with my horrible French, trying to explain myself and to defend Sylvie's honor and my own. I apparently did a rather poor job of it: I was denied any more female "guests" in my room by the seventy-some-year-old matron who owned the hotel. It was this family atmosphere I liked so much about the hotel, so I made no attempt to change her mind. My French was so limited at the time, it would have done no good anyway.

I deserved as much for having French lessons at eleven on a Saturday night, but with my days consumed by looking for maestro Stephan Shultz and my attention preoccupied by the distractions of a city I truly adored, there remained few hours for language tutorials. Sylvie's employer, a French language agency, had left the working out of details to tutor and student, and so now, given the objections of my hotelier, either other arrangements would have to be made or I would need to smuggle Sylvie up the fire stairs.

At nine-thirty that Sunday morning, I took a run along the tow path of the Seine under a penetrating September sun. Like wings, or insect legs, Notre Dame's flying buttresses caught and carved this light into a matrix of shadows. Sight of the cathedral stole my breath away, despite its familiarity. An imposing structure, stained by centuries of city smog, witness to a dozen wars and God-only-knows how many millions of pilgrims, it loomed ominously, majestically, triumphantly. Though by nature I was not as religious as spiritual, I nonetheless felt a moment of communion with God. In this, of all places.

Construction on the tow path forced me up stone stairs climbed by a thousand sailors, a thousand times that many lovers, by writers and painters too numerous to name, film makers, politicians and ladies of the night. A sense of that which had gone before—of history—oozed out of every crack in every stone, filled the branches of every tree that lined the boulevards, occupied a chair at every café.

Parisians carried baguettes like New Yorkers carried briefcases, only without the handle: secured beneath an elbow outstretched like a lance, gripped like a tennis racquet, or brandished like a cane.

I marveled at the tempo of this city, which, on God's day, seemed more like a sleepy village than one of the world's premiere urban centers.

My appointment that Sunday noon with a former colleague of Stephan Shultz, one Adrian Pascale, professor of music at the university, took place in his cramped, viewless apartment, a walk-up with just enough space in the living room for a Yamaha grand piano, a four-track tape recorder and a CD collection that would have made even my dear friend Lyel envious. Pascale, a surprisingly young-looking man, had dark expressive eyebrows, long hair pulled back in a pony tail, and powerful, inquisitive green eyes. I already knew from having talked with him on the phone that he spoke exceptional English, which came as a great relief. I was scheduled to visit Sylvie at her place at ten that evening—my French was barely beyond ordering bread and butter. Without his English, I would have been lost.

While he brewed me a cup of espresso I looked through his library of CDs and we discussed at a distance several re-recordings of which I was unaware. The rest of the room's décor amounted to a terra cotta urn containing a dusty bouquet of dried flowers, a mirror alongside the piano bench—either to frame the narcissistic or to check and correct posture—and a framed page of a hand-scribed musical score that bore his signature as well as an embossed star with the number one in its center.

"It was a competition I won," he said, delivering the demitasse. "It's how all this got started," he continued, taking a seat on the piano bench and offering me the room's only chair. Pupil and teacher. I was immediately uncomfortable, both because they still haven't made a chair for six-foot-four and because I didn't want him too complacent about who was running things. When you need answers from people, it's best to have them out of their element.

"Competition?" I inquired politely, not really interested.

"I was sixteen at the time. The assignment, it was to fill the gap in a Bach sonata. We were given the page three and the page five. We were to compose the page four, connecting these two. I won. This page, it won," he said pointing. "At the time, I have the visions of being the next Mozart. Instead," he said sweeping his arm, but his face revealing disappointment, "a somewhat obscure chair in musical history at the university." In the blink of an eye, he checked himself in the mirror. "And you, Mr. Klick. You are a liar, which is why it is I have invited you here to my home. I am fascinated by liars. As an academic, I rub elbows with them daily."

I sipped the bitter coffee, drank in his bitter words, and wondered if the heat I felt in my cheeks could be seen on my face.

He informed me, "The media calls him Steven Shultz, just as you did over the phone when we spoke. However, if you know the man—and you *do not*, despite your claim to the contrary—then you know it is actually Ste-*ph*-an." He raised his finger at me, as teachers tend to do. Then he lit a non-filter Gauloise without offering me one. I took that as a compliment. "Curiosity is a funny thing. I was immediately curious about you."

"My business with Mr. Shultz is confidential," I said.

"You're working for his wife," he stated flatly. I had no idea what he was talking about. I tried not to show it.

He sucked on the cigarette, collapsing his cheeks. When he next spoke, gray exhaust chased his words. "She should relax. These things have a way of blowing over." I forced a smile. Shultz was owed a considerable sum of money in back royalty payments withheld from him by a former recording company. My interest and that of my partner, Bruce Warren, was in the finder's fee for putting him in touch with this money.

Adrian Pascale flirted with the mirror again and gassed

himself up with a chest full of smoke.

"Last week I was in Italy," I explained dryly, mention of the wife clicking into place. "The maestro was recently seen at a cocktail party outside of Todi. An area called Beverly Hills after Beverly Pepper, the artist, who has installed a good many close friends in the area. I was left with the understanding that the maestro was currently visiting here in Paris. *Moi aussi!*" I attempted. "Me too."

He asked incredulously, "You are suggesting the wife did not send you?"

"Perhaps you've read about a certain Japanese company which is in the process of acquiring a major Hollywood studio, complete with that company's recording division? An audit of the recording side of things revealed an accounting 'error' in Mr. Shultz's favor. My partner and I make our living matching people like Mr. Shultz with lost property and misappropriated funds, including royalty money."

His expression changing, he said, "I think I read about you." He killed the cigarette with a twist.

"That would have been my partner, Bruce Warren. He's the attorney side of the team." I forced another smile. "He gets all the press."

"So you are not working for the wife."

"I thought we had already established that." I said hastily, "I heard about the fireworks between Shultz and the cello player. It was suggested that he followed her here. Is that where the wife comes in?" As the question passed my lips it seemed rhetorical.

A knock on the door interrupted any possibility of a reply. He rose and answered the door. What followed was a volley of expletives, in French, as four men—my size or better—barged into the apartment and headed straight for the piano.

Beside himself Adrian Pascale danced around the room wildly, hollering at them in French as they disassembled the Yamaha grand. From the hall, one of them grabbed a dolly, a quilted pad, and some straps. What little of the conversation I understood had to do with Adrian Pascale's astonishment that they would do this on a Sunday. He was appalled that they had tricked him in this way. "*Dimanche?*" he kept shouting, moving from one corner of the tiny room to the other, but not interfering with their work.

The repo boys paid him no mind. They were numb to such complaints. In a matter of a very few minutes the piano, and its legs, had been wrapped, placed onto a dolly, and moved out to the landing. Adrian Pascale attempted to shut the door in disgust when one of them returned for the bench. Pascale finally slammed the door shut.

I stood and offered Adrian his only chair. He glared at me and lit another cigarette. "On a Sunday!" he exclaimed in French. "Two months is all I owe. It's *nothing!* But now, how am I supposed to tutor? My God, I have a student tomorrow night! They came on a Sunday!" he added hysterically.

Bruce and I were not above paying for information—when needed. I considered cutting Mr. Pascale a deal, but I wasn't sure how much he could help, and I feared his hysterics and present concerns would force him into inventing information for me, solely to save his piano. Again I offered him the chair. This time he accepted.

"What is the cellist's name?" I asked, towering over him as he fueled the ember of his cigarette with a disgusting inhale.

He seemed to have forgotten about me.

"Stephan Shultz's woman friend," I reminded.

"Woman? She's not much more than a *girl*, that one."

"Her name," I repeated.

"Allison Star."

"She's here in Paris?"

Numbed by his loss, he mumbled, "Julia is putting her up at her flat. Julia's number is in . . . hand me that small directory, there . . . yes." It was a photocopy of a listing of the music department students.

A minute later I crossed the hole in the room previously occupied by the piano, and reached the door. I had lost him for the time being.

"Who was to expect such trouble on a Sunday?" he asked.

I left him still sitting in that chair, struggling with his cigarette pack, tearing it, giving up on it, and tossing it across the room. He was staring at himself in the mirror. In another minute or two, he would be crying.

CHAPTER 2

The Parisian subway system—the Metro—proved as pleasant as my memories of it. Though old, the rubber-wheeled cars were quiet, the ride smooth, and the spider-webbed network of tracks covered the city like a blanket. Around every corner there seemed to be another Metro stop. The music of street musicians filled the access tunnels. An army of humanity marched past them indifferently. I tossed a few francs into an open violin case.

I had arranged a rendezvous with Allison Star's roommate, Julia, in the gardens of Palais du Luxembourg only a dozen blocks off the fashionable Boulevard Ste. Germaine. Late, I was in a hurry.

We met at the center of the garden, but only after I had sat on a bench for five minutes. Julia had seen too many spy movies.

She explained, "I wanted to make sure you were who you said you were." She was American with curly blonde hair, a pinched chin, and plucked eyebrows. She had the longest fingers I had ever seen on a woman.

"Piano?" I asked.

"Violin. I called your partner as you suggested. I woke him up because of the time difference."

"Bruce is used to it."

"He said you were moderately handsome, very big, and occasionally impatient."

"He's not at his best when he first wakes up."

"The impatience I saw—the way you were tapping your foot."

"That wasn't nerves," I corrected. "That was Brubeck."

"Brubeck?"

"Never mind." I had probably lived enough years to live her life twice.

"There are two others," she said as if it explained something.

"Giving you a hard time?"

"Two of them. Big, like you. They think I'm lying. They think I know where Allison is."

"And you don't." I made it a statement. Her nod confirmed my second dead end of the day. We walked. The French are as particular about their gardens as their cooking. This garden, actually a park, consisted of private lanes and paths, of trees, shrubs, and flowers, all tended in the most minute detail. And sculpture! Sculpture everywhere: a nude, a prince, a lion. We passed a twelve-foot replica of the Statue of Liberty. I stopped and stared.

"Reminds me of home," she said.

"You don't seem worried about her," I observed.

"Allison can take care of herself."

"And these people looking for her?"

"They want *him*, I think."

"They were hired by his wife," I informed her, testing.

A few of the leaves had yellowed. Some children kicked a soccer ball down the path toward us. I let it roll past wishing they would include me in the fun. Their laughter faded behind us.

"Is it love?" I asked sarcastically.

"You think it's so impossible?" she questioned.

"Stephan Shultz," I said, pronouncing it correctly, "has conducted one or the other major orchestra for more years than Allison Star has been alive. When a man in his late forties runs off with an eighteen-year-old, love is often mentioned but rarely practiced."

"Oh, they've been practicing quite a bit. *You* try sleeping in the room next to theirs." We walked on. "Listen, Mr. Klick. They've barely come up for air. She was the first chair in Salt Lake where he guest conducted. He went crazy over her. She managed to keep it professional, but he knew she liked him. She was scheduled for the Pan European University orchestra's performance in Spoleto. He suddenly shows up as the guest conductor—a last minute substitution. As I understand it," she added as an aside, "the work for him back in the States has not been so great, but don't quote me."

"For a week of rehearsal he's hitting on her, and she resists. Then, through a complete coincidence—although I'm no longer so sure about that—they end up at a garden party together near Todi. They eat at the same table. They both drink plenty of wine. This is late August and we're in the same country where Dante wrote *Inferno*. Stephan is in a guest house with a pool. Alone, until he invites Allison for a nightcap. Stephan Shultz. *The* Stephan Shultz. The one hitting on her. Can you understand that? Allison is as good on the cello as any of the Japanese—better, she plays with soul. She sees the pool; she's feeling no pain; she gets naked and takes a swim. Stephan is after her like a shark. Or maybe a torpedo. He professes all kinds of love for her. They make music on the patio furniture, on the living room couch, and he drags her off to bed. My opinion? He had had this planned since Salt Lake. He knew what he wanted.

"She misses section rehearsal—it's her second offense—and the director expels her from the program. Sends her back to Paris. Stephan intervenes and she's reinstated. He's dropped ten years. A critic for the *London Times* says Spoleto is his best Beethoven of his career despite the young orchestra—he's conducting with 'vitality,'" she said, drawing the quotes. "Allison has shown him the fountain of youth. Maybe he has one last shot at a major orchestra back home. But then it's all over. She's scheduled for some studio work here in Paris. Something important—British, I think. He's supposed to close the Aspen festival with the *1812*—the *student* orchestra.

"Stephan *hates* the *1812*. He returns home and cancels, to Aspen's horror. He follows Allison here to Paris and they do their best to keep me up for two weeks straight. Look at this face!" she said. "You see these lines?" she asked, pinching her eyes shut. "They weren't there a month ago."

I didn't tell her so, but she was right. As hard as she tried, she would never be pretty. Her bones weren't right for it. But the lines at her eyes added character—something she might not believe.

"And where is Allison now? With Shultz?"

"No. With her parents. They're on vacation in Sweden. She called the other night—she is seriously love-sick. Stephan can't even call her; her parents don't approve of the romance. They want her in school."

"School?"

"She's due to start Oxford shortly." She answered my puzzled expression. "A compromise. She wanted Juilliard; they were pushing for Michigan State."

"And where's Shultz in all this?"

"No idea. In a way I'm glad they're gone, although I miss *her*. He's not my type. Pompous doesn't begin to describe it. And the drinking. . . ."

The light in Paris is what makes it so beautiful. It was that light that gave the world the Impressionists, that light that colored romance, that light that warmed the grapes and made them fat and sweet on the vine. It laid itself out like a carpet across the park, and it seemed to cleanse everything it touched. It painted our faces a pale yellow, like fresh butter.

All I wanted was to locate Shultz and give him his $190,000—which as yet he didn't know he had coming. My share of our fee—after my partner Bruce's sixty-six percent take—would be somewhere around $15,000. That would buy me a winter in my friend Lyel's guest cabin back in Ridland, Idaho, a ski pass at Snow Lake, and a lot of evenings by the fire. Lyel was one of those friends who, as kids, would have become a blood brother. A former NBA center, now with bad knees, he had enough family money to add several zeros to the lucrative sports retirement package. He dabbled in investments, wined-and-dined young women he seldom bedded, and occasionally played Watson to my Sherlock though our roles were not so clearly defined. He was generous to a fault and as full of good spirit as his cellar was of red wine. He was the kind of friend one missed when away, and one tolerated when close at hand.

I was carrying the paperwork necessary to close the deal. A notarized signature and Stephan Shultz could put his baton wherever he wanted to as far as I was concerned.

"I did hear a rumor," she confessed somewhat ashamedly, "but that's all it is, I'm afraid."

"I make my meal ticket out of rumors," I informed her. She laughed, and I felt it was *at* me. I said defensively, "Fact is substantiated rumor. Have you ever looked at it that way?"

"The thing is, we all brag, you know? Musicians."

I, too, was a musician. But when you played electric bass in country bands and soft rock bands you didn't mention it to people like her. I bit my tongue.

She said, "Impress each other, hope to get some work out

of it." She hesitated. We walked in lock step. "He's bassoon."

"Is he?"

"Eastman graduate. Freelance. Claimed he recorded with Shultz just last week. Here, in Paris. A piece for a Brit composer. It may have been Allison's session."

"Name of the composer?"

"Don't know."

"The studio?" I asked.

"No. Afraid not." She said, "I told you: it's just a rumor. Probably nothing to it."

I pulled out my notebook. She said something about me being a walking cliché. I mentioned a loss of brain cells in one's late thirties, but it didn't land. I wasn't even sure if she heard me. I wrote down what little there was. "How about the bassoon player?" I asked. "You know his name?"

"Randy."

"Randy? That's all?"

"It was in a café. It's not like we're close friends or something."

"You learned he was from Eastman."

"It came up," she told me. "Listen, I don't even remember which café to be honest."

It didn't feel like honest. It felt as if she was being cautious, not involving friends. I told her so. She didn't like it. I felt her eagerness to be done with me. The feeling was mutual.

I asked the obvious question. "How many studios are there in Paris where a person like Shultz would agree to record?"

"There can't be many. Unless I'm right about Allison's

involvement."

She shrugged. She was "Generation X"; the title suddenly made sense to me. "I haven't recorded over here. . . . Not at that level."

"Allison may know," I said. "If you speak to her—"

"I'll ask her. Sure."

I tore off a piece of notepaper and handed her the name of my hotel. She wouldn't ask Allison. It was visible in her body language. She apologized for not being able to help more. It was her way of ending our meeting.

At Lyel's place in Idaho, in order to grow anything in the gardens, one first has to sift the soil to remove the pebbles and river rocks. Back in the heart of the city, I walked for miles: from Notre Dame on the Ile de la Cité, across the Seine, past the Louvre, through the Tuileries Gardens, and finally to the Champs Élysées, all the while sifting. Waiting for something to grow. I grew an amazing thirst for a beer, which I quenched in a tourist café along the boulevard. I had heard it said that if you sit for an hour along the Champs Élysées, you will see someone you know.

I saw Nicole Russell.

At first I didn't believe it. Two years earlier I had helped Nicole find her Labrador Retriever, alive—and her husband, dead. In the process, she had used me as a diversion, as a way to avoid looking at her loss, of denying her husband's culpability in a scam, of avoiding the truth of their marriage: that it had never really meant anything to him but a way at her money. Nicole had lots of money. She had left me those years before to wake up alone on a sheepskin rug in front of a cold wood stove in Lyel's guest cabin. More alone than I had ever known. I had solved a case for her; she had solved a lot more for me.

I was not accustomed to being walked out on. Parting was an act of negotiation, not retreat. We had talked of permanence. By running away, she had confirmed the seriousness of these discussions. We weren't through. And though there had been diversions in the past twenty-four months, my heart knew that Nicole was no diversion.

I didn't react immediately because this was not the first time that I had allowed myself to see her face in a crowd— I had suffered many embarrassing moments surprising complete strangers.

But when she stopped and smiled at a child—a young girl dressed in a pink floral dress with white shoes and a white bow in her hair—that smile gave her away. Self-conscious. Demure. Had she been in costume or disguise, I would still have known her. I knew the sound of her laugh, the way she toyed with her silverware before being served. I knew how effortlessly she took to her own pleasure and how unselfishly she pursued the pleasures of others. I knew she was afraid of lightning and of fast driving. I knew how she smelled after a shower, and how she showered after every ride, and how she rode as often as possible. The others in the street stood still. My head swooned.

I ran after her. Tormented. Incredulous.

She crossed the wide boulevard amid a disorganized army of strangers, the crosswalk's light impatient and fickle. I battled my way through the cameras and Michelin guides, the sandals and the wide-eyed faces, feeling all the while—because of my substantial height—like a lifeguard in his chair. The ocean I looked out upon was made of hair and hats, bald spots and Hermès scarves. I was the odd man out—the long straw. As a result of this advantage, I was able to monitor her progress across the congested boulevard to the sanctuary of the opposing side. To my horror, it was at this moment the lights changed, stranding me on the far shore of a rapidly running river of multicolored metal: of oddly-shaped Citroëns, the box-like Renaults, and the unimaginably tiny Fiat 500s, all unwillingly involved in a race with unshared finish lines. So great was my desire for our reunion that I numbly stepped out into the traffic, saved only by the constraining hand of a stranger.

In the early months of the two years that had passed, I had written a symphonic poem for Nicole entitled just this "Reunion." Having never heard it performed, I heard it now as I heard it then—fifty-four pieces in melodic harmony, sweet, rich, and thoughtful—as close a reflection of her as I could summon given my limited skills as a composer. The arrangement filled my head as visions of her filled my eyes. It was only as the crush of pedestrians surged past me that I realized the lights had changed once again.

She was nowhere to be seen.

Carried away by memory and imagination, I had lost her!

Over the course of my recent career I had found twenty-seven people, male and female, young and old, who had "disappeared"—most through no intention of their own, but as accidents of distance, time, and the failures of an increasingly mobile society. Only a handful of them (I was beginning to put Stephan Shultz in this second category) had not wanted to be found. Nonetheless, and despite an abundance of acquired skills in this department, finding a single woman on the Champs Élysées on an early Sunday evening in the first days of September challenged me to the best of my abilities. Or the worst. People do not vanish. They do not disappear. They end up somewhere you aren't looking. And the trouble with the Champs Élysées was that there were too many places to look. The place swarmed with tourists; the cafés bulged; the side streets offered the illusion of escape and so were equally as crowded. From my genetic crow's nest I scanned the horizon over the waves of humanity. In all likelihood, one of these heads was hers. My adrenaline-charged excitement intruded on my patience—a prerequisite for this type of work on which I typically prided myself. My eyes wouldn't settle long enough on any one spot to articulate judgment. They skipped across the surface like a flat stone hurled across the water—randomly, and with a life of their own. Panic prevailed where usually I could maintain control. There is a science to such situations that dictates the creation of search quadrants on the outermost fringes, and requires an organized progression through the ranks of people. Thus one contains what or who is about to escape. But such systems are valueless to eyes fueled by emotion rather than logic. I had no thoughts of sector sequencing or divisional proportions. I had the poignant memories of happiness to battle. I had the palpable reality of her skin against mine, of her wine-scented breath laughing from across the pillow.

I had an erection.

In the middle of a million strangers, in the midst of an anxiety attack measurable on the Richter scale, I found myself engorged with an unbridled desire—a physical, undeniable desire—to be reunited with my soul mate. I was in love.

CHAPTER 3

For two days I wandered Paris in a stupor. I had no idea where I was going or why I had come here in the first place, only the memory of a face and a repeated series of failed attempts to match it with a living, breathing woman. I tried a dozen of the more fashionable hotels, and although she could afford them, it occurred to me at some point that they were not her style. She would be down a narrow street in a room with a view. Her hotel would have the finest patio garden in all the city. The room would have exposed beams and a wrought-iron bed that squeaked if you made love too passionately. It would have lace curtains and a deep bath, no TV, perhaps not even a phone, and no one in the place would speak English.

I would never find her. This I began to believe by the end of the second day, soaked through as I was by an afternoon rain shower, discouraged and hungry. I had slipped back into my swamp of hallucination and fantasy where every woman I passed took on her features in reflection. I saw her through shop windows, across the street. I saw her hailing a cab and blurring past on the Metro while I stood, stationary, on the platform. That any human being could be so single-minded as I was for those two days would confound even the most highly acclaimed experts. I suffered from a singular psychology: monism. Finding Nicole meant everything. Food, shelter, sleep—these were for those without purpose. On four separate occasions, I returned to that very crosswalk where I had first spotted her. I allowed the same stream of humanity to rush past me, me a full head higher. I sifted them as I had previously sifted my ideas—by weight, shape, and importance.

Numb, blind even, I wandered nomadically through the city sights on a private pilgrimage. I was the returned war veteran in shock: I drew looks of concern, consternation, and outright fear. The Parisians shouted what had to be insults. Even a man I interrupted as he peed against a building found me frightening enough to zip himself up and hurry away. Several messages went unanswered. When the manager of the hotel showed up at my room with a doctor in tow, I knew I had trouble.

I was examined, fed some soup, and put to bed. Two hours later, I sneaked out the back door and continued my search.

In our brief time together, I had infused Nicole with a love of bird watching and jazz. Concept or reality, I firmly believed her enthusiasm genuine, and so I thought I might find her in Birdland, a jazz club named for Charlie Parker. My clothes were fresh, but my appearance, hardly. In a jazz club, I fit right in.

Birdland was divided into two clubs, alto and tenor—upstairs and down—both with live bands. The restaurant was downstairs. And tonight, Scott Hamilton: one of the best in the Ben Webster school of tenor sax. Scott is an American, and I had met him once, a long time ago, in Providence before he had hit the big time, and before I had fallen short. His playing charged the room. You couldn't have gotten more people in the club with a shoe horn, not with all the olive oil in Italy. Just standing there was a two-pack-a-day habit. A busty waitress in a micro skirt squirted through the horde with a steaming pizza hoisted overhead.

We were briefly intimate—that pizza and I. An air traffic controller would have put my face and that pepperoni pie as a "near miss."

A benefit of height is that you never long for a better seat. I was standing, but it's all the same thing. I was alone, up in the smoke belt, the upper atmosphere of the cave like club where my only obstacles were the funnel lamps and the *"sortie"* signs. I drank a dark rum and tonic and saw God—I needed more food in me before I tried that again. A sweaty girl of eighteen, wearing bicycle shorts and a halter top, somehow ended up straddling my leg from the side. She was even hotter where her legs met, and if she started pedaling I was in trouble. She dismounted, as embarrassed as I was, and punched her way across to a table.

She sat down next to Adrian Pascale. Seeing him, I recalled the section of his CD collection devoted to jazz. By the look of him, he'd been drowning his sorrows, perhaps over the loss of his piano. The woman who had accidentally humped my thigh was his companion. She placed a beer in front of him and took the chair he had been defending. She stuck her beer bottle under the halter top and held it between her breasts. If you believed her face, that felt pretty damn good.

I navigated a route toward their table, elbowing my way through the crowd. Scott soared through a ballad, which helped everyone relax. If it had been a swing tune, I never would have made it.

I reached Pascale's table, but he didn't notice me; his full attention seemed to be on this young woman's casual and revealing efforts to cool her chest. I had the better view from above.

When the ballad finished, Scott took a break and everyone seemed to move at once. I shouted down, *"Bonsoir*, Monsieur Pascale."

He peered around for the source of the greeting, found me, and looked blank.

"Chris Klick," I said. "Stephan Shultz."

He nodded, but I could see he still didn't remember me. His teenybopper looked up and smiled. She withdrew the bottle and allowed the halter top to hold her snugly again, but by then I knew her intimately. Her smile grew wider. *"Bonsoir,"* she responded. Pascale looked at me again and tried to place me.

I reintroduced myself, "Chris Klick. Your apartment. I'm looking for Shultz."

He nodded. I was pretty sure it registered. I squatted alongside the woman with a view of Pascale.

I had a headache and still suffered from my two days of disorientation. The rum made the room louder. I found it hard to concentrate. Stephan Shultz and his bedroom melodrama didn't stand up well next to the thought Nicole was somewhere in this city. Or had she left? That possibility was so unbearable that I ruled it out completely. A couple of postcards is all I had had in the past two years. And then a thought struck me like a thunderbolt—what if she had seen *me* that afternoon on the Champs Élysées? What if she had deliberately run away?

They were both staring at me.

"They take your piano too?" the bimbo asked.

"Mr. Klick is looking for a person, not a piano," Pascale informed her, speaking English for my benefit. "It is not

26

going so good, I will assume," he said to me.

"Not well at all," I confirmed, thinking only of Nicole.

"You have come here to find me?"

"Someone else," I told him. But to look at him he didn't believe me.

"A woman," the bicycle enthusiast proclaimed, drilling me with her eyes. She was no bimbo. You look a person directly in the eye, and you know. She introduced herself as Ami. We shook hands lightly. Hers was cold, from the beer. Her eyes were a smoky gray with hard black outer rings and large absorbent pupils. "An *important* woman," she qualified in a throaty voice.

I said to Pascale, "There are men looking for Shultz. Have they contacted you?"

"Stephan Shultz?" Ami said, incredulous. "*You* know Stephan Shultz?"

"Would I tell them anything?" Pascale asked, shaking his head. "These men were twigs," he said.

"Thugs," I corrected.

"The wife, she is to want only the money. Only the money." His face went apoplectic. He looked quickly away and in doing so announced his slip.

"The money?" I inquired.

"What money?" echoed Ami. "*The* Stephan Shultz?"

Pascale displayed the shifting eyes of a mind busy in damage control—his imagination was hard at work assembling a believable story line to feed me. Thankfully, I had experienced such tactics often enough that I could move a square ahead while he was busy fitting pegs in holes.

To me, the royalty money owed Shultz was "*the money.*" But Pascale was talking about Shultz's wife. Her pursuit of her husband was not about love. "A woman scorned," was one thing. Scorned and broke was another. Jealousy combined with poverty is a dangerous combination.

"He took money from his wife?" I asked. "Cleaned out the accounts?"

Pascale shrugged. He looked a little too drunk to trust.

I tried again. "That is why she's after him? The money, not the running away?"

"Why should I talk to you? Why don't you go away?"

"Why don't I buy the next round?" I offered.

"So stay if you like."

"Shultz recorded here in Paris recently," I said, looking for any kind of response, but not picking up much.

"Did he?"

"You could get your piano back," I told him.

His eyes cleared noticeably. He studied me distrustfully. "My piano?" he asked. "How?" A drowning man reaching for the piece of driftwood.

"The name of the studio where he recorded," I suggested.

"I could do that," he sounded surprised.

"I'll pay the back rent."

"You call me tomorrow," he said, blinking furiously, trying to quell the double vision.

I said to her, "Will you remind him of this, please?"

"You think I'd forget my piano?" he asked me. But I checked with her; she was far more clear-minded. She nodded and smiled sympathetically.

I left some francs for the next round. I had lost my thirst. Nicole had come back to haunt me. From her, there was no escape.

CHAPTER 4

To my surprise, Pascale came through.

The studio's address was a long Metro ride from the center of the city. The air smelled of fall, of burning leaves. As in so much of the city, no structure stood over four stories, lending a sense of town, of community.

I walked through an open market where small stalls, manned by men and women with weathered, expressive faces, offered up everything from live birds to Duracell batteries. I bought some postcards and an apple so hard and tangy that I returned and bought two more and ate them both. I finished up lunch with fifty grams of goat's cheese and a baguette. The French make the best cheese in the world. I was going to have to increase the length of my morning runs.

Opera poured out of an open window where an old woman looked down at me with cataract eyes. I called out the address to her. She pointed right and signaled a right turn.

After four attempts, I found the studio down a narrow lane of cobblestone. From the outside it looked like a warehouse front from an earlier century. The inside included a full sound stage with three grand pianos, a dubbing room, and an engineering room teeming with the latest digital equipment. There were five chain-smokers at the controls. They spoke pidgin English, but far better than I spoke my pidgin French. They were in the process of mixing what sounded like a jingle. Two of them, it turned out, were clients.

When I mentioned Stephan Shultz, a fat one pointed to a

previous date on a calendar. The recording session had taken one day, the mixing, three more. Shultz had conducted a large orchestral piece. An original piece.

The room swam in smoke and reeked of burned coffee. Two of them continued mixing. If my translation was correct, they had recorded an advertising jingle for a toilet bowl cleaner. They treated the mix as if it were Brahms.

"Stephan Shultz," I repeated, just to make sure we understood one another.

The fat one, a man named Henri, nodded vigorously.

"A woman with Shultz?" I asked.

He nodded. *"Mon dieu!"* he said. I only caught pieces of what followed. "So young, no? She trouble for him. All men like this girl, yes? Very pretty. Very sexy."

"She flirts?" I asked.

He smiled and shrugged, not understanding.

"Lolita," I said.

"Yes, yes," he agreed.

"Where is Shultz now?" I tried.

He shook his head no.

"The composer?"

"David Thompson," he said.

"The American composer?" I asked.

"Thought he was a Brit," Henri said. "The two are close friends. This much is obvious."

"Thompson was the composer," I said, pointing to the studio monitors to clarify. "Shultz, the conductor."

Henri grinned. "Of course!"

"Where is Thompson now?" I asked.

"London, I assume. Where else?"

London. This came as a relief to me. Since seeing Nicole

I had begun to dislike Paris for hiding her from me. I needed to get away from the city or else I was doomed to keep looking around every street corner for her. London. I liked the sound of that.

"An address for Thompson?" I asked.

"Yes." Henri led me into a cluttered office and dug through a Rolodex. He had a phone number, but told me it was a service. The London address was in Knightsbridge.

I thanked him for his efforts. He gave me a cassette tape that had been recorded in his studio, and a business card.

CHAPTER 5

The woman was a stranger to me. She waited in the hotel's small sitting room reading a paperback. My proprietress directed me there and headed off to bring us some tea. When you're six-foot-four, you don't enter a room quietly no matter how little noise you make.

She looked up and set the book down, marking her page. She had long nails and soft hands. Her tan was Hamptons dark. Her bleached-white teeth, with their perfect bite, reminded me of a toothpaste ad. I wondered how long it took her to ready herself in the morning—she had the look of a record-setter. Every hair was in place, every piece of clothing pressed and starched. She had money written all over her. "Mrs. Shultz," I tried, hoping to surprise her with my insight.

"The point is," she began, as if we'd been negotiating for the last hour, "we both want the same thing—to find Stephan." She glanced up at me. "You're not going to stand there the whole time, are you? Why are tall men always so

. . ." She couldn't find the word.

I interrupted. "We have different motives," I told her. "You want to take money *from* him, and I want to give money *to* him."

"Yes, well have you thought about giving it to me instead?"

"I wouldn't mind, but I need your husband's signature."

"I could forge it." She was only half kidding.

"You've hired people to find him. They talked to Adrian Pascale and to Allison Star's roommate. They're making my job more difficult. People don't like them."

"You don't mind me saying so," she said, "you look as if you could use some help."

"Pigmented contacts have the same effect on me." My wandering around in search of Nicole had taken its toll. I wasn't in a mood to apologize. "What if I promised to let you know where he is the minute he's signed my papers?"

"No good. What he took is legally mine. Every penny. And I'm getting it back."

I didn't believe that Shultz would walk away from that kind of money—unless he thought it was bait intended to trap him. "You'd be smarter to call off your dogs and let your husband burn himself out. He'll come back on hands and knees."

"He'll come back in leg irons," she corrected. "I don't want him back. I want the money he stole."

"*Your* money?"

"Family money, Mr. Klick. My family's money. Money protected by a pre-nuptial. Stephan spends *much* more than he earns."

"I'm sorry," I said, "but don't maestros command considerable fees?"

"Only those who have a home, and Stephan lost his. He has a reputation as a drinker. St. Louis passed. Seattle. San Diego. The only money for him is in composing for film—and he needs to be in LA right now for that. He's a drunk, Mr. Klick . . . and *a thief!*"

"I need his signature."

"I've lost a husband to a tart with an overactive F clef and a tightly strung bow who is apparently willing to accept an older man's seed for the hope of climbing the international concert ladder. I intend to recover what is legally mine regardless of where Stephan's mid-life crisis and his drinking habits take him. He cleaned out everything that wasn't nailed down—over three hundred thousand dollars in cash including a line-of-credit. Electronic transfers, forged signatures—the man's a thief. At present, I'm living off of credit cards and the charity of a few close friends while he's burning through my liquidity. It's an embarrassing, uncomfortable, and compromising situation. The sooner it's over the better."

"You won't find him," I said honestly.

"Stephan is a public figure, Mr. Klick. He can't hide forever."

"Just long enough to bury your inheritance," I said. She paled noticeably, causing me immediately to reevaluate my assessment of her tan. "Certainly you've considered that possibility," I suggested. "My partner and I have built a business on finding hidden assets. It's the crime *du jour*. Monkey with a few numbers and you're suddenly a lot richer. If your husband is given enough time, that money will disappear."

"Exactly right. So why don't you take a short vacation?"

"Because I'm ahead of you," I answered. "You need *me*, not those goons you've hired. Are you aware your husband did some studio work while he was here in Paris?"

She seemed flustered. "Studios are on my list of course." She fidgeted. "In truth, I believe I have a far better chance of finding Stephan in a hotel bar than in a studio. He loves the ambience of the grand hotels, and he loves being recognized—which happens quite often given the clientele— and even better, he loves it when the other person is buying. My husband has champagne tastes. He doesn't own a single piece of wash-and-wear clothing and he doesn't drive himself anywhere—not that he minds driving, but when he arrives he expects doors to be opened for him. His suits *and* shoes are custom made in London and he owns six pair of reading glasses, not for home use, but because scores are printed in a variety of type sizes and Stephan has only a few scores committed to memory. That is a vanity reserved for youth, and for those who drink less." She was looking right through me. I made no attempt to stop her. Knowingly or not she was feeding me information, some of it extremely useful. "You know, his *real* genius is composition—or was. I'm afraid he's lost that now. He's drunk it right out of himself. *That* is the source of the drinking—the composing. The loss of a brilliant talent. It pains him to conduct the work of others. His true love has always been the pen, not the baton. He has an amazing mind, Mr. Klick. In many ways I feel sorry for him. He has had plenty of offers from Hollywood—sound tracks. But he abhors the idea. What he fails to realize is that this is the only viable option for symphonic composers. The film industry is what the church once was in terms of sponsoring art. But Stephan will have none of it. He's a purist. And he has watched far less talented composers rise to heights he never dreamed possible. We are all governed by dreams."

Her talk of dreams made me think of Nicole. Was this love that I felt, or a three-year-long "knee-jerk" reaction to rejection? I feared the answer. I feared trying to win her back as much as I did the idea of a future without her.

"Composing," I said.

"Exactly," she replied.

"And by being here, what is it you hope to accomplish?"

"It has been extremely frustrating to be so far removed. On the off-chance we find him and he's willing to talk to me . . ." Her voice trailed off, and her eyes grew distant.

"These things can get rough, you know?"

"Rougher than they already are?"

"Let me explain how it works. Your husband comes to realize that you and your representatives are in pursuit of him. He's taken all the money, so the stakes are plenty high. He has hired representatives of his own—and here's where it gets sticky. You put a couple of opposing generals in the same room and lock the door, you think they'll fight it out? Hell no, they won't. They negotiate. But if each of them sends troops into the battlefield the result is bloodshed. History books are full of it. Same thing here. Instructions get fuzzy. Messages get blurred. These troops are itching to do something *other* than deliver subpoenas. If they don't get results, they get leaned on by whomever you're paying." She seemed to be elsewhere. Her eyes wandered. "Are you bored by all this?" I asked.

"I can't see that happening."

"Let me ask you this: What do you suppose happens to people when they fear they may lose their job?—and *all* so-called investigators think about such things constantly. What happens if they locate your husband, but he is guarded? What happens if the guys on your husband's side find their position weakening? I'll tell you what they do— and they do it without any permission—they cut to the source, to *you*, Mrs. Shultz, and they take action to convince you to call off the hounds."

"Violence?" she barked. "Directed at me?" Said with the innocence of a child.

"Money and love are two of three reasons people *kill*," I informed her. People in her position seldom consider such things.

"And the third?" she asked in her best pupil's voice, more interested in trying to complete the test rather than to understand its content.

"Power," I said. "The point being that both your husband and you have put the other at risk by involving so-called 'professionals.' "

"The firm I have employed would *never* take such tactics," she said.

"It's like insurance companies," I explained. "Each is underwritten by the other. You hire company A in New York who then enlists the services of company B in Paris, who, because they are overworked, seek the temporary assistance of company C. This kind of work is subcontracted. But violence is just the most extreme example, not by any means the norm. If I'm working for your husband, how do I get you to call off your boys? I pressure you. How do I do that? Metaphorically, sometimes literally, I search your closets. Are any of us so clean we can't be pressured? Only card-carrying Mormons and children below the age of five are *that* clean, I'm afraid. Are you so pure, Mrs. Shultz? I'm not. And it's worth thinking about before you take this too much further. Ironically, the closer you get to your husband, the greater you put yourself at risk."

"You're trying to scare me. To scare me off! Are *you* working for him, Mr. Klick?"

"If you don't have it already, I'm sure that soon enough you'll have the report on me. And I doubt you'll find it very interesting. How many of us are really so interesting that we make good reading? Not me, that's for sure. I'm single, of limited net worth, of a dubious background in the field of popular music—a former dishwasher, pizza chef, and crew member for the America's Cup—we were knocked out of competition by a torn spinnaker, which, by the way, was proved months later to be the result of sabotage. And that brings me right back to where we started. It's an imperfect world, Mrs. Shultz. As to whose side I'm on: I'm on my own. I am keenly rooted in selfishness in all of this."

"You have a job to do," she said cynically, drumming her painted nails on the tea cup. "I don't think I like you, Mr. Klick."

"Attitudes change," I said.

CHAPTER 6

If there isn't one, there should be a maxim about not voicing one's concerns for fear of living them—a distant cousin to "Be careful what you wish for." By explaining things to Mrs. Shultz, I had called to the spirits. I just didn't know it yet.

My intention was to enjoy a moment of my own charity. I selected a café across the street from, but with a good view of, Pascale's apartment. If I had my French straight, the piano was scheduled to be returned within the hour. I ordered a kirsch. It went down comfortably. I ordered a second while I mentally ran down a list of calls to make in preparation for my departure to London. I owed Bruce a report. I hadn't spoken with him since being sidetracked by Nicole and I needed to justify the expense of freeing Pascale's piano. There were the usual travel arrangements to be made. I kept David Thompson's name off my list. The composer of the recording Shultz had conducted was not for the telephone—I wanted to speak with him in person. I did want to check if he was in London at the present. I decided to call Lyel for that one. Lyel knew the right people to ask. Of the two of us, Lyel was the opera house half—I was more the road house variety.

When I first spotted them, I didn't know if they were hers or his. But because there were two of them, and because Julia, Allison's former roommate, had mentioned a pair, I decided they were on Stephan Shultz's payroll, not hers.

They wouldn't have had much trouble spotting me, so in a way we were already introduced. I watched them directly; they played it more subtly.

The piano was delivered one hour and thirty minutes late; that passes for on time in Paris. I was into my second espresso at that point and was debating a third except that each one cost four U.S. dollars; and even though on an expense account that seldom went questioned, that was rich for my blood.

I left the café and walked the ancient streets of Paris, down narrow alleys with wood-painted signs, past milliners and bistros and dress shops and the ever-present *boulangeries*. I avoided tourists; the Parisians avoided me; we all avoided each other. Life in the big city.

The minute I left the café, that somewhat trustworthy sixth sense of mine told me that my two friends were going to want to chat with me.

I had no desire to be roughed up, and I could feel it coming. They probably thought I knew more than they did. Perhaps they even knew about my meeting with the maestro's wife and believed us professionally connected. That could hurt my efforts—I needed it straightened out. Competition has ways of turning everyone ugly. I had to pee badly, but I thought they might try to "debrief me" in the men's room. No better time to confront a person than when he's exposed to the porcelain.

I stopped at another café to force them into a commitment. Would they pass me by or stop? They stopped and took a table. I drank another espresso. A few minutes later, I surrendered to my nagging bladder. The toilet was something to behold—a porcelain "squatter" with no lid, no seat, just two textured treads on either side of what amounted to a hole in the floor. In the middle of my relief I heard the handle of the door rattle behind me, and I guessed it was one or both of the men following me. A bathroom is a great place to isolate a target. I knew Mickey Rooney couldn't have fit through the room's window. The only available weapons I could find were a plastic-handled toilet brush and a canister of a white powdered cleanser. I

39

flushed the toilet by yanking on a long chain; it sounded as if I had let loose Niagara Falls.

These Frenchies were polite. They waited for me outside the café. I paid for my coffee with my right hand. My left hand remained in my pocket clutching my handful of detergent.

They both wore city clothes. One guy was thin in the face but thick elsewhere. He looked as if he were at a carnival and was poking his head through a cutout of a weight lifter. He had prematurely graying hair, eyelashes as long as Mrs. Shultz's, and enough five o'clock shadow to require two shaves a day. He wore a gold chain instead of a tie. He looked a little glassy-eyed—they both did—which I hoped was the result of coffee, not drugs.

His partner looked a little dumpy. Not as stout. He had puppy-dog brown eyes and a rebuilt nose. Despite his partner's size, this was the one who worried me; he carried a disturbing confidence and an unflinching stare. He had smooth, almost feminine skin, soft features, and a long neck. He kept his hair slicked back and wore a pretty good imitation silk suit—some kind of synthetic I hadn't seen— penny loafers without a dime to their name, and a snappy pair of multicolored socks.

I complimented him on those socks first thing. I tried English as a test. When the one with the weight-lifter's body grinned, I knew we wouldn't have to try French. The one in the synthetic suit remained impassive. He finally said, "Why don't we walk you to your hotel?" in an accent I envied. The French speaking English is a beautiful sound to the ear, even when made by thugs.

We started on our way as a trio, my left hand still in the

pocket. They escorted me between them, each standing just out of easy reach. Professionals. A spark of heat shot up my spine.

"So how can I help you?" I asked.

"We have much to discuss," said the synthetic suit, who walked on my left.

"You're wondering about my association with Mrs. Stephan Shultz," I told him. Weight lifter wasn't talking; he seemed to be enjoying the walk. He lit a cigarette and seemed hungry for the smoke. I didn't know what to make of him.

The suit said, "That is a good place to start."

"Your English is quite good," I said.

"Better than Pascale's?" he asked, supplying me with information whether intentional or not. Questions are loaded with information; that is why it is so important to choose them carefully. Maybe he was tired, maybe he was letting me know they were keeping an eye on me.

"Listen," he said, "you are very big, but there are two of us. Why don't you show us your left hand." I hesitated— caught! "If you do not do this, then things will become most unpleasant. You understand?"

I kept my hand in my pocket, mainly out of obstinacy. I also hoped to draw at least one of them closer to me so that left hand might be effective. "You know, I think I would rather walk alone."

"The left hand, please."

"Fellas, it's just not a night I feel like company."

"Please . . ." the cheap suit added, his impatience mounting.

The weight lifter continued with the cigarette.

Out of the corner of my eye, I saw the cheap suit give a slight nod. They steered me down a narrow alley that smelled of male cats. My heart raced.

They were going to have to come awfully close to me if they were going to force my hand out of my pocket. The limited light of the alley played nicely for me. I withdrew my left hand as requested and was able to wipe it quickly on my pants before exposing it as empty. Satisfied, the short man in the synthetic suit actually thanked me. We stopped, the two of them facing me.

"You are here in Paris in what regard?" he asked, unwilling to stand too close to me. More professional than I might have guessed by their looks.

"I'm looking for your employer. But *not* for the reasons you think."

"You would be best to let this business go," he said. "It shouldn't concern you."

"It *does* concern me. You could do me a tremendous favor," I suggested. "You could ask Mr. Shultz to telephone me at my hotel. You boys know damn well that I have no way to trace the call, so what's the harm? One phone call."

"The reason, it does not matter. You understand? You should go home. You should forget all of this. No? Much better for you."

They had lulled me into a false sense of security by getting me talking. I never saw the cue, if one was given. The weight lifter moved with speed of a person half his size. He turned me and hit me hard in the lower back, then once in my left ear. I reached into my pocket and dusted his face with cleansing powder. He screamed like a stuck pig. My ear rang, sounding as if I had been swallowed by a crashing wave. The other one kicked me on the outside of my left knee. I folded up like a deck chair. The top of his foot caught me in the forehead and laid me open like a *chaise longue*. He rolled me over and took my wallet. To my surprise, he tossed me all my cash, and a Visa card, but kept the wallet.

I was still trying to orient myself as I heard the sound of loafer leather on cobblestone. The one guy was still moaning—and not seeing real clearly, I had to guess. They were gone by the time I rolled back over. Age and experience had long since taught me to assess my injuries before jumping to my feet.

I was going to have trouble peeing for a few days. I wouldn't be running any marathons. For that matter, I wouldn't be *walking* very well. But the knee wasn't broken; he could have easily broken it had he wanted to. My forehead felt bruised.

I limped back to the hotel in considerable pain. Holed-up in my room, I took a bath to soak out some of the pain. I went to bed angry and sore. All I wanted to do was give a guy some money. Why did everyone want to make that so difficult for me?

In the morning I got a call from American Express. My wallet had been returned to one of their offices. The call surprised me—I thought it might be a trap—until I realized I had used my AMEX card to secure my room. It was an advertised service.

Don't leave home without it.

CHAPTER 7

S hultz and his goons now knew my name and my Los Angeles address. Probably a lot more than that as well.

One of the reasons I often retreat to Lyel's guest cabin in Idaho after a job is to stay away from my business mailing address. Why assist the enemy? This work carries with it some of the attributes of war: even when declared over, not all the parties necessarily know a truce has been called.

Because of my mentioning her, they probably thought I worked for the wife. Maybe they had even seen her visit the hotel; I couldn't be sure.

On the other hand, if they were good little Boy Scouts, they would earn their merit badges by finding out what Bruce and I did as an incorporated entity. I had proper business cards in that wallet. This did not require computer searches. Shultz or his goons could call Bruce Warren and confirm my purpose. I wasn't in Paris to sightsee, after all.

If truth be known, my first priority remained finding Nicole. How I longed to hear the melody of her voice, to witness the music of her movement, to measure the quiet cadence of her heartbeat. I knew what gentleness lay inside this woman. I had previously been its focus, and under its penetrating warmth had experienced a profound sense of enchantment, of unequivocal satisfaction, of deep, soothing rest. It had touched me like a drug, this comfort. Was there fault in wanting more? Folly? She had walked out on me, but some forms of rejection, I allowed myself to believe, were a sign of affection.

Qu*'y a-t-il?"* Sylvie asked me in French. I had just gotten off the phone with Lyel, who had made me explain everything in detail. Lyel couldn't stand to be away from what he loosely termed "the excitement." He had agreed to hunt down the composer David Thompson for me. "Your leg," Sylvie said, pointing out my limp.

"I twisted it, running."

"And your forehead?"

"Did we have a lesson scheduled?"

"Yes." But her cheeks blushed and I didn't remember any such lesson. She wasn't carrying any books. She looked around my hotel room impatiently. Uncomfortably. "I came up the back stairs," she explained.

Silence, for being so empty, can carry extraordinary weight. We both spoke at once, though neither of us said anything much.

She went to the door, and locked it. I swallowed hard. Then she turned around and aimed her huge brown eyes at me. "I thought we could eat dinner," she said still in English. English! Why lock the door, I wondered, if dinner was the call?

"Dinner sounds good," I admitted. I hadn't eaten in days. My stomach was running on coffee.

"Maybe work up an appetite first," she said nervously. She stepped up and opened her arms. Europeans were different, I reminded myself. I held her, I could feel her trembling. I could feel myself respond. We embraced long enough for the Jello to leave my legs and the tremors to quiet down.

"I don't usually do this," she said.

"No," I agreed.

Loneliness is so easily calmed by an embrace. I hadn't realized how empty I had been until that moment. It creeps up on you, emptiness. It's a parasite that sucks you dry with you none the wiser. And all the beer with the Lyels of the world couldn't fulfill the promise of a single hug from a woman like Sylvie. For a long, dreamy moment, I considered what it would be like to sleep with her, and I imagined the whole more than the sum of its parts. But I eased away, and she mistakenly took this as the next step and began unbuttoning her blouse. Her bra hid little—two triangles of gossamer silk. She had flawless skin and a coy smile. I wasn't sure how to stop this without hurting her feelings. Thankfully a knock came at the door. I called out, "*Un moment!*"

Blushing severely, Sylvie recovered her buttons quickly, stepping out of the door's line-of-sight in the phone-booth-sized room. I moved to the door, expecting Shultz's goons.

Behind me, I heard Sylvie duck into the bathroom. I placed my right foot on the floor just inside the door in order to block it should my visitors attempt to enter uninvited. I prepared myself for the possibility of self-defense. All these measures, each in proper order, fell neatly into place in an almost effortless, automatic way. Even so, I prepared myself for nearly everything—except what I saw next as I opened the door.

I stood face to face with Nicole.

She had never looked more beautiful.

Memories and images mutate in the subconscious given enough time. Over the last two years, I had reinvented

Nicole in my mind. Now, face to face, I saw that time had indeed been her friend. She had not aged, but ripened. Her skin glowed, her eyes shone, vivid with excitement. Anticipation jumped from her like hot sparks. I could smell a sweet musty fragrance, like a greenhouse in full bloom. I felt terribly afraid of her.

She offered a timid look of puzzlement. We embraced. She sputtered something about having called Lyel on a whim and discovering I was in Paris. I told her about having seen her on the Champs Élysées. We both laughed nervously, and let go one another.

"May I come in?"

I hesitated, but she pushed past me. She stopped at the foot of the bed.

"Sylvie?" I called out, trying to sound innocent but feeling my face flush. I told Nicole, "My tutor is here. Sylvie?" I repeated.

She looked around, and I knew immediately that it was for books or note pads. Seeing none, Nicole asked, "A tutor?"

"Friends," I answered, as I felt her withdraw. I could sense it unraveling.

"This was stupid of me," she said. "I should have called up from the desk . . . She said women aren't allowed. I said I was your sister."

Sylvie opened the bathroom door, looking incredibly guilty—actually embarrassment over coming-on to me. She introduced herself, extending her hand.

The magical feeling of a reunion, of a *rendezvous*, was shattered. My mind was scrambling to save the pieces.

"I am teaching Mr. Klick the French language," Sylvie

said, made nervous by the long silence.

"Yes," Nicole replied, her eyes now cold, her voice fragile.

Sylvie came off as a child caught by her parents. Nicole seemed shell-shocked. I was tongue-tied. She had this all wrong. Did she know how long I had waited for this moment? My feelings for her had compelled me to walk the streets of this city for days on end in search of her. I had a hundred things to say waiting on the tip of my frozen tongue. The three of us seemed to be awaiting stage direction.

"Nicole," I said, my voice a little too pleading.

"Bad timing." Nicole did not look at me. She turned and walked out.

I should have followed, but my legs would not move.

Sylvie edged uncomfortably toward the door. "I'm sorry for this," she said in English.

I nodded.

She kissed me lightly on the check, said, "*Enchantée*," and left.

I drank enough for six that night, alone in a small Greek restaurant in the Latin Quarter. I decided to work through Lyel. He could get to Nicole, make her hear the truth.

In the meantime, work was all I had. I set my sights on London. I was gone from Paris within twelve hours. Good riddance.

ENGLAND

CHAPTER 8

In London I was nearly killed—twice—by forgetting to look right at the crosswalk, and I spent more money than I should have in those first few days because my mental calculator was stuck somewhere between francs and dollars. I went to three plays in four nights. I stood on the steps of the British Museum, then drank in the splendor of Trafalgar Square. I walked from Chelsea to the Tower, from Hampstead to Bond Street. I wore my legs out. I took a two hour walk across the Heath, in the *dark*, and dreamed up visions of bogeymen and ladies in petticoats. I purchased an umbrella for £40—hickory shaft, Fox frame, all-cotton fabric—and learned to live with it on the end of my arm. I ate pub food and had diarrhea for two days. I drank warm beer and ordered more—enough for a party of four.

My size actually frightened people. They avoided me on sidewalks—or rather, pavements. They stared and pointed at me in restaurants. I felt heartbroken and lonesome. I regretted not chasing after Nicole. I maintained a constant internal dialogue. I waited impatiently for Lyel to call. Meanwhile, I played tourist.

I was staying in a Hampstead ground floor studio apartment that belonged to Jane Modisette, a friend of Lyel's. The apartment was a ten-minute walk from the Hampstead tube stop and a wonderful tea shop that served world-class pastries. It had a television with eight channels and a British Telecom telephone that rang repeatedly. I monitored the answering machine. If it wasn't Lyel, I didn't feel like talking. Like the finest British tea, I was steeping.

Messages from Bruce stacked up on the answering machine. He wanted to know how things were going. I wanted Lyel.

On the fifth day, I took a walk from noon to midnight and cleared my head and heart.

At noon on the sixth day, Lyel arrived bearing a smoked Scottish salmon and a fifth of single malt.

Lyel is so big he looks uncomfortable with himself, even a little goofy at times. The Jazz's program used to list him at six-seven, but that was short by an inch or more. He has a big forehead, a hard, protruding brow, and a nose that has taken its fair share of elbows while in the paint, chasing rebounds. He was never much offensively in his short-lived career, but in his rookie year he placed third in rebounds in the NBA. It's a stat he cherishes. His clothes are custom tailored—in part because of his substantial frame, in part because that's who Lyel is: unique, one-of-a-kind.

He spoke in a low but modest voice, as was his way. He used his large brown eyes to express himself. After a brief hello, he broke the seal on the whisky.

For an hour Lyel and I sat drinking, and never said a word. He let me break the silence.

"She caught me at a bad time."

"She caught you. I heard all about it. Just remember: she loves you. If she didn't love you, she wouldn't have walked away."

"She *ran* away," I clarified.

"That too."

"All over a misunderstanding."

"Time heals all," he said.

"Am I supposed to feel comforted?"

"Yes."

"I don't feel comforted."

"You are my guest," he said, "at dinner tonight." He stood. "I'm going to take a nap. Call Bruce. He's worried sick about you."

I secretly believed that Lyel had set things straight with Nicole, and I harbored expectations of a surprise. I couldn't taste my dinner, but the wine was magnificent. I could picture her face across the room as we caught eyes, but the more I thought about it, the more I came to realize it wasn't *my* fantasy but a scene from a credit card ad on the French television. In this depressed state, my imagination was reduced to instant replay. Dinner dragged on, me craning my neck toward the front door.

"Are you expecting somebody?" Lyel finally inquired.

"I was hoping maybe . . ." but I cut myself off when Lyel's disappointed expression offered me a silent lecture. "I know. I know." I told him. But I didn't know.

"What did Bruce say?" Lyel asked, trying to help.

"Stephan Shultz did in fact leave his wife high and dry. He raided their liquid assets—securities mostly as well as a five figure line-of-credit. She has filed criminal charges. Allison Star's parents have filed a civil suit that alleges brainwashing and abduction."

"And he's in love," Lyel said skeptically.

"Aren't we all?" I replied.

"Good," Lyel said, "I think he'll deal."

I felt a prickling sensation on the nape of my neck. "You have a hidden agenda," I suggested. I found my glass of wine and drained it.

"It's a vintage, not a table wine," he scolded.

"It's something to do with me, isn't it?"

"It's meant to be drunk slowly."

"Not Nicole. Not Shultz. Something else." My skin was hot now, and it wasn't the wine.

"It was you who got us into this," he explained. "You said Allison Star might be headed for Oxford. It's a tangled web, Oxford is. I studied there. You've heard the stories a hundred times. So I took it upon myself to gain you an entrée, because without it, you're a tourist, and as a tourist in Oxford you'll never find either Allison Star nor Stephan Shultz. My studies were at Magdalen College, but I've remained good friends with a don at Wadham called Binyon—Tim Binyon. So that's whom I called. Tim Binyon knows *everybody*. That's what got us into this."

I didn't like those last words. I could hear it coming. I looked away from him. I didn't want to be looking him in the eye when he asked me for the favor because he was so damned *sincere* that I would never be able to refuse him. How many times had *he* come to *my* rescue. And me with so few chances to reciprocate. It was one of the great problems of having a friend as close as Lyel—this *weighing* of the friendship, this constant checking of the scales. And he knew me well enough to know that I would never refuse him, if humanly possible. All because he would never refuse me—never *had* that I could think of—not when it *counted*. And I knew that whatever came out of his mouth next was not what I wanted to hear.

He continued, "The thing of it is, it's *Oxford*." He added, "And she *is* due there—you're right about that. It's just as you suspected. So you have to go up there anyway. Right?"

"Do we know she's going to attend?" I asked.

"She's to read this term at Christ Church. Yes. Due any day."

I looked at him then, as he must have known I would. He seized the moment. "A Fellow has gone missing." He allowed me an opportunity for exclamation, but I refrained. "One of the Wadham dons." He explained, "Tim's concerned. He needs your help. And besides, Tim already knew all about you."

"*Me?*"

"We correspond," Lyel said. "I've written about you."

"I'm touched."

"What was I to do?" he asked.

"What *did* you do?"

"I offered your help. An objective eye. Someone *outside* the Oxbridge system who very badly needs to be inside. You see the way this fits for you? His friend has gone missing. You have to understand what it's like there. Very closeted existence. Incestuous, really. As political as any university—*more* so. And very *British* obviously."

"Lyel . . ."

"The Warden claims that this don, this Fellow, took a leave of absence and it very well may be just that, but Tim has his doubts and he could use our help. I *did not*," he emphasized, "commit you to anything more than a conversation or two. At least not at first . . ."

"Lyel . . . Let's have it all."

"We talked about the *possibility* of our—you, actually— staying in college for a while. For a few weeks. Long enough for you to locate this missing friend of his as well as your own Ms. Star and Stephan Shultz. But from the inside, Klick, not the outside. You understand? It's the only way it's done."

"He wants me to find this missing Fellow," I suggested.

"It's not a bad trade if you think about it," Lyel reminded tentatively, cautiously testing me. "Tim is the Russian Literature Fellow. But he's a mystery writer and a reviewer. Wadham hosts something called The Raymond Chandler Research Fellowship. This year's participant has returned to the States on a family emergency. Tim suggests pawning you off as the replacement."

"A writer?"

"You don't have to actually write. Just drink a lot. You're certainly qualified for that."

"Don't start with the compliments."

"It's not forever," he said. "This is a Michaelmas term fellowship, with two weeks already used up. Tim points out you've got until early December if we need it, seven weeks."

"Seven weeks!?"

"Only if we need it. We can cut it short."

"We?"

"You'll like Wadham," he tried.

"What have you gotten me into, Lyel? Raymond Chandler?"

"More wine?" he asked as accommodating as possible.

"Another *bottle*," I suggested.

"It's an entrée," he reminded. "Over here, you have to have an entrée."

"I'd rather stick to the wine," I whined, "and skip the entrée."

"Oh, very punny," Lyel said. He barely lifted a finger, as

subtle a move as I could imagine. It brought the wine steward to his side instantly.

Things were different over here.

CHAPTER 9

David Thompson met me outside the tube stop. He was a tall man, though a few inches shorter than I, with classic tall-dark-and-handsome looks accented by a slight squint caused by contact lenses that suggested serious concentration and keen interest. An American, he had an expatriate's accent. I guessed him at forty-five. He wore a camel hair overcoat, a stiff-collared blue-and-white-striped shirt, black trousers, and black loafers. He walked me across the street and described the history of an Egyptian monument that included two enormous bronze lions keeping watch on the Thames. We kept the wide, dark river to our left. A barge and tug moved slowly down the river, passed by a quickly moving tourist ferry that interrupted the city sounds with an occasional belch of a nasal public-address system and a tourist guide's unintelligible description of the historical site.

"Stephan and I," Thompson pronounced it correctly, "go back quite a way. I studied under him at Tanglewood. This session in Paris came up. It's a new work of mine commissioned for the Queen's birthday, but recorded in Paris because the studio is less expensive than anything over here. The piece is a big Elgar kind of thing, and though I would normally conduct myself, Stephan surfaced out of nowhere. He's fantastic with the larger orchestras—his Tchaikovsky might be the best ever—I mean *ever.* I brought it up with the execs and they pounced on the idea. I must say, I had more difficulty with the factions on *this* side of the channel, but since I'll conduct it for the actual event we struck an acceptable compromise."

"Shultz was paid?"

"Of course. And quite well."

"And the young woman with him?"

Thompson eyed me, "You do get around, Mr. Klick."

"Did she play?"

"Stephan wanted her as first cello, but she was booked as third, and we kept it that way."

"But you met her."

"Of course."

"And how did their relationship strike you?"

He stopped walking and looked me over. "I've known Stephan over fifteen years. I've known you less than fifteen minutes. What makes you think you can ask a question like that?"

"Arrogance."

"Indeed." He started walking again. "Are you a reporter?"

"No, I'm the tooth fairy. People have royalties under their pillow, and I bring them money. In Stephan's case . . . ," now *I* pronounced it right, "it's quite a *lot* of money."

"Then why ask about Allison?"

"When the bitch is in heat, the male dogs tend to congregate at the door."

"Are you always this poetic?"

"The sooner he signs a few papers, the sooner my job is done."

"You could be the press. You could be someone hired

by Tina . . ."

"Mrs. Schultz?"

"He doesn't wish to see Tina. You do not strike me as a tooth fairy, I'm afraid."

"He took her money," I informed him. "He followed the girl over here—to Italy actually. And he apparently planned to stay. Finders keepers."

"What?"

"Cleaned out several accounts and ran off after Allison Star. Tina, as you call her, is not so thrilled about that."

"You've met her?"

"She was in Paris. She's hired some people to find him. They are in my way."

He considered this a minute. "Well, Stephan has *always* been at the center of controversy." He pronounced it like a Brit: con-tróv-ersy. It took me a second to realize what the word was. "He thought she had hired someone."

"Can you arrange for me to see him?"

"Me?"

"Perhaps you could act as middleman for the signing of the papers. I don't actually have to *see* him."

"I have no idea where he might be."

"No idea at all?" The tourist ferry cut a large white U into the water as it reversed directions. Some sea gulls dove down into its wake—white flashes silently bombing the surfaces.

"Does he have friends here?" I added, "Allison is to study at Oxford."

He answered me with a look. I was certain he didn't mean to. I had said the Secret Word. He looked away just as quickly, but the damage was done. "He has friends there," I said, probing. Thompson was frustrated. He knew he had given it away. "Colleagues. Did he study there? Is that it? Did he *say* something to you?"

"Did you meet Tina?" he tried.

"You could act as go-between for me," I reminded.

"She is a lovely woman. Hard to understand some things, isn't it?"

"I don't need to actually meet him."

"How did you ever get into such a business?"

"Just lucky I guess."

"You could leave me a number to ring. If I see him again, I could try."

"Wadham College, Oxford," I said, making up my mind on the spot.

"How's that?" he inquired.

"I've been awarded a research fellowship at Wadham," I informed him. All lives have to start somewhere.

"You?"

"I write mysteries on the side. A pseudonym. I use a pseudonym."

"You?" he repeated.

"You can reach me there starting next week."

"Are you published?" he asked still not believing me.

"I'll be doing research while at Wadham."

"Do you have a title?" he asked, clearly playing along. "For the book?"

"A working title is all," I answered. "*Concerto in Dead Flat*. What do you think?"

"Sounds intriguing." Maybe he was starting to believe me.

Maybe, even, I was beginning to believe myself.

CHAPTER 10

The train from Paddington to Oxford carried Lyel and me through the lush countryside that one always imagines as England, a dark green that no film has ever managed to capture. Fields. Cattle. White stucco farm houses with chimneys spouting smoke the color of the sky. Straw and stone. Draught horses. And more rich, chocolate mud than seemed possible. The trees were changing colors, but the leaves were not yet falling.

Two well-dressed women sat across the aisle from us in club seats, a table separating them. One of these women talked, almost incessantly except to catch her breath. The other remained fixed to every word, uttering only, "Umm . . . umm," when the other paused. This acknowledgement, "Hmm . . . umm," punctuates all British conversations, male and female alike, indifferent even to class. I caught Lyel doing it and reprimanded him.

"Well," he said, "if you don't want to talk!" And with that he pulled out a deck of cards and dealt himself a hand of solitaire.

I wasn't sure why I had agreed to Lyel's volunteering my time. I felt as uncomfortable as if I were headed out on a blind date. Finding musicians owed royalties had placed me in any number of difficult situations over the past several years, and on rare occasion I had even gone "undercover" posing as this or that, but *never* as an author, and never at such a prestigious institution as Oxford.

"There's a first time for everything," Lyel said, rolling over a card. He didn't look up. He didn't give me that Lyel eyeball that warned of other things he knew I was thinking. He just went about his game, lazy and indifferent, as only Lyel could.

"The only thing I know about Raymond Chandler I learned from Humphrey Bogart."

"It's a Chandler Fellowship, but that doesn't mean you're a Chandler expert. It's where the money comes from, that's all. Chandler's estate put up the money on the centennial of his birth. His papers are divided between UCLA and the Bodleian at Oxford. One year a Brit goes to UCLA, the next an American to Wadham. You're the American. If anyone asks, you're researching and outlining your next novel."

"My *next* novel?" I felt terrified. They were sure to find me out: the Great Imposter.

"Don't worry, very few Brits read American mysteries. Theirs are better—or at least so they think. Academics are used to obscurity. At best, only a few of the dons will be mystery readers, and it won't surprise any of them to have never heard of you. Make up the names of a couple of titles and you'll be fine."

"I'm terrified."

"It builds character. When was the last time you were scared?"

"At my age it builds ulcers, not character. Do you have any antacids?" Lyel *always* carried antacids. He offered me two. I chewed down the chalk and felt better immediately.

"You're going to love it," he said.

"Then why do I hate it already?"

"Stage fright."

"I don't have stage fright," I reminded. Eleven years of

playing rock music in clubs and concert halls had cured me of that ill.

"Maybe part of your research is to interview Allison Star—one R."

We had already discussed this possibility. One thing about Lyel, he knew when to retreat to safe ground. "Where did a former NBA center get such debating skills anyway?" I asked.

"You wouldn't *believe* the things that are said between players while under the rim," he answered.

But thanks to Lyel, I had sat front row for many games, and I *did* believe. He flipped over another card, looked up and smiled at me, and quickly dispatched the game. He had won. Surprise.

"People are staring at us," I whispered.

"Maybe one of your readers recognizes you," he suggested.

"Don't push it, Lyel."

"Get used to it," Lyel advised. "The British are impressed by anyone published."

We took a taxi to Wadham College. I was sorry that the taxi was a European Ford sedan, not the stereotyped English taxis like those in London. Oxford had a few of these London taxis, but the majority of those in line awaiting passengers at the train station were nondescript four-doors offering good gas mileage and small, sturdy frames.

A lot of the road surface was still cobblestone, and I couldn't help but be reminded of this city's substantial history, the sheer *age* of the place. The shops and store fronts, the banks and churches, were so picturesque that, except for the electric street lamps and occasional plastic sign, the streets looked more like Hollywood sets depicting the idealized past rather than real-life. Something out of *A Christmas Carol.*

The current day streets *swarmed* with pedestrians and bicyclists. They teemed with students and tourists making crowds like Fifth Avenue at lunchtime. Crowded double-decker tourist buses awkwardly negotiated the narrow streets and tight turns. Unarmed policemen with ruby cheeks and amusingly tall "Bobby" helmets directed traffic and patrolled the footpaths. We passed a Lloyds Bank where casually dressed students were lined up twenty deep awaiting a shot at the ATM cash machine. In a four block area we passed three pizza shops, two movie theaters, and a department store. I felt my heart beating fast. Oxford. The minds that had walked these streets, inhabited these halls, crowded these pubs. People had been studying here *centuries* before America was even discovered! Stained glass leaded windows relating biblical stories. Towering spires. Intricately ornate stone friezes. Gargoyles glaring down at you. And it could not have looked much different then than it did now. We had stepped back in time. I had been here five minutes. Already, I didn't want to leave.

"I'm glad you talked me into this," I thanked Lyel. The two of us barely fit in the back of the cab.

"Just wait," he said.

"Just visiting?" the driver asked.

"Mr. Klick," Lyel replied, indicating me, "is a visiting Fellow at Wadham."

"Is that right?" the driver said in his gluey British accent, clearly impressed. He caught sight of me in the rear view mirror and I could feel him re-appraising my worth as a passenger in his cab. "Dining at the High Table, will you be, Sir?"

"Sir," he had said with so much respect that it gave me gooseflesh. High Table was clearly some kind of litmus test. "Yes," I replied, though somewhat tentatively. He obviously knew more about it than I did.

"An honor to be driving you, Sir," he said sincerely. New York this was not. "My distinct honor," he repeated.

Lyel glanced over at me and lifted an eyebrow as if to say, "I told you so."

I settled back for the ride, wondering exactly what I had gotten myself into.

CHAPTER 11

From the street, Wadham College looked like a cross between a monastery and an ancient fort. Towering chimneys—too many to count—reached up for the gray sky. At ground level a wide, slate sidewalk bisected two immaculately tended grass lawns, clipped as close as putting greens, and contained in symmetrical perimeters by frames of rusted steel bands. The entrance loomed beneath a large archway of sculpted stone—a huge face of nut-brown wood with a smaller, but still grand, door cut into it. I could picture this archway without the wood filler, horse-drawn carriages of a hundred years earlier pulling into the courtyard.

This ancient door, harvested from an oak forest hundreds of years ago, was over two inches thick and was held open by a stout chain. It led into a dark, but short tunnel that entered into Wadham's fully contained courtyard where yet another perfectly tended lawn acted as a large island. **PLEASE KEEP OFF**, a sign requested.

Lyel steered me to my left and into the porter's lodge where several students were picking up their mail in alphabetized pigeon holes. A reception area, with an open counter like that of a nineteenth century bank, separated the porter from the chaos of the students. The air was thick with cigarette smoke. Lyel stepped up to the counter and addressed a red-cheeked man who reminded me of Clarence, the angel in *It's A Wonderful Life*. He had excited blue eyes and white hair. His cheeks bulged with his smile like St. Nicholas.

"And what can I do for you gentlemen?" he asked cordially.

Lyel introduced himself and then me. When he reached the words, "Chandler Fellow," the porter's face lit up and he beamed.

"Yes, yes, yes!" he roared. "Jane!" he called to the back. "It's the Chandler Fellow!"

A warm-faced woman of older but indistinguishable age came out of a small back room, drawn by the summons. She also beamed at me. "Welcome, Sir. Welcome," she said, heading for a large rack of keys. "Delighted to have you!"

John, as the porter introduced himself, located some papers and organized them before placing them on the counter for me to look over and sign. They had to do with responsibility for the keys. While I signed the papers, Lyel asked after Tim Binyon. John placed a call, but there was no answer.

John shook my hand strongly and once again welcomed me to "college." He produced an overly photocopied map, circled my room, King's Arms 11, and drew a route for us to follow. "There's anything you need, anything at all, John is here to help you," he said, referring to himself in the third person.

Locating my room took us through another stone passageway and across a second courtyard to a distant wing that appeared to be ancient wood-frame construction. We ducked our way up a rickety set of wooden stairs covered in a slippery linoleum. Number 11 was a corner office on the third floor over the old pub. Its door had been trimmed out of square and was perhaps six inches shorter than me— ten inches shorter than Lyel. We fiddled with the lock, forced the door open with a slight kick of the toe, and ducked into a suite of rooms, the first of which was my office. The carpeted floor had slanted from centuries of the building settling. The room was roughly square. The views took my breath away—the New Bodleian to my right, and nearly straight ahead, the impressive Sheldonian Theater. The drapes, somewhat neglected, were made of a heavy red linen. Each window hosted an interior storm window—a necessity, I soon realized, because the window frames themselves were probably as old as the building, and just as out of square.

My sleeping room was half the size of the office, with a single bed about the age and size of the office door. My feet would be cantilevered off of this one—another hazard of size.

"What if I don't want to leave?" I asked Lyel.

"I told you you'd like it."

"It's like stepping into another century."

"Agreed. It's quite special. You're lucky."

"And what do I do to earn this?" I asked.

"You continue to be polite to your good friend Lyel."

"It was a serious question, Lyel. I meant it."

"My suggestion is that you *use* your situation here to make the most of things, which is to say that a mystery writer would be interested in *anything* mysterious. This could give you the entrée you're looking for to explore the various aspects of Tim Binyon's missing don."

I teased him, because if I didn't tease Lyel every now and then he began to get this haughty air about him that bordered on snobbery and made me incredibly uncomfortable. "You're so creative," I said. At this moment I tugged on the lid of a built-in piece of furniture in the corner. The lid came up, revealing a porcelain sink with separate faucets and a rubber stopper on a small length of chain.

"The better to soak your head with," he said. I had offended him. He could be like a puppy dog when his feelings were hurt. "I have an appointment with a letting agency," he informed me. "I'm going to rent a flat for a month, and reserve a second just in case"

"A *month?*"

"A month in a flat is cheaper than a week in any hotel." He moved toward the door.

"You're not going to leave me," I protested.

"You're a big boy."

"What about Binyon?"

"I'm sure he'll return at some point. The porter can tell you about dinner in case Tim is gone for the day."

"You *are* going to leave me," I said, stunned. "I could help you pick out a flat," I suggested. I didn't want to be left here. Lyel's presence lent a sense of security that I couldn't quite put my finger on.

"I don't think so." He leaned down heavily on the door-knob and the door opened smoothly. "Get to know the place," he said. "It's going to be home for a while."

He left. I was standing there, the sink's rubber stopper between my fingers like a worry bead. I suddenly realized how expertly Lyel had maneuvered me into this spot. Perhaps he had left, sensing that at any moment I might come to this realization. All I wanted was a signature on a document. Was that so very much to ask? All I needed was a brief encounter with this enigma, Stephan Shultz, and I would have enough money to take a prolonged leave of absence from the world in Lyel's guest cabin. Some skiing. Some time in the backcountry. A signature. And here Lyel was talking about a *month*.

He was right: I needed to find my way around.

I needed to find Ms. Allison Star—one R. Quickly. I could feel the door of Lyel's clever trap closing on me. He had promised me to someone.

And I could tell by my present surroundings that I was in over my head.

CHAPTER 12

I banged my head on the door frame again. Some people are slow learners. The thing was, my mind was else-where.

That first day at Wadham was a memorable one. I used the map that John, the porter, had provided me and found my way to the great hall where the meals were served. When I looked in, some students, young men and women, were studying there on long dark tables, oil portraits of former wardens looking down on them. The stained glass and leaded windows reminded me of a church. I caught sight of a date engraved in a brass plate on one of the portraits. It read: 1622. People had been studying in these halls for a long time.

I found the chapel, the refectory, the student bar, and the library. I spent nearly an hour wandering the college's main garden where a variety of flowers bloomed. A crushed-stone path led around the perimeter of another island of that neatly cut grass, perhaps an acre or more. On the outside border of this path hundreds of varieties of bushes, shrubs, and flowering plants—each one labeled carefully—formed a ten-foot deep skirt, backed by a high stone wall. Three quiet men in coveralls tended to a high bush in the far corner. There was not a twig misplaced, not a dead leaf in sight. I circled the garden several times, more enchanted with each lap. Students occupied benches, reading or talking quietly. Others studied in one of the "rooms" formed by the vegetation. It was one of the single most peaceful places I had ever been. I felt the history, the many great minds that had walked this path, had heard the gentle crunch of rock and pebble beneath them while contemplating some leap in human knowledge. I didn't belong here, but that did nothing to limit my appreciation. I was enchanted.

A large man with thinning gray hair, wearing a navy blue blazer and a worn black sweater, stood in the stone archway that led into the garden. As I drew closer to him, I could see that he had blue eyes, bright red cheeks, and a five o'clock shadow. He smiled at me. A thin lipped smile that brightened his eyes. "You must be the one called

Chris," he said, offering me his thick hand to shake. "Tim Binyon." His smile widened and I could see tobacco stained teeth. "Have you seen the Fellows' Garden yet?" he asked, pointing toward a white door along the far wall. It was nearly hidden by the trunk of the garden's impressive copper beech. He motioned me back into the garden.

He told me, "We Fellows have our own garden. That includes you now, Chris."

He led me past the beech into the far corner, removed a heavy skeleton key from his pocket, and admitted us into a second, breathtaking garden. Smaller than the college garden, it was beautifully planted and planned. "Just for the Fellows?" I inquired, unable to conceal my thrill and disbelief.

"Someplace to think," he replied. "Strictly private."

We met eyes, and I could tell immediately that the emphasis was on *private*. Tim Binyon had something to tell me. We walked on. It felt as if he wanted to get well away from the wall that communicated with the college garden, well away from ear shot.

"I trust we will have many opportunities to talk," he began, "but in case we should not—I am frightfully busy, I'm afraid—I would like to tell you as much as I know about Aiden Sinclair, the Fellow who's gone missing. Mr. Chandler spoke to you of this, did he not?" He meant Lyel.

I told him what little I knew about the situation.

"Yes, well. Aiden enjoys his drink, Chris." He chuckled. "We *all* enjoy our drink here, ehh? You will appreciate our cellar, I should think. Following dessert—supper time, I am talking about—the Fellows take their coffee in the Senior Common Room. Have a smoke. Play some bridge on occasion. Aiden prefers a walk. Loves an evening stroll. He rejoins us after his walk. Claims it aids his digestion. He's a little gassy, Aiden is. Nearly two weeks ago now, it was. Yes, I'm quite sure of the date. We had had a particularly decent port for dessert, and Aiden knows his port. On that evening, he knew his port quite intimately." Another chuckle. "And he took himself an extended stroll, I should think. Gone quite a while, he was. Nothing cloak and dagger, mind you. But when he came back from his walk, he was covered in mud. He had taken a fall, perhaps even struck his head—or had his head struck," he added, training his blue eyes at me for emphasis.

"He was quite drunk—or dazed," he continued again offering me those intriguing eyes, "and went on about some discovery he had made. About how important a find it was. Aiden's field is herbs," he emphasized the "h" in the English manner, to my ear making it sound more like a person's name. "Herbs and dyes. I suppose—and I thought this at the time as well—that he had discovered some species of plant while out for his stroll. Aiden is always stopping along the footpaths, inspecting weeds, shrubs, and the like. Smell the roses, what? This, despite the dark. He's a queer sort, Aiden is. But then again, we all are, I suppose. He is well-liked. I do not mean anything by it. In part, you see, this assumption of mine—of ours—explains the mud he had gotten all over himself. Wandering off the footpath, as he always does, it is easy to get mucked up and muddy. Aiden always has weed seeds stuck to his clothing or mud on his boots. Goes without saying."

We had come three quarters of the way around the Fellows' garden. He pointed out another painted door, explaining that it led to the Fellows' private parking area. Parking in Oxford, I was told, was at a premium. The wall directly in front of us communicated with the Warden's private garden. It seemed to me that there was more garden than college here. While we walked adjacent to the high wall shared with the college garden, Tim Binyon kept the conversation to an introduction to Wadham, filling me in quickly on meals, and some of my responsibilities as the Raymond Chandler Fellow.

Once out of range of the other garden, he launched back into his discussion of the missing Aiden Sinclair. "The next morning Robin Fiddean saw Aiden on sixth stairway. Aiden also said something to Robin about this fantastic discovery of his, though was not specific. That was the last any of us saw of him. He missed his classes that same day. Missed a choir rehearsal—he's quite musical, Aiden is. He may have returned to his rooms, but he was not seen doing so. And not a word since. Not one word."

"What does the Warden say about all this?" I asked.

"I spoke to him about it—I'm sub-Warden here at Wadham. Honestly, he did not seem the least bit concerned. He reminded me that Aiden had been hollering for some research time—time away from the college—and suggested that Aiden, as independent a thinker as he was, had probably made some discovery that needed bearing out by field research. When I suggested that one would think he would have at least cleared such a thing with the Warden, the Warden was unfazed. I must tell you, Chris: *that* was when I *first* suspected something was not on. I *know* this Warden. His reaction was not his at all. He is hiding something."

"The Warden?" I asked astonished. "You think the Warden is involved?"

"He *knows* something—I promise you that. But your reaction is quite appropriate I assure you. Our wardens at university rarely come out of academia. The private sector or civil service is more common. The occasional Royal. But rarely academia. And they are quite above the rest, just as you have indicated. Hmm? Yes. Quite above. It would not do at all—*would not do*—for one of the Fellows to initiate any inquiries on Aiden's behalf. Not as concerns the Warden. Would not do whatsoever, you see. But you, on the other hand. Well, you are new to Wadham. You are an *American*. You see? Quite a different story entirely. You can explore his disappearance with impunity by the nature of your research. Let us say, for instance, that the plot of your mystery was to include some reference to seventeenth or eighteenth century herbal inks. Well then, Aiden is the foremost authority on the subject. To whom better to turn for your research than Aiden Sinclair? And a Wadham Fellow at that! You Yanks can be quite the persistent lot. It is a known trait, so there too you are qualified. See? Do you see how it can be done?" He grew increasingly excited, the pace of our stroll approaching a light jog.

In a more sober volume, he said, "In the meantime: quid pro quo." He removed a piece of paper from his pocket and unfolded it. "Mr. Chandler passed along a name of a young woman in whom he said you were interested. The results of my preliminary inquiry are that Miss Star is expected at college shortly. She will be reading music at Christ Church with Julian Rasner. Julian, as you may know, is the Mozart scholar—*the* Mozart scholar—and I must say that Miss

Star must be quite talented to be reading with Julian. He has, for the most part, directed himself entirely to research. This will be her staircase and room number." He handed me the piece of paper. His handwriting was difficult to read. I stuck it into my pocket.

"Did Lyel say anything about Stephan Shultz?"

"He asked about him, yes. I fished about for you. Quietly, as Mr. Chandler requested." He lowered his voice to a complete whisper. "He *was* seen, again at Christ Church. He attended High Table, as Julian's guest, you can be sure. Not seen since, to my knowledge."

We had reached the door that returned us to the college garden. He walked me along the wall that was shared with another college, explaining, as I asked, that the university was made up of thirty-seven separate colleges, and that the university, as such, was nothing more than an administration center and testing facility. Back in the college garden, we came to a small statue shaped like a chair. If you were small enough to fit, when you sat down you were sitting in the lap of a former Warden. "I served under Maurice Bowra," Tim Binyon explained. "A *marvelous* man, loved by all. He is sorely missed." The stained-glass windows of the elegant and ancient chapel looked down on us from our right. A small grass courtyard was formed between the chapel and the main dining hall.

"Quiet," I said.

"Quite," he answered. After a moment he added, "I'm terribly sorry to say that this is all rather urgent, you see. This Aiden Sinclair business. It's not on, I can tell you that."

"Not on?" I asked, unfamiliar with the phrase he kept repeating.

"Not a bit. No, indeed," he answered, not realizing my confusion. "I'm the cellarer, you see. And though our bottler has a tendency toward red cheeks, it's only a bottle now and then—drawing down the partials, that sort of thing. Never a case. Nothing like that. And that is just the thing, you see. Ehh? A case of port. A *case* of our finest port is missing, you see." I didn't see at all. I could barely keep up with him. "Went missing right along with Aiden Sinclair, I might add. And no surprise. Not to me. Aiden has a fondness for port. It was port that put him into the mud that night, I can promise you that. And who keeps the key to our cellar? you might ask. And I can answer that, sir. The bottler, myself, and the Warden—just the three of us. No other keys. And if not the bottler, then it leaves only one other person who removed that case of our finest. Hmm?"

"The Warden," I replied.

"Exactly."

"He gave a case of port to Aiden Sinclair?"

"Not just any port, mind you. Our finest! What of that? Some of the finest port at university! The value of which would be *quite impossible* to estimate, I might add. Why do it? That is the question, don't you see? Why would the Warden gift Aiden a case of our best, and then pretend it had never happened?"

"A bribe?" I asked.

"I am worried for Aiden, I must say. He is a bit in his cups most of the time, easily misled, I am afraid. Not at all himself since the wife passed on. Oh, five years past, must be, if it is two. Hmm? Not at all himself. No, sir."

Binyon snapped his head quickly around. I looked up in time to see a quiet, pale face recede from one of the fuzzy-glassed windows. Male or female, I couldn't be sure, although the eyes seemed a vivid blue. Had this person been watching us, spying on us, or merely looking out a window when Binyon sensed the intrusion?

"Do you know that person?" I asked.

"I know *everyone* here, Chris. Spent over half my life here. However, I didn't recognize him, if that's what you mean. It is the chapel, my boy, and I can tell you it's not a terribly popular place this time of day. The chaplain, if I had to guess."

"Friend or foe?" I inquired.

"I have never had to think in those terms," he admitted, a disturbance knitting his brow.

"But if you had to?" I persisted.

"Friend, I should say. Most definitely a friend. A good man, our chaplain."

"And this mud?"

"I beg your pardon?"

"You said Aiden Sinclair was covered in mud the night he returned for coffee." I pointed to a muddy patch beneath a formidable tree where the grass had long since died off. "That kind of mud?" I inquired. "Or," pointing now to a large pile of excavated dirt just barely visible on the far side of the Hall—the construction hidden by a contractor's fence—"*that* kind of mud?"

Tim Binyon didn't have an answer for me, but I could tell by his expression that until that moment, he had not considered the source or quality of the mud collected onto garments of Aiden Sinclair. He had not given that mud a second thought.

For me, the mud was the most important of all.

CHAPTER 13

I didn't see Binyon for another four days. Didn't see *anyone*. Or rather, I saw *everyone*, but spoke to no one. I ate lunch in a kind of bubble, a few words spoken to me in passing, but very few, and then only out of that social consideration where, if one is unavoidable, you speak to him or her. I had yet to attend High Table, electing pub food at the King's Arms directly below my office instead. I had stomach cramps for two days and kept to myself. Lunch was an intimidating event, held in the former law library. Huge nut brown tables set out in two long Ts, an excellent hot and cold buffet set up at the end nearest the entry. A grand, intimidating room with a vaulted ceiling and ecclesiastical leaded windows. The Fellows apparently used lunch to catch up on their newspaper reading. There were a few isolated conversations, but not many: the only sounds, loose chewing and the flapping rattle of newspaper pages being turned.

On my first day I chose a seat closer to the buffet because I sensed I would require several trips in order to fill myself. A man with wild gray hair and a cardigan sweater buttoned incorrectly leaned over my shoulder and whispered to me, "He who sits apart, *is* apart." He made a head motion indicating I should move in next to the newsprint boys, which I promptly did. I introduced myself to the man sitting adjacent. He was studying the bare breasts of a very well-endowed young lady on page four of one of the tabloids. He folded the paper quickly. He greeted my introduction with, "Umm," and returned, somewhat stealthily, to his light porn. The man across from me offered the same, "Umm." It seemed that no one was into returning an introduction. They were happy to know my name but saw no reason to offer me theirs. After three days of eating lunch with the dons, I knew absolutely no one. Zero. But I learned that it was always page four, and I kept up on my "reading."

Lyel visited me on day four, just after lunch. He pushed the door to my office closed and stood over next to the electric fire to warm himself. The fire was like a huge exposed toaster, two red-glowing vertical coils that dried the air enough to fool you into thinking it was warmer in the room. Other than a complaining steam radiator, which operated at the whim of a thermostat several floors below, the electric fire was it.

"Where have you been?" I asked.

"Catching up on my jet lag. Paying visits to old friends. Reminding myself how good warm beer can taste."

"You could have called," I suggested.

"Yes, I could have. How is it going?"

"Horribly. I met Tim Binyon—but only briefly. Since then I've learned absolutely nothing about the missing Aiden Sinclair other than what his official write-up in the university literature has to say, and it's entirely academic."

"And what's *that*?" he inquired mischievously, pointing to the open journal on my desk.

I closed it quickly. "It's nothing."

"You're *writing*."

"What if I am?"

"You're actually *writing* something! How cute," he said. He knew how I hated that word.

"Was there some particular reason for this visit?"

"And what *exactly* are you writing?" He was positively thrilled by this discovery. I hadn't seen him this animated in recent memory. He waved his arms about like an actor, exaggerating each and every statement. "A mystery, I suppose. It would *have* to be a mystery, wouldn't it? My god! A writer! What have I *done?*"

I attempted an early defense, just to shut him up. "It *is* the reason I'm here," I reminded. "The *reported* reason. And really, what better way to get my ideas down than on paper? I should have thought of this years ago. How many people have I tried to find over the past five years? And *not once* did I sit down and put it all out on paper. It's amazingly clear on paper, I'll tell you that."

"Shultz or Sinclair?" he asked.

I hadn't thought about this, and I was a little embarrassed to answer, "Aiden Sinclair."

"So you like what Binyon told you," he proposed. "It intrigues you."

"It *is* interesting, if that's what you want to hear."

"Of course that's what I want to hear. It's my job in life to keep you interested—mentally occupied."

He was teasing, of course, but he struck closer to the truth than either of us would have wanted to admit. Since he had left the Utah Jazz basketball team and moved to Idaho, Lyel had spent an inordinate amount of time involving himself in my business. He had more money than he could ever spend and an insatiable sense of curiosity that had, for the past several years, manifested itself in my occupation of connecting musicians with their overdue royalty checks. He was fascinated with each and every case, and with me, in his own peculiar way. Whenever I bottomed out on my emotional roller coaster, Lyel was there with some sort of challenge that he knew I would not pass up. With all of this swirling in my head, it occurred to me that this stint at Oxford had followed closely on the heels of my mishandling of Nicole—and Lyel, more than anyone, knew how deeply my feelings for Nicole ran. Perhaps this stay here was nothing more than an emotional lifesaver tossed my way. It wasn't so strange a thought, he had done such things before in the name of our friendship.

"There are some curious elements to Sinclair's disappearance. The most obvious of these is that the Warden apparently had some role in the procurement of a case of port, possibly intended for Sinclair, and yet he disavows any knowledge of Sinclair's whereabouts."

"Have you spoken with the Warden?"

"Me? I can barely get the steward at lunch to acknowledge my presence! The Warden? You have got to be kidding me!"

"It *is* a closed society, isn't it?"

"Closed? Do you know that when I introduce myself, they don't introduce themselves back? Aside from Binyon, I don't know the name of one single Fellow, and I eat lunch with these people, I pass them on the sidewalks—"

"Footpaths," Lyel corrected.

"There! You see? The light switches are backwards," I pointed out, demonstrating on the wall switch—down was 'on,' up was 'off'—"they drive on the left; they eat with their left hands; and they call sidewalks footpaths or pavements. The only thing we share with these people is the language, and even the overlaps there are preciously small."

"You're shouting."

"I'm out of my mind!"

"I can see that." He added, "Your element, too. You're made more for barroom fights and women who work for tips."

"They're too classy for me? Thanks. I needed that."

"I suggest you ignore as much of it as you can. Make the best of your time."

"You leave phone messages, no one calls you back."

"Have you tried sending notes?"

"Notes?" I asked.

"It's how it is done over here. Not phones: notes. You will recall the Fellows' pigeon holes that John referred to?"

It was a small mail room for the Fellows, also used to park bicycles.

He continued, "You should try leaving notes. The Brits respond quite well to the written word. You'll see." At this point he produced a stiff card and twirled it between his fingers like a card shark showing off. "Case in point," he said.

"What's that?"

"It's our invitation to tea."

"Tea?"

"The Warden has invited us both to tea. I wrote to him— wrote him *a note*—making reference to the Proctor of St. Katherine's—a friend of mine. His invitation returned in the morning post. We're expected at four."

I checked my watch. "But it's three now."

"That's why I came early. I thought you might want to shower." He sniffed the air, annoyingly. "And shave," he added, scrunching his nose distastefully.

"You just thought you would pop in and tell me? What if I had been out?"

"You only leave for supper," Lyel said. "You've barely left your room in the past three days." He had his spies.

"I haven't felt well." I asked suspiciously, "How do you know any of this?"

"You should be attending High Table, you know. That is where you will meet people. The Fellows like to drink. You'll have something in common with them! They like to talk when they drink."

"I'm a slow learner," I offered sarcastically. "John," I suggested, referring to the porter. "John would know my movements, wouldn't he?"

Lyel just stared at me. He stared at me in a way that was intended to tell me something. And then I got it: John would know the movements of *all* the Fellows. It was part of his job to know. Maybe even the movements of Aiden Sinclair on the night he disappeared. It was a place to start.

I nodded.

Lyel said, "You're not as dumb as you look."

"I'll try to take that as a compliment," I said, reaching for my towel. The shower was across the hall.

CHAPTER 14

Sir Frans Tuttle was a clear-eyed, soft-spoken man who radiated intelligence. He shook my hand firmly—"delighted to meet you"—and showed Lyel and me into a sitting room cluttered with furniture. A coal fire burned. The room looked out on the Warden's garden. His wife brought us tea almost immediately and stayed through the tea service which included a piece of delicious lemon-and-rum pound cake. This social time was consumed with British politeness that included inquisitive questioning from both sides. Lyel offered a lengthy explanation of his time at Oxford focusing mostly on his rowing and rugby. As it turned out, one of Tuttle's good friends had rowed the same eight as Lyel. The talk was amiable and warm. When Mrs. Tuttle left us, Lyel gave me an eye cue, and I knew I was on.

I said, "Sir Frans, the novel I'm working on—my mystery novel—is set here in Oxford. It deals partly with ancient scrolls, subterranean vaults, and long-held secrets that the villain doesn't want exposed. Wrapped into this is the college wine cellar and some of the traditions of the college—all of which I hope to learn more about while I'm here."

"Extraordinary," he said, doing his best to sound enthusiastic. Sir Frans' background was in the arts. He had been director of a London opera company for three years prior to his appointment as Warden of Wadham. An American mystery novel was so far outside his experience that he probably had very little idea, or interest, about what I was telling him. But true to his character, his eyes did not wander from me; to look at him, one would have thought that I was the most interesting visitor he had ever entertained.

"One element of the plot will involve ancient inks. I was hoping to speak with Mr. Sinclair in that regard."

Reference to the missing don drew the first discernable reaction from Sir Frans. He glanced quickly to Lyel and then back to me.

I continued, "Over the past few days, I have made numerous attempts to contact Mr. Sinclair. None of the other Fellows seem to know where he has gone off to." To my surprise, Sir Frans allowed a slight grin.

"Who put you up to this?" he asked. "Tim Binyon?"

"Put me up to what?" I asked innocently. One thing I had learned over time was to control my voice, my facial expression, and body language.

He studied me, perplexed. "Aiden Sinclair has evidently taken an expected leave of absence—most likely for research. Autumn, you know. It's an excellent time to collect seeds. It's landed him in a good deal of trouble with students and faculty alike. Myself included."

"He's *missing?* Is that what you're saying?"

"Aiden Sinclair often goes off. Briefly, you understand. He has a wanderlust, Aiden does. But he'll turn up. I shouldn't worry too much, Mr. Klick. My advice: focus your research elsewhere."

"Would you have any ideas where I might find him?"

"Allow me to ring up a colleague at Magdalen who may be able to put you on to another Fellow in a similar discipline."

"Wonderful!" Lyel interjected in his friendliest voice. "On another note, I heard a rumor that the conductor Stephan Shultz has been seen at university. Any truth to *that?*"

"Yes. Yes. Saw him myself. At High Table at Christ Church. Quite the colorful personality is Mr. Shultz."

Lyel asked if Sir Frans had ever run into Shultz during the Warden's stint as head of the opera.

"Well, that's where I came to know him, certainly. We

had our disagreements, mind you. When you oversee the finances, as I did, you *always* have disagreements with people of Stephan Shultz's caste."

"You must have known David Thompson as well," I added.

"Absolutely. Splendid man, David. And he has a wonderful career going for himself. He has been commissioned for the Queen's Birthday, you know? That is, arguably, the most prestigious commission in all of England. An American, no less! Do you know him?"

"We've met," I answered.

"Do I sense a musical interest in the both of you."

Lyel and I glanced over at each other. Was I to tell him that I had once played electric bass on a Steve Miller cut? And if so, how quickly would the cordiality come to an end?"

"A little bit," we both answered, nearly in unison.

"And you know David Thompson's work?" he inquired.

"Not terribly well," I admitted. I wasn't going to get myself caught in a quiz, and Sir Frans seemed the quizzing type.

Lyel offered, "I was hoping you might surprise us by informing us of a Holywell appearance by Mr. Shultz."

He looked terribly upset all of a sudden. "Who told you?" he inquired, then checking me out as well. "About the Holywell, I mean? And don't deny it, if you please, Sir, for we all know that if Stephan Shultz were *ever* to conduct at university, it would not be in the Holywell but in the Sheldonian. Ehh? And yet you so accurately name the Holywell. This, when it is intended to be a *closely* guarded secret. For security reasons, I am afraid I must request that you divulge your source."

"There is no source, Sir Frans," Lyel said apologetically. "I wish there were, if only to satisfy your request. Quite the contrary, it is merely a product of intuition."

"Intuition?" he exclaimed. He wasn't buying any of this.

"In that there is a young woman involved, *n'est-çe pas?* It's the talk of the town, this liaison. London. New York. The world over. Svengali, and his prize cellist, amorously involved. Have *you*, of all people, not heard the rumors? The brilliant young cellist and the seasoned maestro! My god, it has all the tongues ablaze. And would this cellist, this university student, premiere at the Sheldonian, breaking who knows how many centuries of tradition, or would it be, more properly, more predictably, at the Holywell Music Room? And, since the scheduling of the Holywell falls under the jurisdiction of the Music Fellow at Wadham, and, I would assume, the Warden would be consulted whenever someone of Shultz's stature was to guest conduct—and, from the aforementioned tongues, one can only assume that where the chicken roosts the fox will follow, then, I can only presume that Shultz is to guest conduct. These are the reasons I ask such a question, Sir Frans. Please forgive me."

"What college did you say?" Tuttle asked Lyel, referring to his earlier years here.

"It's of no importance."

"What college?"

"Magdalen," Lyel said—pronounced "maudlin."

Tuttle grumbled. He seemed impressed with Lyel. I couldn't be sure what he made of me. His eyes darted nervously. "What *exactly* is your interest in Mr. Shultz?" he inquired somewhat sharply and I hoped that Lyel hadn't somehow given us away. This wasn't the first time that I had found it difficult to give a person money, but that didn't ease my frustrations any. Tuttle picked at a wart on the back of his hand.

"His dynamics," Lyel answered. "Wouldn't you say, Chris?"

"Definitely his dynamics," I replied. "And his feel," I added. "He has a feel for an orchestra the way Horowitz had a feel for the keyboard. Something passes through him and right out to the players."

Sir Frans clearly appreciated our analysis. He nodded, "Yes. Well-said. Couldn't agree more, actually." He tried again, "Musical, are you Mr. Klick?"

"I appreciate good music, that's all."

"Then you'll like it here in Oxford, I should think. There's always a performance worthy of one's attention." The wart was a stubborn little thing. His scratching turned it white. It looked like a piece of plastic glued to the back of his hand. "If there's anything you'd like to hear, please let me know." He seemed to be dismissing us.

We shook hands all around. Sir Frans welcomed me to Wadham once again and promised Lyel to keep him abreast of any performances involving Stephan Shultz.

As we passed the open door to his study, I acted on impulse, for there, framed on his wall, was what appeared to be a *very old* sheet of music manuscript, and the musician in me could not resist having a look. I entered the study without asking his permission—it's one of the drawbacks of substantial size: from an early age you tend to go where and when you wish, for no one wants to try to stop you. It turns you into a bully, without your ever knowing it.

"Is it Haydn?" I asked.

"Very good!" Sir Frans exclaimed, by far his most animated moment of our visit. "It is indeed Haydn."

"Original?"

"Of course. It was discovered in nineteen-sixty-eight in a family bible in Munich. I won it at an auction later that same year. It's my most prized possession."

"It's invaluable."

"Everything has a price," he corrected. His voice was cold. It turned my head toward him.

All at once, I caught a brief look of panic in his eyes, an expression I had witnessed in peoples' faces so many times that I had no doubt what I was seeing. His eyes had dropped just to my left—they had caught on something and that had caused this reaction.

His right hand was moving toward my left shoulder. He was trying to turn me while showing me to the door. Very smooth, this one, I thought. Very polished. I feigned a catch in my throat, averting my face, fist to my open mouth, and barked a little cough. Just long enough for my eyes to make a snapshot of what turned out to be his desk. Then, as expected, he gently turned me and we were out in the hall again and he was rambling on about the joys of Haydn and his pride at owning the manuscript.

I was still assimilating the mosaic of that frozen moment as Lyel started to speak, the two of us now entering the main courtyard. I raised my index finger. Lyel knew me well enough to cut himself off mid-sentence.

In my mind's eye I saw a letter opener and a stack of bills. Red leather with tooled gilt borders. Mahogany and brass. I saw a telephone and an address book. I saw the back of a picture frame and a jeweled paperweight made of clear Steuben Glass. I saw an in-box and an out-box. My eye hesitated on this out-box and, as if through the zoom lens of a camera, the image enlarged, occupying all my sight. I stopped walking, my vision fully fixed on my memory of the Warden's desk.

I said aloud, "It was a letter in the out-box." Thankfully, Lyel remained silent. Yes, we knew each other well. Click, click, click, went the zoom feature of my mind's eye. "An address in Devon. There was a postal code." All at once the image was gone; Lyel's curious face looked down at me. I said to him, "The letter on the Warden's desk was addressed to Aiden Sinclair."

CHAPTER 15

I could not be considered a professional locksmith. I had taken lessons once from a smith in San Francisco who had responded in a road call to my locked car rental. We had gotten along well, and somewhere in the four minutes and eighty-five dollars it had taken him to open my rental, I had inquired how one obtained such knowledge and he allowed that, for a fee, he would be happy to pass along some basics to me. Those basics turned out to include Slim Jims and Speed Keys and other technologies that advanced the art of quick, unforced entry. But actual picking required a set of expensive tools that looked like dentist picks, about four hands, and a good ten minutes for the simplest of locks. The more complicated locks could take a half hour or more. This image of someone convincing tumblers in a fraction of a second to part like the Red Sea, presented so often by Hollywood, turned out to be a fantasy invented by, and affording, screenplay writers an easy mode of entry into and through the most difficult of situations. Still, as this smith of many years before had advised me: "It's always easier just to steal the key."

That was what I did.

My friendship with John, the lodge porter, had quickly developed into something bordering brotherly love when he had discovered that I lacked my college degree. He had found me out by offering to order me a black robe for my High Table dinners. Knowing a little something about this tradition, thanks to Lyel, I inquired if that meant that I needed a sheepskin on my wall, which it did. John, a blue collar Irish sort of man, delighted that someone like me had attained dining privileges *without* a degree, and we became fast friends.

This new found friendship enabled me to join John and Jane on the back side of the porter's counter and share stories while I suffered through the indignity of second-hand cigarette smoke. I learned more about Wadham College from John than any alumni history would have told me. I also learned the filing system John used for the key cabinet. Here, behind a plywood door that was left open during working hours, hung duplicate keys for every room on college grounds.

Aiden Sinclair's key was number seven, staircase six. When John turned to answer an undergraduate's question, I seized the opportunity to borrow the key. I rationalized my effort by convincing myself that if John were to knowingly cooperate with me he could lose his job. This way went my reasoning, I was actually protecting him. And so goes the rationalization of most criminal acts.

Staircase six was accessed off the left side of the central courtyard. The tarnished copper numeral "6" was fixed neatly in the center stone of the archway that led into darkness and up a flight of silent stone steps toward a landing where a low wattage bulb glowed dimly. Hundreds of years earlier some student had no doubt ascended these very stairs with a candle clutched firmly in hand. You could see where his footfalls had worn the smooth stone. A young woman with thick curly hair wearing black Reeboks bounded down past me, flashing a smile and white teeth. I heard the rapid slap of her rubber soles fade below as it echoed through the chamber of the staircase. I rounded the landing of what the Brits called the first floor and climbed to the second, wondering why our two cultures couldn't even number floors the same way.

Aiden Sinclair's rooms were to my left where a recently installed white door prevented my entry. I alerted my ears to warn me of anyone approaching, slipped the key in and twisted. A moment later I was closing and locking the same door behind me. I was in.

I reached for the light switch, but thought better of it. The students and Fellows were certain to know which rooms lay behind which windows, and to illuminate Sinclair's lights might invite curiosity. Instead, I moved down a short, darkened hallway, passing a water closet to my left—he had his *own* I noted; I did not—and turned right into his office/study. Slowly, carefully, I drew open the drapes admitting as much of the ambient light cast from the "yard lights" that lit the courtyard as possible. The light was soft and yellow. It played off an old couch, a door table supported by file cabinets used as a desktop, an entire wall of packed bookshelves, an electric fire, several standing lamps, an overstuffed chair with no relation to the couch, and a black cube on a low bench that I took for a television. The secret was to give it a few minutes. I stood like a sentry, pressed into the near corner of the room. The nine o'clock bells tolled clear across the city from St. John's. Other than those bells, it was the complete and total silence punctuated by my own elevated heartbeat. Why is the dark more quiet? I wondered as my eyes slowly adjusted. Then it was almost—almost—like the room was bathed in candlelight. Enough for me to move around. Enough, even, to read bits and pieces of the papers scattered everywhere. More paper than in Ryman's stationary store, all of it covered with information. Hand written, photocopied, typed, computer generated. More information, it appeared, than one person could possibly assimilate. But there it was. It leant me the same sense of awe as when I had entered Wadham's grounds for the first time; the dons and Fellows here were, as the Merrill Lynch commercials had once said: "A Breed Apart."

The papers on the desk were stacked in a half dozen piles. I sat in the chair, took the top paper from one of the stacks and aimed it toward the window, finding plenty of light by which to read. The first three stacks were clearly work from his teaching and gave me insight only into the specificity of his work as an herbal ink expert.

I leafed through a stack of correspondence because correspondence has that same voyeuristic payoff as rummaging a person's medicine cabinet. Judging by Sinclair's correspondence, he was about as interesting as an owner's manual for an electric can opener.

Next stack. And the one beneath it.

There, an equation, written on a Post-It that was stuck to the base of his desk lamp. It read:

Music = Misc.

I puzzled over this. Music equals Miscellaneous. What could it mean? A file system? A reminder of what? Posted as it was, on his desk along with a half dozen other notes, I knew it held significance for Sinclair—something he might forget and need later.

Music equals Miscellaneous. It made no sense.

Another Post-It caught my eye, this one attached to the phone's handset. It listed three names: Randall Bradshaw, Lester Tilbert, and Henry Hagg, each followed by his two digit phone extension. Fellow Fellows. I borrowed a piece of Wadham note paper and duplicated the contents. I tried desk drawers, bookshelves, and a good look at Sinclair's vast filing system. No "misc," no "music." Boring and of no use to me.

I checked my watch. Forty-five minutes had passed. I left the study, entering Sinclair's bedroom which had more the feel of private chambers. The outside light shone brighter in this room. There was an unmade, undersized single bed pushed into the far corner, a well-used reading chair with an accompanying standing lamp, a straight back chair, a dresser, a foot stool, a portable heater, and a counter with several electric cooking devices: a hot plate, an electric kettle and a toaster. In the near corner to my right, at the foot of the bed, was what appeared to be a wicker hamper. Dirty laundry rates right up there with medicine cabinets. I opened the hamper.

I experienced that quick-paced fluttering heartbeat of an archeologist who sees the gray glint of bone in the dirt beneath his brush. From within the wicker hamper, a pair of muddied trousers stared back at me. Dried mud, as in falling down. Mud, as in the night a drunken Sinclair appeared in the Senior Common Room excited by some discovery that he would not openly discuss. Mud. Perhaps it would offer some clue as to where Aiden Sinclair had made his find.

I returned to the office, stole an envelope from his trash can, and then sampled the mud from the trousers into the envelope, folding it carefully and pocketing it. My reconnaissance around the rest of the bedroom provided little else except a look at Sinclair's present academic reading preferences and the discovery of an intensely pornographic magazine in the drawer of the bedside table. Black and white shabby stuff, close ups that embarrassed me.

Interestingly, I could find no toiletries in the W.C. This returned me to the bedroom. No suitcase. No underwear. Only two pair of socks. Each drawer of the dresser seemed to be a little too empty. What I failed to find told me as much as what I had found. Each of these discoveries helped to ease my mind. Odds were, Sinclair had not been abducted or, apparently, harmed in any way. Instead, he appeared to have taken an unannounced trip, which had been the Warden's claim all along. Perhaps this was nowhere near as serious as it had originally seemed. Enough was enough. It was late. I decided to leave.

Leaving was not as easy as entering, for I had no idea what, or whom, I might encounter in the hallway. When entering, you can always knock first; it doesn't work to knock going out. I placed my ear to the door and listened: I heard fast footsteps fading quickly, someone descending past the rooms. I turned the knob and slipped outside. The deadbolt lock mechanism required me to use the key from the outside in order to close the door fully, and that took a second. All the while, I felt the eyes of guilt boring down on me—surely I would be caught.

No one. I made it.

I tucked the key into my pocket and hurried down the staircase, keeping my head low. As I passed through the stone arch into the main courtyard, I encountered a tall, willowy figure, arms crossed and silhouetted by the flood lights. When a room light came on from behind me, I saw it was the chaplain.

"Evening," I said.

Only then as his quiet, peaceful face remained fixed in a stare did I realize he had been waiting for me. He pointed toward the chapel. "Have you toured the chapel yet?" This was not an invitation, but an order.

I walked with him the short distance to a tunnel-like passageway that led to the student garden. Inside this passageway was the chapel's massive wood door with a thick black iron hoop handle. The door was small. We ducked through into the vestibule. This marble floor was also bowled from centuries of church-goers. A long elegant bell rope hung in front of us stretching twenty, thirty, forty feet to the wooden ceiling. A grand piano, elaborate lead work in the stained glass windows. To our right a huge pipe organ dominated an entire wall. Only two lights were lit, the chapel glowing colorfully from outside lights pouring in.

"It was completed nearly four hundred years ago," the chaplain's calm voice proudly told me. I could make out his face now. Early forties. Green eyes. Dark hair. Strongly handsome. He caught me staring at him. "I'm called Jake," he said.

I introduced myself and we shook hands.

"We can talk safely in here," he informed me, arousing my curiosity, adding, "Very few people use the chapel this time of evening."

"Safely?"

"We can discuss your visit to Aiden's rooms without fear of being overheard."

"Oh."

"The draperies," he clarified. "I saw the draperies move and I knew someone was inside. I am not the adventurous sort. Nor is it my job to police the college. My calling is to observe and advise where I can." He lifted an eyebrow to indicate either curiosity or tolerance. He motioned to one of the stained glass windows and described its history to me.

"I'm a mystery writer," I said.

"Yes. So I've heard. The Chandler Research Fellow. Some of us have been looking forward to your time with us here. I'm a mystery fan myself. Can't get enough of them. What do you make of Elizabeth George?"

I had never heard of her. I made a face like I was considering how to answer.

"I think she's splendid," he added.

"A little old-fashioned, perhaps," I stated with an intentional lack of enthusiasm.

"Perhaps she is at that!" He seemed pleased. "Perhaps

that explains my fondness for her work. Yes. I suppose that's right. Good. Very good!"

"What about John D. MacDonald?" I asked, naming one of the only mystery writers I had ever read.

"Never heard of him," he declared condescendingly.

"Travis McGee?"

"Don't know his work either," he replied.

I declined to explain the connection. Better to leave well enough alone.

"Do you know Aiden?" he inquired politely.

"It's research of a sort," I explained vaguely.

"Then you don't know him."

"No."

"And yet you were in his rooms. How is that possible?"

"It wasn't me in his rooms."

"You might consider your surroundings before making such a statement." His hand swept toward the altar and the huge bronze cross there.

"I stole the key from the porter's lodge," I confessed.

"Fortunately, I'm in the salvation business. You've come to the right place."

"He has disappeared."

"Yes. Aiden and I, well, we talk often, you see. Aiden could use a little salvation."

"His drinking?"

"Then you've heard."

"Port, isn't it?"

He chuckled. "Maybe you do not require my help."

"We all require help," I suggested.

"It's just that there is something going on here at Wadham that, well, who is to say? If I knew what it was, I wouldn't . . . But you see, I don't know, do I? And that makes it impossible to say."

"And Aiden Sinclair is involved?"

He shrugged his shoulders. "By nature of my role here, I am a neutral party, Mr. Klick—"

"Chris," I corrected, "or Klick. But not Mr. Klick. He was my father."

"I saw you in the cloisters speaking with Tim Binyon. You can trust Tim."

"Is there someone I can't trust? Someone I should know about?"

"Be thankful it was me who saw those curtains move. You would be asked to leave for what you did tonight. The Warden would not tolerate such behavior from a Fellow. Or from a student, for that matter."

"I am grateful," I said. "I want to find Sinclair. I'm thinking about writing my mystery around his disappearance. It would make for a good one, don't you think?"

"Depends how it turns out," he cautioned, leading me back in silence toward the heavy door and the chill night darkness that lay beyond.

CHAPTER 16

My British Telecom phone purred from across the room where I was huddled in front of my glowing electric fire. With a coffee mug a quarter full of Drambouie, I was trying to warm myself and collect my thoughts following my visit to Sinclair's rooms and the chaplain's.

On the other end of the phone call, Lyel said calmly,

"He's gone."

Lyel had taken a field trip to the Devon address I had seen on the envelope in the Warden's study. "Gone?"

"He *was* here, up until this morning. It's a cottage on the Devon coast. Lovely place."

"Spare me the real estate description. Gone *where?*"

"No forwarding address."

"Tuttle warned him," I said. "Tuttle knew that I had seen the envelope."

"Same thought crossed my mind."

"But at least he's all right," I tested.

"We don't know that," Lyel corrected. "He *was* all right, up until this morning. That's as much as we can assume."

"I see what you mean. And are we *sure* it was even him to begin with?"

"Trash can contained three empty bottles of vintage port 1947."

I whistled. "That's fairly convincing." I somehow couldn't connect Lyel with rummaging through trash, but I didn't want to discourage his enthusiasm so I let it be.

"I haven't had a chance to get a look inside his room, and I haven't found out who owns the building. After this long a trip, I'd like to come away with something."

"You searched his trash," I reminded. Lyel had a way of challenging me; he made me work for evidence, teasing with bits and pieces, but forcing me to see the connection before he would volunteer the whole. Knowing Lyel, knowing that tone of voice of his, I suspected the empty bottles were not all he had found in Sinclair's trash.

"Very good. I did indeed."

"I hope you weren't observed."

He said, "Sinclair is no criminal—correction!—if he *is* a criminal, he's new to it. He took absolutely *no* precautions with his trash. None whatsoever. He's been eating poorly, drinking well and, by all appearances, has only had one letter from Sir Frans."

"You *have* a letter?"

"I'm missing the second page, and therefore the signature. We don't know for certain, although I suppose we could do an informal handwriting comparison. But, by the content, I'm pretty sure it was from Sir Frans, yes."

"What did it say, Lyel? *What did it say?*"

He read to me,

RE: Your recent discovery.

Your find here may—and I can't make out the words—*but, as we discussed, it comes at a most inopportune time. I thank you for your cooperation in this matter, and trust you are enjoying your current research. Please know that—*

and it stops there," Lyel finished.

"Your *find*," I quoted, emphasizing the latter.

"Inopportune time," he quoted back.

"They're hiding him. Someone is hiding him for some reason."

"And they're keeping him drunk—very drunk, by the look of it. Expensive drunk, which must also be for a very good reason."

"What could it be?"

"That's the problem," Lyel pointed out. "It could be *anything.*"

"Something in his field? Herbs? Ink?"

"I wish we had that second page of the note," Lyel said.

"I paid a visit to his quarters," I informed him.

"Did you?" he asked.

"I have some names to run by you . . . hold on a minute." I had written down the names that I had found scribbled onto a Post-It note. I read them back to Lyel: Randall Bradshaw, Lester Tilbert, Henry Hagg.

"I know Hagg! He's a musicologist. I read for him twenty years ago," Lyel said, referring to the Oxford tutorial system I had yet to understand.

"What about Lester Tilbert?"

"Don't know him."

"Why write down the names?"

"Nothing mysterious about one don having written down the phone numbers of other dons."

"The chaplain says there's something mysterious going on. He wouldn't elaborate."

"What did he say exactly?" Lyel asked. He didn't believe me capable of translating from the British.

"He's not right about any of this Sinclair business. He's overly cautious about saying anything."

"Scared?"

"Could be. Could be he knows more. That was the feeling I got."

"But trustworthy?"

"He's the chaplain, for Christ's sake!"

"No pun intended. The question still stands," Lyel said.

"Yes, trustworthy. Helpful, I think. He'll help if we need him."

Lyel instructed, "We need to know if Sinclair struck up

these friendships recently."

"Agreed."

"Binyon would know."

I told him about my discovery of the muddy clothes. I finished by warning him, "If Allison Star is coming to the university, as Binyon said, then as we agreed, Aiden Sinclair takes a backseat after that. Do you want to brief Tim Binyon now, or would you like me to wait for your return?"

"Who said I'm returning?"

"*After* you get a look inside his room," I corrected myself.

"I'm going to find him, Klick, whether you help me or not." I knew that Lyel tone.

"I didn't say I'm quitting. I said it would take the backseat."

"Same thing. It's okay."

"Lyel, it's *not* the same thing."

"We're closer than we were to finding him."

"Agreed."

"And Sinclair only has a one day jump on me."

Lyel had helped me out on any number of occasions— sometimes getting me out of some very tight jams. But he was not meant for the kind of work he was now suggesting he undertake. I said, "Something tells me *you* should have been the Raymond Chandler Fellow. This end of things is much more suited to you."

"You'll learn."

"That's not exactly what I mean."

"I can do this, Klick. This is nowhere near as difficult as you make it out to be."

"But it's not the safest undertaking. We've talked about that."

"You're worried for me. I'm touched."

"You're touched alright."

"I'll *be* in touch." I could hear him laughing—laughing at his own cleverness—as he hung up. But he was right, I was worried. All because I knew one thing Lyel didn't: amateurs were the most dangerous sleuths of all.

CHAPTER 17

The following evening, dressed in sports jacket, tie, and gray flannel trousers, I entered the Senior Common Room. It sported a low ceiling and red leather furniture, a circular antique card table, leather couches and padded window seats. In the far corner, a small wedge-shaped cabinet served as the bar. Tim Binyon caught me by the elbow and offered to buy me a cocktail. It was a warm gin and tonic—the Brits didn't believe in ice.

"How's your *research* coming along?" he inquired. It was a decent sized room, but this time of evening, as the Fellows gathered for High Table, it offered no privacy.

"Just fine, thank you. Making some wonderful headway."

"Anything that I can help with?"

"There may be. I'll certainly think about it." I did think about it, and I immediately suggested, "Perhaps you could make introductions for me. I would appreciate meeting messieurs Bradshaw, Tilbert and/or Hagg." I didn't know Tim Binyon well, but I knew a strange look when I saw one.

"Those names mean something to you?" I asked softly.

He replied in an equally hushed voice, "In any contained social structure the alliances and friendships are constantly shifting, constantly changing. It is human nature. Hmm? However the three men you just mentioned are most unusual bedfellows—three entirely different people: different tastes, different disciplines entirely. And yet those three men, the very same three you just mentioned, have recently been sharing time together—extraordinarily often, now that you mention it. At functions like these. High Table. The garden or cloisters. A most unusual alliance."

"And Sinclair?"

"Yes, Aiden too. You're right!" he crowed, draining his gin and edging away from me to pour us both another. As he filled mine—and he *filled* it—he said, "Sinclair too!" We stood off to one side of the room. Tim Binyon studied the faces. "Well," he said, "it looks as though I shall be sitting at the head of the table tonight." As sub-Warden, he explained, he presided over High Table unless the Warden showed, which wasn't often. "I'll ask you to sit to my left, Chris, unless there is a female guest, in which case I'll put you to my right. That's Randall, by the coffee." He nodded toward an exceptionally thin man with bad teeth, a full beard, and narrow-set eyes. Randall Bradshaw reminded me of a scarecrow. "I'll suggest to Randall that he join us. I'll place him next to you, no matter." He glanced at his watch. "Is that alright with you?" he inquired.

I was a little overwhelmed by the formality and by the idea of one man controlling the seating of his peers so carefully. Clearly the implication was that if he told Bradshaw to sit next to me then that was where Bradshaw would sit.

He must have seen the disbelief in my eyes.

The sub-Warden reminded, "This is England, Chris. I imagine it takes some getting used to."

"Yes," I answered. *And then some*, I was thinking. We clinked our glasses together in toast, and killed the remainder of the gin.

I was half in the bag before I ever got to dinner.

CHAPTER 18

Before we left the Senior Common Room, all the Fellows, except me, had donned their black robes as required of them for this ritual. The robes had subtle differences. One or two had a fringe work that looked like some kind of lace running up the borders and on the cuffs of the three-quarter length sleeves. Others had worn elbows or frayed seams, the dons proud of their tattered state and wearing them like a badge of honor. There was no particular order to who went first, but there we were crossing the main courtyard toward the majestic entry to the dining hall, surrounded by the ancient yellowed stone quarried five hundred years earlier, the wind spinning the ragged hems of the gowns as clusters of Fellows, in twos and threes, formed a loose procession headed for dinner. Through the soles of my feet I could sense the Augustinian friars whose grounds these once were. I could taste the history here as certainly as I could breathe the chill autumn air.

The Fellows, who long since had come to take this as nothing more than a stroll to dinner, seemed to miss the elegance, the sense of drama that welled up in my chest. Perhaps it was the gin, perhaps that brutal English wind that stung my eyes—but I felt a certain reverence for a ceremony that had been practiced for centuries. I stood in the shadow of history, an outsider allowed not only to glimpse, but to *participate* in a ritual that held all of the wonder and formalities of England, the British Empire, Oxford University and her world-famous dons. I was a visiting Fellow. Me! This hit me hard as we formed single file and strolled down the aisle between the impossibly long, electric-candle-lit tables where the undergraduates went after their food like pigs at the trough, but who, on seeing me—for clearly I stood out—would raise their eyes and stare, their heads turning as they tracked me. *Who is this new one to High Table?* their questioning eyes said. A few of the young women smiled warmly at me and I felt myself stir. No way! I cautioned myself.

The dining hall seemed to stretch forever. Huge, life-sized oil portraits looked down on us. With its uniquely vaulted roof, this room felt more like a cathedral. The lot of us stopped and chatted by a large stone fireplace where a coal fire burned brightly. I saw Tim Binyon shaking hands with guests and composing the seating arrangement closest to him. When he felt confident we were all in attendance, he took a single step up to the small platform from which the High Table looked out onto this room. The signal. We all followed—those of us with "assigned" seating and those of us without. The chairs were tall ladder structures that seemed as old as the wood overhead. There was more silverware on three sides of my plate than I had ever encountered. Exactly how was I going to negotiate *that?* I wondered. Enough forks, knives, and spoons for a family of five. And all for me! There were two wine glasses, a water glass, and a bread plate—or was it for salad? There was a gigantic silver bowl of steaming bread. There was a head waiter, a wine steward—whose sole job was to keep our glasses topped—and four servers, two of whom I recognized from lunch. Another, Margaret, was responsible for cleaning my rooms. When the women had been seated, I sat down and tried to look comfortable. It wasn't easy.

Tim Binyon said, "Chris Klick, may I present Randall Bradshaw."

The man to my right—for indeed, Tim had placed me to his right so that I had a full view of the enormous room—offered me his hand and we shook. He *felt* like a scarecrow as well. The bones in his hand felt like the spines of a garden rake. "Pleased to meet you," he said.

"And you," I answered, regaining my strength.

I had work to do.

CHAPTER 19

T he first course, a fish course, was cold salmon with hollandaise on butternut lettuce. It was served with a fruity white wine slightly above room temperature. That, dessert and coffee, and I would have been fully satisfied.

Randall Bradshaw smacked his food and slurped his wine. The table was abuzz with the hum of congenial conversation punctuated only by the wine steward's gentle intrusion as he checked to make sure another pour was desired. You were charged for your wine consumption by the glass. Presumably the wine steward kept score, although by the look of him he practiced his trade himself.

I doubted whether, in that state, he could count to ten, much less keep straight the drinking habits of thirty Fellows and their guests. A white-gloved hand, a bottle extending from it like a prosthesis, would slip in alongside me and miraculously fill my glass, retreating as silently as a snake, a voice hissing only the single interrogative, "Sir?" A slight nod from me and the bottle tilted downward. So simple. So sloshed. So quickly.

"What's your area of expertise?" I asked my scrawny-necked neighbor, Randall Bradshaw. His starched shirt collar was a size or two too large, leaving a dark gap in which his neck pivoted. I was well aware of (though confused by) his stated expertise, but one of the intriguing parts of my role here was to know nothing; I was pretty damn practiced at playing dumb. I had spent a lifetime at it.

"I'm a diplomat," Bradshaw responded.

"Civil service, you mean? Government work?"

He looked at me curiously and his fork sank to his small plate.

"Embassies? That kind of diplomat?"

"Oh, I *see!*" he said emphatically in a most British way. He smiled. He was amused with my American ignorance. I remained confused. "No, no, no," said with all the grace of a teacher. "A *diplomat*. Diplomas. *Scrolls*."

"Oh, I *see!*" I echoed.

It appeared he liked my teasing response. He slurped down some wine, peering over the glass at me.

"Scrolls," I said.

"Exactly. I study scrolls pertaining to a forty-year period in the mid-eighteenth century."

"Scrolls?" I repeated, curious. I couldn't quite wrap my

mind around this concept. "Catacombs, that sort of thing?"

"Libraries now—environmentally controlled rooms—but yes, originally they were stored by the church or local government. No telephones in the eighteenth century," he enlightened me. "Communications were sent by messenger from sheriff to sheriff—the equivalent of a governor in *your country*." There were those two words that everyone at Wadham seemed so eager to attach to me. A day wasn't complete unless someone reminded you of where you had come from—that you were a *visitor* to England. Some salmon bubbled onto his lip and he missed it with his napkin. I felt tempted to help him—like a mother with an infant child. "What is interesting—to a scholar—about these scrolls is that each sheriff had his own identifying language and structural format. No matter what the length, given the first ten words of a communiqué, I can identify *who* sent it, therefore, approximately *when* it was sent, and, more often than not, the gist of the message—the *intention* or *purpose*—you see."

"But the paper—the parchment—has held up on these scrolls?" It seemed amazing to me that a scroll two hundred years old would not have decomposed.

"Well, then, you've hit upon my specialty *exactly*. The parchments. Indeed, one of the identifying factors in any diploma is the paper upon which it is written. Paper manufacture was a highly skilled craft, and each craftsman had his own identifying mark—thread count, pulp quality, watermark. The paper alone can tell you where and when the diploma originated. Sometimes from whom."

"Then you can judge authenticity as well," I said offhandedly.

He hesitated. "Indeed," he said, finishing the last of his salad. We didn't talk for the next few minutes. Bradshaw worked his way through his glass of wine and, giving the wine steward a sharp eye, was soon poured another. He downed this one as well. I was using the other Fellows to gauge my own consumption, and Bradshaw was suddenly ahead of the rest of us by a good deal. I tried to engage him in conversations, but after several tries it suddenly occurred to me that I must have made a misstep at some point and that Randall Bradshaw had lost any social interest in me.

The main course was a thick piece of beef, boiled carrots, roasted potatoes and a rich Bordeaux. I hesitated a moment, adjusting my napkin while I waited to see which fork was to enter into play. Three people all went for the same fork at once and I realized we were working our way in through the service, course by course. Maybe this wouldn't be so difficult after all. The gravy came around in a silver boat, and briefly the conversation waned as food replaced loose tongues. I caught Tim Binyon's curious eye. He came to my assistance by asking Bradshaw, "I say, Randall, have you heard anything from Aiden?"

The question turned several heads, not the least of which was that belonging to Randall Bradshaw.

"Me?" he asked.

"Well, yes," Binyon continued. "See you two together quite a bit these last few months."

"Me?" Bradshaw echoed. He turned a shade of red that matched the wine and he glanced around the table as if someone might come to his rescue and answer the question for him. I paid particular attention to this frantic searching on his part. When he found a set of eyes across the table and down a few people, I made a mental note of that particular face. The face belonged to a man who had made supper but had missed the Senior Common Room. "Why on earth ask *me* such a thing? I know as much—as little—as the next man."

"It's just that you two seemed to have been getting on, that's all."

"Getting on? Aiden and me? Not a bit. He's the tree-hugging sort. Hmm? Not at all my lot. You know me better than that, Tim."

He signaled the wine steward who was working his way down the other side of the table. The man didn't seem in any particular hurry to reach Bradshaw—probably worried about losing count. Bradshaw added, "Just as curious as the next chap. More so, I should think!" Again, he briefly caught eyes with the man down the table. This man had an older face with a darker complexion. His narrow-set eyes didn't stay on Bradshaw long before he caught me staring and stared right back at me. I averted my eyes, but too late: he had caught me studying him, and we both knew it. I was strangely drawn to look one more time at him, but I fought this urge, directing my attention to my beef which was proving difficult to cut and even more difficult to chew.

Bradshaw added nervously, "I should think he's off on some research trip, what? Just like Aiden Sinclair to leave unannounced. Probably a bloom coming off in York and Aiden is out chasing the damn thing down for its pigment. What?" He smiled, but it seemed forced. He drummed his finger heavily on the rim of his wine glass, again signaling the steward who had finally reached us.

I said quietly to Bradshaw, "This Aiden Sinclair thing is

of great interest to me. You can imagine how excited I was to literally step into a mystery."

"Mystery?" Bradshaw protested.

"I write mysteries," I said convincingly.

"Oh, yes. Quite. But listen here: mystery? Aiden Sinclair? No, no, no. I should hardly think so. Aiden goes wandering off like this all summer long. Off into the hills and such. But what's to it? Hmm? Crushing berries and such! Hardly out of character for Aiden to wander off. Don't understand all the fuss, actually. The Warden's not too concerned; why should the rest of us be?"

Tim Binyon heard that. He seemed ready to comment, but refrained from doing so, planting a carrot in his mouth instead and catching my eye. He chewed slowly and deliberately.

"You must know Aiden well," I said, mimicking the extremely quiet voice which everyone else was using.

"How's that?"

"Scrolls," I said. "He's an ink specialist in a way, isn't he? Herbs?" I used the American pronunciation by mistake and he didn't seem to understand the word. Remembering to make it sound like a first name, I repeated the word and Bradshaw nodded.

"Yes, I suppose we do share similar fields in a way." Then quite sternly he said to me, "We at Wadham keep pretty much to *ourselves*. Between teaching and research there is not the time—nor the desire, I might add—to wonder about the next man's business."

I took the rebuke like a man. I stabbed another piece of beef, impolitely told Bradshaw to pass the gravy, and went back to an aerobic bout of chewing. My eyes drifted to

Bradshaw's colleague across the table, where, thankfully, I found him engaged in conversation.

Maybe it was the wine. The steward just kept circling the table. I asked him, "Have you and Sinclair ever collaborated on any research projects?"

That deep red that had so magnificently colored his cheeks vanished like a curtain being lowered, leaving him ashen white. Bulls eye. They *had* indeed worked together, I decided.

Tim Binyon overheard this. "Have you two been working on something, Randall?" To me, Tim Binyon said, "Randall and Aiden were responsible for ferreting out a fake diary several years back. Perhaps you read about it. It was said to have belonged to a monk of some cloistered order and challenged the ecclesiastical canon, implying a book of the bible had been drastically rewritten for political concerns in the Middle Ages."

He asked Bradshaw rhetorically, "Wasn't it Christ Church?" To me he said, "Wadham and Christ Church ended up in a kind of contest. Their experts against ours. They challenged Randall's findings. Wasn't it Christ Church?" he repeated.

"Indeed. You know very well it was," Bradshaw answered.

"And?" I asked.

"Oh, Randall came out on top of that one! Your Yale University backed them up. Eventually Christ Church came around as well. The thing was a fake. Isn't that right, Randall?"

"A complete sham." He sipped—gulped—some wine. "The thing of it is," he explained proudly to me, "the paper was authentic enough—you see, the forgers had to *create* the actual diary itself—but the binding glue was all wrong. Aiden spotted it right off. They had done their research, but not thoroughly enough. There was a drought of several years up prior to the time the diary—the physical diary I'm now talking about—came into existence. The drought caused a shortage of a particular pitch used in binding leather to the covers. The pitch they used wasn't available for another six years and wasn't used commonly by religious orders for another ten to twelve. The diary had been clearly dated, you see, which was a big mistake on the part of the forgers, for without a date the whole thing might have passed muster."

"He's being modest," Tim said. "Wasn't the paper sideways, something like that? I thought *that* was the crowning blow!"

Bradshaw's chest swelled—he glowed—he said proudly, "The only way to create such a forgery is to cut the paper from an existing work. You can't *make* the paper, in part because the materials just aren't available, and in part because it won't test correctly. So you take the paper, sheet by sheet if necessary, from existing volumes—blank end papers, that sort of thing—and you assemble your own book. In this case, however, in the laboratory, that procedure was noticeable. Inconsistencies in the discoloration along the freshly cut edges. Also, they used a two-bladed cutting tool that was far too sharp, and not common for this period. Again, that dated the forgery and aroused our suspicions."

Binyon, too, was feeling the wine. "It was a proud moment for Wadham, is what it was. Not every day one gets a leg up on Christ Church."

Bradshaw swelled with pride and worked on his wine. Binyon had broken the ice. The man was no longer suspicious of me. He lectured me for another ten minutes on the specificities of his work, though was temporarily interrupted by the arrival of third course: a piece of crustless toast, soaked in butter and covered in melted cheese with a slice of hard-boiled egg. The way they dished out the cholesterol here, the Fellows were all walking time bombs.

When this course was finished, Binyon allowed a moment or two of idle conversation before banging the table and coming to his feet. All the Fellows rose, nearly in unison, most clutching their napkins. Tim mumbled a benediction in Latin so fast as to be incomprehensible, "*Benidictus, benidictum . . .*"

There was a loud scuffling as the chairs slid back. At least three people, including Binyon, reminded me to bring my napkin with me. I followed the robed procession out the great hall, down some stone steps, and up toward the old law library, now the lunch hall.

The hall was bathed in a gentle candlelight. The exceedingly long train of tables was laid out with silver bowls overflowing with fruit and *seven* different wines presented in various bottles and decanters. We took our seats—again assigned by Tim; it was improper to sit adjacent to the person you were near during supper, so it took some reshuffling of the deck to accomplish the proper seating arrangement. Once seated, the bottles came around, one by one, in a strict procession. I chose my poison—port, in honor of Aiden Sinclair—and passed the bottles on to the man to my left. This man quickly corrected me. He said politely, "*Always* pass the lighter wines first. If you pass them on in the order you receive them, then all is well." He added, "Or at least it is the other chap's fault." He winked at me. I winked back, which, I feared, he took as an offense. I introduced myself to him. "That's fine," he said, shaking my hand reluctantly and not offering me his name. I had the feeling I might never know many of these men by name.

I counted five laps of the wine brigade. I stopped pouring for myself after two, electing to pass the bottles on without partaking. But, to my surprise, many of the Fellows filled up on every lap. It was true—the glasses—we each had *three* of varying sizes—were quite small, but even so, the volume of conversation was growing louder with each lap and the smiles were beginning to look pasted on. The Fellows were drunk. Quite drunk. And me, along with them. It would be a day or so before it would occur to me that they did this *every* night.

Following dessert, which lasted about forty-five minutes, I took a stroll hoping to sober up. The night air was damp and cold and was tinged with the smell of smoke. I walked fully around the main garden and tried my new key to the Fellows' Garden, but was too drunk to get the door unlocked. I walked over into the shadow of a small beech tree, to the statue of the former warden, and perched on his arm. The cold metal actually felt good to me.

When I reopened my eyes, I was staring at Randall Bradshaw, who was standing in the uppermost window, framed in a rich green. This was the only window lit in the building at this hour. His mouth was moving: he was speaking to someone. A second or two later he was joined at the window in a hot discussion with the dark complexioned man I had seen, but had not met, at High Table. They both had a drink in hand. When Bradshaw moved to my left, and temporarily out of my sight, a third man could be seen. He was standing farther back in the room, visible from the waist up. I could guess the names of the two strangers: Henry Hagg and Lester Tilbert.

There I was, lounging on the arm of a former Warden, witnessing what appeared to be an emergency meeting of the three men whose names I had found in Aiden Sinclair's office. Despite the cold, despite the wine's dizzying warmth, I felt a distinctive pounding in my chest—there seemed to be one, and only one, reason these men might be up in that room: I had said something to rattle Randall Bradshaw at dinner, or he had said something to me he shouldn't have.

The problem was, I had no idea what I had said. At that particular time of night, I couldn't remember much at all of dinner. I could barely remember dessert, except the nearly endless circling of wine bottles—in the proper order please—and a kiwi fruit I had peeled on my plate to the amazement of several men around me. The kiwi's at Wadham were not peeled, I was told, they were cut in half and eaten with a spoon like a section of cantaloupe.

I found myself climbing a narrow, cold, spiral staircase made of ancient stone. I had come completely around to the main courtyard and had entered through the central arch that, to the right, leads to the Hall. To the left, through an extremely low door, was this spiral staircase that wound its way up to the old Fellows' dining room, a room still used for off-season dinners for the dons. Tim Binyon had toured me here on my first day. As I recalled, there was also a balcony overlooking the main dining room. But this staircase was the only way up or down and I knew from experience that the first rule of eavesdropping is to *always* allow yourself two different modes of escape. Entering a cul-de-sac of any kind was the mark of an amateur.

But I wasn't thinking very clearly. I had the wine to thank for that, as well as the adrenaline pumping through me. And there I violated another cardinal rule: never mix booze and adrenaline.

I sneaked my way up the claustrophobic staircase, bent over like a hunchback, angled sideways to accommodate my wide shoulders, prepared—or so I thought—to make a quick exit. My full intention was to place my ear on the door to the Green Room, as it was called, and hear what it was none of my business to hear.

I was one step away from the door when I saw the oversized doorknob turn and a crack of light jump from the ever-widening opening.

With my reaction time numbed, I lost my chance at the stairs. The angle was wrong—I stood a good chance of being seen.

Instead, I took a giant stride right past the Green Room's door and kept right on going, up a single step and through the door to the grand hall's small balcony.

I made it through to the balcony, and I nearly had the door shut behind me when I thought better of it. I was too late; it would be seen closing. Of this, I was convinced.

I heard a few protesting words from a voice that wasn't Bradshaw's. "We haven't resolved this, Henry! Walking away is no kind of answer."

An equally unknown voice—presumably that of Henry Hagg—said, "Good things come to he who waits. Patience, my boy." He added, "This too shall pass." I wondered if he meant me. "Was this door open?" he asked.

The Brits are peculiarly sensitive to doors left open. Not only do they like their doors shut, but locked. Many a front door to a British home has no doorknob at all on its exterior—only a key hole and a knocker. A door left open was a red flag for these Fellows.

I could hear him approaching.

He intended to check the balcony.

A balcony is a strangely naked place to want to hide. It is, perhaps, the worst of all cul-de-sacs, for it ends in mid-air. But if I didn't move quickly, I was going to be discovered, and I didn't care for that idea one bit.

I raced to the far end of the tiny balcony, vaulted the stone rail, hooked my hands around two of the ancient balustrades and lowered myself to hanging. Only my hands remained on the dark balcony. The rest of me dangled out of view, suspended twelve feet above an electric candelabra and a giant dining table. Even with my six-feet-plus of body height and my just-shy-of-three-feet arms, I had about a four foot free fall to reach the table top. This would not be a dainty, quiet drop but would instead sound more like a traffic accident.

The door swished as it came open. "I don't remember this being open," echoed the voice of Henry Hagg. Footsteps. I couldn't tell their direction, but I suddenly caught sight of his shadow, back lit and stretched to an impossible size, cast out across the vast space of the empty dining hall. He looked like a praying mantis. Another, equally disgusting, insect joined him.

The familiar voice of Randall Bradshaw, his chewed words rolling together from over consumption said, "Oh, God, Henry—we've turned you into a paranoid! Look at you. The balcony is *empty*, dear boy. What exactly are you looking for?"

"I tell you, this door was closed."

"As drafty as a barn, this old hall. Good God—just *look* at you!"

The image of the praying mantis stopped. It turned and retreated toward the door.

To my astonishment, I heard a key turn. They had *locked* me on the balcony.

The crash heard later that same night in the dining hall was never fully explained.

CHAPTER 20

I *saw her from the corner when she turned and doubled back*. Lyrics—even Chuck Berry lyrics—intruded into my thoughts more often than I ever admitted. Music was a part of me. I had long since willed my body to science and someday, when I was dead and gone and the chemical engineers disassembled my DNA, they were going to discover a few quarter notes attached somewhere along my chain. Some sharps and flats.

This particular lyric was inspired by the magical grace of Allison Star—one R. You can be told how beautiful a woman is, but nothing fully prepares you for the Allison Stars of this world. It seemed as if a spotlight were singling her out from the crowd. I caught myself holding my breath, this tingling surge of energy passing from my groin up through my chest and flushing my cheeks. "Jesus!" I spoke aloud to no one.

She wasn't *Glamour* magazine beautiful. Not a bit. She was dressed like a vagabond, like all the Oxford students dressed—ill-fitting clothes loosely hung off bad postures and fragmented hair cuts that totally lacked any hint of style. Allison's hair was the exception, and perhaps it helped to single her out. It was a clean strawberry-blonde, cut just above her shoulders and curled in at the bottom so that it cupped her ears. She carried herself magnificently—proudly and with a deliberate, careful stride. She had very square shoulders, an exceptionally thin waist, and long, graceful legs. But it was her hands that gave away her beauty and her profession. Outrageously long fingers, soft smooth skin, and perfectly manicured nails. No jewelry. No nail color. Tiny little wrists. She wore a starched white man-tailored shirt and a huge sport coat, baggy and awkward. The shirt was tucked into oversized heavy wool slacks gathered at her waist and bunched by a brown leather belt. Her face was too round to qualify for the cover-girl look, and her eyes a little large—but the effect on me was like seeing Audrey Hepburn in *Roman Holiday*: breathtaking. What's more, she possessed that spirited intelligence that grew bigger than life as I approached her. She had an aura, a persona that drew you in like steel filings to a magnet. When I was ten feet away, and closing, all else slowed down, so that only Allison Star existed. This, I thought, was the same phenomenon that had women accused of being witches. This power. Men feared it because it reduced them to sniveling wimps incapable of getting out a coherent sentence.

"Allison Star?" I said, when alongside of her.

She took one look at me and doubled her pace. My size had frightened her. It wasn't the first time I had had this happen. It's strange to have people look at you as if you're some kind of monster, when inside you feel so differently.

I kept up with her.

"Don't," she said. "Go away." She continued to walk at a frantic pace, forcing me to dodge other students or risk knocking them over.

"Don't follow you? Or don't go away?" I asked. "I'm Chris Klick. I'm a mystery writer. I'm on a research fellowship at Wadham."

She stopped abruptly. Her chest was heaving. Nice chest at that, now that I was closer. Her face was scarlet. She looked at me once, but then gazed down at her shoes. "That's original."

"It's true."

"*She* sent you, didn't she?"

"Who?"

"Oh, come on! Just leave me alone. Please. I don't know where he is."

"Who?" I repeated.

"What are you, an owl or something?" She snorted her discontent.

"You're Allison Star the cellist, aren't you? I heard you perform in Italy with the youth orchestra." One of the problems with being a good liar was that I learned to really hate myself now and then. The huge sense of relief I saw in her eyes—the flattered touch of conceit—made me feel like a schmuck. But I had a job to do, I reminded myself—and somehow, as always when Lyel was involved, I was quickly getting away from it.

"What?" she asked.

"The youth orchestra."

She studied me then, head to foot. It wasn't a sexual examination, but that was how my hormones mistook it. She sized me up, shook her head in disbelief and said, "No."

"No, what?"

"I don't know. Just no. You have 'no' written all over you."

"Are you flirting with me?" I tossed this out there because I wanted to catch her on the side of the head with something completely unexpected. It was my only hope of dislodging her suspicions. She had good instincts, this woman, and my job was to dismantle them.

She coughed up a laugh. "Don't flatter yourself." We were back into our foot race, though with my long strides it was no contest. Perhaps she *was* flirting. What a heady thought *that* was. I stopped walking. She went right on going. I waited. When she glanced over her shoulder at me—just to check—I knew I had her interest.

I caught back up to her at a run. "Coffee. I know this is your first day. I know a *lot* about you." Flattery, I hoped, might get me somewhere. This had to be one lonely, frightened woman. "Have you been to the Nose Bag."

She laughed. "The *what*?"

"Best cheap food in the city."

"The Nose Bag?"

"Exactly. What they lacked in naming the place, they made up for in their desserts."

"Desserts?"

"Chocolate cake?"

"No kidding?"

"And I'm buying."

"Why should I?" she asked.

"Because it's *good* cake."

"I don't think so," she said, clearly reconsidering. "Besides," she added, stopping at a door. "This is my lecture." She pulled the door open. The room was teeming with students and noise.

"What if I wait?"

"Tell her I don't know where he is."

"Who?"

"There you go again."

She disappeared inside. The door closed behind her.

I headed to the Nose Bag. I knew that look in a woman's eye: This one had a real relationship going with chocolate. Me—she could care less about.

CHAPTER 21

I was four cups of coffee into my buzz when she entered the second story restaurant. New to university, she came alone, having not yet established a social set. She had bought the cake and coffee before she ever saw me, and when she did, she headed straight to my table. "Are you following me?" she asked.

"I was about to ask you the same thing." I pointed to my crumb-littered plate. "This is my fourth cup." I nudged a chair with my foot. "Join me?"

She looked at me skeptically. Her jaw fell open slightly and she shook her head. "No."

As she walked away I said, "You keep saying that."

There were no empty tables in the place. All told, the Nose Bag held about ten tables. Four of them were large clear-finished picnic tables and were used as family dining, strangers sitting alongside strangers. The smaller tables were shared as well, but only at peak hours. As it was, she was going to have to ingratiate herself into a table of complete strangers or accept my offer. Men were staring. She made two full laps before surrendering.

She took her seat, saying nothing to me, and went to work on the cake. She cut her pieces delicately, keeping them small, stretching out the experience. "This is *really* good," she allowed about five minutes into it. She glanced up at me occasionally, as suspicious and skeptical as ever. She said, "You're too old for a fellowship."

"Thanks."

She smiled and wiped chocolate off her lips. "You're staring at my hands."

"They're nice hands."

"No one has ever stared at my hands before."

"Don't kid yourself. You just never *caught* them at it."

She shot me one quick, hot glance. I felt it down in my knees.

"Nice eyes, too," I said.

She blushed. "I don't even know you."

"And we're already having coffee together." I added, "What do you think of Elgar?"

"He's never done anything wonderful for the cello."

"How about Barber?"

"Melts me. Absolutely melts me. Physical. He's extremely physical and passionate. It's very hard to play the ones that affect you physically. I tend to overplay Barber, which is bad. Every now and then there's a composer like that—you know? Lights you up like a Christmas tree."

"Like Stephan Shultz?" I asked. She didn't like that. "More coffee?"

"Sure."

I grabbed her mug and refilled both of ours.

"Why did you say that?" she asked when I returned. "Who are you?"

"There's a rumor going around Wadham that you're going to play the Holywell and that Stephan Shultz might conduct. He conducted you in Italy. Even an *old* man like me can do simple math."

"It's not so simple," she said.

"It's no coincidence, is it? Italy and then here? You and Shultz."

She stabbed at the chocolate cake. After all the care she had taken with it, it seemed to be a kind of violation. "No coincidence."

"So there *is* going to be a concert?"

"I'm scheduled into the Holywell. Yes. I have no idea if Stephan Shultz will conduct."

"And the program?"

"The rumor line didn't know?"

"Know what?"

"You've heard about the Mozart, haven't you?"

"*The* Mozart?"

"The missing manuscript page? The page that was found. From the *Liebespaar* cello concerto."

"They found the missing *Liebespaar?*"

"Christ Church is verifying the work. I'm to be the first cello player in two hundred years to play the concerto in its entirety," she said, radiant with pride. "Scholars have been arguing about that page for the better part of this century. The Holywell is significant because as a child Mozart played there. Did you know that? He wrote the *Liebespaar* not long after that, while still here in England. It's a very significant find."

"I know the *Liebespaar* very well," I exaggerated. Lyel would know all about it. Lyel knew *everything* about classical music, opera, and ballet.

"Dozens of scholars have written that missing page—for the sake of performance. Now, finally, we will all see the original."

"You haven't seen it then?"

"Oh, no. It's not been published. It has to be authenticated first. I'll see it in rehearsal. Then the world will hear."

"I can see why Stephan Shultz would be anxious to conduct something as important as that."

"He was born here in England. Did you know that? That is about his *only* hope of being part of this. They would never let a full-blooded American conduct. Not the premiere."

"But you are American, and they're asking you to perform."

"True, but I think that is because my competition for such a performance, in terms of cello, would be a Japanese and the Japanese have enough clout and influence here at Oxford already without giving them something like this. It's a very difficult piece."

"*The Lover*," I translated. "It had better be difficult. Relationships are certainly tough enough."

She nodded, suddenly sad. I imagined she was in the

midst of one of the most difficult relationships possible. Twenty-some years younger than her lover. He, an international celebrity. Stolen monies. Lawsuits. Investigators. I felt myself growing sympathetic to her problems and softening in a way I couldn't allow myself. I would have to watch her now, and hope she led me to Stephan Shultz. The sooner the better. If I stayed around much longer in Oxford, the Aiden Sinclair mess was going to trap me—I could feel it. I was getting sucked into that. Lyel wasn't helping matters any, running around the country trying to find Sinclair. The more effort he put into this, the harder it was going to be for me to quit.

I finished my coffee. "Well," I said, unable to think of what to say. It was her hands doing that to me. I couldn't keep my eyes off them. "If you're going to be giving a recital—anything like that—I hope you'll let me know. Chris Klick at Wadham."

"I remember," she said. Did she want to me stay a while longer? Was that what I saw in her eyes?

"If the Fellows invited you to perform—you know, informally—maybe a string quartet, something like that, would you do it? Could you put something like that together?"

"Does that play into your mystery?"

"Pardon me?"

"Your mystery—the one you're writing."

"Oh, yeah. Sure. The mystery. Fits right in," I acknowledged.

"Is dinner involved?"

"At the college, or with me?"

"Both?"

"High Table?"

"Do you have dining privileges?"

"Absolutely."

"I would *love* to do a High Table."

"We'll do it up," I told her.

"Will we?" she asked dreamily. She was young; I had allowed myself to overlook this, but now there was no mistaking it.

"The Fellows drink like fish. It helps make up for the food."

"Perfect. But I better perform *first*." She grinned.

"Be careful. I'm going to set this up."

I was standing, looking down at the way her fingers curled around the warm cup.

"I hope you will," she said, looking me in the eye. Yes, nice eyes.

I decided right there and then I didn't like Stephan Shultz. I didn't like him at all. I didn't like myself much either. Misleading a young, confused woman, all in the hopes of getting my job done. Or *was* that all of it? Maybe the smart thing to do was not give Shultz the chance at the royalty money. Leave him to work out his sordid life without my help.

Then again, I wasn't known for doing the smart thing.

CHAPTER 22

I move through life from error to error, victory to victory. I tend to forget those times in between—and the in-between occupy the largest portion of my life. But it is the mountain tops and the river bottoms that I remember, that I cling to for dear life, treasuring every second, not the long, strenuous hike up or down. Life, it is said, is not the destination, but the journey there. For me it is a series of stops along the way, a series of stellar moments that have little relationship to either the journey or the destination except that these moments exist on that same fragile time line.

One such moment occurred that afternoon as I cleared the final squeaking stair and turned to face the trapezoidal door to my Wadham office.

Nicole was sitting in a formed fiberglass chair waiting for me.

I laughed. Laughed aloud. One quick, sharp, nervous peal of unconfined emotional release. To my eyes, she looked as lovely, as peaceful—she was as welcome—as any person on earth.

She smiled.

I said, "All the pain, all the hurt I have endured since Paris is small payment to enjoy even one of your smiles."

"Keep talking," she encouraged as I approached my office door, not knowing if she would allow me to take her into my arms. I fumbled with the key and opened the door.

I said, "The joy of this moment, the lightness of my heart, is something I will always treasure, always remember. Even if you've come here to get rid of me—which is itself an impossibility—my only regret would be how long it was between your smiles."

"That's not why I'm here. I'm here because I'm a sucker for your purple prose, your quiet eyes, and the sound of your voice. I'm here because I reacted wrong in Paris and because even a brief amount of time with you—which is somehow all we ever get—is among the best times. I'm not here to forget or to remember, though I wish we could do both. I'm just here, I guess."

"I have an electric fire in my office."

"You always were a romantic."

"When it really gets cooking, it smells like a toaster on the fritz." I smiled. I couldn't help but smile around her.

"Any coffee?"

"Tea. There's coffee in the Common Room."

"Tea's fine."

"Are you going to come in?" I asked.

"My legs won't move."

"I could serve you out here." I added, "Or I would gladly carry you inside."

She stood and took a tentative step toward me.

I dropped the keys and pulled her into my arms with enough strength to squeeze the air out of her. She hugged me back, her face turned into my chest, her hair scented like fresh cut flowers. She began to shake—she was either crying or laughing. I didn't care which. I was crying; I knew that much—watering the flowers in her hair.

Laughing and crying, it's the same release. Joni Mitchell. More lyrics. Music swimming in my head. Big orchestral stuff. Butterflies in my stomach.

"Who's your carpenter?" she asked, noticing the peculiar slant to the door.

"The place has settled some over the centuries."

"Haven't we all," she added nervously.

We made it inside. I switched on the electric fire. She peeled off her coat, rubbed her hands together and studied the place as I went about filling my electric kettle from the hideaway sink. "Interesting reading," she commented.

"The man is on sabbatical. He's a chemical engineer or something like that."

She had reached the windows. "Fantastic views," she said.

"It's a great location," I agreed.

She drew each of the drapes after inspecting the view. She headed back to the door, and for a moment I thought I was to lose her again, but she depressed a button on the lock and the springed latch sprang into place, locking us inside. By this point the electric fire was in full blaze. *Put another log on the fire.* She pushed the two awkward chairs out of the way, clearing a space on the floor in front of the wall toaster. My pulse was somewhere around one-sixty. My heart was lodged just below my Adam's apple. Our brief physical relationship in Idaho, several years earlier, had ended in front of a fire. Were we to pick up where we had left off?

She removed an afghan throw from the back of one of the chairs, shook it and spread it in this cleared space. Then she knelt down onto her knees facing me and began to unbutton her blouse. She said, "I know we should probably do a lot of talking, a lot of catching up. Right? Talk until two in the morning? But what if we say things we don't mean? What if we hear things we don't want to hear? Somehow I think that in *our* case, it's not the right approach at all." She unbuttoned the last button. Her blouse remained closed, but open. She unfastened her belt, unbuttoned the waist of her dark pants and unzipped the fly. The kettle whistled. I was frozen. "That will have to steep, won't it?"

"There's a bed," I pointed to the other room.

"No. Beds are for later. This is where we left off—in front of the fire." She had clearly treasured that moment as much as I had—realizing this meant the world to me.

I poured the water and capped the tea pot, sliding a cozy over it. I took a cautious step toward her—this was her choreography, not mine. I didn't want to misstep. "This thing hardly qualifies as a fire."

"It's quite warm," she said, parting her blouse.

I had no memory of losing my clothes, although I did remember removing hers. I drank in the smell of her skin where her neck met her shoulders. I absorbed the quiet cooing sound she made as my fingers roamed her skin. I treasured the purring deep in her throat when I kissed away one of her tears; the taste of her lips; the shifting color in her eyes, altered slightly by the orange glow of the electric fire as she squinted in pleasure. Her nails raised goose bumps as they raced down my spine. She welcomed me lusciously in a smooth pocket of warmth and tenderness, locking onto me, holding us immovable for several long, wondrous minutes before we began even the slightest of movements. Then it was all an expression of what I felt inside: adoration, empathy, forgiveness, gratitude. It was Us, not me, not her. I had everything at that moment. Take my wallet, my experiences, even my music. This surpassed passion, the tactile realm, the physical plane. It was instead, all-encompassing. The ultimate connection, the surrender of one's soul. This was the summit—a view from the highest mountain.

The wall heater hummed. Traffic moved below. Her heartbeat increased and finally approached mine. She clung to me greedily. I treasured the moment.

CHAPTER 23

When I opened the door to the hallway, mid-morning, I found Lyel sitting uncomfortably in the formed fiberglass chair. He didn't even turn to face me. He said, "I figured I had better wait." This was to help explain to me why he had not knocked.

"You figured how?" I asked.

He pointed to the floor where my keys lay in a pile. "Even you don't forget your keys unless it's something important."

"I have you to thank for this, don't I?" I asked sincerely.

"It was she who sought you out. I merely aided the effort. May I come in? I'm getting arthritic in this chair. Or do you need to clean the place up first?"

"You can be really vulgar when you try."

"I'm tired. I have traveled great distances in the past few days. I'm worried because I assume Ms. Star has arrived on campus—as it were—and that, by definition, will distract you from the more pressing troubles of Tim Binyon and the elusive Aiden Sinclair."

"You're one of those people who begins to sound British the longer you stay here. Did you know that? Talk normal, Lyel, would you?"

"I am talking normal. *Listen* normal, would you?"

He stood and ducked through the doorway. His eyes lighted on the downed afghan. I kicked it aside. "Good for you," he said. "*Both* of you," he added. I had no comment. It was none of his business, despite his involvement in getting us together. "May we talk?"

"She's sleeping," I said, indicating the other room.

He gave me one of his patented—"Oh, how cute"—grins. Condescending and jealous at the same time. I had no comment.

"You didn't find him?" I said, extrapolating from his earlier comment that Aiden Sinclair remained elusive.

"Indeed I did. Sort of."

I knew that look of his. Defeat. Fear. How had I missed it, up until now? My knees betrayed me. I sank into a chair. "Lyel?"

"It confounds me that human nature is to get rid of something when it worries you, rather than resolve the worry. You see, he had telephoned ahead in preparation for taking a room at a small B&B on the Cornish coast. And, it so happened that the landlord . . . well, I won't bore you with the details. Suffice it to say I obtained the phone number—at no small cost, I might add—and was later able to locate the establishment that belonged to that phone number through an *exhaustive* search of Fodor's *Guide to B&Bs*. I called ahead, attempting to establish that Sinclair had indeed taken up residence there, only to be told no such man had registered. However, a description I provided, which, in fact, was the description Binyon provided us, was immediately associated with a gentleman who had taken a room beginning the night before. I allowed that I was to pay the gentleman a surprise visit and that it would not do at all for him to know in advance of my arrival. I thought the proprietress was with me on this. She's a woman by the name of Moorehead. Have you got a drink?" he asked. It was only the middle of the day, but I dutifully served Lyel a sherry and warmed water for tea for myself.

After a few sips of the drink, he continued. "This is not my game, Klick. You know that. I'm not particularly good at this sort of thing. Rather bad at it, actually, I'm afraid to admit at this late date. The only explanation I can give is that I must have been followed. Of course, there may be some other explanation, and it would relieve me a great deal to learn of it, but I somehow doubt it. The point being that by the time I reached the small coastal town of St. Agnes, our dear friend Sinclair had been away from the B&B for some eighteen hours. What is most troublesome is that his belongings—his bag, some paperwork—were to be found in his room. I insisted that Mrs. Moorehead take a look you see. Sinclair had gone for a walk up the National Trust's coastal path late afternoon the day before. Mrs. Moorehead believed she had missed him during one of her errands into town. Never mind, she thought, he's gone to supper. They have wicked fogs along the Cornish coast, and St. Agnes has a lovely old lighthouse with a deep, resonant fog horn that can be heard for miles. So the theory goes that even if Sinclair had wandered off the path—presuming now that he *did not* head into town for supper as Mrs. Moorehead supposed—the fog horn is sharp enough and clear enough to lead a true Englishman back to town. Don't look at me like that. I didn't say it was *my* theory." I made my tea strong and added a half teaspoon of honey, something that drew a painful wince from Sir Lyel.

"The fact of the matter is that Sinclair never returned to his lodgings—although, and this is pure speculation on my part—his things had been gone through, and, quite likely, some papers removed from them. How do I know this? I can see it in your eyes! I know this—I speculate—because

I discovered a paper clip on his bedspread and his case zipped shut leaning against the bedpost. That's all, just a paper clip. But entirely out of place. And everything *inside* his case was neatly paper clipped. Dozens of bunches of papers, all neatly paper clipped, and one stray paper clip. Anyway, I suppose there are any number of explanations for his disappearance. He may have innocently slipped from the path and fallen to his death. I'm told it happens—and not infrequently in the bad fog—and that bodies are rarely discovered. The water's extremely cold there. The bodies go down fast. By the time they bloat and return to the surface some days later, they're miles out to sea—caught in a fisherman's net if they're lucky. Left to God, in all his wisdom, if not."

He had been drinking before he came here. It was the only explanation for his long-winded, overly dramatic presentation. Lyel had never handled death well. It went back to his father, who had been an MIA early on in the Korean conflict.

"Of course, he may have been *assisted* in his fall—if he took a fall. He may have indeed gone into town for dinner as Mrs. Moorehead believes, in which case, it's likely he was abducted somewhere along the way. By whom, and to what purpose, remains a mystery, at least to me. Or he may have, in fact, been caught by the tide. There is a wicked tide there—twelve feet or more in the matter of little more than an hour. It's swallowed little children in the past. You have to move your parked car, or it too will be drowned by that tide."

"This sounds like a wonderful place."

"It's actually quite charming. Depressed economy, like all the coastal villages, but lovely to look at." He sipped the sherry again.

"So we've lost him for the time being."

"That's the optimistic attitude, yes."

"I'm feeling optimistic today."

"No surprise there." Lyel reached out with his long leg and toed the afghan.

"So long as you're in such a lucid mood . . . how about I throw a couple of ideas past you?" I said.

"I'm intoxicated."

"That's what I meant."

"Oh."

"I believe I have identified a trio of fellows, who, it would seem, have only recently, after years of opportunity, found a common friendship. These same fellows had the good fortune to be written up on a Post-It note alongside Aiden Sinclair's office telephone."

"We've already discussed this."

"Yes, but I was able to meet one of these fine men. At High Table no less."

"How did you like it?"

"Meeting him?"

"High Table, you idiot."

"The one area of your intoxication that I take issue with is this propensity for denigrating comments about my intelligence. Can't we leave that out of it?"

"How was it, Your Majesty?"

"Ceremonial. Filling. Sumptuous. Splendiferous. Scintillating conversation, an awe inspiring spectacle. But! More to the point, I engaged in an exchange of words with one Randall Bradshaw, diplomat extraordinaire. Diplomat," I repeated, "in the original sense of the word."

"Scrolls," Lyel answered, annoying me with his knowledge of such things.

"It took me a while to cotton-on to that concept, but yes, scrolls."

"And what was he like, this Randall Bradshaw?"

"At first charming, interesting, a little drunk. But later, reserved, withdrawn, edgy, and even more drunk."

"They do like to drink, the dons," Lyel said.

"Somewhere during the conversation, Bradshaw tuned me out, either because I'm me, or because I struck a nerve. By his increased consumption of wine, and because of a situation that occurred later that night, I think it may have been the latter, but I too was drinking heavily and I'll be damned if I can remember what it was I said that set him off."

Lyel advised, "They're temperamental, those dons. It may not have been you."

"There's something I haven't shown you."

"Do tell."

"Show-and-tell time." I excused myself and went into the bedroom. She was asleep, her bare back to me, hair spilled across the pillow. Sight of her took my breath away. For a few seconds I just stood there staring. Then I located the sample of mud from Aiden Sinclair's clothing and returned to show it to Lyel.

After my explanation of its discovery, Lyel studied it for several long minutes, turning it over and over in his huge fingers. "It's a unique color, I'll say that."

"Identifiable, I dare say," I said, mocking an English accent.

"Don't even *pretend* like that," he scolded. He studied it again. "I think they call this a clue."

I said, "Great minds think alike."

CHAPTER 24

I debated leaving a note for Nicole, but decided it was far too impersonal. Instead, I awakened her by gently rubbing her back. She rolled over, and I then gently rubbed her front, and we nearly lost another hour. I was going out, I told her, but there was no reason for her to react to that. I hoped she would continue sleeping until whenever and leave a note or be around upon my return. I began to explain where the women's shower was located but she stopped me, reminding me she had a hotel room in town, and that she would, most definitely, leave a note.

Lyel and I attempted to retrace the footsteps of the missing Aiden Sinclair on the night he had arrived at the Fellows' Common Room so covered in mud. It was not an easy task because, from everything we had been told, he tended to roam on extended walks after dinner in an effort to wear off the effects of the port. The first route we took was along Parks Road, north, away from college and the center of town. It was a lovely stroll along a tree-lined flagstone footpath, following, for some distance, a high stone wall surrounding various University properties. This same wall, however, prevented much wandering. Lyel kicked back the leaves and grass until we could see clearly the color of the wet earth here; even given allowances for moisture content, we both agreed it was no match whatsoever. We continued on to a large park, where even on a cold autumn day students were involved in all sorts of frenetic activity, including use of the American Frisbee, which amused Lyel to no end. Here again, try as we might, we failed to find any matching mud samples.

Lyel, who professed to know something about geology, suggested that with the appearance of all of the top soil being so similar, there existed a good possibility that we were looking for a *deeper* soil, something dug up.

Being geniuses, both of us said, in unison, "The gardens!"

The return walk to college was accomplished in less than half the time of our original sortie, both of us long-legged and eager competitors. We headed directly to the student garden, located a worker busy beneath a leafless bush, and consulted him on the color of soils in the area. He must have forgiven us our ugly-American abruptness and tendency to speak over each other—in our excitement, even Lyel lost his manners. Unlike an American college campus worker, who would be only too happy to stop work for whatever reason, for whatever time period, this British counterpart was a true gardener in the sense that he appeared, in fact, to merely tolerate the interruption. He had no intention of engaging in a long-winded explanation.

"Aye, the soils certainly change colors, lads," he said thickly. "Depending on where you be and how deep you stick the spade."

I could barely interpret what had been said, but Lyel seemed to grasp it quickly. He asked, "How deep is the top soil—on average?"

"Better than several feet. You bury a fellow, you'll find some different soil, I should say. You should be talking to the grave diggers." He laughed. "Those buggers'll know 'bout the earth, now won't they, lads?"

It was a ghastly thought, but both Lyel and I thought it at the same time: one way a person could become so absolutely covered in mud was to fall down into a hole. This too might have explained Sinclair's excitement about his unmentioned discovery.

Lyel and I both thanked him. This most recent possibility had brought a sudden silence over both of us. We were a good twenty feet away from the gardener when he called out, "Lads! If you want a good look at the different soils, might I suggest the new dormitory?" He answered our curious expressions with, "The construction on t'other side of the chapel." He pointed.

The connection went off in both our heads simultaneously. He must have been surprised to see two grown men wave enthusiastically and then take off with a sprinter's start toward the chapel cloisters and the construction beyond.

We reached the barrier surrounding the pit in the ground out of breath, breathing fog like fire-breathing dragons. We could hear workers shoveling on the far side of the huge concrete stem walls, but on this side there was no one to be seen.

The construction site was perhaps one hundred by two hundred feet, an absolutely enormous hole cut deeply in the ground, now with fifteen-foot-high formed-concrete walls reaching up toward ground level where we stood. Rising from these walls at regular intervals, bunches of steel reinforcement rod reached upward, ready for the next pour of concrete.

"That's twenty-five feet down at least," Lyel said. As with most other subjects, Lyel considered himself an expert on construction. Those venturesome enough to ask him would be told that in the days immediately following his limited run as an NBA center forward, he had "dabbled" in both real estate and, later, construction contracting, and had, at the end of his short building career, erected the largest log home in North America—twenty-seven thousand square feet, near Sandpoint, Idaho. All of it was true, though it didn't make him any better a judge of distance.

"I believe you," I said. With Lyel, it's often best to agree. I was guessing the hole at more like twenty feet.

"And look there," he said pointing out the strata of soil levels where a mechanical bucket had surgically sheered the earth. It *was* intriguing, like something from a junior high field trip. I could clearly make out three separate layers, three different colors and textures to the soil composition. The first, at ground level, was dark and loamy and ran to a depth of about four feet; the second, cratered with great chunks of black rock, carried on for another two to three feet; and the third, made pale by limestone, ran as deep as the hole had been dug. This last section was, to the eye, the closest relative to the sample I had removed from the trousers of the missing Sinclair. The similarity was not lost on Lyel who was already looking for a way through the saw-horse barrier and into the pit.

"Interesting, isn't it?" he asked, now pointing to the recent construction of a plywood wall about ten feet high, the purpose of which was unclear.

"The partition?" I asked. "For safety, don't you think?"

"But examine its *placement*," Lyel chided, as if to say: *Do I have to tell you* everything?

He was right—of course—when one examined the area of excavation protected by the plywood wall, it seemed to be an odd choice. "There are far more dangerous, more troublesome spots than that," I concluded.

"Exactly."

"Unless that is merely the start of the barrier. Maybe they intend to wrap the whole site."

"Let's have a look," Lyel suggested.

They had done a good job of it. Where the barrier was erected there was no chance of an accidental fall. My mind wasn't working well. I had Nicole to thank for that. "Do you suppose this thing was inspired by Sinclair's fall?"

That comment invoked a withering look from Lyel. "I guess so," I answered aloud.

"But there is more here than meets the eye," Lyel suggested. "Do you see it?"

We lived in this state of perpetual challenge, Lyel and I. It wasn't good enough to just make a statement. You had to throw a teaser out there and invite comparison, entice some competitive hormones in the other man. Embarrassing the other scored big. To look like a fool was the ultimate failure. Such interrogatory provocations did keep the mind sharp, the eye hungry, and the conversations moving. We were rarely bored when in each other's company.

I sought out as quick an answer as I could, compiling as many as possible, sorting them according to likelihood, so as to have back-ups available if my first attempts failed. This was war and you didn't leave the entire battle to the front line. "The excavation is a funny shape," I proposed.

"Very good," came his answer, indicating I was only partially there.

"It's cut away right there instead of running parallel to the poured foundation."

"Yes. Exactly," Lyel agreed.

"Excavation of this sort is typically done in a straight line, unless some part of the construction *calls* for a curve at that location—say an entranceway, terraced stairs, or a fountain."

"Okay . . ." he said.

"You're keeping something from me," I said, detecting as much.

"You're keeping it from yourself," he chastised.

"Meaning?"

"The Senior Common Room. You've overlooked the Common Room."

I had to bend my mind out of shape, for at that moment it couldn't have been further from the Senior Common Room. Slowly some images took shape in my mind and I exclaimed, "The model! The plans!"

He smiled patronizingly. The common room contained a beautifully constructed scale-model cardboard replica of the future dormitory and, framed on the walls behind it, prints of the various floor plans. Only a mind such as Lyel's could not only recall its existence, but also the specific details of the building itself. I didn't even know when he'd been inside the Common Room—Lyel was full of such surprises. He said confidently, "There's no such bulge called out in the plans. I promise you that."

"Maybe they hit a pipe or something. Can you imagine digging around a place as old as this?"

"Perhaps," he said, though sounding thoroughly unconvinced.

"If not that, then *what?*" I begged.

"Just a thought, that's all." He circled around the construction site then, leaving me little choice but to follow like an obedient dog. For all his charming sensitivity, Lyel could be an insensitive brute when he worked at it. He stopped abruptly, turned and asked, "What did you say just now?"

"A broken pipe."

"No, after that."

"Digging in a place as old—"

"Oh, yes." He continued around the structure, with me taking up the rear.

It was somewhere during our orbit of the construction that I first noticed that prickly sensation at the back of my neck that warned me I was being observed. It's as keen as a sixth sense; you either have it or you don't. It had cropped up enough over the years that I had learned to trust it. I had learned to react to it.

Lyel, for his part, felt nothing, and continued his goose-walk around the perimeter, which worked in my favor as the man watching us went right on watching.

He had an observation point up the veranda of the library, a concrete bunker of a building built in the mid-sixties. Dressed in an olive green oil-skin overcoat, he wore heavy gloves, his hands clasped in front of him. He was just high enough above us, and partially obscured by a cement rail, to have that same haughty, indignant appearance of one of the Politburo posing beneath Lenin's image during the May Day parades of yesteryear. Red hair escaped a wool cap on his head. An aluminum clipboard was tucked tightly beneath his left arm. For all I could tell, he didn't see me see him. I took one all-encompassing look and forced my eyes back to the unsteady ground in front of me that Lyel was negotiating effortlessly.

I said to Lyel quietly, "There's a man whose full attention appears to be fixed on us."

"Is there?" he asked, knowing better than to look. "A big man. Oil-skin coat?" he asked, stealing my thunder. When I failed to answer, Lyel said, "Saw him earlier. He was staring then, too. I like making a scene, don't you?"

"I'd rather know why he's so interested in us."

"Because we scare him," Lyel said, coming to a stop and looking up, not at our observer, but at the east wall of the completed foundation. "They do good work, I'll say that much."

"It's just a chunk of concrete, Lyel."

"But it's a *nice* chunk of concrete," he insisted.

"If you say so." We were approaching the workers, all of whom were involved erecting a continuing line of heavy wooden forms to contain the poured cement. There were metal braces, plywood, metal forms, and there was a lot of noise. We stood on a tiny strip of ground. Behind us was the library, in front of us the open hole and foundation. Did Lyel remember having crossed though the barriers at the last corner? We were about to get yelled at, and he didn't seem to realize it. Or did he?

"There, you see?" he asked, indicating the first clear look we had *inside* the erected screen that had so interested him from the other side. Only from this small piece of ground could you get a good look down in. This area had been excavated wider and deeper than the original construction hole. It lacked the teeth marks in the clay made by the mechanical digger, and instead appeared to have been shoveled by hand. And this, the only view of the area. Even from well above, where the oil-skin clad man stood watching us, the poured foundation walls would prevent any view. Lyel said to me, "Mark my word, Klick. By tomorrow, there will be a wall here as well."

"Hey there, you two!" a gruff voice called out angrily from the crew.

Lyel beat our hasty retreat.

And he was right: The next day a plywood wall had been erected clear around the site, including the very ground where we had been standing.

CHAPTER 25

The Bodleian, like the U.S. Library of Congress, houses at least one copy of most hardcover books published in England. There a comparison of the two institutions stops, however. The Bodleian is private, owned by Oxford University, is not open to the public, and is far older. Its benefactor, the Elizabethan diplomat and Oxford proctor Sir Thomas Bodley, so loved books, and was so dismayed by the sad condition of Duke Humphrey's Library which had been given to the university by that nobleman a century or more earlier, that he took the proper housing of books in hand in 1598 and began construction of what is today called the Old Bodleian Divinity School. Used mostly for research by scholars from all over the world, it requires you to be "recommended" to the Bodleian in order to apply for, and obtain, a pass. Most passes issued are temporary, lasting one academic year or less, except those awarded to the University Fellows who generally are "in" for life.

I filled out the appropriate form and delivered it to Tim

Binyon who had offered to sponsor me. He added a few hand-scrawled lines in writing I could not read and signed it, along with his title, sub-Warden. "You've nothing to worry about," he promised. "They won't question the authority of the sub-Warden. However," he cautioned, "it will cost you a fiver"—a five pound note. He apologized for this fee several times, as if I might be crushed by the loss of the eight dollars. This, in a country where a small frozen yogurt cost three dollars, U.S. I was still puzzling over this when I sat down across from the enormous woman in the Bodleian's "admission's office."

The brochure told me that the Bodleian consists of three principal buildings: The Old Library, The New Library, and the Radcliffe Camera. Of all the buildings in the City of Spires, perhaps the Radcliffe Camera is the most memorable. It is certainly covered well in the postcards. Shaped like the dome of the US Capitol, but without the rest of the building, huge columns support its second story—what the British call the first floor. It is an ornate example of perfect stone work, complete with a cupola on top. Of all the memories I would take with me, the most impressive was that of the Radcliffe Camera covered in autumn's first snow.

Because of its tremendous age, to an outsider the Bodleian appeared to have grown and expanded with little attention paid to a "system." I was to learn that in fact an underground rail system exists deep in the bowels of the place, with routes that run under the city streets used to shuttle books and manuscripts from one building to another without the works being exposed to the harsh Oxford elements. There are ancient dumb waiters and other conveyor systems in place, and, juxtaposed to this, an extremely sophisticated computer system to help with electronic searches, both for here at the Bodleian and across the whole of England. There is an Oriental reading room, a blind students' reading room and a music reading room—map rooms and three rooms of classics.

At each of these rooms the patron consults a catalogue, fills out a request, and then submits this request to the attendant. Twenty minutes to three hours later, your request arrives and you find a place to study.

At this point, I discovered that Tim Binyon's easy assurance that it was only a matter of paying a fiver came unstuck. Sir Thomas had been a farseeing, and worrying, sort of man. To protect his library, an elaborate Bodleian Oath was, and, seriously updated, still is, required of any scholar wanting admission. I was to be no exception. With all ceremony, I raised my hand before the formidable female dragon, terror of admissions, and swore: "I hereby undertake not to remove from the Library, or to mark, deface, or injure in any way, any volume, document, or other object belonging to it or in its custody, not to bring into the Library or kindle therein any fire or flame, and not to smoke in the Library, and I promise to obey all the rules of the Library."

I was consigned by the admissions office to a map room in the New Boldeian, the building directly across the street from my Wadham office. This, Tim Binyon had assured me, was where I would find what I was looking for: Randall Bradshaw's most recent research.

The "diplomat," Bradwhaw, had aroused my sense of curiosity, first at High Table, and then by apparently calling a meeting of the Group of Three—Bradshaw Tilbert,

Hagg—in the Old Senior Common Room.

I wasn't sure how Binyon had discovered what Bradshaw had last been researching, but I wasn't going to ask. Perhaps he had been able to access the Bodleian computers. Perhaps he had a graduate student who worked at the Bodleian. One thing I had quickly learned about Oxford was that an unspoken network existed between Fellows of various colleges. Some had gone to school together years before, some sat on university committees together or shared a research interest or a sport or art. But the networking was extensive, and Fellows were known to keep tabs on one another—to spy, where necessary—in order to protect their budgets and maintain their curriculum or canon. It was an intriguing and mysterious place just beneath the surface, and, in typical British fashion, no one *ever* discussed this "other world" quality to the place.

Binyon had provided me with a typed list of eleven volumes that Bradshaw had requested. The last three were from the map room, and that's where I started by clearing the New Bodleian's main entrance, showing my photo ID pass to the guard, and walking through a metal detector. The older man behind me was required to leave his briefcase checked with the guard. They were extremely thorough about inspecting materials entering and leaving. It was only as I passed through this surprising security that I realized that some, if not a good deal, of the contents of this venerable library were no doubt priceless—literally priceless.

The building's interior was old and unglamorous, its bare stone walls interrupted only by the occasional stunning oil portrait of men—all men—dressed as Lords. I passed a W.C. on my left, turned left, and the map room was on my right.

The map room consisted of six long tables of various materials placed end-to-end in the center of the room. Against the windowed wall that looked out at Wadham, an archaic gunmetal gray machine sat unattended, a relic of a different era. Perhaps it had been used for film strips or some other cataloguing device, I couldn't be sure. It looked like a cross between an overhead projector and a canister vacuum cleaner. One long wall and part of the far end of the room were devoted to stacks of narrow shelves that held dozens of oversized books that turned out to be the Bodleian form of card catalogues. Card *books*, instead. This was all so new to me.

I was told by the attendant, a sharp-nosed young man who carried an air of boredom and pretension, that I could request up to four different works at the same time, but that I would only be allowed to physically handle them in pairs. When I returned the first two volumes, I could then request two more, and so forth. I asked advice on how to fill out the requests properly. He tolerated my ignorance, though somewhat impatiently. When I finally submitted the three Bradshaw titles, he studied them thoughtfully and told me, "These may take an hour or two. You might want to come back after the meal time."

I returned to my office, grateful it was directly across the street, made some tea, and tried to think of something fun to do with Nicole—other than the kind of fun we had been having, that is. I spotted a notice for a concert at the Sheldonian. It was a string ensemble playing Dvorák, and it occurred to me that it might be the very thing that Allison Star would attend. Lyel had successfully caught me up in the Sinclair disappearance, and I was neglecting my duties to my partner Bruce and Ms. Star. I left a message at the hotel for Nicole inviting her to the concert and dinner afterwards, finished the pot of tea, and returned to the Bodleian.

The ritual involved with collecting one's research material lent an added importance to the material itself. Along with this came a different librarian's words of caution, "Do be careful, please." She was a slight, wisp of a woman, no older than nineteen, with bad teeth but alabaster, creamy skin like raw milk. I wanted to touch that skin to see if it was real. I attributed her warning to my size. To her this was probably like handing a Steuben vase over to a gorilla.

The works were contained in outsize gray cardboard boxes, marked neatly on the outside with a code and description of the contents. I had no idea exactly what I was inheriting until I found a spot to sit down and opened the first of the two boxes. I gasped aloud and drew her attention as well as that of a few others in the room.

Inside this plain gray box I found a remarkably ancient leather-bound volume, hand-tooled and painted. Also large. Just the cover of this volume was breathtaking. *Do be careful*, I heard echo inside my head. Indeed. And now I understood why. It had to be two hundred years old at least. I had no education in such things to know its value. I *carefully* removed it from the box, set it down in front of me, and opened the cover. For the second time in as many minutes I let out an audible gasp. I was holding, in my very hands, the original manuscript to Gluck's *Alceste*. A human's handwriting pouring creativity onto the page. Why the Brits had this in *their* library, I did not know, nor did I care. To a musician, even of my lackluster caliber, this was a treasure indeed. I savored every note, every scribble, turning the heavy yellow pages one by one and reading along. The smell of the paper, dusty and *ancient*, the haste with which the notes had been drawn. I felt myself transported back two and a quarter *centuries* to some dimly lit room, where a man hunched over a quill pen created a masterwork by flickering candlelight. Give me the opportunity to pen one such phrase and I would gladly sell my soul, I thought. An unexpected knot formed in my throat as a particular flourish of tightly drawn sixteenth notes scurried up the staff. I *knew* this moment. A man wearing khakis and crepe soled shoes under electric lights, reading it a million miles in time away from the man who had created it, and yet it was part of their shared artistic language and experience. One of these men was immortal, his mind, his ears, having left an imprint that would outlast me by another few millennium. It was a concept difficult to grasp, and one that I found overwhelming.

I was humming the lines to myself. A young man across from me asked me to please be quiet. I smiled. I didn't have an irritable bone in my body. I hummed internally, imagining the notes, savoring the lines, actually hearing it in my head as it played out before me on the page. For me, this was akin to stepping into a sacrosanct tomb. This was gold and rare gems in portions not to be believed. Page after page of it, some with notes written in the margin, erasures, second thoughts. This was *brilliant*, as was the British saying for anything too wonderful to be described.

I spent over an hour glued to this manuscript. It went by in about five minutes. A born-again scholar. Suddenly I understood the thrill that a Randall Bradshaw underwent each time he accessed such a treasure as this.

A voice whispered my name from deep within the base of my skull. This voice always sounded too much like Lyel and too little like me, considering it occupied *my* head. "Klick," it called out, assaulting me as some kind of third person of whom it was no part. I recognized its purpose, which was to alert me to some fundamental mistake in logic I had just made. I was familiar enough with this voice to understand that much. I reviewed my most recent thoughts, trying to identify my slip before that internal voice felt compelled to set me straight. I had been so deep in admiration of this manuscript that I was actually *high*. My pulse was elevated, I felt vaguely warm, as if having finished a cup of Egyptian coffee. I negotiated my way through the slash-and-burn debris of my memory, side-stepping the smoking fires of forgetfulness. My memory was about as trustworthy as a mine field. No place to go dancing in the dark. "Klick," the voice nudged, growing louder. Pretty soon it would be shouting at me, denigrating me for my inability to problem solve.

"Randall Bradshaw?" I asked myself.

"*Warm,*" my other self answered.

"Manuscripts? Diplomat."

"*Warmer still.*"

"Music manuscripts?"

"*Bingo!*"

"What was a diplomat like Randall Bradshaw doing spending time with a Gluck manuscript?" This repeated in my head several times.

The idea flamed. Chestnuts roasting on the open fire. You're there!

The little voice vanished, allowing me to think in peace. By his own admission, Randall Bradshaw's field of research and teaching was *political* scrolls, messages sent to and from squires and sheriffs in the halcyon days of olde. It wasn't so much that Bradshaw didn't have the right to view such a stunning object as that which then sat before me, but it didn't seem in his nature to wile away his time at the Bodleian humming harmonies of Gluck to himself. He seemed more the tone deaf type.

Trying to remember every detail of my conversation with Bradshaw at High Table, I carefully put away the Gluck and opened my other gray box. To my delight, and consternation, I found that this too contained an original musical score. *What was going on here?* The composer, a Brit, was unknown to me, and on examination, the work seemed a little formulaic, someone borrowing heavily from Handel but hoping not to be noticed. The British composers of this period were full of such lifeless tricks. By other accounts, however, the manuscript book itself appeared nearly identical to the Gluck. It too was leather-bound and appeared to be the exact same size.

I kept the Gluck—Bradshaw's last and most recent object of borrowing—and turned in the other box for another that the attendant was holding for me in reserve. With the exchange accomplished, I returned to my seat and opened this box as well. Yet another musical manuscript, the same vintage, and though wood-bound, not leather, it contained similar pages and an equal amount of artistic flourish on the part of the composer or his scribe. The lines I read were nice. Neat. Melodically confident. I checked the edge of the box again. It was indexed as "Hay-Grt-

MaEflt." I pondered that a moment before committing the intractable error of once again speaking aloud in such a room. "Oh my God!" I said. And that was it exactly. No wonder it read well: it was Haydn's *Great Mass in E-flat*. I had missed that on the first go-round. Terrified of damaging it, I returned it gingerly to its gray box, most of the eyes in the room silently reprimanding me for my outburst.

I couldn't begin to estimate the value of the manuscripts I had so casually requested. Several hundred thousand dollars, I guessed. Perhaps that for the Haydn alone. And clearly, it seemed to me, I had Bradshaw all wrong. He had requested all of these before me—he had to be a musicologist of some repute.

And that, I decided, deserved checking.

CHAPTER 26

Waiting beneath the huge stone busts of Roman emperors that boldly fronts the north curve of the Sheldonian Theater—something of a misnomer as its primary function is to house the degree-giving ceremony, the annual Encaenia, which before Wren's daring construction took place in St. Mary's Church—I marveled at the hundreds of bicycles randomly lashed together outside the King's Arms pub, at the eclectic variety of clothing parading past me—everything from white-tie dinner dress to slovenly genius student, black robes to dog collars. There were soft-hearted giggles carried on the cool night air along with strongly voiced intellectual argument. A motor scooter coughed up foul-smelling exhaust, followed in turn by an open-topped double decker tourist bus from which the amplified voice of the tourist guide berated the passengers with dates and figures. A deep-throated man in his cups struggling with an uncooperative bow tie mumbled something about "castrating the bugger." After an historical accounting of the Sheldonian and the Bodleian, the bus burped its foul discharge and continued on to insult some other attraction. I had grown uncomfortably accustomed to the buses. They stopped directly beneath my office window every twenty-six minutes, ten hours a day.

To me, the open-air tourist buses and the offensive odor of vehicle air exhaust were the two clear strokes against that charming city. The crush of tourism placed a distant third. I had heard talk of an intentionally-excessive downtown car duty; and the argument existed to enclose or do away with the buses altogether, but I feared it was only talk. Offending tourists or discouraging dollars and Deutschmarks was an unlikely action from an elected city counsel.

"You look a little glum," Nicole said, interrupting my thoughts.

"Nothing that a drink couldn't cure."

We drank champagne at a champagne and dessert bar beneath a pizza and pasta restaurant located in the oldest food hall in all of Oxford.

"What are you thinking?" she asked.

"That this structure has stood here since 1053. It seems impossible."

"Think how many nights that is. How many full moons. How many mugs of beer and broken hearts."

My poetess was something to look at tonight. She wore a dark velvet jacket patterned with deep purple flowers, worn over a pleated blouse with a single strand of pearls. Her skirt was an equally rich fabric, as jet black as coal. She wore black stockings with small white stars, and patent leather flats. She was ready for the Sheldonian. Her hair was glossy and pulled off her face, lending her a regal neck and somehow enlarging her curious eyes. When she giggled it sounded like a bell choir. She seemed interested in everyone who came and went and made up implausible stories about each: here, an aristocrat's escaped son; there, an Indian princess carrying an illegitimate child. There was no end to her imagination, no end to my devotion to her.

"House of Lords," I whispered to her, indicating the same over-indulged fellow I had stood alongside outside the Sheldonian.

"Royal family," she agreed.

He ordered a Pims quite loudly.

"Are you looking forward to it?" she asked.

"What?"

"The concert."

"Of course."

"Are you sure?"

"Positive. Why?"

"You seem a little preoccupied."

"Only with your beauty. It seems such a waste to share you with the world. I want you all to myself."

"I'm yours."

"Are you?"

"Tonight I am. I think so, yes. Ask me later."

We laughed. She ordered us two more glasses of champagne. An American couple sat down nearby. We recognized each other for our origins immediately and exchanged pleasant smiles. They were our ages and didn't strike me as tourists.

"And who are they?" I asked conspiratorially.

"Hit men," she said. "Hit *persons*," she corrected herself. "They're to kill someone tonight during the concert. He's to create a diversion. She does the actual deed."

"Hitchcock," I suggested.

"Oh, very Hitchcock, indeed. They've seen them all. They know all the lines."

"All the lines?"

"All. Yes. And she's a dancer as well. You can tell by her legs."

She had stout legs. It was an unfair comment.

"And him?" I asked.

"A sailor. Track and field when he was young. Expert driver. Knows everything there is to know about Roman architecture."

The waiter was standing alongside of us, waiting for us to finish talking. Nicole would say later that that was why they called them waiters. He had our glasses of champagne on a tray. He leaned in privately and asked in a concerned voice, "That chap over there?"

Nicole and I glanced at each other and burst out laughing. I froze a memory of that moment in my mind, for it was rich, honest laughter, the kind impossible to manufacture. Her head was tilted back, her teeth gleaming, and her cheeks red. It was a moment as honest as two people could ever be with each other. It was placed away in my secret vault, my permanent collection, saved for the days that the wind blows impossibly cold and you haven't a friend in the world.

CHAPTER 27

The Sheldonian was built by Wren on order from Gilbert Sheldon, Archbishop of Canterbury, who was so shocked by the licentious nature of the university's degree ceremonies that he decided to move them out of St. Mary's Church into a theatre. What they wanted was to build a structure in the manner of the classical amphitheater which of course had no ceilings. So how was Wren to use standard timbers to roof a theatre of classical shape and size? It had never been done. His solution was to essay the semicircle, the ceiling eventually turning out to be 70 X 80 feet, and using a fore-shortened painting to heighten the effect. The interior has boxes and pulpits and galleries in Wrenish carpentry, all adapted for the curious ceremonies of the university where degrees are given, Latin compliments bandied, and prize poems read. It is also used as a recital hall, a lecture hall, and houses musical events. The seating is not especially comfortable and temperature control is a nightmare, it being like a furnace inside in high summer and very cold due to the stone in winter. It is very British to put up with discomfort for the sake of grandeur and tradition.

Our seats were second from the top, up where the birds fly, up where, along with your program, they also give you a bottle of oxygen. On the way up to our seats, every male head within twenty yards turned to catch a glimpse of Nicole, and there I was with this object of desire clinging to my arm seeking balance. I had no right to gloat the way I did.

The program was a poor photocopy on cheap yellow paper folded in half. It reminded me of church. It listed the players and the pieces and thanked a bunch of people in a typeface that didn't copy well. We had arrived a few minutes early, following our taste of champagne. I was keeping an eye out for Allison Star, whom I had been wise enough to mention and to describe in detail to Nicole beforehand. I was entertained by the ornate surroundings. Slowly the room filled up.

A hand-painted sign informed the careful observer of an observation deck in the building's cupola, accessed via a stairway through the west door. It cost you fifty pence and, I assumed, a fair amount of stair climbing. Daytime hours only.

"That her?" Nicole asked, nudging me. It was her third such try. She had turned the surveillance into a game.

"No," I said regrettably, "but you're right on the money with that one. Hair just a little longer, face just a little more classic."

"She must be a beauty," she said. This, for the *sixth* time.

"She's okay," I returned quickly. Ever cautious. Trying to sound uninterested.

I was on tentative ground with Nicole. I had learned once before that intimacy and emotional alignment were no guarantees of the steadfastness of our acquaintance. She had left me once before, left me cold and alone in front of a burned out woodstove with only the scent of her on my hands and an image tucked safely behind my eyes. I was like a pilot fish swimming alongside of her, wishing I might have been born a suckerfish instead. How I wanted to attach myself and not let go—not be let go. My increasing march on middle age had left me cursing my precious solitude that I had for so long sought. It followed me now like a shadow, and I longed for a brilliance of light to banish it: intimate company. I longed for her to replace it, or me to replace hers, to effect that ephemeral condition of oneness that proves so elusive the older we get. I ached to take hold of her hand and never let go, to learn to love her snoring and her endless brushing of her hair, to learn tolerance and forgiveness and to negotiate them as a two-way street. I had been traveling one-way for so long that I no longer followed directions very well—I just chased the traffic lights and signs straight on. Straight on.

"How about her?" she asked, squeezing my hand.

I looked down at hers, hoping I would never have to remember what it looked like.

As I raised my eyes and followed her gaze I was looking at Allison Star. "Bingo!" I said.

"Really?"

"It's her."

"Nice clothes."

"I wouldn't be surprised if he bought them for her. He covets her."

"Lucky her. We should all be coveted."

"Seconded."

She squeezed my hand again. Perhaps, I thought, in this age of cosmetic surgery, there was an operation available for two people to be joined at the hand like Siamese twins. I wanted it, if there was such a thing. We could feed each other, wash each other, and no one could possibly cut in on us while dancing. We could learn to play three handed piano—write pieces for it.

Allison Star had come with a friend, a girl of like age but nowhere near the same beauty. It seemed to me that the really gorgeous women didn't care to be seen in the company of equal beauties, didn't care to be compared, and so surrounded themselves with less delicate flowers.

"Nice row," Nicole commented.

"Just because she's at sea level?"

"I'd feel better if there were seat belts up here."

"Those aren't the kind of seats you buy," I noted. "Those are *given* you."

"She's a VIP?" she asked.

"Yes. She is perhaps the most prominent musical student at university, considering her connections."

"Will he show?"

"I think so, yes." I answered.

"What makes you think so?"

I wasn't sure how to put it.

"Chris?"

"Put yourself in his shoes. Easier for me than you, perhaps. Some months back, you have seduced a young woman . . . Well, there she is, at the bottom of the stairs there. You've just seen her. You've seduced *her*. That kind of youthful beauty. Youthful *energies*, if you will."

"Oh, I *do*," she reminded. The champagne had made her playful.

"You have toured part of Europe with her, filling her head with empires won and lost, her stomach with the best champagne, and her . . . You get the picture."

"Vividly. You border on the gross from time to time."

"But you have *owned* her. She is your concubine, your Lolita. You are her Svengali. You have even been on the run with her, adding to the sense of adventure. Your physical relationship is in that savage stage of infatuation and exploration."

"All systems go."

"Exactly. You do a little freelance work, but not much. Most of your time is spent in devotion to this fountain of youth you have accidentally acquired. You feel *years* pouring off you like garden soil in the shower. Better than ever."

"And then Oxford for her," she said, catching on. "Yes, I see."

"Boys her age. The added attention because she is no *normal* student. She arrives a modest celebrity even *without* him. And despite his reputation for being a workaholic, despite the dozens of bookings he's canceling worldwide, can he tear himself away? Does he *dare?*"

"I think not."

"No. He watches over her. He stays in touch. They make love clandestinely. Hotels. Friends' apartments."

"If you believe this, then why aren't you following her? Watching her?"

"Because I don't think it's actually started yet. I think *he's* watching her. And if I take up the game as well, then he's just as likely to spot me as I am to spot him, and then I've lost my edge. No. The point is, *she* is not going anywhere. She is the bait. And until the trap is properly set— until *tonight*—I saw no reason to take such risks."

"Tonight?"

"Look at the combination. His lover and his favorite music. He's expressed it openly, you know? Despite all the tremendous symphonic orchestral work he does, he began as part of a string ensemble. It's his true love. And so is she."

"Tonight?"

"Probably," I said more confidently. "I suspect, in fact, that he is living right now in the Oxford area."

"And she *knows* this?"

"Doubtful. No. I doubt she knows he's been keeping such a close eye on her. He's waiting to make their reunion a natural progression of events. But he's here at university. Somewhere. Working, if I know him. Waiting. Nervous. Wondering if this budding flower will close her petals to him."

"Spare me."

"It's the environment," I said, sweeping my hand to include this ornate structure. "I wax poetic in places like this."

"You can wax," she allowed. "But you don't have to drip all over the place." She kissed me then, just in case she had hurt my feelings. Which she had.

CHAPTER 28

The first piece, middle of the first movement. Lights down. Ensemble in black and white, bows moving in unison as if controlled from above by invisible strings. They are lighted and gleaming. Nicole and I sit uncomfortably on the hard wooden benches. Those around us have perfected a Sheldonian slouch. Every so often I can hear her humming. I want to put my head against her neck and feel her tones reverberate through me. I want to be inside her.

She faces me with a giddy smile, not one approved by her vanity censors, but one that she's let slip in an unchecked moment. The room swirls with the warm color of perfect harmonies and the rise and fall of the composer's emotions. To hear it, you would think he wrote it in a single sitting, it is so precise and coherent. It probably consumed him for the better part of a year, laboring with a quill pen and a small glass well of black ink. Working by candlelight sometimes, by the window at others. Working at the keyboard where he sits on a bench, bent and crippled from the years of composition. Working drunk. Working hungry. But nearly always working.

While Nicole absorbed every note, every nuance of movement offered by the first chair, I watched the shadows of the upper balcony, ever the optimist. Ever the worker bee. I knew firsthand the pain felt in a lonely heart—this woman sitting next to me had caused me plenty. It is often innocent, and unintended, such pain, but it sears one's arteries and veins. It turns one's breath cold—one's bed cold. It carries with it an emotional winter. And if grief is the snow of such a season, it falls heavily, it drifts deeply. One is lost in the whiteout of the storm, and seeks shelter and warmth wherever available, at whatever cost. And that is why I *knew* he would come.

My eyes patrolled the reaches and depths of areas out of bounds, alert for an unexpected flicker of light, or evidence of movement. He was the voyeur. It was not me, nor the men hired by his wife from whom he hid, but from *her*. She was his everything, his universe, and stealing this time with her, even separated by the distance of this great hall, was critical to him and yet a violation of privacy for her.

Who knew exactly such a man's thoughts? Did he find himself wild with desire? With jealousy? Longing? Happiness? How desperate was Shultz to keep Allison his?

I placed myself in his position, well aware there was no way to predict the reasoning or emotions of another. I knew that in his position *I* would be at the Sheldonian hoping to steal a glimpse of her. I would be thinking that both hormones and time apart would work against me. Young men her own age were certain to pursue her unabashedly.

Given the combination of the musical program and Allison Star's attendance, I felt certain he would come.

"Excuse me, Nicky." I squeezed past a line of knees and into the aisle, feeling embarrassed about my size. Once in the aisle I took my bearings. The ushers were students, the security light. At the entrance a few elderly patrons of the Sheldonian Society had collected our tickets, the only adults involved. So typical of youth, once the performance began, all ushers duties were abandoned, placed aside until intermission. Everyone's attention was fixed on the ensemble. All but mine and the elusive Stephan Shultz, who I assumed was in a location enabling him a view of Allison.

I headed up the aisle instead of down to avoid interfering with people's line-of-sight and to make myself less visible, not more.

Strategically, I would have preferred the ground floor in order to lessen the chance of Shultz's escape. But staying high in the dome I afforded myself the advantage of the patrons' attention being trained downward and away from me. In the uppermost tier, I was able to move freely. Few, if any, would notice me. And I was working under the confidence of experience. For the years of my musical life I had practically *lived* in such places. Just as *he* had. I was comfortable with the physical restrictions imposed upon me by such a place, and perhaps even a little more familiar with *this* side of the stage than even a veteran like Stephan Shultz. Furthermore, I had the warmth of the champagne to thank for an unqualified sense of relaxation and contentment. I was moving smoothly and quietly. I felt suddenly bulletproof.

Buoyed by the knowledge that with a face as familiar as his, he could not escape being recognized without dealing with the public, I felt confident that he would avoid sitting amid the audience. Amid the peons. His recognition factor demanded he find a place to himself or wear a disguise, and his sizeable ego suggested the former. Stephan Shultz's vanity would not tolerate disguise. He would demand exclusivity. Isolation. A hushed whisper into the ear of the matron at the gate, a small but firm handshake of appreciation, and the hall was his. I focused my attention on the upper reaches to my right, an area blocked off because of the staging of the performance.

Moving quietly through the dark in a building that is over three hundred years old was not, as I discovered, a skill I had yet attained. The Sheldonian was built for, among other things, theater in the round. The upper balcony seating continued fully around the structure, bisected on the far wall by an enormous pipe organ that for the performance served as a backdrop. Seats behind and to the side of the orchestra had been roped off with a braided red cord that ended in gold tassels. I ducked under this meager, and unattended, barrier and slipped quietly into the dark and unoccupied area.

The centuries-old plank flooring creaked beneath me.

It was here in these darkened upper reaches that I expected to find Shultz. The audience to my back and below me, I moved cautiously, exploring each footfall tentatively for complaint. The thought had occurred to me that Stephan Shultz might have brought along his knee-breakers as a precaution. I had no desire to allow a couple of thugs the jump on me. I had met two of them in Paris. I still carried a few bruises.

I edged my way smoothly and silently along, hugging the back wall where I was the least likely to be noticed and where one side of me was protected. With the harmonies of Dvořák wafting into the upper rafters, I moved in a cryptic dance, consumed by melody. The wall curved around the internal perimeter, leading me away from the occupied seats.

Expectation beat strongly in my chest, defying and contracting the musical score. I could not claim any clairvoyance or prescience as my own. If anything, I was naturally inclined toward *distrusting* any such flashes. And yet on this occasion *I knew*. Shultz was here. I would find him. If anything was predictable, if anything was familiar to me, it was the behavior of a middle-aged man hopelessly in love.

I spotted a man below me. He was sitting alone, tucked into the darkness, arms raised, a pair of opera glasses trained down. I saw only the shape of him, and yet I knew it was Stephan Shultz. I froze, careful now, like a hunter. I assessed my surroundings, absorbing every nuance, every motion, every sound, alert and alive. I lived for such moments. My senses heightened, the music suddenly louder in my ears, my heart heavy in my chest. I took one tentative step forward, alert and aware of my immediate surroundings. I cocked my head slightly and listened. Again, I paused.

My biggest advantage came from the restrictions enforced upon Shultz's peripheral vision by his use of the opera glasses, the small black rubber eyepieces cupping his eyes like a horse's blinders. His focus was also many yards in front of, and below, him, not above and behind. I was too big to come off as an autograph-seeking fan. If he saw me, he was likely to run, or, worse, summon his henchmen, who, if anywhere near, were most likely on the other side of the doorway that led to the stairway and the lower level exit.

I debated waiting him out, using the cover of the audience's applause to approach, but I feared that with his knowledge of the piece, he might choose to exit a few dozen bars from the finale, forcing me to rush him. An open field tackle in the upper balcony of the Sheldonian, my target one of the most revered conductors in the world, seemed one hell of a bad way to make an introduction. Jail seemed more likely. A fit of panic seized my chest: what the hell was the plan? So close and yet so far.

Stephan Shultz, *in the flesh* ten yards away, voyeuristically enjoying sight of the lovely Allison Star. And there I was, the Incredible Bulk, lurking in the shadows, ready with a small fortune in royalty money littered between the lines of the weighty documents I needed him to sign—documents that remained under lock and key in my quarters at Wadham. The frustration, the uncertainly, the angst, the anxiety built to a fevered pitch, echoing the music below.

Had I not been so focused on him, I might have listened more closely and realized this was the conclusion to the opening piece. The final crescendo and climax threw the audience into an explosion of applause. I took several strides toward Maestro Shultz, grateful for the cover. But in my excitement I rushed it.

As he lowered the binoculars, he swung his head, sensing my approach. His response was immediate. He sprang like a cat out of his seat. No middle-aged, lethargic man, he. Vaulting the last three rows of fixed benches like a hurdler, he darted through the open doorway toward the stairs. He caught me with my feet planted. I had not expected him to be anywhere near so quick or sure-footed.

A beat late, I sprang into action, motivated more by competitiveness than a desire to do my job. I would not be so easily beaten by a fifty-plus baton twirler. I would chase the bastard and overtake him. I would *win*. I too hurdled the benches—a little more quickly than he had, I convinced myself. Raced through the exit door, descending the stairs three at a time.

Intermission. Was it possible? Already? Had my surveillance allowed time to pass so quickly? Or were these people at the bottom of the stairs late arrivals? Either way, Stephan Shultz and I were immediately engulfed in a mob of well-dressed people. He pushed rudely through them, making for the final door to the outside. I heard his name called out in discovery as he turned victim to his celebrity. One man was bold enough to grab hold of him. Wielding my outstretched forearm like a sword, I hacked my way into the throng.

Murmurs of, "It's *him* . . ." "Shultz . . ." "It *is!*" bounced off the lobby's stone walls.

His admirers quickly closed in around him, defeating my purpose, blocking me out. Accustomed to such assaults, Shultz arrogantly charged ahead. I encountered an increasingly impenetrable wall between us. He glanced but once over his shoulder to confirm my pursuit; his expression gave away nothing of the concern he surely felt. Instead, upon seeing me, he seemed energized by his discovery. With one last surge, he broke through the doorway and out into the evening.

"Stand aside," I said, in my best imitation of a British accent, which accomplished all of nothing. I finally resorted to relying on my size and strength and created an exit for myself.

People panicked as I challenged from behind. There is nothing so contagious as panic. It spread, electrifying the air and triggering a mass exodus. Pushing. Shoving. Cries for help. Protesting voices rising increasingly louder. Everyone straining for the exit. A young woman tripped and fell immediately to my right. She grabbed for a man's leg and was denied purchase as he instinctively kicked her off. I elbowed open a small hole, stooped, and offered an arm to the fallen woman. I knew something that no one else here did: there was nothing to panic about.

I pulled her to her feet and she clung to me desperately. "Hold on," I advised, abandoning my phony accent. I turned my back to the door and leaned into the crowd, driving the stopper out of the neck of the bottle. Once outside, I stumbled on a stone step, lost my balance, and went down hard. The woman fell atop me. My vision inverted an upside down Stephan Shultz making for the street. In order to pursue him, I would have had to jettison this woman onto the gravel courtyard. Instead, I helped her up as several others offered us both a hand.

Shultz escaped. I spent fifteen minutes looking for him, but to no avail. When I returned to the Sheldonian, Nicole had saved me my seat although she seemed upset by my desertion. Allison Star stayed to the program's conclusion. Nicole and I followed her back to her dorm. At no point did Shultz make contact. Nicole's hotel was more private than Wadham. We had a late drink in the bar, and a long wonderful night in her room.

CHAPTER 29

Human memory is a funny thing. Perhaps some day all the doctors and researchers will figure out why one day we can't think of what it is, and yet the next day it—whatever it was—comes pouring out as if a dam has burst.

Somewhere between being told by Tim Binyon that Randall Bradshaw had no known interest in music of any sort and Nicole's innocent use of a blank page at the back of a Barbara Kingsolver paperback, upon which she jotted down a note, I recalled a piece of my High Table conversation with Bradshaw.

That at the time I was once again attending High Table, on this occasion with Lyel in tow, might have had something to do with it as well, at least in terms of my enormous consumption of wine while trying to keep up with my fellow Fellows. Perhaps the wine disgorged some impediment to thought, some "writers block" of the imagination.

At this level of intoxication anything was possible. The Fellows drank like there was no tomorrow. High Table after High Table, in an endless string of News Year's Eves, little boys let loose in the cellar. The volume of consumption amazed even Lyel, who could drink most under the table. On this night, Lyel reached there first—eyes glassy, an awkward smile pasted on shiny lips. These dons had livers destined for research labs.

I did not, and by my fifth glass of claret, and the sight of Randall Bradshaw across the table—staying well away from me—I finally remembered a snippet of our earlier conversation that proved most enlightening. Bradshaw's voice returned to my drunken ear: "You can't *make* paper," he had said. " . . . the materials aren't available. . . . So you take the paper, sheet by sheet from existing volumes— blank end papers, that sort of thing . . ." *from existing volumes*, my mind repeated several times.

Nicole, writing on a blank end paper in the Kingsolver novel . . .

The feel of the Haydn in my hands . . . *The yellowed parchment!*

"Chris?" Lyel inquired. "You don't have a bone stuck or something?"

"Oh my God, Lyel. I said it right to his face without ever knowing. *No wonder* he came unglued—no pun intended." I hissed into his huge ear. "No wonder they had that meeting up there in the Old Common Room. Hagg or Tilbert heard him explain it to me! Heard us right across the table as Bradshaw handed me everything I needed— only I was too drunk to catch on."

"You're not exactly sober now," he cautioned. "Nor are

you making much sense."

"I made some off-handed comment about how a diplomat could judge the authenticity of a scroll. *That* was when Bradshaw started hammering the vino."

"What the hell are you talking about?" Lyel whispered back at me.

I cupped my hand to his ear. "Forgeries," I said, at which point Lyel dropped his fork to his plate and won the attention of all twenty-three dons seated at the massive table.

CHAPTER 30

For fifty pence I was allowed to climb an endless set of rickety wooden stairs ascending to the Sheldonian's cupola. I arrived a few minutes early and enjoyed the view. From there, the City of Dreaming Spires became an all-encompassing three hundred and sixty degree panorama of slate rooftops and gray stone fingers pointing to God. Across the intersection, I could see into my own windows at Wadham, could see the desk at which I worked. Directly across the street: the New Bodleian, where I intended to go immediately following this meeting.

The slate roofs looked like reptile skin. Red chimneys, some emitting a black coal smoke, provided the only color. Churches. Colleges. And in the far distance the lush rolling hills of farm ground, framed by fences and stone walls. I spotted several head of cattle and a few lazy horses grazing on the heavy grass; they looked like toys in the muted, shifting sunlight that battled with the ubiquitous clouds.

Her footsteps announced her. She was energetic by the

sound of those footfalls—not in keeping with the statelier paces of the other Wadham dons. She was light and lithe. She was about my age. She had dark hair to her shoulders, a narrow, thoughtful face with a pronounced nose and chin, thin lips and delicate eyebrows. She had a full figure and wore simple clothes. Very little make-up. She was careful with her pronunciation of my name, as if I might have trouble understanding her accent.

"Mr. Klick?"

"Dr. Abernathy?"

"I prefer Julia, if you don't mind."

"Chris," I countered.

"We're lucky to be alone," she said, crossing to me, tugging on her coat nervously. "We should speak, whilst we retain our privacy." She used the soft "i" on *privacy*, which reminded me what a gentle language this could be.

"Lovely view, this. What?" she asked.

"Terrific."

"Yes. I thought you would enjoy it. Better than a common room. What?"

"You're a diplomat—scrolls, right?" I asked. "Tim Binyon speaks very highly of you." He had also said Julia Abernathy could be trusted to never say a word about our discussion.

"Tim's an old friend." She stared out at the spires, clearly as enthralled with the view as a first-time tourist.

I asked her, "If you needed a sheet of parchment from the late eighteenth century—hypothetically speaking . . . something for a forgery perhaps . . ." This turned her head. "Would the New Bodleian make sense?" I asked, looking over at the building. "Hypothetically," I repeated. "As a possible source?"

She glanced around carefully. I felt heat spike up my spine.

She swept her hand across the horizon like a stage actress, as if about to explain something about the town. Then her hand fell and her eyes bore into me hotly, speaking with excitement. "We use the term 'paper' quite loosely, Mr. Klick," she said, ignoring my request to be called Chris. "The composition of parchment was, and is, a science. An *exact* science. Oxidation, fiber content. You offer our university laboratory a particular piece of parchment, a particular diploma or scroll, and if they are any good at't'all, they can come back to you not only with the approximate date of its creation, but the country, the province, even the city where it was made. Made, not manufactured. It was, and is, an art, you see—an *art*—the making of such parchment by hand."

"Water stamps?" I asked. "That sort of thing?"

"Much, much later than the period you mentioned. No, not at all. Water marks? Nineteenth century perhaps—letter writing stationery, that sort of thing. But eighteenth century? No. I believe you have missed my point, actually." She waited. I said nothing. Clearly, I *had* missed her point. When she spoke quickly it was hard to understand her. "You see, there is precious little blank paper remaining from the eighteenth century. Ah! There! I saw a flicker of something in your eyes, didn't I? Yes! Splendid! You *do* see where I'm headed, don't you?" I felt like a student who raised his hand too quickly before being able to fully articulate the answer. She looked over at the New Bodleian herself and quizzed, "Where do you turn if you *need* a quality piece of parchment from a given era?" she asked.

"The New Bodleian," I answered, hazarding a guess.

"To the *archives*, of course." Her hand was pointing now down at the moss covered, gray shingle roof of the Bodleian Library. "Blank pages fall at the end of the early bound manuscripts, same as they do today. It must be cut exceptionally cleanly. Easily missed if you are careful enough."

"But it *is* done?" I asked.

"Allow me to tell you how it is accomplished, this surgery. It is not easy, you see, for there is almost always a librarian in the room somewhere nosing around his or her business. Around *your* business. And this is not something to be taken too lightly, this surgery. No, it is not. You are defacing a work of art, and any historian, any academic engaged in such an activity, is well aware of this fact, believe me. It is not something to be taken lightly. Not only is it larceny, it is certain to result in one being made redundant by university." Her excitement was contagious. My heart beat more quickly. She spoke so softly, I could barely make out her words. "You carry the razor somewhere easily accessible, for when you're given your chance, you must act quickly and surely. If you push too hard," she said, indicating a spreading motion with her hand, "you will crack the spine and the book will fall open to your crime each and every time. Most importantly, it will fall open there *the next time*, and that is something you hope to prevent most of all, for your name is the most recent in the records."

"Or you accidentally cut the page behind it," I spit out.

She nodded, though acted as if she hadn't heard me.

"You calculate the pressure required to cut through this single sheet, yes, careful not to score the sheet that follows. There are so many mistakes to be made, and you have reviewed each and every one a dozen times. Perhaps, in the privacy," there was that pronunciation again, "of your flat, you have even *practiced* this.

"You make your cut cleanly and quickly," she continued. "One chance is all you have to do this correctly. No trimming. No time to repair any mistakes. You cut; you remove your trophy and you quickly sequester it where it will, and does, accompany you from the library. To be caught with it in your possession is the end of your academic career."

"So why risk it?" I asked aloud, my mind churning.

"It is a *treasure*," she exclaimed. "A blank sheet upon which history can be rewritten."

Footsteps ascending toward us. Her head snapped in that direction. Our moment was over. American accents. A husband and wife, perhaps. Vacation. A trip to the top of the Sheldonian. Julia Abernathy said nearly soundlessly, her glossy lips mouthing the words, "History rewritten, Mr. Klick. The *power* of it."

Her timing was impeccable. She turned away from me and headed for the stairs, passing the tourists just as they huffed up to the top and spouted, "It's *gorgeous!*" nearly in unison.

All I saw of her was the sway to her hips, the motion of her body, and the lingering image of her fading from my vision like the dying orb left from a camera's flash.

CHAPTER 31

Allison Star's angelic skin caught the yellow light of the hallway's bare bulb. The King's Arms staircase had hardly been designed with a woman like this in mind. Seeing her there was like coming across a Botticelli in a dank and dreary cellar; the hallway was twice as bright because of her.

"Hello," I said. Brits preferred this to "hi," a greeting some apparently didn't understand, distrusting the familiarity. Britain is not a familiar place; it is a formal place. Formal gardens. Formal people. Formal language. I had found that if I kept this in mind, I could negotiate my way around the social structure and could avoid making a complete ass of myself all the time. Part ass, part of the time, I had learned to live with.

"Hello," she answered, twisting her hands in her lap like she was washing them. Nervous, or a ploy? I wondered. Women, even young women with looks like hers knew all the games, all the tricks. If she had been selling something, I was prepared to offer my wallet. Nicole had gone off to London for the day and a play that same evening with "a friend"—something she wouldn't elaborate on. I was expected to accept things with Nicole; I was trying.

I invited Allison Star into my rooms and seated her on a couch, taking a hard back chair across from her. She finally gathered the strength to ask angrily, "Was that *you* last night?"

I didn't have to ask what she was talking about. "Yes," I answered honestly.

"You terrified him, you know. He thought it was . . . He worried it might be someone else."

"An emissary from Tina," I answered. "No. He was lucky it was me. It might have been them."

"You have to drop this, Mr. Klick."

"One signature is all. This can be done so easily. How difficult can it be to look over a few documents? He takes them to London, signs on the dotted line, and the money is his. I may not look that much like Santa Claus, but I'm close."

"He's not going to sign anything."

"Does he know about my offer?"

"In a roundabout way. I didn't know the particulars. He'd like the money. Who wouldn't? But he doesn't believe you would travel all the way over here just to give him some money, and he isn't even convinced that the money is real. He wonders how, if the money is owed to him, you could have access to it."

"My partner is the attorney, Allison. All I do is find the person owed the money."

"You just have to drop it. Please."

"I'm like a dog with a bone. I don't get my share until he signs. I'm like a benevolent bounty hunter: no prize, no payola. But in my line of work, everybody wins. All I need is twenty minutes, just long enough to get Shultz in front of a notary public to sign the papers. I've spent too much tracking him down. If he wants to be rid of me, the smartest thing to do is to sign the documents."

"Give us some time, Mr. Klick."

"You think I'm *lying?*" I asked innocently.

"Through the teeth," she answered bluntly. "And so does

Stephan. All we want is peace. You've driven him into hiding again. He doesn't trust anyone, now. Coming to the Sheldonian was a big risk for him."

"It certainly was," I confirmed, then repeated, "All I need is twenty minutes. It's really not so much."

She seemed to be talking to herself when she added, "Julian told him he'd be fine in the upper deck, and now he thinks that maybe Julian put you up to it." She glanced up at me. "They had a history of playing practical jokes on each other when they were undergraduates, you know. So now he doesn't trust Julian either."

Mention of Julian Rasner had me sitting up as straight as the chair's back. It only made sense that two men of approximately the same age, and wedded to the same occupation in their different ways, would know *of* each other, might even know each other well. But it had not occurred to me that Shultz and Rasner would go back twenty or thirty years together. Music was a business of favors. Of networking. Perhaps Shultz had come to Oxford with more than this woman in mind—although with her only a few feet away, alive, a blue vein pulsing in her elegant neck, this was difficult to imagine.

I took a wild stab: "I thought the practical joker in the bunch was Randall Bradshaw." He seemed to me to be of the same age as these other two, and I knew he had attended the university.

"Randy? Oh, no. He's the *conservative* one! He was always the *target* of the jokes." She smiled at that thought, but then realized her mistake in sharing it with me and blushed. She couldn't take it back, and she didn't want to direct my attention to it; she was much smoother than I might have given her credit for. Nonetheless it sat there like a piece of spinach stuck in her front teeth.

She steered around it deftly, returning to her favorite subject: me. "Will you give it up?"

"No," I answered. All I could manage was a monosyllabic response because of the sudden connection made between Shultz and Bradshaw, the blushing diplomat who completed the trio of men who seemed somewhat frantic about my looking into the disappearance of Aiden Sinclair. These colleges were clubby, and with Shultz's past association with the Christ Church scholar, Julian Rasner, and now with Bradshaw made clear, I had to wonder how much Shultz's avoidance of me was based on fear of his wife's collectors catching up with him, and how much on my poking around Sinclair's disappearance. I decided to play hard ball; a fellow American would appreciate the sport. "I'll tell you what I'll do, Miss Star," I said, addressing her formally, a technique used by police who want to shake-up a suspect. "I will give your Mr. Shultz twenty-four hours to make a decision: he can deal with me and have this over with, or he can face the wrath of his wife." It hadn't occurred to me to play nasty, but now, seeing the leverage I had on him—Allison Star was *stuck* here at the university, after all—it seemed the strongest hand to play. "I have no intention of calling his wife and revealing Shultz's whereabouts. But I will gladly do so if he gives me any trouble about this royalty check. Let's not forget," I said, frustrated, "that I'm trying *to give him money!* Money that he didn't even know he was owed." I took a deep breath. "Pass that along to your Svengali, will you please?"

She blushed. Just right. She didn't like me. Fine. At least we had a relationship now. I didn't like that aspect of the job, but there was nothing to be done about it. I had run around the runaround long enough. My legs were tired.

"Knock, knock?" I added, attempting to disrupt that distant gaze of hers.

"I'm right here," she said, quietly, still thinking.

"Did you hear my offer? Would you like me to repeat it?"

She fired back at me, "Your *ultimatum?* I don't know where he is. We hardly see each other at all, and when we do, it's by his decision, not mine. There's nowhere I can call him, no way to reach him. I have no idea if I will see him or hear from him in this arbitrary time period you've imposed, so I suppose that means you'll end up informing his wife where *I* am. And this means in turn," she said, her eyes dancing in pools of tears that she wouldn't allow to run, "that I'll have to tell him *not* to see me, *not* to contact me again. And quite frankly, *that sucks!* Why can't all of you *just leave us alone?*"

"Impossible, I'm afraid." I said this quickly, before I weakened under the pressure of her convincing emotions. "But what I can do," I added, my foundation crumbling, "is tell you that I won't call *anyone* until I hear from you." I lied, "I'm going to watch you, Ms. Star. I'm going to make your business, my business. He's going to contact you, and you're going to pass my message along. And if you fail to do so, then *you* are the one who is the cause of your own problems, because I'll be expecting to hear from you *immediately*. Not twenty-four hours later. Not *two* hours later. Immediately. And if you think that I won't know when he's contacted you, you're wrong. I will know. I'll make it my business to know. It *is* my business to know. Am I getting through?"

She nodded. Intimidated. Slightly scared of me. That was okay. Maybe it was even right for the moment, even though I felt like hell. You say things you wish you didn't have to. And if they work then you use them another time. And another. And pretty soon you are that person you didn't want to be, doing things you never wanted to do, and you can't quite figure out how it is you became that way.

But it's there. You're stuck with it.

And when you close the door to the room, listening to her footsteps echoing as she descends the stairs, you too descend, down into the darkness of your being, wondering who you've become.

CHAPTER 32

Dessert was a hallowed institution at Wadham. The elegance of the former law library, converted into the Fellows' Lunch Room and host to High Table's dessert, was never more apparent than when the long walnut dining tables were placed end to end and covered with silver bowls brimming with fresh fruits, several different wine glasses, a myriad of dessert wines, and a small white plate and tableware setting for each Fellow and guest in attendance. The table glowed in flickering candlelight, and shadows waved against the white walls that were interrupted by immense windows blackened by another rainy night.

As did my colleagues, I arrived at dessert somewhat worse the wear from a dinner punctuated by the efforts of our generous wine steward. After the guests were reshuffled, the rest of us scattered to the nearest available seat, falling into it heavily and then looking around ourselves, taking a reading on whom we were to share small talk with on this particular evening. I sat to the right of Robert Applebalm, Wadham's senior Victorian historian, a man who wore smudged eyeglasses and a soiled tie. To my right was Dillard Brookner. I didn't know what Dillard did at the college, and I wasn't sure I cared. He was a young man who tried to act fifty, forced an upper class accent, and always had shined shoes. This latter classification set him noticeably apart from his peers, and warned me to be wary of him. Dillard was clearly moneyed, and, as such, at a distinctive disadvantage here. It was one of Oxford's little foibles.

While the others had slumped into the nearest available chair, I had been an intentional heartbeat behind, successfully placing myself directly across from Henry Hagg, the college's Music Fellow. When he spoke, requesting the bowl of grapes, I knew the voice from my eavesdropping on Hagg and the two other Fellows whom I now viewed as co-conspirators in something I had yet to fully understand. I allowed us all to settle in comfortably. The Fellows had a way of taking their time. They basically ignored anyone who didn't matter to them, focusing instead on their fruit plates and the far more important progression of the wines. The dons tolerated the old-timers, those red-cheeked emeritus Fellows who returned to High Table once or twice a week. The dons held contempt for those who frequented the hallowed halls too often, drinking wine to which they had no real right to drink, thirty years of teaching or not.

Once a month was considered too often for these retirees.

Henry Hagg passed the wines to Phillip, a man I took as Wadham's comptroller, though I wasn't sure I had that right. I didn't want to rush things with Hagg. Dessert typically lasted forty minutes to an hour, and this acclimation period seemed important to a Fellow's mood. The British were only slightly more talkative drunk than sober, but I wanted to give Hagg every chance to loosen up. He short-circuited my attempts by addressing me first. "Mr. Klick, isn't it?"

"Yes."

"The Chandler Fellow," Phillip informed Hagg.

"Yes. I am pleased to make your acquaintance." He didn't introduce himself. I was used to this by now. I was simply expected to know who he was. Lucky that I did. He asked, "How is the mystery going?" loading this question purposefully, meeting my eye with an unspoken challenge.

In my peripheral vision I caught sight of Randall Bradshaw, two seats to Hagg's right, who, by the snap of his head, had clearly overheard this question.

"Better than I expected," I answered. "What a surprise to find such a wealth of useful material right here at the college." I smiled at him purposefully.

"The British love a good mystery, Mr. Klick." He used a pair of stainless steel surgical scissors provided with the grapes to snip off a cluster. He laid them carefully onto his empty plate, as if worried about bruising.

I said, "When you were a student here, you must have known Julian Rasner." It was a long shot. I knew that Rasner had graduated from Oxford but not when. Still, he looked to be about the same age as Shultz. Shultz and

Rasner were contemporaries. In private he might have lied to me. But it wasn't worth his lying about in present company. The fellows knew *everything* about each other. Academics, the world over, were an inbred bunch.

"What makes you say that?" he inquired, stripping grapes carefully from the stems, and collecting them on one side of the plate. He had no intention of eating them until this ritual was complete. And he was in no hurry.

It wasn't a denial. I smiled cordially, attempting to be just as challenging as he had been with me a moment earlier. "And Stephan Shultz," I added. "Shultz and Rasner were good friends, so I have to assume you must have at least *known* them."

"Known them?" questioned Robert Applebalm, whose neck suddenly extended from his shirt collar like a turtle's from a shell. Without any warning, his curiosity-ridden expression invaded my airspace, crooked teeth and all. He pressed his nose within an inch of my own, his face contorting like a rubber mask. "*Known* them?" he repeated, the sour alcohol coloring his breath. I leaned away from him, mistaking this as an attempt at a kiss. "Hmm?" he questioned. I half-expected his tongue to shoot out between his clamped lips, mimicking a snake's or lizard's. His neck recoiled and sucked back into the collar. "The best trio at the university. What was it, Henry?" It came out as *'Enry*. "Piano, cello, and horn?" To me he said, "Melted the knickers right off the girls, ehh? Hmm? Made you wish you studied the flute or something." This won a chuckle from several of the men around me. All but Henry Hagg who looked desperate, as if Applebalm had just revealed a state secret.

"I remember this one performance at the Holywell—"

"Robert!" Henry Hagg chastised sternly. "It was twenty-five *years* ago."

"Well what's ever the matter, 'Enry? Phillip, pass 'Enry the port, what? Hmm? Was only going to mention that splendid Beethoven—that's what. Whatever *is* the matter? Ehh?"

Phillip did in fact pass the port, but Henry Hagg's attention was divided between me and Robert Applebalm. I risked one quick glance in the direction of Randall Bradshaw and confirmed his keen interest in this conversation and his apparent concern over Hagg's outburst. He seemed ready to shout something down the table, but contained himself.

"The interesting thing about a mystery, one thing that makes a good mystery," I suggested to Hagg, "is the relationship between the characters. Don't you think so, Robert?" I said, addressing the man adjacent to me.

The man's elastic neck wormed out of his collar once again, as his face came to within inches of my own. I immediately regretted involving him. "Oh, yes, dear fellow. Though some, no doubt, will argue differently. Ehh? Hmm . . . Emphasis on the plot. Plot is everything. Body needs a strong skeleton, and all that. Ehh?"

This prompted what amounted to a heated discussion among those in our immediate vicinity. As the challenges began to fly, Henry Hagg popped a grape into his mouth and bit down on it. We met eyes and I saw that he was a stronger man than I had suspected. He made no effort to look away, or to break eye contact. This was something of a staring contest, with the first to break contact the weaker of the two, and I was willing to play. Applebalm proved himself to be ever the gentleman as he picked up on this tension between Hagg and me. He stopped himself mid-sentence—something about the creation of tension through the manipulation of character—and said, "Everything all right, 'Enry?"

"Fine," Hagg said, reluctantly losing our contest and diverting his glare to his colleague.

"Said something wrong, did I? Bit in the cups, I am. Pay no attention. Hmm?"

"Shultz and Rasner certainly went opposite ways," I said to Applebalm.

"Stephan and Julian had a falling out over a composition of Stephan's. Can't remember exactly what that was all about. Too long ago. I say, Randall," he shouted too loudly across the table, but winning the man's full attention. "Whatever was that row about between Julian and Stephan? Do you recall? Accused him of plagiarism, wasn't it?"

Bradshaw called out, "Don't have the slightest idea what you are talking about, Robert! Muck-raking again, are we?" But he didn't wait for answer. He teased, "More wine, ehh?"

A few of the dons chuckled at this as well.

"Splendid suggestion. Splendid! Who *is* slowing down the wines? Hmm? Ah, it's you, Chris! Hurry them along please."

It *was* me. The wines were grouped to my right, looking like bowling pins. They were making laps more quickly now. Hagg crushed a few more grapes between his teeth, eyeing me tentatively. I helped myself to a sauterne and forwarded the ensemble to my left. Wax from one of the candles flooded onto the table and Phillip tended to it. Phillip tended to *everything*.

"Stephan Shultz is a composer, is he?" I asked anyone.

The heads bobbed. Henry Hagg glared at me and checked quickly to his right. From down the table Randall Bradshaw looked on like a referee.

"I only know him as a conductor," I said, testing.

"He was quite accomplished at one time," Henry Hagg told me. I had not expected his participation in this, and it immediately caused me to consider his motives: Was he trying to reduce my suspicions, or was he less concerned about this line of inquiry than I had first believed?

"Still composes under a pseudonym, doesn't he?" It was a statement, made by Phillip. "Film scores and like, isn't it, 'Enry?"

"That's right." The man was staring me down again. I was a little too drunk to register all this. I was beginning to feel some of it was getting by me. I smiled at him. It was all I could think to do. He didn't smile back. He was angry with me. I felt from him a bubbling hatred that carried a vague warning. Henry Hagg was no pushover. His look said, "Don't spoil my fun." I wanted to know the nature of that fun. I wanted to know what it was he and Randall Bradshaw had to protect and how it involved Stephan Shultz and what it had meant for the missing Aiden Sinclair. What it meant for me.

Allison Star had stated that Shultz avoided music scores—that she had tried to talk him into composing more. Where was truth? Where were the lies?

The small dessert book circulated. We marked down our

names and how many glasses of which wines we had consumed. We would be charged accordingly. Only Wadham had such a charge system for dessert wines and it was a cause of much grumbling among the Fellows. It was an honor system that, according to Tim Binyon, was nearly always abused.

Henry Hagg challenged Robert Applebalm over a university committee decision that I hadn't heard about and didn't understand. It was a deft bit of manipulating, for the topic of Stephan Shultz disappeared entirely, and for me to bring it back up, when I finally got the chance, would have been in bad taste and would have directed attention to it in a way that I had no desire to initiate.

I sat quietly, sipping my wine until it was empty. Dessert ended and we adjourned. I was invited to join everyone for some coffee, but my head was spinning, and I came to understand why Aiden Sinclair took his short walks after dessert. I said how I would join them in a few minutes, and excused myself.

Robes slung over their weary arms, the Fellows formed a loose procession, out through the stone arches, into the gray swirling mist, silhouetted by a brilliant light mounted high on the roof. Save for that, it might have been a night a hundred years earlier. Perhaps two hundred. This same procession had been repeated for centuries, and there was something about my intoxication that made note of this, that caused shivers up my spine and down my arms. I was living in an historical time capsule. The stone worn into bowls by the leather soles of a million footfalls—I couldn't escape this image. It was always the worn stone my mind returned to. But this image of the dons, chatting casually, walking stiffly, was imprinted firmly in my brain. They disappeared into the mist, only their voices lingering in the echoey confines of the courtyard, and for a moment, I secretly hoped they might ask me to stay here forever.

CHAPTER 33

I spent some time wandering the construction site in the dark, trying to clear my head. I was walking unsteadily and carrying a running conversation with myself. I made a full loop, crossed through the darkened gardens and, as I passed the opaque doorway leading into the chapel I heard a familiar voice say, "Chris, could I have a word with you?"

It was Jake, the chaplain, just his face revealed partially in the shadows. He swung open the heavy wooden door that arched over his head. It groaned on its hinges. I hit my head going through, ducked, and tried again. He had been at dessert too, sitting to Dillard's right. He walked almost as drunk as I felt. We made an interesting pair. "Jake," I said, my voice suddenly amplified by the chapel's high stone walls and gambled arches.

He heaved the door closed behind us. It acknowledged with a booming thud. We walked toward the altar, our footfalls like a baby clapping. When he spoke, it was with a reverend's hush, but his words carried effortlessly in the chancel. Like the other Fellows, he was remarkably adept at concealing the degree of his intoxication, speaking without the slightest slur or misbegotten inflection. I could only assume we were alone, for there was no speaking confidentially in here, given any volume. Those hinges would warn us of our privacy being compromised. Color over-flowed from the towering stained-glass windows, lit by exterior floodlights. Biblical lessons surrounded us. The large brass cross adorning the altar glowed. Aside from this, it was dark. No candles burned, no electricity was in use.

"After a few glasses of wine," Jake said, "I find it is not so difficult to speak my mind. I saw you in the garden and thought this might be a good time for both of us."

"If we can't make time for God, Jake, then what's it come to?"

"This has little to do with God, my friend. Though I assure you: He's watching over you. He *must* be." He sounded a little surprised by this possibility.

"I'm listening." Lyel and I occasionally engaged in heated theological debates, though I doubted that Jake would appreciate my side of those arguments. Half-crocked, it was easier to listen.

"How are you enjoying it here at Wadham?" he asked.

"That's why you asked me in here?"

"You and your friend made a bit of a scene at the new dorm."

"Just looking around, is all."

"Everyone at college has heard about it," he said.

"Just a small misunderstanding over crossing some lines."

"People can find themselves in trouble by crossing certain lines."

"Are we talking about the construction site?" I asked.

"Indirectly."

"Maybe we should try for a little more direct," I suggested. My head was ringing. I either needed another drink or some sleep.

"It is not easy funding a college. No easier here than in your own country, I suspect. Perhaps *more* difficult here. The Thatcher years saw our budgets cut drastically. *Drastically*," he repeated for emphasis. "And the result, at least for Wadham, has meant some unusual alliances for some strange bedfellows." He smirked, proud of coming up with this expression.

"Among the alumni?" I asked, thinking of the new construction project.

"A Japanese businessman," he answered.

"One man?" I asked, unable to conceal my astonishment.

"Yes. Only one."

"But it must be costing *millions*."

"Over ten."

"Ten million *pounds?*" I started doing the math, converting into dollars.

"More."

"One man?"

"We needed a dormitory. He needed college enrollment."

"Want to run that by me again?"

"We accept the money for the dormitory. Quietly. In turn, we agree to accept five top students from Japan. Five each year, for the next fifteen years."

"That's all?" I asked.

"But we *must* accept five. You see?"

"No. I don't think I do."

"It's the prestige of the university. It's the *guarantee* of that prestige. Placement within society is extremely important to the Japanese."

Even in my drunken haze I thought I understood what he was saying. "Five students of *your* choosing, or five students of *his* choosing."

His eyes flashed in the ambient light. "The dormitory will solve some overcrowding and allow us to offer several additions to the curriculum. It's very important to Wadham. We're not one of the bigger colleges, you know. It's not easy."

"How many other colleges at the university have such 'alliances?' "

"You're a mystery writer," he said mistakenly. It had been several years since I had misrepresented myself. It made me feel a little cheap to have a preacher unloading the truth on me, and me not reciprocating. But I quickly overcame any moralistic tendencies I might have felt. I nodded, and swallowed once to keep from smiling. I had a horrible urge to laugh at that comment. "It means you're curious by nature. An explorer. Both into people, and situations, I would imagine. Just a word of caution is all: direct your energies elsewhere. This much money, these kinds of alliances, are quite complicated and involved. You must realize: the Fellows vote on these matters. Yes? We are uncomfortably acquiescing in our present situation. Other colleges, you say? Yes, I would imagine it's everywhere if it's at Wadham."

"The Japanese are buying influence at Oxford University?"

"It's not exactly the Vatican." He added, "The Japanese are busily buying up *everything, everyone*, my dear boy. Look around you. It's worse in your own country, I should imagine. They've become cleverer about how they do it.

That's all. They were a little too visible for a while; they got their backsides singed and it taught them a lesson or two about public relations. If you have no relations with the public, it's better for all. So they go about what they do privately. Though not too privately. Not if it can be converted to prestige at home. Buckingham Palace honored this chap who gave us our library. Did you read about it? It caused quite a stir. He must have felt it was worth the noise it was certain to generate—and he knew his stuff: the university connection never *was* revealed. Being the first Japanese so honored by the Queen. You see they value that kind of thing terribly. Damned important to them what the other chap thinks."

"You want me to stay away from the new building."

"I want you to realize that Fellowships can be terminated quite quickly. I enjoy having you around. So do many of the others. But you keep on doing as you are now, and we'll be corresponding by letter, I'm afraid." He coughed. "Better to direct your energies elsewhere." Then he looked up at me and asked, "Fancy a night cap?"

We drank Drambouie from goblets in his small office and he told me about a sweetheart he had once had on a visit to Scotland. The way he talked about it, it sounded like fifty years ago. Perhaps to him it was.

It made me miss Nicole. I returned to my rooms to attempt to reach her in London. She had a habit of getting away from me. It occurred to me that she might have left me again, and that I was as yet none the wiser.

CHAPTER 34

My concern over Nicole, heightened by my inability to locate her by phone, steered me toward a beer which I drank in solitude sitting before the warm glow of my electric fireplace. I hadn't heard from Lyel, and I was worried about him, too. I was working on some considerable self-pity when my telephone rang. I jumped toward it, expecting it to be Nicole.

It was a woman's voice. A stranger. Young. A student. I marked the time: 2:00 A.M. She offered no name, but said, "You are the mystery writer, are you not?"

"That's correct."

"Forgive me for calling so late."

"It's not a problem. I'm up."

"Could I come up to your room for a few minutes, please? It will only take a minute."

"*What* will only take a few minutes?"

She told me, "You spoke to the chaplain tonight—a few minutes ago." She caught me off-guard, and I hesitated, unsure exactly how to respond to this. I sampled the beer. "I was *inside* the chapel at the time. I heard what you discussed, and I have something to add." It was her turn to hesitate. "If I would not be disturbing you."

"King's Arms, eleven," I instructed her.

"Won't be a minute." The line went dead.

It seemed possible that someone might have been hiding in all that darkness. It also seemed *likely* that Jake, in his drunkenness, had not conducted the most thorough inspection of the chapel before summoning me inside.

I showed her inside. She was a small woman with pale white skin, soft dark eyes, and hair that hung flat on her head. She carried some of that late teen puffiness that was certain to be shed in the coming years. It was doubtful she would ever be beautiful, but that was to her favor. Meeting her, one focused on her intensity. There was a lot going on behind those quiet eyes. She wore grungy clothes with a large, intentional hole revealing the smooth side of her left breast and another exposing her abdomen. She had five tiny gold hoops through her right ear giving it the look of a spiral notebook binder. She had a little too much hair on the sides of her neck. She showed no uneasiness. To the contrary, the first words out of her mouth were, "Have you got another?" She had a pretty thick accent, distinctive. And had I known more about the country, I might have pinpointed her origins.

I brought her a beer and she straddled a chair backwards, facing me with her chin on the top slat of the chair's back and her legs spread.

On closer inspection, the whites of her dark eyes appeared bloodshot. Either she was stoned, or she had been crying.

"I was in the loft," she said, answering what would have been my first question. "The balcony. Up there because I didn't want anyone to see me. I wanted to be alone. I wanted some privacy. The chapel is a private place for me."

"Sorry if we disturbed you," I said, taking my chair by the electric fire.

"I heard what you said, you two, didn't I? Heard everything you said."

"You might have announced yourself."

"I had a thing going with him, you know?"

"The *chaplain?*" I asked.

"Aiden." She drank a good bit of the beer. A surprising amount, really. "Courage," the Brits called it. "Don't ask me why I'm telling you this, because it's just something I decided I had to do. Had to do it quick-like, while I was thinking about what you two talked about."

"Aiden Sinclair," I repeated, just to get that straight.

"They think he's soft in the head, don't they? I *know* they do. What do I care? He's charming, really. Really, he is. Honestly. And we just sort of—you know, it just sort of happened." She fired me a terrified look. "Bollocks! I was going to get you to promise you wouldn't say anything about it, and now I've gone and forgot!"

"I won't."

"You promise? Do you? Could get him tossed, you see. They'd chuck him. Probably chuck us both, wouldn't they? Mum and Da wouldn't like that, would they? Whip my backside is what my Da would do."

"I promise." It made me feel like I was in Junior High.

"Was up there praying for him, is what I was doing."

"For Sinclair? Praying?"

"He kept in touch with me, Aiden did. Right up until Tuesday last. Wouldn't tell me nothing, the little creep. But I still love him, you see. And he knows it. It's not so good when they know it. You know?" She seemed to be thinking aloud more than talking to me. I switched the electric fire to half heat. My left leg felt about medium rare. She said, "An' when you two started in on that business about the new dormitory, I almost jumped up and screamed."

"But you cried instead," I suggested.

"I *did* cry! Shows, does it? Never could hide a good cry.

Not me. Wear it all over me face, I do. Don't I?"

"I'm told Sinclair disappears like this from time to time. Is that true?"

"Disappear? Who told you that? The Fellows, I suppose. They *would* say that. He tells the Warden, he does. He's a good man, Mr. Klick. Don't make him out to be nothing else. A *fine* man. An *honest* one, which is more than you can say about most of them."

A student not liking her professors was nothing newsworthy. I looked her over again and tried to picture her with Sinclair and I thought the man was lucky to have her: there was kindness in her face, a shy simplicity to her smile, and yet she carried herself confidently, which was something peculiar to the girls I saw around the University—they seemed much less inhibited than their American counterparts. She said, "I saw you and that other one out there t'other day."

"Out where?"

"The new dorm, I'm talking about. That miserable construction. They go at it all day, they do. I didn't know about the Japanese bugger 'til tonight. The money. But I'm not surprised. The Fellows will do whatever's necessary to keep their jobs. They live like kings, they do. Drink like fish, live like kings. Protect that however necessary, they will. More and more Orientals there are. Don't see half as many Africans, do you? And so I suppose the Father was right when he told you what he did—'bout going easy and all, because I can see how what he's saying would be true and all, wouldn't it? How they wouldn't like no poking around out there, nothing disrupting their precious dormitory." She nearly finished the beer in her next go at it. She set it on the floor and leaned back over the chair, and my eye wandered to that hole in her shirt and the bluish pale skin that showed there. "And what none of you knows—what you couldn't know, could you?—is that Aiden was out there, too. Out there the night before he disappeared. Was out there digging around, he was."

I recalled the mud I had found in Sinclair's room. I didn't tell her that Lyel and I had already reached this same conclusion. "Digging around?" I asked naively.

"Was in his cups, he was. He likes to tip a few, he does. And he got disoriented, you see—a little lost is what he was—what he always is—and he went and fell right into that works area where they were digging it up, he did. Came to my room all filthy and excited 'bout something. That's the way he is, you know. He's energetic, Aiden is. Always going on about something or other. Was a little too buggered-up for me to understand exactly what he was talking about. But filthy as a rat, like I've said. I think it had something to do with that bottle. He kept going on about that bottle."

"A bottle?"

"Not grog. Don't mean like that. A *dirty* bottle. An *old* one it was. That's his research field you know? Archaeology, not herbs. All excited, he was—going on and on. Went back to the Senior Common Room, he did, but not before talking me into joining him later. Two o'clock it was before we went back out there. Aiden digging with a spade and me holding the light for him. Couple of kids after buried treasure we were."

"Digging?"

"Drunk, mind you. Both of us drunk. Just old bottles,

mostly. Looked like a bunch of rubbish to me. Who cares about a bunch of rubbish? But that's Aiden for you, isn't it? Gettin' all excited about old dirty things. There's no fig-uring 'im, Mr. Klick. I'll tell you that right now. No fig-uring him 't'all."

"Bottles?"

"And then you and that other one are out there, you see; and then the Father tonight, and I figures you had better should know about Aiden nosing 'round there too, because he's gone missing an' all." She reached down for the beer. She didn't sound very disturbed to me. "Wouldn't want you to go missing as well."

"That's very thoughtful of you."

"So, that's 'bout all I came to say, unless you'd happen to have another beer I might have."

I thanked her. Then I brought us both another. She pulled her chair up to the electric fire, still straddling it and leaning over its back. We sat there for a while in silence, both of us staring at the glowing red coils. I felt her look at me several times. "You're a big bloke," she said. "So's your friend."

I knew she wasn't hitting on me, but I was at a loss for words.

"I don't really see you as a writer," she added. "Who *are* you?"

I felt myself blush alongside the heat of the electric fire. "Did he say anything about the bottles? Anything at all?"

"You're not going to answer me?"

"Did he mention any names?"

"Who *are* you? Do you know if he's all right?"

We suffered through another long silence.

"And who's your friend?" she asked.

"We *are* trying to find him," I admitted, wondering immediately why I would admit such a thing. I stared at the beer in my hand, regret filling me.

She looked up, eyes sparkling, and then seemed to force herself toward the fire again. "I knew you were a good person," she said. "You have the face of a good person." That should have made me feel better, but it didn't. Maybe I was more intoxicated than I was admitting to myself. She said, "I think he said something about Remmington—do you know Herbert Remmington?"

"No."

"Magdalen College. Though he spends all of his time at the laboratory. That, or the pub. He and Aiden are mates, they are." Still looking at the fire she asked, "Why you looking at me like that, then?" She sipped the beer. "Are you thinking what I think you're thinking? It's not that I'm a prude, you know! Don't want you thinking like that. We British girls are a hell of a lot more relaxed about it than your American girls—can tell you that. Truthfully, wouldn't mind boffing you if I wasn't so sweet on Aiden. But it wouldn't be right, you know. Have I embarrassed you?" she asked, glancing over at me.

"I think you have."

"Did I get it wrong?" she asked, amused. "Oh God! Now it's me embarrassed."

"No," I admitted uncomfortably, "I was probably staring."

She glanced down at the hole in her shirt. As if we were discussing a football score, she asked, "A tit man, are you? You Americans like tits, don't you? It's different over here, you know?"

"Yes." I wanted to vanish, but these were my rooms.

"You have got a girl, do you?"

"Yes."

"Got one here at the college?"

"No."

"Never much for that long distance stuff myself. Like it a bit more physical than that." She smiled. "Have you got a loo in these rooms?" I pointed. "You tired?" she asked, coming out of the chair. "Am I keeping you up?"

"No."

She used the bathroom, which was out in the hall. When she returned she sat down and said, "Do you like it here?"

"Yes, very much. You?"

"Not the same for me, is it? Classes and all that rubbish." Her zipper had not fully closed. She tugged it shut, not the least bit modest or uncomfortable. "Look," she said softly, "it's not like Aiden *owns* me or anything. Can't explain it. So either I stay or go, but I think it's best to be on the ups about the way a person feels." She shoved her hands tightly into her front pockets. They barely fit. "What do you think?" she asked, rocking nervously on her heels.

I didn't want to offend her. "I think you're very kind. Pretty, too. But you should go."

She stood and took my chin in her hands and we met eyes and hers were smiling. We stayed this way for quite some time before she said, "Well . . . I'm off then. You'll tell me if you find him, won't you?" She didn't wait for an answer.

I heard her going quickly down the stairs. It was then I realized that I didn't even know her name.

CHAPTER 35

It was raining the next morning when I awakened late, my mouth tasting like an old sock. I hadn't dreamt about anything that I could remember. I hoped that Lyel might call. Or Nicole.

I resolved to take a run. I had missed yesterday, and if I went out and put in a hard four miles I knew it would make me feel better. The rain wasn't too bad—an Oxford drizzle. I donned a pair of sweat pants and a sweatshirt with the sleeves torn-off just above the elbow. I waved to John, the porter, on my way out. He was sorting mail in a cloud of cigarette smoke, and his ruddy cheeks brightened with my greeting.

I turned right out the entrance onto Parks Road and made for the park which lay about a half mile up on the right. The street was alive with bicycles and too many cars. The footpath was an undulating sea of umbrellas of every size and color, some in better shape than others. The students traveled in groups, everyone talking loudly at once. This was an age I remembered well—when politics, ethics, and philosophy were still worth discussion. This desire had tempered somewhat in me, which probably explained why I didn't write much music these days: I had nothing left to say. Only my fireside conversations with Lyel evoked much creative thinking in me anymore, and I wondered why that was.

Someone tripped me from behind just as I made my cut to enter the park. I blamed the collision on my day-dreaming—there were times during runs when I wouldn't remember anything at all about the last several minutes of a run, and perhaps that was why I enjoyed it so much. But as it was, I went down hard, spilling into the wet grass and landing my left hand in a pile of gooey mud, which I knew instinctively was not mud at all, but the discharge of the rear end of a dog. It was the warmth and surprise of the dog shit that distracted me and kept me from immediately recognizing that the collision had been intentional.

He was a big man in running clothes meant for someone smaller. He leaned over and struck me once squarely in the center of my chest, immediately below the V in my rib cage, knocking the wind from me and paralyzing me at the same time. Then there was another guy at my side, and suddenly I was being dragged. My head hit the edge of a car as I was indelicately stuffed inside so that my face came down on a fuzzy velour seat. Dark blue, with white cat hairs.

They tied a blindfold over my eyes. The door thumped shut. The car buzzed off. I wasn't allowed to sit up for the rest of a fifteen minute drive that had me sliding around the back seat, my left arm twisted well up my spine.

"I don't recall hailing a cab," I said into the seat.

"Sorry for the treatment, mate," the man breaking my elbow said. "Won't be too much longer."

It wasn't. Perhaps fifteen minutes in all. The car drove over a rough cobblestone and came to a stop. I was led out of the car—they protected my head this time—and I heard a heavy door groan on hinges that needed oiling. Then it was a wooden floor creaking underneath my feet, and suddenly I realized that my escorts were gone, and so I untied the blindfold.

He was smaller than I had expected. Celebrity makes

people larger than life, and I had imagined him the way I had seen him on PBS: standing tall in front of sixty tuxedoed musicians, majestically waving his arms about—big, and in control. The white hair I recognized, the spirited, mischievous eyes, the wry, intelligent smile: the same man I had pursued in the upper reaches of the Sheldonian. The voice belonged to an orator, as rich as Devonshire clotted cream, and yet entirely American. "Let me apologize for the treatment, Mr. Klick. This entire situation is rather tawdry." He stepped forward, "Stephan Shultz," he said. I took hold of his strong hand—the one with which he held his baton—and we shook.

"It wasn't exactly a scenic ride. Blue velour is not my favorite."

"Coffee?"

"I need a signature is all. Does the figure one-hundred-and-ninety-thousand dollars do anything for you?"

"It's creative," he replied. "Inventive."

He moved into a small sitting room with a low-ceiling and a fireplace that was made but unlit. There was dog hair on the carpet, but no animal in sight. I excused myself to the bathroom and cleaned off the dog dirt. When I returned, escorted of course, the drapes were drawn—to keep me from seeing where I was, no doubt. A somewhat dim bulb burned in a lamp in the far corner. He sat into a large wing-back chair that sighed under his weight. I took the couch and sank a little lower than I had expected.

"You've checked me out, or I wouldn't be here. You know I'm for real: I have one-hundred-ninety-thousand dollars with your name on it."

"Minus your cut."

"Twenty-five percent plus expenses, which, I might add, are running into some serious money the longer this continues. Of course, you've liberated your wife's trust," I said bluntly, "so maybe you can skate by without the money, but it's how I earn a paycheck, Maestro, so I'm not about to give it up. Right now, you're the best client we've got. Until another comes along, you're my paycheck."

"I'd like to believe it. I really would. And it's one hell of a good story. Sincerely. But it's not true, is it? Why bother Randy and the others if you're here to do me a good deed? Hmm? It's confusing to me, Mr. Klick. See? And as for checking you out: you're something of an enigma. No credit cards. No bank accounts. No living family. What are you, CIA or something?" he mocked.

"I pay my taxes," I replied. "And I vote. And I give money to the Snow Lake Animal Shelter."

He picked at the fingernails of his left hand. "Exactly what will make you go away?"

"Your signature—your notarized signature."

"Notarized?"

"At the embassy in London. If we were home, any old notary would do."

"The embassy?" He laughed. "You must be kidding. It's *her* isn't it?" He looked a little frightened. "You're cleverer than I gave you credit for. The *embassy!*"

"It's *not* her. And it's not Allison's parents either. What you do between a woman's legs is of no concern to me." He bristled. "You want to chase the fountain of youth, that's your business. My business is giving people money they earned, and you'd be surprised how difficult some people like you make it. When I got into this work, I thought it would be so easy—I mean who's going to turn down hard cold cash that someone basically stole from them? Well, you'd be surprised! You think you're the first to run me all over hell and gone, sic goons on me and stuff me into cars? Hell, this is old hat for me, Maestro! I'm just getting warmed up. What amazes me is how people just *won't believe* a stroke of good luck. Most of my job seems to be convincing people. And I'm not a salesman. I'm not particularly good at the marketing side of this work."

"I'd say that you're *quite* a good salesman. You almost sound convincing."

"One trip to the embassy. That's all it takes."

"Not a chance, Mr. Klick. The American embassy? You have *got* to be kidding. It would be better for everyone if you just went away."

This was his second reference to *others*, and though it slipped past me without much notice the first time, this time it rang loudly in my head: "Better for everyone." He had mentioned Bradshaw. My presence at Wadham was not appreciated, and pressure had come to bear on Shultz to get rid of me. I liked that. The pest in me appreciated this—Lyel and I were bothering someone. Good. "As I've just explained, *you* are paying me to stay at Oxford—the expenses," I reminded. "And I'm enjoying the hell out of it, thank you very much. If you think I'm—"

"There won't be any expense money forthcoming if I don't sign on the dotted line. Correct? You're not spending *my* money, you're spending your own. Don't fool yourself."

"You are going to turn down one-hundred-and-ninety-thousand dollars? Is that what you're telling me?"

Poor Shultz looked confused. I knew he wanted the

money; he clearly didn't trust me, or the situation, and yet I could understand how he would want to avoid the embassy at all costs—if there were some kind of domestic warrant issued for his arrest, perhaps the embassy had the legal authority to exercise it. We were in a stalemate—except that he was right in my fear of the expenses. I told him so. "I have passed the Fail Safe point, Maestro. I *have* to get you to sign to cover my costs on this. You ran me around Paris, now Oxford—my God a cup of coffee is nearly five bucks. You think I'm going to give up on you? Did you kidnap me to tell me this?" I asked in astonishment. "Are you *aware* of the laws you've just broken? You think the Brits don't have kidnapping laws? Do you have any *idea* of the trouble you're in? That is, unless you plan on *killing* me—which doesn't really seem your style."

"Nonsense. Nonsense to all of that."

"What if somebody saw it? What if I can deliver a witness? Are you thinking clearly, Maestro? You know what I think? I think you're out of your element—that's what. You've lived a pampered, chauffeur-driven life for too long to know how to deal with anything but a first chair and the lighting director. You've hired a bunch of goons—God knows at whose urging—and you think they'll help you to make it out of this cleanly. But Allison is a marked woman. Your wife's people are, or will be, watching her; I'm watching her, *everyone* trying to find you is watching her. You've targeted her—intentionally or not. And she's a mess, in case you haven't had time to notice. You have to climb into darkened balconies to even get a *glimpse* of her. Nice healthy relationship, isn't it? And what about her college-aged boys?"

"Shut up."

"You think they know about you? You think they would *care* even if they did know? An old guy like you. You know how the sap runs in that age group?"

"Shut *up!*"

"It worries you, doesn't it? Would worry me too. Definitely."

"You don't know anything about Allison."

"I've visited her dorm room. Have you? You think I'm the only male to have called on her?" I let that fuel his thoughts. "The sooner you straighten this all out, the sooner you can go back to living. Or maybe you *like* it like this. On the run. Stealing a glimpse on a rare night. What I have a hard time believing—what I imagine *everyone* has a hard time believing, even Allison—is that you'll give up the performance stage for very long. At some point you'll return to conducting, providing anyone will give you a shot at it. Or maybe *that's* the problem. Is Allison just a distraction—something to keep your mind off the fact the phone just isn't ringing anymore?"

He viewed me with contempt. "Leave Oxford," he ordered.

"You didn't actually think you could steal her inheritance, did you?" I asked, dumbfounded by the idea. I assumed him to be the civilized, highly educated, responsible maestro I had met on video and in newsprint, on CD, and over Texaco Theater. But as his nostrils flared and his eyes went wide, I sensed an adolescent under the white hair, a horny choir boy caught lifting the skirt of the organist. His indulgence in an extravagant lifestyle was legendary and well-documented in every interview. It was not too difficult to imagine that he had squandered huge sums with such pretensions. I asked, "What if I could put it back for you?" His eyes sparked with excitement, and I sensed a man who had sobered, if only briefly, to realize the desperation of his current situation as an international fugitive.

"I'm not a thief, Mr. Klick." He said this, but I sensed it was a lie. "I've committed no crime."

"Then you have a very bad press agent," I informed him. "My partner, and friend, is extremely good at dislodging money from stubborn accounting practices. I don't know that he's ever tried to reverse the process. But what if the money just suddenly re-appeared in whatever account or accounts from which it came? Would that reduce the heat any?"

His eyes smiled, though he fought them, and I realized I had been had. My face must have betrayed me, for he inquired, "What is it?"

I answered, "That's what you brought me here for, isn't it? To ask me the very same question I've just asked you." I laughed. "You've *conducted* me, haven't you? Wave your magic baton and I draw back my bow and I play for you." I felt both embarrassed and angry—I didn't like being used like this. My nose ring hurt. I challenged him, "Did you use these same techniques on Allison? Was she, too, just another score to conduct? Lean over her, wave your baton of sympathy—lonely, tough life at home—and take the place of the cello between her legs? Is that how it started?"

He stepped forward, red-faced, and reared back his right arm to strike me. Then he dropped his hand and his lips twisted into a churlish smile and he said, "You're a poor loser, aren't you?" He walked over to a side table where a bottle of gin kept company with several inverted crystal tumblers. "The Brits don't take ice. Do you?"

It was still before noon. "None for me," I told him.

"Nonsense. Of course you'll have some. You won't let a man drink alone, will you?"

"Absolutely. I allow myself that luxury often enough. Live a little," I said, adding, "I could call myself a cab if you're too busy. We wouldn't want you drinking and driving."

"Have you always had that mouth of yours?"

"Near as I can remember."

He poured himself a light gin and tonic, no ice. I asked for some Gatorade, but he only grinned at me. "What about it?" he asked.

I suggested, "You have to sign off on the royalty money so we can replace whatever you've spent. We'd have to do that first."

"I can offer you a larger percentage than usual. And yes, it would *all* need to be returned. None of it's mine."

"I'm not real eager to help granddads who rob the cradle."

"There's that mouth again."

"There it is," I agreed. "I think you're right: maybe it is time for me to leave Oxford."

He sampled the gin.

I said, "You took your wife's money—cash—out of the country on your person. You failed to report it anywhere along the way, leaving or entering the various countries you've visited." I waited for him to deny this. He did not. I asked, "Were you just born stupid, or is it something you acquired?"

"Maybe I've got the wrong guy."

"By my way of thinking, you've got *a lot* more wrong than just that."

He had gained some *courage* from the gin. "What I propose is that you leave Oxford immediately and make arrangements for all this in London. Exactly how we arrange your fee is up for discussion—but the timetable is not." He collected himself and said, "I acted impulsively, it's true. I prefer to think of it as passionately. It is imperative I return the money as soon as possible, however, to avoid any further legal actions on my wife's part."

"They're catching up to you," I said.

"If it were simply a matter of returning into the country and making a deposit, I wouldn't deal with you. But that is no longer a viable option. I need it put back. I need it to simply reappear, with no traceable connection to me whatsoever. And that means a person with your particular talents—or perhaps, those of your partner. I am not a humble man—I am quite aware of that. But this is business. This is something from which we both can benefit."

"There are considerable risks."

"You and your partner work it out. You will pardon me, but I do not travel in your circles. Finding someone to return this money for me is not the easiest thing. I have made a mistake—perhaps a serious one. One must pay for such mistakes. I understand this quite well.

"What is of the utmost importance to me is the timing," he continued. "This cannot wait. You see? There is a very real urgency here that I'm not sure you understand. If you agree to work with me, it must happen immediately— within the next few days at the latest."

I wanted to think of myself as shrewd and observant—a negotiator who knew his stuff. After all, I had been in similar situations often enough. And yet I felt as if the maestro had his hand in my back pocket: the alarms were ringing. On the verge of agreeing to work with him, I forced myself to refocus and see him for the manipulator he was—a monster of the cultural elite intent on checking the oil of his first cello while paying for dinner off his wife's inheritance. One didn't enter into agreements lightly with such people. He was too polished for me. This was one of the problems of trying to do business with performers: the distinction between the stage persona and the "real" persona dimmed, and I never knew exactly who I was dealing with. "Message received," I said.

"Is that a 'yes' or a 'no?' "

"That's a 'message received.' " I grinned a photo booth grin for him. I looked into his eyes and said, "The next time your power brokers get pretty with me, at least some of us are going to need medical attention. That's not a threat. It's just so you know."

"Tough guy, huh?"

I shrugged. My temper flared, but I vowed to contain it because I wanted out of here and I sensed he would let me go now if I was a good little boy. Even so, a flash of heat zipped up my spine and I felt feverish. Given the opportunity, I would have hurt him if he had pushed me any farther. "I'd like to leave now."

"I need an answer."

"You'll get an answer."

"How?"

I answered, "Blackwell's—the music store, not the main

bookshop—come by each afternoon at three. No goons."

"Every afternoon! You're setting me up!"

"You could give me a phone number," I suggested, knowing he wouldn't.

"Blackwell's at three."

"As soon as I have an answer, you will."

He nodded, and called out for his boys, arranging for my departure.

They blindfolded me again. On the way out the door, remembering that the driveway had been gravel beneath our feet, I intentionally stumbled going down the stone steps and fell hard into the drive, picking up a pebble in the process. Two of the boys helped me to my feet, and once again I staggered, this time to my left as I heard the pulsing beep of the car's key alarm grow loud enough to tell me we were only feet from the vehicle. I smacked into the right rear fender, and, as I made contact, dragged the stone, digging into and scratching the paint of the vehicle. I dropped the pebble quickly.

"Be careful with him," Shultz called out from behind us.

The boys actually apologized to me.

I remained quiet and content on the ride back, well aware of that scratch, and that if I got lucky, Stephan Shultz was no longer in hiding.

CHAPTER 36

Turning right through Wadham's arched stone entrance, I entered the faculty mail room with its thirty gray-painted pigeon holes. I dodged the Fellows' bikes stashed there and reached my box which contained a university newsletter, a notice from the bursar to remember to sign up for dessert wines, several phone messages and a letter from Sir Frans Tuttle, Wadham's Warden:

You are cordially invited to join me at the Warden's Cottage for tea at four this afternoon.

Until then,
Sir Frans Tuttle

This wasn't so much an invitation as an order. No RSVP. I tucked the note into the pocket of my sweatshirt and hurried up to my rooms to catch a shower before lunch. I was starving. On my way out of my clothes I placed a call stateside and caught Bruce just coming home from dinner.

"Someone's been making inquiries into us," Bruce informed me.

"Shultz," I explained. "It's why I've called. He wants a favor from us."

"Does he?"

I explained the offer to Bruce.

"No way," he answered.

"I thought as much."

"He violated international monetary law. That's seven years at Club Fed *with* good behavior. Maybe we eat this one, kiddo," Bruce said. He waited for my agreement. When it wasn't forthcoming he said, "You're willing to risk that?"

"I'm on the wife's side. I think it's salvageable."

"Do you?"

"Bottom line: if he gives her back her money, then he

needs ours. I think if we could help him out, and if we could find a way to waive the notary thing at the embassy, he might go for it."

"Power of attorney," Bruce said bluntly. "He assigns you power of attorney for this one transaction. One transaction only. It's a big word, and it will scare him, but you can handle the paperwork if he'll do it. I could fax you the necessary forms."

"Let's try it. Go ahead and fax them."

"Can you get to him?" he asked, knowing this had been my biggest obstacle.

"Yes, I think I can." I waited. I asked, "Can we do it? Is there some way to get that cash back into U.S. accounts without it having to be physically *carried* through customs?

"That's called laundering."

"We let them *do* it, we just tell them *how*."

"That's called abetting," he said.

"Just sketch something out, would you?"

"I'll get back to you."

I swelled with pride; it was as good as a "yes."

CHAPTER 37

As I entered the old library for Fellows' lunch, I spotted Randall Bradshaw, Lester Tilbert, and Henry Hagg all huddled around a copy of a newspaper like coaches on the sideline debating the play. They were too engrossed with whatever they were reading—or looking at!—to glance up and take notice of anyone. Maybe it was the bare-breasted model on page four of the *Sun*—the Fellows *never* missed their news. But there was a conviviality among them that won my attention. If the object of their attention were a nude, they were counting freckles. As I worked my way down the hot buffet, helping myself to two Bratwurst, sauerkraut, a cold roll, Stilton cheese and a string of grapes, I kept one eye on the trio, still wondering what they were reading, and I decided to make my way down the west side of the room, cutting behind them in hopes of peeking over their shoulders.

Henry Hagg noticed me first. He smiled widely, though falsely, at me and greeted me in a big, warm voice that I didn't trust. "Our mystery man!" At the same time he pushed aside the newspaper and Bradshaw organized it and folded it neatly. *The Independent*, I noted. No bare breasts in *The Independent*.

"Gentlemen," I said.

Tilbert looked incredibly pleased with himself. "Enjoy the meal," he said, but his expression issued a gleeful warning, the twinkle in an opponent's eyes before checkmate. The content of the warning escaped me, but I nonetheless took note of it.

I headed directly to the news table where multiple copies of the seven or eight daily papers were piled. I took a copy of *The Independent* and sat on the other side of the room from the trio. Searching the front page headlines I didn't find any easily identifiable item of interest to the three, whose academic subjects, personalities, and interests seemed so varied as to be completely disconnected. I continued further into the paper, enjoying the Bratwurst tremendously, and stumbled onto an interesting news article on page four.

JAPANESE INFLUENCE ON OXBRIDGE QUESTIONED BY MINISTERS

Oxford and Cambridge, collectively referred to as Oxbridge, were constantly the source of newsprint, but rarely the subject of Parliamentary review. The article fell short of making any accusations about the trade-offs for Japanese "investment" in the two universities, but it did mention the state honors received by a certain Japanese businessman, Mr. Royan Fujiami, and it went on to mention Wadham in particular, though again fell short of citing the current construction project. It seemed peculiar to me that the three dons would find this subject matter amusing, something worth celebrating, but when it came to dons and politics I was learning there was no telling. Perhaps they had opposed the Japanese influence and were now gloating at the bad press it had incurred. Competition was not something lost on the dons.

The article opened up a number of possibilities, all of which, it implied, would be the subject of the upcoming review by the ministers. It also, however, pointed out that many of the nation's bond issues had been underwritten by heavy Japanese investment, and the author openly questioned the objectivity and scrutiny any such inquiry would receive. The last paragraph was openly cynical, criticizing all foreign investment and the influence it wielded.

I leafed through the remainder of the paper, interrupted occasionally by a Fellow nearby. I fielded several questions about health care, the space program, and the current president—the dons tended to view me as something of a U.S. litmus test, and used me alternately as a reference manual, a sounding board, and a dart board, depending on their mood. There was nothing in the paper that jumped out at me like that article on the foreign money flooding into the colleges and the profound effect—"the threat"—it posed for those institutions. By the time I was into the Stilton, water crackers, and the grapes, I glanced up to see Hagg glaring across the room at me suspiciously, attentive in a way that went beyond anything attributable to simple curiosity. It was a penetrating stare, one broken the moment we met eyes. Bradshaw and Tilbert were no longer sitting with him, and I got the feeling that Hagg remained solely to keep an eye on me. As I thought back to my brief visit with Shultz earlier in the day, and his mention of my disturbing "others," *my* curiosity was piqued.

These men were actively involved in Sinclair's disappearance. I had no way to fully explain it—yet—but I felt it in my bones. Somehow, also unexplained, there was a link to Shultz that I didn't understand.

I needed Lyel. He had a way of listening that allowed me to hear my own thoughts.

I needed some beer, some time, and some discussion. And a copy of *The Independent*. I went down and stole one from the Fellows' Common Room before heading back to my rooms in King's Arms. I reread it three more times but nothing jumped out at me and slapped me in the face.

CHAPTER 38

Your research fellowship is terminated, Mr. Klick. I am sorry to have to be the one to deliver this news. Typically, the bursar would have told you. But I feel something of a responsibility towards you."

I ducked when entering the sitting room of the Warden's Cottage. A large gray mutt slept by the roaring fire, under a gloomy oil portrait of a witch of a woman whom I took to be Dorothy Wadham. I couldn't imagine anyone would elect to live with such an image, so perhaps it was required of the Warden to tolerate this one piece of decor. On the other hand, perhaps the room remained the same and only the wardens changed. Or worse: perhaps Sir Frans *liked* the painting. It was a cozy room with rich fabrics, antique furniture—dark brown and nutty—and limited lighting. From where he sat in front of me, the Warden's face was caught in a hemispherical silhouette like a half-moon. I could see his entire face, and yet only that one lighted eye existed after a few minutes, wet and bright blue, only half a nose and half a twisted smile. The Brits were impossible to read—probably great poker players, and even more difficult to understand. Despite my keen ears and the shared language, words slipped by occasionally. It required me to pay special attention.

"Terminated?" I asked, heart pounding.

"Yes. You'll have some tea?" he asked pleasantly.

"Terminated?" I repeated.

"We are short the rooms, you see. Terribly sorry."

I felt as if the wind had been knocked out of me. I needed

access to Wadham and its Fellows if I was to help find Aiden Sinclair. I still owed Tim Binyon that effort. "Rooms?" I echoed. My brain wasn't working. Like a myna bird, my only capacity for conversation seemed to be to repeat everything I heard.

"An administration problem is all. An oversight."

"An oversight."

"Exactly."

It wasn't often that I was at a loss for words, but Tuttle and his cozy study intimidated me, and this news had come completely unexpectedly. I felt above begging, but I was surprisingly close to it.

"I've barely begun my research."

"Yes. Well . . . Nothing to be done."

He looked into the flickering fire, his expressionless face a screen reflecting the shifting light. To him, I was lower than his dog. His wife, a stately, handsome woman with high cheekbones, a matronly figure, and fifty years she could not hide, delivered a pot of tea, two cups and saucers, a pot of hot water, and half a lemon poppyseed cake. We were not introduced. She acknowledged my presence with the slight nod of her gray hair, addressed the tea service, handed each of us a cup, and departed.

The door clapped shut. I began, "You don't under-stand—" The wrong words to speak to Sir Frans.

He interrupted, "My good man, the situation is quite simple: your association with Wadham is terminated. We simply don't have the room."

"The new building," I mumbled.

His eyes twitched, though he remained stoic. "Say what?" He glanced at me. "I suppose so. Yes. If Bruckner

Hall were completed, then things would be different, wouldn't they? More room all around."

I studied him. "What exactly are you afraid of?"

"I beg your pardon?"

"Warden, you are probably a very good administrator, but you're a bad liar."

"Nonsense!" he said emphatically.

"You're a *good* liar?" I inquired.

He flushed.

"The article in the paper. The Japanese investment. You think I had something to do with it."

"You are a fraud, Mr. Klick. You misrepresented yourself to me." He looked over at me. "I would prefer to keep this *civilized*, if you don't mind."

"Civilized?"

"You are *not* a published author. Of mysteries, or of anything else for that matter, although I have uncovered several copyrighted musical materials under the name Klick. Is that you? Are you that Christopher Klick?"

I had not figured that Sir Frans would have me checked out. Lyel had assumed Binyon's recommendation would be enough to sell me to the college, but now, apparently, I had been found out. My proclivity for quick rejoinders deserted me. How much did he know?

"Hmm?" he asked, attempting to establish the high ground, and inciting a competitive urge in me.

I said, "You *must* know that I publish under a pseudonym if you've done any research whatsoever. So, I assume instead that, knowing I'm here to research, you must have something to hide, something you're afraid I might uncover. What you don't understand about me, what you couldn't possibly know, and obviously didn't think to consider, Sir Frans, is that by trying to get rid of me, you've only made me angry, and there's nothing worse than an angry writer. The pen really is mightier, you know."

He reddened. He clearly didn't like being addressed in this manner. The truth lingered somewhere inside of him. I could see it spread into his eyes. Desperate eyes.

"This wouldn't have something to do with my paying a visit to the construction site, would it?"

He fumbled for his words. "You . . . you had a young woman student in your rooms until well past two in the morning. That's simply not on."

He was having me *watched!* Enraged, I prepared to blast him when a sharp knock snapped on the front door, followed by Tim Binyon in long strides. "Frans," Binyon said, barely acknowledging me, "this is absurd!"

"I beg—?"

"We will put it to vote, if need be—the Fellows. We will override you, if put to the test. And then where will you be? Eh? Leave us alone, will you please, Chris?"

"No, I won't," I objected.

They both looked at me with surprise.

"No," I repeated. "I am not a dog to be shooed away!" I protested.

Binyon said to Tuttle, "It's Fujiami, isn't it? This news story?" To me he said, "He thinks it's *you*, you see?"

"I see perfectly well. What you don't realize, Sir Frans," I continued, "is that if *I* had uncovered the Fujiami connection, I would have saved it for a novel."

"The fellowship is canceled," he said to Binyon. "And what do you mean by storming in here? This is my *home!*"

"You *invited* him here," Binyon reminded. "We receive funds for this fellowship. How do you intend to handle *that?*"

"He is disrupting the administration of this college."

"Ridiculous!"

The two men continued their discussion; the British aplomb with which they went after each other could hardly be called arguing. They barely raised their voices. I was focused on Tuttle's reference to my disrupting the 'administration of this college,' for I took it to mean my questioning of the three Fellows—Hagg, Bradshaw and Tilbert—and my poking around the construction site. Another possibility was that the young woman who had visited my room had been a plant. I doubted that—you don't fake eyes bloodshot from tears.

Tuttle settled something with Binyon and asked me: "Would you care to explain yourself, Mr. Klick?"

"I don't see what it is I have done to deserve this," I complained in the whiniest voice I could muster. Ignorance, I decided, was the best tack. Tuttle would prefer to think of me as dumb; his British superiority could live with that. If I was conniving, or overly confident, I was in trouble. "I've been researching and outlining—a *terrific* story, by the way—and all of a sudden you want me gone. I can only think there has been a misunderstanding, and as far as that goes, I'll do whatever I can to clear it up." I checked with Binyon, whose tired looking eyes viewed me with some admiration. "But 'disrupting the college?' I don't see how writing a mystery—a piece of *fiction*, after all—can be invasive to the administration of a college of Wadham's reputation." I tried my best to look sheepish and contrite.

"It is the nature of your research that I am interested in, specifically. It would seem to me rather idiosyncratic, this research of yours. You seem to be here one day, over there the next. What *exactly* is this mystery of yours about, Mr. Klick?"

I chanced a glance at Binyon, who appeared extremely nervous, and answered in a naive way, "A Fellow who goes missing." I leaned forward earnestly, and really worked on sounding southern California-dude-stupid. "What I've done is take this Aiden Sinclair thing to the extreme. Maxed it out. 'Cause it seemed so perfect for a story, you know? Like this don is working on something kind of top secret and disappears, and no one knows exactly what was going on. That kind of thing. So, what I'm doing—maybe what you're referring to—is that I'm talking to the dons a lot, trying to come up with a story that might make sense—like what it was he was working on, and who did him in." I smiled my best shit-eating, dumb luck look. I had to explain my questioning, because he clearly knew about it—but in a way that he could stomach. If I was dead-on the truth, but didn't know it, he might take this as the best possible situation and allow me to stay. My trust remained in his sense of superiority; I had to count on his believing me so stupid as to not fear me.

Tuttle knew something about Sinclair's disappearance. That much was apparent. He lost a shade of color before quickly regaining it, along with his confidence. He studied me with searching eyes.

Binyon slipped into a leather chair whose frame chirped like birds and immediately began picking dog hairs off his sleeve with an overt amount of distaste. The dog eyed him as if this chair were his. Binyon repeated, "I'll call for a vote if you force me to, Frans. This Chandler Fellowship is important to the department, important to all of us. It gives us international recognition and enhances our standing among the other colleges."

My chance to remain at Wadham lay stretched between these two men like a rope in tug-of-war. I wanted to reach out and grab Binyon's end and pull it hard—but it wasn't mine to grab. I was ever the outsider, and I felt this distinctly and knew to keep my mouth shut.

"You must be a bit more discreet," Tuttle said, providing me with a ray of hope.

"And *we* must allow him to do what he came here to do, Frans," Binyon corrected. "The charter of the fellowship specifically calls for research. Are we to dictate the direction of that research? Do we dictate the direction of *any* university research—given existing budgetary guidelines? Is it Fujiami? Is that it? Fujiami can go stuff it: he's getting what he wants—and *then* some. If he wanted a low-profile existence, he should never have actively sought the attention of the Royals. He has only himself to blame for all the press he is receiving. I should like to think that we at Wadham look after our own. Isn't that so? Chris is one of *us*. Let's not forget that. We have a duty to support him, not challenge him."

This was clearly Binyon at his best. The art of debate. Of pressure.

"Yes, yes," Tuttle agreed, the decision weighing on him heavily.

"We foster creativity, we don't stifle it," Binyon went on in his best pep talk tone of voice. For a Brit, he sounded almost animated.

"Yes, of course," Tuttle mumbled, his mind elsewhere. He said emphatically, "Aiden's absence is *not* a mystery. I explained that when we first met." This was directed to me, I realized, despite the fact he appeared to be talking to the dog.

"But it's my job to make it one," I replied. "I'm not after the truth," I explained. "I'm after a good story. The truth— although allegedly stranger than fiction—is usually far too boring." I coaxed a slight grin out of him. "Without meaning to sound rude, the dons of Wadham are hardly a barrel of excitement." He smiled widely.

"No," he said, glancing toward the expectant face of Tim Binyon, whose eyes were trained onto him. "Very well," he said, conceding.

"He stays," Binyon said.

Tuttle nodded. "But I honestly feel it would be far better for Mr. Klick to confine his research to the Bodleian. Disrupting the Fellows does not benefit the college in the least."

"Well, I for one could use a spot of sherry," Binyon said to me. "Will you join me?"

It was barely afternoon.

"Certainly," I agreed.

"Are we clear then?" Tuttle asked.

"I think so."

Binyon said, "I believe we are."

"Splendid. No more disruptions?"

"I'll do my best," I said.

"All we can ask," Binyon contributed, taking me by the arm and literally dragging me from the Warden's den.

CHAPTER 39

The strangest things can set one's mind at work. On that blustery fall day, as I was walking off the sherry's I had enjoyed with Tim Binyon, I passed the Holywell Music Room with its white doors and church-like appearance. The wind was swirling dust balls and litter in its chilly air, and as a vortex of soot approached, I stopped and turned my back to it. My face was flushed and warm from the sherry and my fingers cold. I heard a bicycle bell in the distance and the faint barking of a dog. There was the smell of lamb in the air. And there was Mozart.

The piano strains were coming softly from the Holywell, muted but discernable. I knew the passage to be Mozart without thinking about it, though the name of the piece escaped me. La, la, la, la . . . I could hum along in my head. And then, as the vortex passed over me—right through me—I was carried away like Dorothy to Oz. It was as if my entire conscience was briefly exhumed and carried aloft, providing me a moment of omnipotent insight. What some call "a flash of brilliance." For that brief second or two, I knew all.

Perhaps the greatest thing about that moment was that I wasn't actually *thinking*—I was just *allowing*. If anything, I was *not* thinking, but instead getting out of my own way. *Mozart.* Briefly this made all the sense in the world to me, but as the vortex passed by and sucked its way along the footpath, lifting what appeared to be a spent condom, I lost the connective tissue that held it all together for me. It was as if I had had a vision, and just as quickly lost it. And then my thoughts kicked-in—I was no longer *allowing*. "It was only the music carrying me away," I attempted to convince myself. "It was the sherry. It's not a walk that I need, but a nap." All these thoughts conspired to confuse me, and I lost hold of that instant of total and absolute knowledge that I had just experienced. I lost my chance.

I stood there silently, the music flowing over me and passing through me as the spiral of dust had just done, and I tried desperately to get back to that moment of brilliance, but it was gone. It was down the road chasing a student on a bicycle—the one with the anxious bell that I had heard. It was off through the intersection and then up, up, up, into a low, wet sky where it vanished, absorbed, consumed, by the oppressive grayness—the low ceiling of depression that hovered over this city endlessly. And my mood with it. I wanted that moment back, sensing—*knowing*—that I had had it all within my grasp, albeit fleetingly.

But Mozart wouldn't quit. He teased me from the piano keys as the rehearsal continued. The melody danced in my ears and I shook my head to clear my thoughts, and the melodies remained. There was the low, sensuous pulse of a cello in *pizzicato*, and I was immediately reminded of the gorgeous Allison Star and, subsequently, of her aging lover Stephan Shultz and my morning spent with him, and of my meeting scheduled at Blackwell's Music shop. *Mozart. Allison. Stephan Shultz.* And there it was again—just a flicker this time: that flash of brilliance. *Mozart. Allison. Stephan Shultz,* I tried. It was gone, though something unexplainable remained.

Mozart. Loud and clear.

I reversed direction, returning toward King's Arms, passing a news-and-grocery kiosk busied with students coming and going. I crossed the street to be alone, the scent of cooked lamb growing stronger, the Mozart receding until swallowed by the whine of automobiles and the anxious chatter of students on the go. Several sweeping black robes crossed the street and hurried up stone steps, wraithlike, disappearing behind an enormous wooden door that sang on its hinges. I felt like a displaced time-traveler.

I was not following any plan, any guidance. I seemed instead to be being drawn around the corner and back toward Wadham by an unseen force. Then, almost as if I weren't controlling my own guidance, I veered left, dodged a set of speeding bicycles, crossed Parks Road, and bounded up the stone steps to the New Bodleian Library. I presented my pass to a crusty old gentleman with bad teeth and a bulbous red nose who nodded and called me, "Sir." Me.

I found my way down a silent corridor, up a flight of stairs, down another long corridor lined with oil portraits of unhappy looking men in black ermine-trimmed robes and into a room where the wooden floor squeaked, to be greeted by an exceptionally young, vanilla-skinned woman with huge eyes and thin hair. She didn't whisper, but I could barely hear her as she asked to help me. I was directed to a catalogue, and returned a few minutes later with a long list of titles. We started at the top of my list.

"Mozart," she said, copying the titles onto a form. "He's absolutely brilliant, don't you think?"

I lost track of the time, as happens when excitement steals into me. The first few titles proved of little use to me, but by the middle of the list things were picking up. At the time I had no interest in the contents of the books and manuscripts, only in who had signed out for them. I was an investigator again. On familiar ground. Comfortable. Safe. Incredibly happy.

By five-thirty, my alabaster-skinned helper was replaced by a young, acne-ridden man of eighteen who wore three gold earrings in his left ear and smelled like a locker-room after a practice. He helped me through the remainder of my list, indifferent to my cause, but attentive in his service. My heart beat a little more quickly with each and every discovery. I felt as if I were uncovering a tomb, a slight brushstroke at a time. Careful and exacting.

I went about reconstructing my moment of brilliance, building my sand castle farther up the beach where the waves couldn't lick it back to nothing. I constructed a plausible explanation for the confusing behavior on the part of the three fellows that I had witnessed over the past several weeks, an explanation that seemed to tie together all my suspicions, stringing a thread among them and, quite possibly, even the missing Aiden Sinclair. Although an intriguing theory, it remained just that: circumstantial at best. The kind of thing to cause Lyel to howl with glee. I doubted even Tim Binyon would go for it. But I had had my moment, and now backed by some proof positive, I could not be dissuaded. The evidence pointed to a conspiracy to defraud.

Hurried and impatient—displaying my worst American traits—I escaped this reference room in favor of another, one floor down, that carried the day's newspapers. There is no worse offense for an investigator—however amateurish—than misleading oneself, and I suspected I had done just that. I picked up *The Independent* and once again devoured it cover to cover, skimming headlines and titles as I had earlier. It was a small but not insignificant article, a few pages past the article on Japanese influence that had mislead me. I had probably read it three or four times thinking little or nothing of it. But now it jumped out at me. It might as well have been a banner across the top of the page in huge bold type.

"Yes!" I called out triumphantly, drawing annoyed looks from my neighbors and apologizing softly.

I returned the paper and literally ran from the building, turning right down Broad Street. I bought my own copy of *The Independent* to show Lyel, and, clutching it in hand, headed at a quick pace to my rooms. I stopped at my pigeon hole on the way.

There was a message from Bruce, another from Tim Binyon, and a third, received only minutes before, from Lyel scrawled in the porter's hand which read: "Urgent that we meet at The Randolph—ASAP." Keeping the newspaper, I headed immediately to the city's only grand hotel.

CHAPTER 40

The lobby wasn't much: a few nice tables and chairs off to the left where several groups were enjoying afternoon tea, the registration desk and cloakroom to the right. Lyel wasn't having tea.

The bar was straight ahead and down a green corridor to the right. It had a lofted ceiling, green walls and leather chairs and sofa. The bar itself was a deep mahogany with dozens of bottles rising behind it. The bartender was an ancient man with a gray mustache and fuzzy cataracts where his eyes should have been. He had bad teeth and revealed a smoker's voice when he greeted me.

Lyel and a handsome man in worn clothes occupied the far corner. Lyel caught my eye; he was drunk. So was his companion, Herbert Remmington, introduced to me as a Fellow at Magdalen, whose expertise was archaeology. My late night visitor, she of the five earrings and teasing breast, had mentioned Remmington. I had subsequently mentioned him to Lyel, and Lyel had done his homework. I hadn't seen Lyel in over a week.

Lyel said strongly, "Dr. Remmington was just telling me about," and he emphasized for my benefit, "some *artifacts* he received from Aiden Sinclair."

"Artifacts? Is that so?" I said, catching Lyel's eye. He was most certainly tanked, but there remained the keen sense of Lyel's sharpened wit behind it all.

"Yes, you see," Remmington replied in a high, effeminate voice, "Aiden asked me to look them over, you see. Would not say where he had come by them. That's Aiden through and through: protective, isn't he? Hmm? Yes, indeed: that's Aiden Sinclair."

"And you did look them over," Lyel reminded.

"Most certainly, Sir! Yes, of course I did. And as we have just discussed, I found them to be quite authentic. Splendid, actually. Hmm? Yes indeed, quite splendid. Say what? Twelfth century. Hmm? No later. Kitchenware I should imagine by the abundance and the variety. Beer mostly. Bottles, you see. Hmm? Quite a find."

"Bottles?" I inquired, recalling my young visitor's mention of bottles.

"Drink of the day, ehh? Of the times. Hmm? The monks, you see. A rubbish pit is what it was. Toss all the empties, ehh?" He laughed. "Only these are nearly nine hundred years old. The grounds where Wadham now stands once actually housed an Augustinian friary. Several pieces of cookware, pieces of a utensil—perhaps a fork or spoon. Very important find. *Extremely* important, historically, in terms of the university. Really quite fascinating! Just the kind of find we've been waiting for. And Aiden of all the blokes! Who would have thought? A tree hugger! And then to take off as he has and deny us anything more. A tease is what he is. A damn tease."

Remmington drank his wine—port—and held it up for the wizened bartender to see. I ordered a beer. So did Lyel, though he didn't need one.

"He received a gift," Lyel told me, referring to the archaeological historian.

Remmington nodded. "Four bottles of a 1947." He caressed his small, empty port glass, masturbating its stem. "Just a gift."

"From Sinclair?" I asked.

"No, no. Anonymous it was. It was implied that the University had an important announcement to make concerning the artifacts, and I was asked if the four bottles would help persuade me to keep my mouth occupied until the proper time arrived. This presented no problem for me whatsoever, of course. It was Aiden for whom I did the favor, ehh? Aiden's discovery, not mine. Ah, splendid!" Another port was delivered. So were our beers.

"Aiden Sinclair called you? About the artifacts?"

"A week ago Tuesday it was."

Lyel raised his eyebrows at me. The day that Sinclair went missing on his coastal walk. This, no doubt, was what had brought Lyel back to Oxford.

"I see," I said, though I didn't. Not really.

Lyel asked the drunken man, "Who has bottles of '47 in their cellar? Which colleges?"

A brilliant question: Lyel had thought to trace the bribe backwards.

"Ah ha!" Remmington grumbled. "Yes, the same occurred to me, Sir." He repeated this.

"Then you were curious too," I said.

"Who would not be, Mr. Klick? A '47 is not just rare. Rare is too generous a word, too forgiving. A '47 is precious. A '47 is—I will tell you what it is like—an excavation I once had the pleasure of leading along the lower Nile . . ." And off he went for ten minutes, leading Lyel and me painstakingly through a remembrance that included the precise description of brushstrokes that eventually revealed a small gold bracelet of great historical value that now bore his name in the Ashmolean Museum. During this monologue he managed to put away the port without any apparent effect, and he reordered another with an auctioneer's signal to the bartender.

"So you knew someone had gone to a great deal of trouble," Lyel encouraged, reviewing, "to give you not one, not two, but *four* bottles of '47."

"A great deal of trouble and expense." He nodded. "And of course one asks oneself as to necessity. One bottle would certainly have impressed me. Two—sweet luxury! But *four*! It's over the top, is what it is. Indeed, it is this lavish quantity that tickled my fancy. Why *four?* I had to wonder."

"And the answer?" Lyel pursued.

"Well, Sir, I am not convinced I have an answer. The discovery is significant, certainly. Important, to be sure. And as to your question concerning the source—well, who is the most likely candidate for my benefactor but Wadham? It is Wadham's discovery after all. It would not do to have Magdalen College announcing a discovery of this sort on Wadham's plot. Not on at all. No, it is Wadham's gain, and clearly Wadham has a cellar capable of having a '47 tucked away in the cobwebs—one of the best cellars in the whole of the university, and for a smaller college, that's an impressive claim."

Lyel and I exchanged glances. Had Sinclair been shipped off because of his discovery, the college attempting to time the release of the information and worried that a loose-tongued Aiden Sinclair might spill the beans prematurely?

I asked, "What's the point of timing such a release? Is the timing significant?"

"It must be to someone!" he said loudly, amusing himself. "Four bottles of '47 is certainly significant."

There was a long drunken pause of several minutes during which both Lyel and Remmington seemed to be napping. "Let me ask you this," I said, jarring them both. "Would a discovery of this sort, of the sort we're talking about here—the beer bottles, the monks and all—would such a discovery, if part of say a construction project, well, in New York City, for instance there were archaeological discoveries during a waterfront project that, because of their cultural importance and significance, slowed down, actually halted the project for a time. Would that sort of thing be likely to happen here as well? Would a construction project be interrupted if, during the excavation process, an important discovery were made?"

That awakened Lyel. Remmington's glassy, bloodshot eyes enlarged.

"I see!" the Fellow said.

"I take it that's an affirmative?"

But he didn't seem to hear me. He continued, "Yes. Of course. The dormitory."

Lyel sat up more straightly. He said, "And such delays can be extremely costly."

"Extremely," I repeated softly.

"But you see," Remmington said primarily to himself, "this all makes such good sense, doesn't it? What if there is to be no announcement made? None at all. That would, in fact, help explain the offer of four bottles. I should say it would. Or even a significant delay. Of course."

It was worse than what he thought. In my view, the four bottles were merely to buy some time. Ultimately, if this were to be kept silent, then Remmington would have to be dealt with, in the same or similar fashion that I now feared Aiden Sinclair had been dealt with: permanently.

Reading my thoughts, Lyel said to Remmington, "I think a spot of holiday might be in order."

"Holiday?" the academic inquired.

"Is it possible for you to get away from college for a fortnight?" Lyel inquired.

"What on earth are you referring to, Sir?"

"A research trip," I said, modifying Lyel's suggestion.

Lyel tested, "If it were possible to arrange the financing

for a two week research trip to the city . . ." Remmington's eyes brightened. "Would your schedule allow for such a thing?"

"I have work to do in Paris," he said greedily. "Would be far more productive with my assistant along."

Reproductive, I thought, but I held my tongue. The Oxbridge Fellows had a history of mistresses that dated back to the monks.

Before Lyel could answer, Remmington added, "Afraid I do not fare well on a Channel crossing, mind you. And I *will not* support the Chunnel. Would have to be by air."

"But you could arrange the time?"

"Quite flexible, this term—my schedule."

"Then it's settled," Lyel said, clearly unfretted by the expense. He might have just saved a life. He pushed back from the table. Remmington appeared terribly pleased with himself. Lyel added, "It should go without saying, Sir, that to speak of this openly, to speak of this at all, would present the possibility of entangling yourself further in what appears to be a *difficult* and *troubling* situation."

Understanding this fully, Remmington asked, "Is Aiden quite all right, gentlemen? Do you know of his whereabouts?"

I thought of the green, swirling waters of the Atlantic churning below the Cornish foot trail that Lyel had described so vividly to me. I thought of a submerged body, neutrally buoyant, its pale, swollen arms out like wings as it guided its way randomly through the darkened depths. "We believe we've located him," I answered. Lyel flashed me an annoyed look.

"That's fine," Remmington said, relieved. "You'll

pardon me for asking," he said, toying again with his wine glass. "But a couple of Yanks . . . You see? Government blokes, are we?"

"Friend of a friend," Lyel answered quickly, making sure to cut me off.

"I'm a writer. Researching a novel is all."

"That's *not* all," he insisted. But he went no further, not wishing to push his luck. Four bottles of a '47 port and a trip for two to Paris were apparently enough for Dr. Remmington. We all had our price. He rose to his feet, staggered slightly, and knocked the entire contents of the table to the floor in a deafening crash. He smiled at me. "Nothing to worry about," he said. "Happens all the time."

CHAPTER 41

Back at my rooms, I showed Lyel the newspaper article I had discovered. I withheld the nature of my library work until he had read it through.

"Oh my," he said, sounding a bit British. It was time to go home.

"Do you see?"

"I see the newspaper, but I can't focus at the moment. I've read the article. I assume this is somehow connected to our endeavors or you wouldn't be so excited, now would you? But I'm afraid I'll leave you to fill in the blanks for me."

He was still quite drunk as it turned out, though he could conceal it well enough to make me think about it before recognizing the signs. Lyel leaned well back into a chair when he had had too much to drink. He forgot to don his reading glasses—he had read the article without them. He adopted a wily smirk, self-contented in an intimidating but apparently unintentional way that nonetheless annoyed me. And he allowed his recently-pressed and combed exterior to deteriorate just a little, losing his perfect grooming just enough to step out of character: his double-breasted blue blazer hung open; his collar button was undone; and his sailing club tie dangled slightly askew.

"Aiden Sinclair's specialty is?" I asked.

"This isn't going to be a quiz is it? I don't believe I'm up to it."

"Herbal inks," I answered.

Lyel snapped his fingers, as if the answer had been on the tip of his tongue.

"And Bradshaw?"

He stirred the air with his hand, suggesting I continue.

"A diplomat. An expert in scrolls and paper."

"An herbalist and a diplomat," Lyel repeated. "Well, they fit neatly enough together."

"Coffee?" I inquired.

He declined, encouraging me to continue.

"Henry Hagg?" I asked. He shook his dull head. I answered myself, "Musicologist. And Tilbert? Lester Tilbert is a Victorian historian: an expert on another time— another age."

"I'm aging myself, Klick. Keep it *moving*, please." Irritable. He needed a beer, but I wasn't going to offer him one.

"Aiden Sinclair's disappearance may not have much to do with this, not directly, but he was part of it, you see?"

"Part of *what*?"

"And the thing of it is . . . what's really interesting about it all is that I have a feeling—more than a feeling really—that at the center of all of it, the one missing ingredient, is none other than Stephan Shultz."

"The center of *what?*" Lyel said.

"The newspaper article. . . . I originally thought they were reading about the Japanese investment in the university. But now, come to find out several pages later, it's the article on the missing Mozart manuscript, the one Allison Star told me about. It's value has been estimated at three hundred thousand pounds!"

"But the manuscript page is in fact a fake?"

"Most definitely."

"But Sinclair?" Lyel asked.

"Stumbled into the construction site and came away with souvenirs that threatened to delay the construction project, just as Remmington suggested."

"So the Warden sends him packing."

"Off to Cornwall to pick berries. Yes. Out of the way. What if they were caught knowingly pouring concrete on top of an archeological find of significant historical value? What kind of kink would it put into their benefactor's chain to delay by six months or a year?" I decided on two beers after all. When I returned, handing one to Lyel, I said, "And the others in the forgery were only too happy to see Sinclair go: one less loose cannon to worry about."

"Until you came along."

"Until *we* came along," I corrected. "Yes. They worried that by nosing into Sinclair and Shultz, we might do exactly what we have done: discover they had combined their various talents to forge a missing manuscript page from Mozart's *The Lover*."

"An expert for each field," he observed. "The right ink, the proper parchment, historical accuracy, musical elements that would ring true."

"David Thompson suspects it," I said, mentioning the London composer. "He told me that Shultz's true genius was Mozart composition. It was a hint I think, and I missed it!" I added, "Bradshaw stole the back pages from a Gluck in the Bodleian collection. Aiden Sinclair provided the ink. Every single aspect of the forgery would have to be perfect if it were to hold up under scrutiny. No one person could accomplish it alone. But four or five of the world's leading experts? Who is going to catch it?"

Lyel found his glasses and checked the paper. "Says here that was up to Julian Rasner."

CHAPTER 42

Tim Binyon's rooms occupied a corner suite overlooking the gardens and the Warden's Cottage. Every horizontal space was occupied, stacked high with papers, books, and magazines. His electric fire did not buzz the way mine did, and his chairs were nicer and the paint fresher. The place had a lived-in feel to it—an ancient history could not be easily painted over.

Lyel and I sat facing him. He had served us tea to help sober up Lyel. The elbows of his dark wool sweater were completely worn through and threadbare. He carried a day old white stubble beard on his weathered cheeks.

Lyel warmed him up with some of what we knew and then said, "No one person is capable of forging a musical manuscript and getting away with it. But if you combine all of their talents—"

I interrupted, "Parchment, herbal ink, musicology, calligraphy, historical reference . . . "

Binyon's skin went the color of his stubble. His lips and eyes were wet and shone in the harsh light of the ceiling fixture.

"And the value of it!" Lyel proclaimed.

Binyon muttered, "Value?" His voice strengthened. "You don't think for a minute that this is about money do you? I shouldn't be fooled if I were you. This has little if anything to do with money. This is a *challenge*—an intellectual challenge. This is a boyish prank: can the dons of Wadham pull the wool over the eyes of Julian Rasner and the like-minded experts at Christ Church?"

"That may be how it began," Lyel granted the man, "but *The Independent* placed the value of the piece at three hundred thousand pounds."

The figure clearly astonished Binyon. "Is that right?" he asked. He repeated, "Three hundred thousand?"

"Aiden Sinclair provided the ink," I explained. "But he got drunk one night and fell into the construction site at the new dorm and made an archaeological find dating back several centuries. An important find to the university's history. . . ."

"But such a find would delay construction by weeks, perhaps months," Lyel picked up, "and that was unacceptable to both the Warden and the money behind the construction."

"Fujiami."

Lyel and I nodded in unison.

Lyel said, "The Warden lured Sinclair away from the college to keep him quiet, but not before Sinclair passed along some of the artifacts for verification to a friend at Magdelen, making the Warden's job even more difficult—he had to delay this verification as well. I think you will find the college's '47 port reserves substantially lower than expected. And you will find that excavation at the construction site was enlarged for no legitimate reason except to empty the site of artifacts. My guess is that they worked nights to remove them."

Binyon said sadly, "And Aiden is not known for keeping quiet about his discoveries."

"We know he was excited by this find," I explained. "There's a young woman here at college. . . ."

"Once he reached Cornwall and sobered some," Lyel said, "Sinclair more than likely wanted to return to Wadham in order to get on with his discovery."

"Tuttle must have let slip to Fujiami about Sinclair's find," I theorized, "and left him to deal with it."

"Good God." Binyon's lips trembled.

Lyel said softly, "He disappeared while on a coastal walk. Hasn't been seen since."

"It's a hell of a lot of money, this construction," Binyon said. "The dormitory. If it's a significant find, it might have mucked up the schedule badly."

I said, "Sinclair's partners in the forgery grew worried when I began nosing around. They saw trouble and pressured Tuttle to terminate my fellowship."

Lyel said, "Without a believable explanation for Sinclair's disappearance they may suspect that one of their own group is attempting to reduce their numbers—especially if they're planning to split the money from the sale of the manuscript. At this point there's a very real temptation to do just that."

Binyon nodded.

Lyel said, "Paranoia breeds foolish mistakes."

I didn't tell him that Shultz's offer for me to return his wife's money to the US was almost certainly a disguised effort to get me out of town. Lyel had realized that this was why Shultz had put the time constraints on his offer. And the time constraints, in turn, alerted us to the implied importance of the next few days.

"Aiden is getting it from both sides," Binyon offered. "From Fujiami's people and from his co-conspirators."

"The question," Lyel said to the man, "is what, if anything, can be done about any of this? If the Mozart forgery is good enough to pass Rasner's scrutiny, then an attempt by a couple of visiting Americans to discredit the manuscript is unlikely to get anywhere."

Binyon nodded contemplatively. "If it's that good, it may stand."

I said, "Unless the fellows involved were to admit what they've done."

Binyon chimed in, "I'm sure that was the original intention—simply a wonderful practical joke on Julian Rasner. But this large sum of money . . . That has most certainly changed the situation considerably. Why reveal the scam at all?"

"Exactly," Lyel said.

"Fear is a strong tool in situations like this," I suggested, adding, "It can loosen tongues, with the right bit of *conducting*."

"What I can't understand," Binyon said, "is Sir Frans' involvement. It isn't on at all. Not like him at all. He's above all this sordid nonsense. He'll be Warden for another year or two at best. I just do not see him condoning any harm done to Aiden. For what, a dormitory? I tell you, it's not on!"

"Perhaps we're wrong about that," Lyel offered. "We assumed the Warden's involvement because of the port. But Bradshaw or one of the others could have bribed the bottler."

"Hopefully," I said, sitting forward and drawing both men's full attention, "we're wrong about Sinclair's outcome."

Lyel leaned in, his eyes riveted onto me. "Perhaps Fujiami's people didn't kill him," Lyel offered, astonishment sweeping his face. He smiled widely. Without Binyon's judgement of Tuttle's character, we might not have caught onto this possibility—the man's possessions left behind at the B&B had seemed so convincing. "They've just delayed his return."

I said to Binyon, "I passed the Holywell and they were practicing Mozart. It's *the* Mozart isn't it?" I recalled the musical phrase. I knew that I was right.

Binyon nodded. "*Liebespaar*," he said.

"I haven't seen any posters about the performance."

"No posters, no. Heavens no! Invitation only. Three quarters of the audience will be up from London. Some Royals have accepted. This is a *major* find."

"When?" Lyel asked harshly. "When is the performance?"

It had not occurred to me that the performance would be

by invitation only and that preparations were already underway.

"Tomorrow night is the final rehearsal, the following night, the performance." Binyon said confidentially, "though *no one* is to know. Security is the main reason. The Royals and all."

I gasped, "Then Rasner has *already* judged the manuscript authentic, despite *The Independent* suggesting his work continues."

"I suppose so, yes. He'll make the formal announcement at the performance. We've restricted the press to just BBC radio. Live radio. Splendid stroke, don't you think? Hmm?"

Lyel glanced at his watch, and then up at me.

"Can we make it there and back in time?" I asked.

"Where?" inquired Binyon.

Lyel nodded at me, though he didn't seem convinced. "It'll be tight," he said. To Binyon he added, "Cornwall."

I explained, "Aiden Sinclair, if alive, is our only hope."

CHAPTER 43

I took Bradshaw. Lyel took Lester Tilbert.

I phoned Bradshaw in his rooms and asked to meet him in the Fellows' Garden knowing this kind of clandestine meeting would trouble him but make him too curious to refuse. In fact he accepted.

I reached the garden first, passed under the towering copper beech and, using the large skeleton key, let myself in, ducking through the low stone arch. The grounds were immaculately manicured, a pebble footpath framing a rectangle of several acres of closely cut lawn, the outside perimeter of which was a botanical garden of bushes and shrubs bearing only their Latin identification. Bradshaw arrived, his eyes bloodshot, his breath revealing an afternoon sherry.

I locked the door behind us.

"Rather cloak and dagger, this," he said brightly, affecting a grin that he felt none of.

"Then you've heard," I said, seizing upon an opening like that.

This caught him off guard. We strolled the pebble footpath amid the cackle of some bird life. "Say what?" he said.

"I'm not making any accusations," I cautioned. "Please allow me to speak hypothetically, because it's not the who of what I have to say to you, but the *what* that is so important."

He looked genuinely troubled then, and I relished the moment. "Go on," he offered.

"Let us say that for the sake of a practical joke, several Fellows here at Wadham combined their resources—their very specific talents—in an attempt to discredit another Fellow at another college."

"Don't have the slightest idea of what you are talking about," said the man who was suddenly carrying a sheen of perspiration on his brow.

"Hypothetically," I said, "let's say these efforts were aimed at creating a single page of musical manuscript."

He caught his toe and lost his balance, though only slightly, recovering gracefully for a man his size. He cleared his throat with some effort.

I said, "A missing Mozart page . . . Something like that."

"Indeed."

"And let us say that these men were able to elicit the genius of a great composer—an American conductor perhaps—to write the actual content of that page. And let us say that it all worked out splendidly, far better than anyone believed possible. Good enough to pass. And let's say that originally the idea was to give up the ruse at some point. But first, the missing manuscript page would be 'found,'" I said, drawing the quotes, "say in Germany or one of the Soviet republics. Found by a Brit and brought to Oxford for verification."

His breathing was audible now, either the result of his substantial girth, or nerves. I hoped it was the latter. I continued. "And let's say that at some point a collector named an approximate value for this treasure, and let's say that the Fellows had never really contemplated the value of such a thing, only the game of it all. But greed is a funny thing, you know?" I asked, winning his worried attention. "Greed really does bring out the worst in people. And maybe it occurs to one or more of these Fellows that the fewer the better—in terms of splitting up the proceeds of any sale of such a document. Reduce the numbers, increase the value of the shares." We walked for a moment in the accompaniment of some small birds. Bradshaw seemed unable to get out a word. I said confidentially, "People who keep secrets too close often die with them on their tongues." Bradshaw looked as if he might cry. This was all too far away from the quiet research of a diplomat. Reminded of this, I said, "Someone would have to supply the parchment, of course. The paper for such a forgery. And really, this person would be committing the greatest of all the crimes, for he would be required to desecrate ancient manuscripts of aesthetic and historical value. The rest of the Fellows are really just in it for a lark. A joke. A contest. But not the man who places a razor to a Bodleian manuscript and removes a page from the original. That's an actual crime."

"What is it you want?" he demanded, his voice cracking. He stopped abruptly and glared at me, his expression reduced to a boyish fear.

I stopped too and faced him. "It might have begun as blackmail—one working the others. Who knows? But it would most certainly have worried these Fellows when one of them went missing—take an ink specialist, someone like Aiden Sinclair. Ups and disappears. You would have to ask yourself why. And come to find out he left a B&B for a walk one day, a walk along the Cornish coast, and he never came back. Never came to get his things."

The man looked horrible, his pasty skin blotched with orbs of red rash.

"One down," I said. "Three or four more to go."

"Do you know what you're saying?" he gasped.

"And the thing about situations like this, is that one of the parties inevitably wises up and confesses his or her role in whatever took place—and *inevitably* it is this person who is treated by the courts with the most leniency. The *last* to speak up is always assumed to be the most guilty."

"I know *nothing* of Aiden's disappearance," he proclaimed.

"It's hypothetical," I reminded. "Strictly hypothetical." We were back at the gate having come fully around the garden. I withdrew my large key from my pocket, but

Bradshaw blocked my attempt to open the door just then.

"Is he alright?" he inquired.

"The thing is," I said, disregarding the inquiry, "the fewer the participants, the larger the split." I then said, "Have you heard anything of Lester Tilbert lately?" I nudged him aside and used my key to unlock the heavy door. "I thought I saw him at the Warden's cottage this morning. Is that possible?" I asked.

"You've got this wrong," he said unconvincingly. "I don't know anything about any such forgery."

"Hey, it's all hypothetical," I reminded, stepping beneath the arch and leaving him. "Nothing to get too worked up over."

CHAPTER 44

My friend John, Wadham's porter, appeared flushed and filled with excitement. As arranged, we met at the King's Arms pub, directly below my offices. I bought us both a pint.

"I don't know what you are up to, Sir, but it's rather intriguing," he said.

"Were you able to do as I asked?"

"Oh, yes, Sir. Quite able. It's not so very complicated, the college phone system. Old is what it is. Had enough trouble with it over the years to make me something of an expert." He consumed his drink in just a few bold gulps. I ordered him another. He lit a cigarette.

"And what did we find out?" I asked.

He lowered his voice. "Mr. Bradshaw telephoned Mr. Hagg's rooms, he did. Just when you said he would, Sir."

He stopped altogether as the barkeep delivered the warm beer. Bradshaw had followed up our talk by contacting Hagg. I felt ebullient. I could hardly contain myself. I sucked down my beer and ordered another. John continued. "Mr. Tilbert also phoned Mr. Hagg, not long after that. I'd say twenty minutes separated the calls is all." Hagg, it seemed, was the leader of the conspiracy.

"And Hagg?" I asked.

"Phoned out of college, he did. An Oxfordshire number, though I can't tell you whose it is."

I pictured Shultz's bungalow retreat with a scratched car in the driveway. Perhaps Shultz was the top of the food chain. Was Aiden Sinclair being held right here in Oxfordshire? Were his fellow Fellows behind his detention? It didn't seem right to me. It was "not on," as the Brits were fond of saying.

"And that's it?" I inquired, disappointed.

"I doubt that, Sir," John replied, hoisting the beer to his lips and forcing me to wait him out. Over the top of the glass beer mug he said, "If timing has anything to do with it, then the call to the Warden's Cottage can't be ignored for it followed on the heels of Mr. Hagg's call to Oxfordshire, and it came from *out* of college."

I had also asked him to monitor the Warden's calls. All this I claimed was part and parcel to research for my mystery. I told him that I had a scene that involved the Fellows and phone calls within college and without, and I doubted the porter could know which and what calls were being placed. As part of that research, John believed that I had set up a situation to trick the Fellows into calling one another to see if the porter could be the hero of the story. John supported the idea of the porter as hero. He had assured me that there was little the porter could not find out if pressed into service. So I conducted my "test" and John happily obliged.

"That's interesting. I didn't realize you could determine that," I said, attempting to boost his ego.

"And the Warden followed this immediately with a call to Cornwall."

My heart jumped. "Cornwall?" I repeated.

"Yes, Sir. Cornwall it was."

"You can determine that?"

"If you know how the system works you can. The masters are billed individually for toll calls, they are. That includes the Warden. Outgoing calls are recorded by the system for the purpose of billing. Yes, Sir."

"Cornwall," I repeated.

"St. Agnes exchange it was," he added. "Me Mum's sister, my Aunt Tildey, lives in St. Agnes, she does. I know the exchange by heart, I do."

"St. Agnes," I echoed. It was the village where Sinclair had gone missing. This was no coincidence.

Our little trick on Tilbert and Bradshaw had led us back to St. Agnes. Why? I felt a pounding urgency in my chest: the Warden was in this, up to his knickers.

CHAPTER 45

The U.K.'s road system was just that: roads. There were extremely few divided motorways, with most of them serving the London area. The remainders ran like populated spines to the island's extremities. Lyel drove cautiously through tiny hamlets and quaint stone villages but sped quickly through the countryside on his way to the M4 running west toward Wales and Cornwall. Traffic moved well on the motorway and I slept for the better part of two hours. We traded off the wheel when we encountered some construction, and I piloted us south toward Cornwall, the motorway giving back to extremely narrow paved roads connected by chaotic roundabouts and plain arrow-shaped signs indicating the name of the next town. I was in heaven.

Oxford's rolling hills of green grass and muddy fields of cattle and farming were no longer with us, replaced by the Cornish peninsula's open landscapes and rock cluttered fields. Cornwall's one lane tracks were lined with "Cornish hedges," claustrophobic four-to-six-foot tall stone walls; and with traffic being two-way, precarious negotiation was undertaken when two cars converged. Many of the tiny French and Swedish cars that we passed were lacking exterior mirrors, leaving only broken plastic stubs where they had once been.

Six hours of driving, and the village of St. Agnes poured down off a hill into the green frothing waters of the Atlantic Ocean. Once a fishing village, it now played summer host to British tourists who enjoyed its rare expanse of easily accessible beach. But summer was well behind us, and life in St. Agnes had slowed to pub talk, some commercial fishing, gardening, and the quiet social existence of British village life. The town's only inn had been built high atop a bluff overlooking the beach and the waters beyond. It hosted seven guest rooms and a dining room that could serve fifty. The ceilings were so incredibly low that Lyel and I had to duck out of the way of the rough-hewn timbers. The proprietress was a criminal psychologist from Bath whose weekend boyfriend, Gaylord, acted as barkeep and registrar Monday through Friday.

Lyel and I took two nearby rooms on the ground floor. Mine felt like the captain's quarters of a galleon: the bed was three feet off the floor, forcing me to slouch when I attempted to sit up. The room's only other furniture was a dark chest with a massive padlock, and the rain-splattered windows were the size of food trays and mounted high on the thick stone walls. With a body my size, the postage stamp bathroom became a kind of puzzle requiring me to back-up to enter the shower; I had to drop to my knees to shampoo. Lyel and I met for cocktails upstairs where the psychologist delivered us whisky straight up and warm beers back. Lyel had a crook in his neck and he looked in pain. By the end of the second round he seemed more himself. We had to speak extremely quietly for the roaring fire to cover our words.

He said, "The B&B where our friend stayed is up the High Street about three blocks. There are two other B&Bs in town, and this inn—that's it."

"So if he had visitors," I theorized, "they either stayed here in St. Agnes or one of the other nearby villages."

"They stayed here. I established that last time. One of the fisherman saw them. A pair of men in their early thirties. Stayed here." Lyel signaled Gaylord out from behind the bar.

"Yes, Sir," the fortyish man said cordially. He stood about five foot eight. He had the strong, meaty hands of a butcher.

"In terms of tourists," Lyel inquired. "Americans, French, Germans . . . any Japanese?" Lyel glanced at me— he had obviously asked this question on his last visit.

"Germans mostly. Some Americans. Very few French. Belgians perhaps, but not French."

"And Japanese?"

"You don't see them as tourists, if that's what you're asking. They don't take to the beach or the footpaths. Businessmen is more like it, though I'll be damned to understand what business, other than the fishing, would bring a chap to St. A's."

"But you do see them?" I asked.

Addressing me, the man said, "Had a pair of 'em in not a fortnight ago, I did. Stuck to the red wine and the lamb shanks, they did. Poor tippers are the Japanese, and these two fellas stuck to themselves, speaking all that gibberish of theirs back and forth, and always going out to place their calls when we've got perfectly good phones right here. Cheap is what they are, the Japanese. Don't like 'em much, if I'm being honest with you."

"Here on business?" I asked.

"You'd think so, wouldn't you? This time of year? What else would bring a pair like that? Thing of it is, they took to the footpaths those two. More than once they did. Gone for hours, they were. Made me think a little better of them, you want to know the truth—it's our Cornish coast makes us proud."

To Lyel I said, "We had better go for a few walks if we want to stay in favor."

Gaylord chuckled, offered us another drink and we both accepted. Three whiskies—I wasn't going to need the fire.

Lyel said, "I was told they were here in St. Agnes two days and two nights." He added, "If they've been around more than that, we should certainly be able to find out."

I understood what he was driving at: if Sinclair was alive, the two Japanese were holding him somewhere along this coast. If so, his captors would need to food shop; they would be seen; they would stand out. The Cornish villages were tiny—outsiders, especially foreigners, were easily identified and tracked. Though only in St. Agnes for two days, it didn't mean that Fujiami's team had left the area. Our job, and we had only the one morning in which to accomplish it, was to hope we were right, find Sinclair and liberate him from his captors.

We ate a long, slow dinner over a bottle of Burgundy and then sipped Drambouies by the fire and eavesdropped on the conversations surrounding us. It was the kind of perfect dinner that Europeans treasure and Americans often waste. I placed a call to Nicole from the lobby phone booth and awakened her. She filled me with good feelings, and promised to leave a forwarding number for Kent where she was headed next. I fished for some kind of indication that we might spend time together after my job was through, but I came up with an empty hook. Commitment remained outside of Nicole's vocabulary, and even the hint of it drove her further away from me. I hung up, drunk and slightly disappointed. I went to bed alone and bothered. This life that I had carved out for myself was filled with loneliness and isolation. I envied Lyel the big house in Ridland, Idaho, and the swarm of friends with which he surrounded himself.

CHAPTER 46

Breakfast was dark tea, broiled tomatoes, sausage, eggs, toast and marmalade. I ate so much I felt sick. Or perhaps it had been the drinking of the night before. Lyel, dressed nattily in wool tweed pants and a forest green wool sweater, sparkled with enthusiasm and energy that did little to improve my mood.

"Perfect morning for a walk, don't you think?" He was beginning to sound English. It bothered me.

I glanced outside. Thin fog, not a ray of sunshine in sight. "You're joking."

"It's probably best to divide and conquer," he said. "An awful lot of ground to cover. Not much time."

Lyel leaned forward. He smelled of the sausage. "It seems to me that if alive, our friend must be within walking distance of here. He goes on a walk and disappears, not to be seen again. Unlikely they tossed him into a car and kidnapped him outright. More likely they intercepted him on the trail."

"We've been over this," I reminded. "Where are you going with it?"

"To the car," he informed me, unfolding one of the Brits' incomparable maps. "You, on the other hand, are going south on the footpath. I will drive down the coast, park, and also head south. When you reach the car—right here—you will drive to here," he said, pointing, "and I'll meet you. Check the pub when you arrive, in case I've beaten you." Lyel was the fastest walker I knew, and this was his attempt at a small boast. "Together we should cover about ten miles of coast, and I don't see Sinclair making it farther than that. You'll find that the cottages—and there are damn few of them—are held quite back from the trail. This time of year, most will be empty. But I'm afraid we'll have to inspect each and every one, if we're to know anything. We'll also want to watch for any disturbances along the path itself, indicating the struggle. The grasses are fragile along the trail—they could help us."

"So noted." I waited until we met eyes and I told him, "No heroics, Lyel. As a team we might stand a chance, but solo, we're doomed. If we happen to find the hideaway, we team up and approach it together."

"You're the daredevil," he reminded, "not me."

"I'm serious about this."

"I understand." He looked a little hurt.

"It's a good plan," I told him. That seemed to help. He stabbed a final piece of sausage, chewed it vigorously, and washing it down with tea said, "Let's go."

CHAPTER 47

The coast trail was nothing more than a vaguely marked narrow dirt track edging precariously close to sixty foot cliffs that towered over the surging green sea. Tall grasses, looking like unkempt hair, covered the hard, rocky earth as if carefully planted, uninterrupted by shrub or bush. The sound of the crashing waves was magnificent, a constant chorus of the sea's voice speaking words that could almost be understood. The Cornish coast had been active for centuries, primarily as a source of pirating and smuggling, and with no visual reminders in sight up on that trail, I lost track of the twentieth century—it too was swallowed in the fog and the salty mist, the deafening roar of the breakers below. I could imagine the long boats and the square riggers, the buccaneers and the kegs of rum, the crates of firearms dragged up on rocky beaches. I could hear the cry of shore birds, but because of the fog, could not see them. To my left, the field of green grasses rose steadily, climbing to a bench where the fog thinned. I spotted the first cottage twenty minutes into the hike, when my heart was beating strongly enough to sound a thumping in my ears.

The cottage was incredibly small. It had once been white, with a stone chimney that had lost some of its rock to the on-shore breeze and winter storms. I examined the grasses for any unexpected swath cut in the direction of the cottage, but found nothing of the sort. Nonetheless, I intended to have a look.

I walked another five minutes, up a small rise, and then back down toward a small inlet and cut left into the grass, my route hidden from view of the cottage. The footing was tricky due to the rock, and I took my time because of an old injury to my right ankle that sprained easily. The grasses smelled pungent—an earthy aroma of salt and shore and pockets of rich soil. I remained below the cornice, hiding from view of the cottage, until I ascended and crested the small rise. I could see an unused driveway leading to the cottage, and I made my way there and approached the structure from the front.

The place was closed up tightly, leading me to believe it abandoned, but since this might be the intention of any kidnappers, I had no choice but to pursue it more closely. I knocked sharply on the front door and waited, my words of warning to Lyel fresh in my ears—this was not a one-man job. No one answered, which was no surprise. I tried again and then walked the perimeter of the cottage, pressing my ear to the shuttered windows and straining to try to see through the few available cracks. No one. Nothing.

From up here on the bluff, the foggy coast trail twisted south like a dark string on a green rug. Elevated, I could see down the coast to the next cottage, perhaps a half mile away. I stayed up on the bench and approached it. This cottage, gray with white trim, was also shuttered tight, and again, there was no sound, no indication of life. I made my way back to the trail over difficult terrain and continued south, climbing down a steep slope and up the other side to where a stone wall ran for several hundred yards, demarcating private property. I'd been out for over an hour. The tall stone wall, covered with a creeping vine, held the hiker incredibly close to the frail edge of the sheer cliff looming over the frantic waters below, and I was glad I was not prone to acrophobia. This stretch of stone wall struck me as the perfect place to have trapped Sinclair. Without quickly bounding over the wall, there was no place to escape an attempted attack. With this occurring to me, I slowed and carefully studied the grasses, alert—as Lyel had cautioned me to be—for any disturbance that seemed out of the ordinary.

I discovered just such a disturbance one hundred feet from the corner of the wall, an area where the footpath widened with recently scuffed ground cover, some of the grass torn from the soil, all of it matted down as if trampled. The grass remained bent and broken along the wall line until the subtle signs of traffic crossed through a closed metal gate. The width of the path of broken grass was far wider than could be explained by one person—it appeared wide enough for three, and I could almost picture Sinclair being escorted away from the trail, a guard to either side.

I remained outside the chest-high wall, followed it around the next corner and inland toward what I hoped would prove to be yet another cottage. I walked for ten minutes, gaining elevation, protecting my ankle from the threatening rock outcroppings. The area defined by the wall was perhaps forty to fifty acres, and I came to the southeast corner before long. I could not see a cabin or cottage within the enclosure—perhaps there had once been such a structure, but there was no sign of it now. I struggled up onto the wall to gain some height and surveyed my surroundings, still intrigued by the disturbance I had discovered along the path. The fog immediately along the coast had cleared, pushed off by a light breeze, and my view south was breathtaking—a picture postcard of the Cornish coast trail: rock and the green marble sea, lush vegetation and dark earth.

I did not see the cottage at first, only a gravel cul-de-sac where day-trippers could park and access the trail, the sight of which caused me to wince for I feared Sinclair, if he'd survived, might have been moved to a vehicle and transported elsewhere. But then I realized the dark shape I had overlooked was in fact the peak of a weathered roof of a shoreline cottage set down into the top of a rocky gorge, hunkered down out of the harsh, constant stream of weather that raced ashore. Sight of this roof raised the hair on the nape of my neck, for with the fog lifted and the air cleared, I could also make out the inconsistency in the grass where it had been walked upon by more than one man. This trail of slightly lighter green stretched away from me like an arrow, pointing directly to the roof so easily overlooked. And I knew.

I could have approached and taken a closer look. This was, in fact, my temptation. But the governing force within me instructed me to seek Lyel's assistance first. I dared not alert or alarm whomever was inside this cabin. If it later proved that I was wrong—if I wasted hours of our precious time for nothing—then so be it. If you've come to hunt, you don't spook the big game until you're ready to do battle. My senses, my reasoning, told me that I was right in this. If I was right and I blew it, I not only put myself at risk, but, more importantly, Aiden Sinclair.

Down, off the wall, I could no longer see the roof, and I thought this a clever lair indeed. I hurried back toward the coast trail and, reaching it, took off at a brisk jog, glad I was accustomed to my daily run. I reached the parked car forty minutes later. Twenty minutes later—another hour since my discovery of the secluded cottage—I pulled down a long hill into a sleepy coastal village, arriving just as a fleet of seven small fishing boats took off from a sandy beach into the mean waters, the fisherman clad in bright yellow weather gear. The boats looked too small to brave those seas—mere matchsticks. They bobbed in the high, wind-ripped water, launching white sea spray into the wind. I thought what a hard life some have chosen, and I knew these men would not trade that life without a damn good offer.

Lyel was not to be found in the nearest pub, and so I took off walking toward him, up the coast trail, climbing steeply at first and then leveling off on the high bluff where I got a better view of the fishing craft as they cut toward the vast gloomy waters of the Atlantic, now as tiny as corks. I broke into my jog, warming up the sweat that made my clothes damp, and carefully watched my footing—to trip or stumble might send me over the edge, the trail ran so close to the cliffs. Lyel had a walking stick and was escorting two women, a German and a Swede, who appeared to be in their early twenties. The German had bright green eyes and high cheekbones, the Swede, blue eyes with thick pouty lips. Lyel had a way of attracting young women like this, though he never became involved with them. The three were laughing as I approached, Lyel talking up one of his stories and following behind them like some kind of shepherd. He stumbled through introductions for me, slightly embarrassed, I thought, by his casual pace, knowing perfectly well that as I arrived at a run I was in need of his company. We met eyes and communicated this all at once. Lyel, who had lost his knee to the NBA, was incapable of jogging for any distance without putting himself into great pain, but he could walk nearly as fast as I could jog. Saying goodbye to his young friends, he shifted gears, and the two of us—Lyel looking stiff and awkward, me looking big and slow—made our way back toward the small fishing village. When we were out of earshot, I explained to him what I had discovered.

CHAPTER 48

Adrenaline is not something that can be controlled. In fact, the more I tried to calm myself, the more excited and heated I grew. The cottage, backed up to a wall of sharp boulders, with a stunning view of the craggy gorge that it occupied, was about fifty yards down a steep incline from where I was situated. A quarter of a mile down the left edge of the gorge, a small dirt parking area was carved out of the shore grass looking like a deflated brown balloon. From this parking area a narrow but well-worn trail led down to the cottage. Lyel pulled the rental into the parking area and climbed out. He intended to pass himself off as a travel magazine writer, but he was too big to look like a writer. He looked more like someone bent on repossessing the refrigerator—and capable of carrying it away all by himself.

I waited out of sight, my heart pounding in my chest, my throat dry. The air around me seemed incredibly crisp and clean. Everything seemed to sparkle despite the fact that the sun had not yet showed itself. This clarity, this experience of heightened senses was familiar to me as a precursor to danger—I was acutely aware of what I was getting myself into.

Lyel strolled slowly down the long, occasionally steep path, stopping to drink in the views and fill his enormous lungs with the sea air, trying his best to appear unhurried and curious in case he was being watched by someone other than me. I awaited his arrival at the cottage's front door, and, when this moment finally occurred, made my move down through the boulder field, eyes alert at the cottage's back windows for any hint of movement. The footing was precarious, the going difficult, and yet I had to move quickly. Lyel and I had thrown together a plan hastily—we could only trust that we had done these kinds of things together before, and that sometimes there was no choice but to wing it.

As I reached the halfway point, I heard, but could not see, Lyel knock sharply on the cottage's front door. I stopped to listen, which was not part of the plan, but something that I couldn't resist. If Sinclair were being held by the Japanese, would his captors open the door and greet an unannounced visitor, or remain inside hoping that he might go away? I had to know, for the decision to greet Lyel or not indicated with whom I was dealing. A second thought occurred to me: Lyel's rental car was alone in the parking area. Perhaps Sinclair, if being held here, was only being checked on a couple of times a day and left alone for the remainder of the time. If so, that would make our job much easier.

Lyel knocked again.

The cottage's back door came open quietly and a small figure slipped outside, returning the door closed gently. This person—a man, by the shape of him—headed directly toward me, up into the craggy landscape behind the cottage, then cut to his right, screened from Lyel by the huge rocks. He seemed headed for the parking area—a backstop, someone to intercept Lyel or to sabotage the rental car—a safety valve.

My immediate job became to, in turn, intercept him. Lyel would not know this, would not know our timing had been thrown off. This drove me to hurry, but without haste. My main advantage was that of surprise; my target did not know I was up here amid the rocks.

I crouched and stitched my way through the large rocks on a course to intercept the man, careful with my footing to remain as quiet as possible. He was fast and agile, and from above I could see his dark hair moving through the labyrinth of the gorge, and as he corrected his course, so did I. He forced me to move faster than I would have liked. He was a good scrambler, comfortable in the rocks, and this troubled me—he was small and quick; I felt big and slow.

I dodged around an enormous boulder, circled it, and ran smack into the man. Any opportunity of surprise was lost in the collision. He was a flurry of limbs. He came at me like a meat grinder.

People practiced in the martial arts deliver sharp, penetrating blows meant to interrupt the nervous system more than damage bone and muscle. It is a subtle art, full of finesse. And although I lacked very many skills in performing this art, I had studied several variations thoroughly and, as a matter of self-defense, could practice certain protective postures. He landed an upper body stab intended to invite a block from his adversary; this, in turn, was supposed to open up the possibility of a blow to the knee that would have crippled me for life. But I allowed the upper body blow to land, and I did not flinch, so that as he automatically followed with a vicious swing of the right leg, I was ready for him. As his leg extended, I kicked out and struck his solid standing leg, snapping its knee backwards and filling his face with both pain and substantial surprise. My large hands laced together, I delivered a meat cleaver straight up to the sky, catching his chin in the process and clipping his head up and back. He was going to need a chiropractor. This blow lifted him off his feet before he had a chance to fall to the ground, which he then did. As he crashed, I dropped my knee, and most of my weight, into the V below his rib cage, paralyzing his diaphragm and knocking the wind from him. I took his head by both ears and, in a carefully controlled effort, popped the back of his head against a rock with enough force to make him dizzy, but not enough to cut his scalp or break bones. He wore blue and gray Nikes. I used the left lace to tie his hands behind his back, and the right lace to secure his sock in his mouth. My right arm remained partially numb from the blow he had delivered. His knee was bad—he wouldn't be running the forty yard dash for a while. I left him and hurried to the cottage's back door, hoping that this man had left it unlocked for me.

As I approached, I could hear Lyel's voice rumbling on about something unintelligible. His knocks had been answered.

I tried the door. It opened.

CHAPTER 49

The experience of being inside this cottage was similar to the contrast in feelings between dreaming time and waking time: a person has more courage while dreaming. Hostage situations are nothing to mess with—a misstep can cost a hostage his life. Suddenly, I found myself inside the back door to this cottage, my heart trying to escape my body, acting like a small dog hidden inside a coat pocket when trying to pass Customs. I knew nothing of the layout of this structure, had no clue how many, if any, adversaries I faced. Instead, I held on weakly to the thought that surprise could make up for many of my shortcomings. Lyel was currently standing in the front door, making noise or trouble, depending on whom he faced. That was good. The place smelled of cabbage and rice. It stunk. It smelled as if there had not recently been a window or door opened to the outside air—fetid and sour, like a rarely cleaned locker room. I moved cautiously, fearing that the old plank flooring might give me away. I kept my head low because I was too tall for the door jambs. It was a nice enough cottage—freshly painted white walls, clean windows with stunning views, throw rugs, and Impressionist poster art, done tastefully. I sneaked through the small kitchen and crept my eye around the door jamb into the cottage's sitting room. The staircase ran down the center of the structure, separating this sitting room from a small bedroom. I could see Lyel at the door. He was speaking with a Japanese woman who was about five feet tall. Since I saw no one else, I deduced that her associates—if numbering more than the one I had leveled outside—had sequestered themselves with their hostage either in the adjacent bedroom or upstairs. Or both. It seemed unlikely that a seaside cottage would have a basement of any sort.

My problem was that I had a good distance of ground to cover without being noticed if I were to be of any help to Lyel. The more I pondered this, the more my situation seemed precarious. I was not the dainty type. I was certain to be noticed.

Worse, to my mind, was that Lyel was so much the gentleman that the chances were slim that he might attempt to break inside past this woman. The idea that he might attack her was unlikely, virtually impossible, which again put the onus on me. Furthermore, there was no telling what the arrangements had been with the man I had met out back, and the longer we took in our attempt to locate and free

Sinclair, the worse.

There is that point in all adventure where the participant must take the plunge. You can only stand so long on the edge of the cliff before deciding to jump—if you stand too long you will give it up for sure. Or make a mess of it.

"What I was inquiring about," Lyel said politely, "was the availability of the cabin, this cottage, you see? Or if you knew of others. Quite frankly, I expected an Englishman— I thought I saw him the other night—about this tall, dark hair, kind of the university look, if you know what I mean."

"I'm sorry, you must have the wrong cottage. I would like to help, but—" She began to swing the door shut.

Lyel said loudly, "No, no! Please! No reason to be rude! I've come all this way you see? It's quite a drive from London, isn't it? And I *know* that I have the right place. I just think there's some kind of mix-up."

She continued to shut the door. Lyel put his hand out to block the attempt. Another moment and she would have it closed and locked and I would be in the deep stuff. There is no such thing as good timing—there is merely the moment, and either the decision is a good one or not. I made my move.

I didn't treasure the idea of tangling with a woman— especially one that I suspected was defensively trained. She was small. She would be lightning fast, capable of bone-shattering blows, and was not only familiar with her surroundings, but presumably had back-up nearby. I pur- posely took long strides, attempting to reduce the number of footfalls necessary to reach her. She heard me when I was halfway across the room, and her head came around like a gun turret, her body still facing Lyel—her immediate adversary. *Well trained*, I thought. Her face took on no sudden look of terror, no shock. *Too well trained*, I reconsidered.

I willed Lyel to do something. *Anything*. Make a noise. Break her knee. Deliver one square blow to her solar plexus as she remained with her head turned. At the same time, I knew this was a wish for alchemy. He wasn't going to touch her, would make no effort to physically surprise her or render her silent. Lyel was more likely to talk to her—to politely ask her to refrain from violence as she attempted to sever my head from my torso. It was one of those moments when I wished I could freeze my surroundings while I remained animated and able to lecture Lyel— to remind him that the very reason they had used a woman to answer the door was to lessen the perceived threat; that he was being taken advantage of; that she was also probably their strongest fighter. But there I was, rushing across the wide plank flooring heading for contact with the female ninja; and there was Lyel, a bit florid in the face, looking panic stricken and paralyzed.

Seeing her limbs flail, I recalled a moment as a child when holding a pinwheel I had blown into it, watching its spines race. She looked much the same: legs and arms, hands and feet, all in a blur. I crouched, hoisted my right forearm above and in front of me, and prepared for the first blow. As it came—a hand chop that numbed my arm—I dove down flat onto the floor and kicked sideways, catching the instep of her balancing foot. This fragile appearing woman went down like a pail of rocks, but trained to recover quickly, rolled and recoiled like a spring.

I heard a crack of furniture and assumed that Lyel had

encountered at least one other—Lyel liked using furniture, and with his size was capable of swinging a desk if he had to. I had never known him to damage an antique, but he would gladly splinter a reproduction without a second thought.

The rubber sole of a shoe left its imprint on my cheek and snapped my neck back sharply. She followed this with a high kick to my abdomen and then a second shoe-plant into my face. I knew that she had caught my nose because I had experienced that consuming purple goo before, and I shook it off quickly because to be dulled for more than a split second was to lose this fight. She came at me with another volley of high steps, like the leader of a marching band on amphetamines. I felt like a punching bag. Along about the fifth kick I snagged her ankle, and as I did, I stood straight up like a jack-in-the-box coming out of the chute. I was tall enough to literally lift her off her feet, and in doing so she banged her head sharply on those wood planks. By the look in her dark eyes, she wasn't thinking clearly. I dropped to one knee and yanked *both* her arms up behind her back, knowing that most martial arts programs provided ways out of the single arm placed in this position. I pressed her chest into the floor, placed my knee in the center of her lower back, and glanced up at Lyel.

He had apparently delivered a ladder back chair squarely across the shoulders of this woman's associate as the man cleared the bottom of the stairs. The result appeared to be a dislocated shoulder and, quite possibly, a broken collar-bone—the man sat listing to, and favoring, his right side in obvious agony. Lyel stood over him looking like the little boy who had dropped the cookie jar—Lyel abhorred violence, unless drunk, in which case he excelled at it.

If there had been any others in the small cottage, I assumed we would have heard from them, and therefore, I presumed us alone. Nonetheless, I wanted to verify that quickly.

"Find something to tie her with," I said, hissing at him. It seemed ridiculous to talk softly in lieu of all the crashing and banging of the previous minute, but old habits die hard.

"With which to tie her," Lyel said, correcting my usage—when Lyel was nervous, there was no predicting what he might say. "If you're going to be a writer, you had better learn to get it right."

"He'll live, Lyel," I countered, wondering who, if anyone, was upstairs. My main effort was to settle him down in a hurry.

Lyel located a curtain pull and cut it free with a jackknife he always carried. I tied her wrists tightly, and ran a loop around her neck, hog-tying her so that if she fought against it she would choke herself; I didn't have Lyel's hang-ups.

Towering over his prey, Lyel said, "He's going to need a doctor."

"He'll have to find it himself," I stated clearly. Lyel's tendency to act Florence Nightingale was legendary; it didn't surprise me at all that he might try to help the very same man that would have broken all of Lyel's limbs if given half the chance. "Let's check upstairs. I'll lead."

"What about him?"

"We're going to have to tie his wrists," I informed him.

The Japanese man's eyes went hysterical.

"It'll kill him," Lyel said, disapproving.

"It'll hurt," I agreed. "But it won't kill him."

Despite Lyel's protests, I bound the man's wrists. To my surprise, he did not emit even a peep of complaint as I was forced to jerk his left arm behind him. This impressed me and, at the same time, made me concerned that a few pieces of flimsy curtain cord were likely not enough to hold either of these two. But it was all that we had, and I felt an almost desperate urge to hurry upstairs.

I resorted to hand signals, imparting to Lyel my sense of foreboding while instructing him to remain behind and stand guard while I ascended in search of Sinclair. He nodded a reluctant acceptance.

The stairway was narrow and it held that cottage-by-the-sea musty smell so particular that I could have recognized it blindfolded. The top of the stairs offered three narrow doors. All closed. Two bedrooms and a bath, I thought. A single door down the short hall and to my left—the longest wall of the three—the largest bedroom, I decided. Door immediately to my right—odd place for a bathroom, at the top of the stairs—I guessed this was the second bedroom.

If I'm Sinclair's captor, I keep the bigger bedroom for myself, storing the prisoner in the smaller of the two. I tried the doorknob, which turned, but the door was locked. There was a skeletal keyhole below the doorknob. Sinclair was on the other side of that door—I knew this, but I grew concerned that he wasn't alone. Four people guard him— one stays in the room with him at all times—especially in the event of the occurrences of the last few minutes.

I had no desire whatsoever to encounter another flail of flesh as I had with the woman downstairs. I was hurting over my entire body. I moved quietly to the end of the hall and checked the bathroom—empty. I turned the doorknob to the larger bedroom, pushed, and the door came open—empty.

The blow struck me hard on the base of the neck—a chop, as if someone had sunk an axe into my upper shoulders. My knees went watery, and my arms, my whole body, felt as if I had dived into water fully clothed in winter dress. My neck felt rigid, like a steel pipe had been fixed to my head. I couldn't spin my head around.

The small bedroom was somehow connected to the bath—that was the first thought that surged through me; he had slipped into the bath and out the door that I had stupidly left open.

He followed with two kidney punches that shot so much pain into me that I tried to scream, but the first chop had impaired my diaphragm and I was gasping for air. Dizzy, delirious, aching with pain, I continued my slump toward the floor. At that moment, he could have broken any bone or even killed me—and he might have, had Lyel not appeared at the top of the stairs.

"Quit that!" Lyel said, announcing himself and ruining any opportunity for surprise.

I *felt* the ninja turn toward Lyel—I couldn't see him, and I had to wonder what he thought when he saw Lyel's size. He was so well proportioned that at first Lyel looked quite normal. Then one realized that his shoes were size sixteen, and his hands could cup a basketball like a piece of fruit. He had a reach four inches longer than mine—about a football field longer than this man behind me, for I saw him now as he moved stealthily and smoothly toward Lyel, abandoning me in all my substantial pain. Lyel just stood like the Jolly Green Giant, letting this man come toward him—inviting him to make the foolish mistake of getting even an inch too close, which is inevitable because Lyel's size is so easily misunderstood. At that point, Lyel feinted with his right hand, drew the man's attention, and then leveled a left hook squarely into the base of the man's jaw. Lyel's speed, on and off the court, was legendary, and this man would be telling stories about him. The blow cocked the man over like he'd been broken in half and slammed him down onto the floor. Lyel grabbed him by the ankle, spun him one-hundred-and-eighty degrees and released him, delivering him into the wall, back first, and knocking the wind from him.

"Are you okay?" Lyel asked.

"I can't move," I answered, "but I think I'll be all right."

"I detest this kind of thing," Lyel said.

"I know. I'm sorry," I apologized, my sole intention to remind him that this was *his* doing, not mine. I got my point across. I could see it in his eyes as he nodded. Lyel is really nothing but an extremely oversized teddy bear. There were times like this that I wanted to hug him and tell him it would be okay. He needed that kind of thing. Somewhere, way back, there had been an incident that had driven Lyel's emotions into a cave. Even with me, his closest friend, he had never shared this moment. It seemed to me the only explanation for lack of a woman, a lover, in his life. He had plenty of opportunity, but he never did anything about it. Scar tissue is stronger than flesh.

"I'm okay, Lyel." I knew that this was what he wanted to hear.

"I'm sorry," he apologized, seeing things clearly.

"The difference between us," I said, "is that I don't mind

this so much."

"You're a sick person."

"Yes."

Using some lamp cord, we immobilized the groaning individual whom Lyel had plastered on the wall.

"We're lucky, you know," I reminded. Although familiar with martial arts, we were not experts. We should have been sporting broken limbs.

"We're big," Lyel said.

"True."

We crossed the hall together. I prepared for the possibility of yet another protector. Lyel leaned his shoulder against the door, bumped hard, and the jamb tore loose splintering the wood. Lyel is not far off an elephant at times.

Aiden Sinclair alive! He sat wide-eyed in a ladder back chair looking like a school boy sent to the corner. He wore a week's stubble on his face and his eyes were glassy not with drink, but with relief and joy. "Who are you?" he asked.

"Friends," Lyel replied.

"American," he muttered.

"We need your help," I said.

Aiden Sinclair nodded.

CHAPTER 50

It was Henry's idea," Sinclair explained to Tim Binyon, referring to Henry Hagg, the musicologist. "He and Julian have been at one another since their years at Eton. It was done as a practical joke, that's all."

"To see if Julian could be fooled by the forgery," Binyon said.

"Exactly so. Yes."

Lyel and I sat quietly by and let these two go at it. Binyon's digs were nicer than most. He didn't live in his rooms, but he could have easily. It was five o'clock in the afternoon, the performance just three hours away.

"It appears that you succeeded in fooling him."

"Indeed we did."

"So the game is won. Why perform the material?"

Sinclair looked sheepish. "There's been a bit of disagreement on that account."

"Disagreement?"

"Indeed," Sinclair answered. "It seems the missing page is worth quite a sum. That part of it wasn't expected, you see. Not at all. And well suddenly, with the idea of three hundred thousand quid planted in everyone's minds . . . You understand, Tim." He glanced at us as if we would not understand.

"Divided between you," Binyon said.

"Yes. Exactly right. Nice little retirement nest egg, what?"

"Disagreement," Binyon repeated.

"You may not believe this, but I dissented. So did Lester." Glancing at us, he explained, "Lester Tilbert, the historian. It was Lester's job to discover the manuscript page and bring it to Julian's attention. He and I opposed this idea of not revealing the joke, as did Henry most of all. Henry lived to reveal the forgery. But no one anticipated Julian's enthusiasm. Before we knew it he had contacted *everyone* imaginable. The Holywell was booked, a cellist sought. Ironically, he asked Shultz to conduct. Can you imagine? Shultz *wrote* the piece, of all things! My God! It got out of our control is what happened. And then what? Every week we waited, we were a week deeper into preparations to premier the piece. Suddenly our efforts looked criminal instead of humorous. We put it to a vote and elected to remain quiet."

"That's not on," Binyon replied earnestly.

"No, not at all."

"Won't do."

"No. Of course not."

"It's going to have to be revealed—the truth, I'm talking about," Binyon said.

"Absolutely," Sinclair agreed.

"And your disappearance?" I asked.

"Tuttle's doing," he answered me. "I didn't see it clearly at the time," he told Binyon, then he looked over at Lyel, to include us all. "Gave me some time off, he did. Some port as well. Told me to take a fortnight in Cornwall. I thought he was protecting me from the fallout of the manuscript. I thought he knew something that I didn't. But it wasn't the manuscript at all. I knew that the moment the Japanese showed up. It's the construction site is what it is. My stumbling on to quite a find there. To preserve the site would, I should imagine, have required quite a delay. I took the pieces to Herbert Remmington for examination."

"I spoke to him," Lyel interrupted. "He was quite impressed."

This appeared to thrill Sinclair. "Authentic? I knew it!"

Lyel told him, "He said that it was an important historical find."

"But," I added, "as far as we can tell, they excavated quickly and then boarded off the site."

"So that once you returned," Lyel said, "there would be nothing to find."

Sinclair appeared damaged. "Ruined it? They ruined the site for that bloody dormitory? It's criminal!"

"Perhaps they held on to the artifacts," Binyon suggested. "I can't believe that the Warden would condone destroying the artifacts."

Sinclair was a bright red. "They should have their heads lopped off!"

"Money," Binyon said, with an egregious sense of distaste that could only come from an academic.

"Music equals miscellaneous," I said to Sinclair, reciting from the Post-It I remembered from my visit to his rooms.

"You Yanks certainly do your research," Sinclair said to me.

"What does it mean?" I inquired.

"My laptop computer," Sinclair answered. "The file, 'miscellaneous,' is password protected. The password is 'music.' Didn't want to forget the damn thing."

"So it's relevant," I suggested.

"Relevant?!" He chuckled. "It's the herbal formula for the ink on the manuscript we're talking about. You give that to Rasner and his boys, and they will be singing 'forgery' in no time flat."

"And the laptop was with you," I stated.

Sinclair nodded.

Binyon said, "Rasner gets hold of this . . . It's not on. Wadham's name will be dragged through the mud for years to come."

"My fault, I'm afraid, what?" Sinclair declared.

Lyel offered, "Perhaps it doesn't need to come to that. Perhaps Sir Frans can be convinced to make things right for everyone involved."

This sparked Binyon's eyes. He sat up straight and said loudly, "Just right!"

CHAPTER 51

The burden of the job fell onto Lyel and me. On short notice, there were no other second-story men to be found.

The situation had been reviewed carefully and thoroughly. Sir Frans Tuttle denied any destruction of any archaeological artifacts and was genuinely stunned at the revelation that the Mozart piece was a forgery. With the embarrassment of his college at stake, his memory suddenly returned and he allowed how certain discoveries during the excavation might have been placed in storage. Sinclair and Remmington were allowed access to this "storage"—two dump trucks worth of dirt piles, deposited alongside an Oxfordshire farm road—delighted to find many of the pieces still in good condition. The rest was left to us.

I found Allison Star rehearsing for the evening's performance at the Holywell. She bowed incorrectly when I entered the small, church-like building, and subsequently took a break, attempting to flee the building before I reached her. Lyel headed her off at the back door.

"What's the meaning of this?" she inquired.

"We need to talk with Stephan," I said, pronouncing it correctly.

"I don't know what—"

"He's to conduct tonight. We know that. We know much more about all of this than perhaps even you do, young lady," Lyel explained. "The best foot forward is to cooperate. You just may avoid criminal charges for your friend Mr. Shultz that way."

She turned an odd shade of green.

"Contact him," I said. "Tell him to meet us at Blackwell's, unaccompanied—solo—before six. The music shop," I added. Attempting to come up with something that might explain it to him I said, "Tell him it's about Julian Rasner. He'll understand."

"I don't know how to reach him," she complained poorly.

"You'll think of something," Lyel said.

"His entire career is at stake," I added.

We turned and left. I was in need of a beer. Lyel was hungry.

CHAPTER 52

Blackwell's bookshop on Broad Street is one of the more impressive features of this impressive city. It is sprawling and yet intimate. It is intelligent. It is what the newer American chains have been trying to imitate—a place to get lost in the written word. An orgy of good reading. Having been installed in a centuries-old building, the floors and levels seem added together as an afterthought, stacked as an infant child might do with wooden blocks.

By contrast, Blackwell's music shop, just up Holywell, boasts a surprisingly modern interior. Quite small, it's a treasure trove of music in all media.

Stephan Shultz looked like an advertisement for Ralph Lauren's Country Collection. He wore a houndstooth check blazer and an ascot. He looked absurd. He approached the two of us with the haughty gait of an egoist. We waited at Mozart, thinking it appropriate.

"Gentlemen."

"The proposition is this," I explained bluntly. "You locate where Rasner has stored the forgery. We will liberate it for you. Following the performance, Tuttle will demand to see the original. It will not be able to be found. It will not exist. Your composing the missing page will not be revealed." He was a shade of gray now that I had not witnessed since seeing a dead body hauled out of the Middle Fork of the Salmon river.

Lyel added, "And you will sign Klick's papers and accept this money that he's been trying to give you, and you will donate a portion of that money to Wadham so that it may restore certain archaeological artifacts that are in desperate need of attention."

"You cooperate and we go away quietly," I explained. "You don't, and the forgery will be revealed, including the role of *all participants.*"

Some of his color returned. "We did a good job of it," he proclaimed.

"You got greedy," I said.

He shrugged. "Expenses," he said, meeting eyes with me. His sparkled with humor. Stephan Shultz was one of a kind.

I handed him the fax from Bruce that I had received. It detailed a method of safely laundering his wife's money. The idea was to purchase a rare Stradivarius cello valued at, or slightly above, the amount he'd liberated from their joint accounts. He would use what was left of his wife's money as well as a chunk of the royalty, intended to make up for what he'd already spent. The instrument would be carried into the country by Allison Star. I appreciated Bruce's intended irony—the mistress would provide the wife with the confiscated fortune. If he followed it carefully, he could return the money due his wife and avoid prosecution. He studied it, clearly surprised I had delivered.

Lyel and I had decided incentive was important in Shultz's case. He glanced at his watch, "There's not much time."

"I've never done anything like this," Shultz complained.

"You're a fast study," Lyel answered.

"We think you're up to it," I added.

CHAPTER 53

The call came in at 7:30, just thirty minutes before the performance at the Holywell. Stephan Shultz confirmed that it was me on the other end of the line and, without mentioning his own name, said, "It's locked up in Laboratory B in the Sciences Center. That's as much about location as I could get without raising suspicion."

"That's enough," I said.

"No it's not," he said urgently, catching me before I hung up.

"I'm still here."

"They intend to *display* the manuscript at the end of the performance, which means they intend to—"

"Pick it up," I finished for him.

The compound of science facilities was on the far side of the park that I jogged regularly. My heart felt tight. Lyel and I walked as fast as our legs would carry us. The buildings were recent additions to the university, built in the mid-1960s. The beauty of Oxford's open campus and enormous enrollment was that even a pair of abnormally large Americans lurking around hallways would do little to arouse suspicion. The downside of this was that if we managed to steal the document, we might be remembered. As a result, we elected not to travel as a pair, but to enter the brick three story building containing laboratory B from different entrances.

The halls smelled of unpleasant chemicals, and the lighting cast a green hue on my skin. I felt tension in my chest, and my breathing was short and fast though I struggled to control it. Anticipation is its own drug: it can paralyze; it can turn the weak into giants.

I was anxious. A clock ticked loudly in my head— *Rasner is coming to get the manuscript!*

I pictured a thief as someone short and small, wearing dark clothes, partially bald, with sinister, glassy eyes. I felt like a two-ton gorilla in a toy poodle pageant. Without a coin toss or similar democratic notion as to how the assignments of this attempted robbery were to occur, I ended up with the inside job by default. Lyel was to work the hallway and raise his voice in an inquiring fashion should the need arise to alert me. Meanwhile, I was to attempt to locate and steal the document. To aid me in this attempt I had a few crude lock-picking tools should the need arise—but my lock-picking talents were minimal; it could take a while to decipher and open even the simplest of locks.

The door to Laboratory B was yellow wood with a small glass window mounted at eye height. It was on the British first floor—the American second story. I killed time impatiently studying a bulletin board until Lyel appeared at the end of the extremely long hall. We made eye contact and Lyel nodded, indicating he was ready to stand sentry. I peered through the window—the lights were off and the room appeared empty. I turned the knob and pushed on it gently and it swung on silent hinges. I was inside.

I don't know the biological reasoning behind it, but the body perspires when under stress—perhaps it was once intended to throw our scent into the air or to cool down the system as it chemically overheated, but whatever the reason, sweat cascaded down my ribs in cold drools, feeling as if someone were tickling me from behind. I switched on the lights. The room was a vast sea of stationary lab tables with thick, black surfaces covered in electronic machinery, glass vials and Bunsen burners. It was a teaching lab with thirty or forty stools around fifteen such work areas. The ceiling was acoustical tile, the floor linoleum. One of the walls was windows overlooking the park; one, green chalkboard. The left wall, facing outside, was a teaching desk with a roller chair, drawers and a series of built-in cabinets. There was a door, presumably to an adjoining lab. I approached this area first and began to search for a lock box that might contain the forgery.

I found a two-drawer file cabinet, locked. I returned to the small window in the lab's main door and saw Lyel reading the same bulletin board where I had stood. I knocked lightly on the door, caught his attention, and lifted my hands to the window, indicating the turning of a key—I was going to attempt to pick a lock. Lyel nodded. What a team.

For the most part, file cabinets have extremely basic locks—one or two tumblers. A locksmith might have had it open in a minute or two. It took me five, at the end of which my shirt was damp, and my jaw tight with tension. There is nothing quite as satisfying as the feeling of a tumbler falling victim to one's efforts. There is an accompanying visualization to the process, and I could *see* the puzzle come unlocked as I twisted and picked. I pulled on the top drawer, and it opened. I felt like a child secretly opening a Christmas present when no one was watching.

As the drawer came open I suddenly wondered what the penalty might be for such a crime. It's funny how these thoughts occur *after* the crime is committed. I knew that the British had no bill of rights, that the police could be extremely tough on suspects. I wondered what the university's attitude was to Americans rifling locked file cabinets. I wondered how I had allowed myself to be compelled into doing this, and I realized that my partner, Bruce Warren, would deny any association with me if this went south. Would someone spot the lab lights switched on and investigate? Would Lyel be able to hold them at bay? I would certainly not have time to re-lock the cabinet, given such a scenario, though I might have time to shut the drawer and make myself look busy. What kind of explanation could I invent for my presence here? Why had most of this eluded consideration until the moment of truth?

My fingers hurried through the contents of the top drawer, aware that at the very least I was looking for a manuscript page that was hermetically sealed in plastic—this, to contain the aging process due to exposure to oxygen.

Nothing. The documents were letters and exams and worksheets. Nothing close to a musical manuscript page.

I searched the lower drawer next and found more of the same—but no musical manuscript page.

Discouraged, I shut both drawers and used the forearm of my sport coat to wipe down the handles in case the police dusted for latent prints. I felt stymied. Perhaps Shultz's information was incorrect. I checked my watch—each passing minute brought Rasner closer.

I inspected the cabinets left-to-right, upper-to-lower, opening each and appraising the contents. They appeared to be personal storage areas. Some contained running shoes and notebooks, others, aprons and rubber gloves. No manuscript. Nothing even close to a lock box.

It was then that the only other door in the room intrigued me. Perhaps it didn't communicate with the next lab. Perhaps it was *storage.*

The doorknob was keyed, the door locked. *A far more intricate lock*, I knew from experience. I pulled out the picks, feeling overwhelmed and even intimidated—this was a thirty minute job for me, and only that if I got lucky. I tried to collect myself, to push away the insecurity and steel myself for the difficulty this job presented—I could not attempt this without a good deal of confidence and surety.

I inserted two of the straight, tapered picks, turned my head, closed my eyes and concentrated all my senses on the tactile response of metal against metal. I felt the first tumbler and set the pick in place. I opened my eyes.

The hinges were on the outside of the door.

For a moment, I didn't see it that way—I saw instead an image in my head of the picks, and the tiny spurs of metal that I needed to conquer. Then my eyes refocused and caught sight of the hinges, and I realized that this must have been originally built as a closet, outfitted with a lock later. I jumped up to check the hinge pins to see if they had been welded into place. They had not.

I hurried over to the main door and peered out the window. I couldn't see Lyel, but I could sense his irritability. Lyel was not good at waiting alone—he was probably agitated and as anxious to have this over as I was.

I frantically searched the lab countertops and the cabinets beneath for a hammer and screwdriver. I found a piece of angle iron that would work for my screwdriver and a black-rubber mallet that would serve quite well for my hammer. Returning to the locked closet door, I worked the hinge pins out by beating on the angle iron with the mallet. I took out the top and bottom pins and then, leaning my weight against the door, the middle hinge pin. Easing off the pressure forced against the door, I tried to fit my fingers into the crack at the jamb alongside the hinges, but my fingers were too thick and I resorted to using the angle iron as a pry bar. With a loud *clunk*, the door opened hinge side first. The noise of it coming open startled me—I was unprepared for it. I could picture Lyel in the hallway beginning to sweat. Anyone on the floor below—perhaps even above—would have heard it. I worked fast.

I hoisted the heavy door out of its jamb and laid it against the wall to the side, careful not to allow it to slip and crash to the floor. The room inside had, in fact, obviously begun life as a closet, but had since been converted into a poor man's safe deposit vault. Two of the three walls were shelves cluttered with chemicals, flasks, rags, and even a box of lost-and-found. The wall directly ahead held a small refrigerator—locked with keyed padlock—and a three-by-three stack of half-height metal lockers, seven of which were also locked with keyed padlocks.

The locker in the center of this group held three names inked onto white athletic tape, one of which was *J. Rasner.* I went right to work on the lock.

Padlocks are not easy picks. The tumbler mechanisms are considerably smaller than a door lock, and the lock itself is able to move about making setting the picks extremely frustrating and difficult. The clock running ever louder in my imagination didn't help things at all—I could feel a pressure bearing down on the back of my neck as if someone were looking over my shoulder. This sensation was suffocating. My forehead broke out in perspiration.

I heard voices in the hall, and when I identified Lyel's among them, I nearly lost my final pick. *Rasner!* I thought. *Coming to get the manuscript page.* My heart about to explode, I caught myself holding my breath. *Stall them, Lyel!*

The lock clicked open. I twisted the padlock, slipped it out of the locker's hardware, and opened the locker. There were four shelves. I found the manuscript in a gray card-board box marked with Rasner's name. It was sealed in a thick plastic sheet and marked, "Mozart."

Even though a forgery, the effect of holding this in my hands sent goose bumps through me, for it looked and felt so *real*. Scrawled black ink images of sixteenth notes rushed in a genius-like way across the page—a mind in a hurry to express itself. I took longer than I should have to examine it.

Lyel's voice, growing louder. Nervous. Eager. He was asking directions. The Brits were too polite to ditch him.

The locker went shut, the padlock in place. I ran the man-uscript out of the closet and placed it on the nearest work surface.

Lyel said loudly, "But I'm not *sure* I have this exactly."

I glanced toward the room's door. Lyel was blocking it, standing with his back to it, preventing sight of me through the window, preventing anyone entering. He was being a nuisance.

My fingers felt clumsy all of a sudden. Uncoordinated. I hoisted the heavy door into place and had trouble feeding the locked tongue into the appropriate space in the jamb. On the third try it took. I fed the rest of the door into the jamb and bumped it gently into place so that the hinges matched. I returned the center pin first, then the bottom pin and had to fight with my whole body to make the top pin take. But it did. I rubber hammered them into place.

Lyel had used up every ounce of indignity and rudeness. I caught the light out of the corner of my eye as he stepped aside, thanking whoever was there, again, unnecessarily loudly. *They must think him deaf,* I thought.

As the door came open I grabbed a glance of the manuscript lying out on the countertop amid a ruin of flasks, note papers, tubes, and machinery. I reached for it, but missed as the room door popped open and I crouched for cover. I tucked down into a ball and scurried one row across, staying below the level of the countertops. I heard footsteps—two people. I caught a peek of their shoes and lower legs—men's shoes, men's trousers. I looked up to see the edge of the manuscript protruding from the clutter on the counter of the lab bench adjacent to the one behind which I hid. I saw a possible window of opportunity, but it would mean lightning fast reactions and quick feet.

I caught the backs of heads as the man in the lead—Rasner, I assumed—unlocked the closet. The door came open and they stepped inside, providing a visual block between us for the first time. I lifted my head like a periscope, stood slightly, and duck-walked toward the next lab bench over. Reaching across and through a clutter of glass tubes and beakers I pinched the manuscript between my fingers and attempted to extricate the sheet through the maze of delicate glass in front of me. I could hear perfectly clearly Rasner's key slip into the padlock's slot. I had a few seconds at most.

The manuscript nicked a glass tube and dislodged it, and it was only my quick reflexes that kept the piece from exploding on the unforgiving surface of the countertop. But I caught it, eased it down, and then liberated the manuscript.

I heard the locker door come open.

I turned and faced the room's main door—it suddenly felt about five miles away, like something from a nightmare. I had no choice—I had to go for it.

"Impossible!" I heard a thick British male voice cry out.

Five long strides to the end of the lab benches—I counted them . . . turned left . . . three strides to the door . . .

Mumbling between the men from the closet. "I'm telling you, I left it right here . . . No, no: I have the only key . . . We made *arrangements!*" Rasner was quickly losing control of himself.

I turned the doorknob and pulled. The hallway represented freedom. I stepped through the door, into the hallway, gently, carefully eased the door shut behind me and, through the small window, caught just a glimpse of the two men coming out of the closet, one piping mad.

I turned and walked as fast as a person can walk without running.

Lyel was waiting outside. He looked as white as a ghost.

CHAPTER 54

The Holywell Music Room's high dome reminded me of being inside a white egg shell. Bare brown-wood benches rose steeply like bleachers aimed toward the small stage where Mozart had once performed as a child. On this night the setting was chairs and music stands for a small orchestra. The building was filled to SRO. I searched the backs of heads until I saw a bald spot that I took to be Randall Bradshaw, and then realized that he and his cohorts in crime—the historian, Lester Tilbert, and the musicologist Henry Hagg—were sitting together, all in the same row, as they might be if behind the defendant's table in a court of law.

Sitting in the front row was Sir Frans Tuttle, dressed impeccably. To his left was a Japanese man I took to be his guest by the way Tuttle fell all over the man. Lyel confirmed the man's identity when he said, "Nice and sweet. The one next to Sir Frans is none other than Fujiami."

"This could be a beautiful thing."

"Yes," Lyel agreed. He looked exhausted. We both needed time back in Idaho. Seeing me stretch my neck, he said, "Do you see her?" He meant Nicole; he knew that look of mine.

"She said she'd try to make it."

"You know, Chris—even if she doesn't, it doesn't mean anything."

Lyel *never* called me by my first name. "Chandler?" I said, driving home my point by using his first name. He *always* knew more about her than I did.

"She got cold feet," he acknowledged. "On the bright side, I think that's good news—she's more and more comfortable with you, more and more convinced there's something there, something between you two."

I felt the pain down in my stomach, mistaking it for a leftover of the brawl in Cornwall. "How is it you always know more about her than I do?" I asked, expressing one of my greater concerns.

"She trusts me."

"Oh, that certainly makes me feel better."

He touched my arm. "Here we go," he said, cutting me off.

I turned to see what all the fuss was about. Two Royals— a second cousin to the prince and his dignified looking Lady-Something-or-other with white hair and matching pearls—entered with a guest, a gentleman I took to be the bean-counter in charge of the National Archives whom I knew was slated to attend. Those already in seats watched their entrance and the buzz of conversation rose dramatically as the three took their chairs which had been set up in the front of the front row, partially blocking the view. No one complained.

Then I realized that Lyel was not referring to the Royals and their guest, but to Aiden Sinclair, who had not been on campus for the past several weeks. He saw us and stopped before entering, but I nodded at him and he walked right past us to the front as we had earlier instructed. He walked up to the edge of the platform stage and turned around, as if looking for a face in the crowd, when in fact it was so that his face could be seen by all in the crowd.

I took great joy as the line-up of Bradshaw and friends went into panic.

Sinclair stood there an inappropriately long amount of time before acknowledging Bradshaw and friends and smiling and nodding at them as if eager to join them. This put the team of three into a difficult and untenable situation. They did the only thing they could: cleared a space for him and signaled him over to join them.

But before approaching his associates, Sinclair walked over to Tuttle. Out of earshot, I could only see him extend his hand to both Tuttle and his Japanese guest. A moment later he reached into his pocket and handed the Japanese gentleman a small glass bottle—one of the artifacts recovered from the area that was now occupied by the foundation of the new dormitory. And I knew the words that would follow, for Lyel, Tim Binyon, and I had put them into his mouth—a threat for Tuttle and his present company to produce all of the artifacts, and for the Japanese industrialist to finance the complete excavation of the site; otherwise Sinclair and his American friends, along with Herbert Remmington, the distinguished archaeologist, would expose the kidnapping plot intended to keep Sinclair's find under wraps. When Tuttle glanced back at Lyel at me, not with hate or vexation, but *respect*, I knew that we had scored a direct hit. Tuttle knew when the scrimmage was lost.

Sinclair then went through that uncomfortable act of slipping his way past those people already seated, everyone murmuring the mandatory apologies. He sat down next to Bradshaw, whispered into his ear, and then pointed toward Lyel and me. On cue, we waved and produced our best shit-eating grins. Bradshaw had just been told that Lyel and I knew everything there was to know about the forged manuscript page, and that without full cooperation, jail sentences and fines were certain to follow. Whether or not Bradshaw smelled the port on Sinclair's breath, it seemed fairly apparent that the message had been properly delivered. When he looked over at us for a second time, he looked positively disease-stricken.

Seeing this, Lyel whispered over to me, "Nothing satisfies like satisfaction. I wish I had a beer."

"Contain that urge," I suggested. "But maintain it."

The program that I was handed at the door was Xeroxed onto cheap paper folded in half. Shultz had the schedule wrong—and I wondered if he had wanted us caught. The first order of business was the **PRESENTATION OF MANUSCRIPT** by Julian Rasner, followed by **THE PERFORMANCE** with Stephan Shultz conducting. This first item was the moment that Lyel and I eagerly awaited. Fifteen minutes later, the orchestra assembled and ready, the crowd agitated and restless, it became readily apparent that we had encountered some kind of delay. A distraught face of Julian Rasner was twice seen briefly at the darkened door to the back room.

Finally, with little choice, Rasner clearly faced the music.

Sweating profusely, he showed himself, discouraged the resulting applause, and made a dash for the Royals. Here, he shook hands, head bowed, and then kneeled so that he could speak privately. He spoke for a long time, and the crowd hushed as if to eavesdrop. Impossible, of course. Next, the prince's second cousin leaned over and evidently relayed the text of the message to the representative of the National Archives, who then summoned Rasner to his side. They spoke briefly. All this to an audience of two hundred curious. There were discussions all around, and Rasner finally presented himself to the audience at large.

"Ladies and Gentlemen, welcome. I wish I could bring better news, but I'm afraid the news is nothing but bad." This caused a ripple of speculation throughout and the crowd took a moment to settle. The British were not immune to a love of gossip. "I am terribly disappointed to say that the original Mozart manuscript page, which I had so hoped to present to the National Archives so that it might find a home at Oxford's own Bodleian Library, has, this very evening, been stolen from my laboratory." The subsequent roar was probably heard on the High Street. It took several minutes before the audience settled down. "It has been determined that we will go ahead with the performance, as scheduled," he said with the pronunciation peculiar to the American ear. He looked up at the crowd imploringly, and seemed about to say what everyone understood—that without the original manuscript in hand, to be studied and restudied, its authenticity would always remain open to speculation by scholars, its legitimacy challenged. Only Rasner, who had discovered the document based on a hint planted by Lester Tilbert, and a scant handful of his assistants, had ever claimed to have seen the original. Within days the London press would begin suggesting that Rasner himself had been the author of a hoax, and that when push-came-to-shove he lacked the resolve and the confidence to present that hoax to the National Archives for further scrutiny. Rasner's career was in flames—score one for the Fellows of Wadham.

The performance featured a brief, but stirring, solo by the lovely and extremely talented Allison Star. To my ear the performance was flawless, the unity of the piece seamless in its integrity. As author of the forgery, Shultz's inventiveness and imagination briefly matched that of the great legend, and my guess was that only the most studied scholar had any idea where the missing piece fit into the whole.

CHAPTER 55

Sir Frans Tuttle's resignation as Wadham's Warden made all the London papers. There was no mention of the fact that three of Wadham's most respected dons, Tilbert, Bradshaw, and Hagg, had been required to replenish Wadham's cellar with a case of vintage port, estimated to cost each a term's salary. These same dons would forfeit their High Table privileges for one academic year—the result of a vote by their peers. Ten days later, the night before our flight back to the US, Lyel and I were invited to dinner at a small but lovely cottage some ten miles out of town in the heart of Oxfordshire. The cottage was part of a former manor house that had been converted to five luxurious homes (the word condominium simply didn't fit quarters this grand and historical). We were invited at "7:30 for 8" meaning dinner would be served promptly at eight, and if we wanted a cocktail, 7:30 was encouraged.

A car with a scratch on the fender was parked in the circular drive. I pointed it out to Lyel, reminding him of my kidnapping under Shultz's instruction. As I entered the cottage, I recognized it immediately. I had this sinking feeling that Lyel and I had failed to dot all our i's and cross our t's. I didn't trust Shultz one bit. I walked in with my muscles stiff, on alert.

He offered us his Smile In F-sharp Minor—one practiced for the audiences, certainly not born of any emotion he might have been experiencing. "Quite a brilliant stroke," he said, greeting us with an outstretched hand. "All the time and effort put into it, annulled by a single theft."

We shook hands. "We don't know anything about any theft," I said.

"I'm sure that you don't," he answered. "And I know nothing of any forgery."

"It's better that way," Lyel said.

Shultz was intimidated by Lyel's size. It's the man's forehead that does it to most people. It's imposing. Like Rushmore. The maestro kept backing up away from him. "Quite

303

is lost on youth."

"And your wife?" I asked, turning the knife as sharply as I could. I admired Shultz, but I didn't like him.

"That's where you come in," Shultz said.

Another car pulled up out front.

"Please stay after dessert," Shultz said. "We'll talk more."

Tim Binyon's wife was heavy and pale and charming. It was just the five of us for dinner. Shultz's henchmen probably ate in the kitchen with the cook and our server. Binyon and Lyel and Shultz drank too much. I was feeling nervous and out of sorts. Nicole had told me over the phone that she wanted to come stay with me at Lyel's guest cabin for a few weeks. I couldn't get my mind on much else. I couldn't wait for that plane.

After dessert, the pale Mrs. Binyon led her husband by the arm out the door and assisted him into the car. The word was, Shultz assured us at dinner, that Binyon was to be named Warden. It was extremely rare for a Warden to come out of a college—typically, they were appointed from some prestigious position in The City. The champagne at dessert was what finished off the man. If I had matched him drink for drink, I would have never made it past the salad course. Lyel had tried, and I knew him well enough to see that his eyes would not focus. Another thirty minutes and he would be snoring—regardless of where he fell at the time. I expressed a keen interest to Shultz that we do our business quickly, for instinctively I understood that this was to be business.

"I intend to follow your instructions to the letter," he whispered to me, referring to Bruce's fax. "Allison has

"Theory is better left to the university life," I answered. "This is real world. We're talking eighty-some-thousand dollars for one signature. The cash to be wired within twenty-four hours."

Lyel told him, "We read about the offer of guest conductor in Minneapolis."

"You know how cold it is up there?" Shultz complained. "The Midwest? Me? It's unthinkable."

"It's a living," I suggested. "One signature," I reminded. "The US Embassy tomorrow morning."

"You could always forge another Mozart," Lyel contributed, a bit in his cups. "Maybe you'll get a film offer."

"The embassy opens at ten," I informed him. "You have between ten and twelve noon to have this notarized. They close the notary office after noon."

Shultz stared at the stapled contract.

"All you have to do is sign it," I reminded.

Lyel told him, "There's a pub two blocks east of the embassy—The Iron Pig. Klick and I will be waiting for you from ten to noon. Our plane is the next morning, so this is your only chance."

I stood. Lyel pulled himself out of his chair with some difficulty. "If you don't mind," Lyel said, bending down and confiscating the bottle of port. "We could use a nightcap." He corked the bottle and cradled it like a baby.

I shrugged at Shultz: I couldn't be held responsible to stop a man Lyel's size.

"Forty-five percent?" he complained one final time.

"The Iron Pig," I reminded him.

Shultz nodded gravely. It was the first and only indication I had that he would keep the appointment.

IDAHO

CHAPTER 56

In November the northern Pacific storms track south of the Aleutians and come barreling into Puget Sound and Seattle dumping feet of snow onto the Cascades, rain across eastern Washington, and snow again in the mountains of Idaho. Sometimes these storms line up like freight cars and follow one after the other for two weeks or more, burying the high desert terrain south of Snow Lake and preparing the town's world famous ski mountain there for its Thanksgiving opening.

I had been expecting Nicole who was driving up from Los Angeles, but with the weather as it was my attention focused on the phone instead, fearing a cancellation. Lyel had snowshoed over to his guest cabin, my home away from home. He had beers open for both of us and was stabbing the fire in the hearth more out of boredom than necessity.

"Don't be so glum," he said. "If not this time, another. She said she'd visit; she will."

"Unless she changes her mind," I said.

"Glum! You see? It doesn't suit you. Pull out of it." He motioned toward the green beer bottle. "Man's best friend," he said.

"Do you miss it?" I asked.

"Oxford?"

"I loved every minute," I said.

"Is that why that typewriter is set up in the guest room

"I shut the door so you wouldn't see."

"I saw through the window as I passed by. Going to t

for a research fellowship, are we?"

"Just writing out what happened," I said. "Taking notes."

"Uh huh," he said skeptically. "I bet."

We heard the front loader then. Heavy snow in Idaho isn't moved with plows but with earth movers. The yellow creature with the two white eyes came down the long driveway that led to the guest house, its front bucket dumping a quarter ton of snow at a time into towering piles that lined the road. The machine groaned and jerked and backed-up, slowly cutting a route back to civilization. I had been holed up here for the better part of two days and was loving it. I only wished that it hadn't been time spent alone.

Lyel was out on the front porch waving with his free hand, his breath a steady stream of white fog. "It's Randy," he told me. "Man's an artist with a front loader." A moment later he shouted, "Hey, Klick, come here. I think you're going to want to see this."

"Randy's terrific," I answered. "But I think I'll pass."

"Don't know what you're missing. I'd get my butt out here if I were you."

I knew he meant business. I dragged myself up out of the comfortable chair and joined my friend on the front porch. Snow swirled into a near white out. Beers and a front loader in a snow storm—I was back in Idaho.

The front loader's cab stood five feet off the ground. I recognized Randy as the cab's glass door popped open, and called out a hello.

"Special Delivery!" Randy announced. "Her car went into a drift back by the bridge. But this is one determined lady, mister."

The operator's seat rocked forward and Nicole climbed

out pulling a tweed duffel bag behind her. Lyel hurried to offer her a hand as I stood flat-footed and dumbfounded.

"Is there a fire going?" she shouted out at me.

"You bet," I answered.

"And cold beer," Lyel told her.

"Hot chocolate?"

"That, too," Lyel said.

Nicole kissed Randy on his rough cheek and then jumped down into Lyel's waiting arms. They should have been my arms, but I was still in shock. I heard a few faint strains of music fill my ears.

"Welcome to Idaho," Lyel said.

I finally moved off the porch. Nicole hurried down the shoveled path and threw herself into my arms and we embraced. "Judging by the weather," she said, "it looks as if I'll be here a long time."

"Music to my ears," I said, holding her tightly, not letting her go, still humming Mozart.

Center Point Publishing
600 Brooks Road • PO Box 1
Thorndike ME 04986-0001 USA

(207) 568-3717

US & Canada:
1 800 929-9108

Student Solutions Manual

for

Mind on Statistics

Third Edition

Robert F. Heckard
Pennsylvania State University

Jessica M. Utts
University of California, Davis

THOMSON
BROOKS/COLE

Australia • Brazil • Canada • Mexico • Singapore • Spain • United Kingdom • United States

Printed in Canada
   2 3 4 5 6 7   09 08 07

Printer: Webcom

ISBN- 13: 978-0-495-01807-0
ISBN- 10: 0-495-01807-4
Cover Image: Jack Hollingsworth/Corbis

Thomson Higher Education
10 Davis Drive
Belmont, CA 94002-3098
USA

For more information about our products,
contact us at:
Thomson Learning Academic Resource Center
1-800-423-0563

For permission to use material from this text or product, submit a request online at
http://www.thomsonrights.com.
Any additional questions about permissions can be submitted by email to **thomsonrights@thomson.com.**

TABLE OF CONTENTS

Please note - Supplemental Topics are located on the book CD.

INTRODUCTION

What is This Manual?

This *Student Solutions Manual* is intended to supplement the brief answers provided for selected exercises in the back of the textbook. It includes fully worked solutions to those exercises. It also provides hints, additional interpretation and other notes of relevance for specific exercises, which should be useful for similar exercises as well.

Tips for Doing Exercises Assigned for Homework

1. You instructor will most likely assign exercises that reinforce ideas and methods he or she thinks are important. Therefore, your first strategy for tackling problems assigned for homework is to review your class notes. You will probably find that the instructor either worked similar examples, or at least provided you with the necessary tools for working out the assigned exercises.

2. Sometimes there will be very similar exercises near each other, especially for the "Basics" exercises (with exercise numbers in blue). The exercises with numbers in boldface have answers in the back of the book and are worked out in this *Manual*. Therefore, you might see if there is a boldfaced exercise that is similar to the one you are trying to do, and look at how it is done.

3. The majority of the exercises in the book are listed under specific sections. Therefore, if the exercises assigned are listed as applying to a certain section of the book, look in that section for information on how to solve them. If you are assigned exercises listed under "Chapter Exercises" you can see if there is a similar exercise listed under one of the sections. If so, then you know the relevant material will most likely be found in that section.

4. Whether you can identify the relevant section of the chapter for a particular exercise or not, the next strategy is to look for appropriate "Key Terms." These are listed just prior to the beginning of the exercises in each chapter, and are divided by sections. If you can identify a key term appropriate for a particular exercise, then you can read the material surrounding that term in the book and will most likely find the necessary information to solve the exercise. For instance, suppose you are asked to do Exercise 8.78 in the Chapter Exercises for Chapter 8. The exercise states that you should "The vehicle speeds at a particular interstate location are described by a normal curve." Looking over the Chapter 8 Key Terms, you will see that the term "normal curve" appears under Section 8.6. If you look in that Section, you will not only find the relevant material, you will also find examples similar to what you are asked to do in Exercise 8.78.

Exercises Not Assigned for Homework

Working exercises is an excellent method for studying statistics. If you are using exercises for that purpose you will be better served by *not* isolating the exercise as applying to a specific section of the book until you understand more about the exercise. One of the most difficult problems students have in solving problems is identifying *which* technique is appropriate. The mechanics are often easy once the appropriate topic has been identified.

Therefore, when you are studying a particular chapter, start by trying to solve the Chapter Exercises that have solutions provided in the back of the book or this *Manual*. Try to get as far as possible before looking at the solution. If you are really stuck, then try identifying pairs of exercises that are similar. Use the solution provided to figure out how to solve the first one, then attempt to solve the second one on your own. Another strategy is to first do the exercises in each section that have solutions provided. Then, attempt to do the Chapter Exercises without looking at the solutions until you are finished.

CHAPTER 1
SELECTED SOLUTIONS

1.2   **a.** The observed rate of cervical cancer in Vietnamese American women is 86 per 200,000. This could also be expressed as 43 per 100,000 or 4.3 per 10,000, and so on. In decimal form, it is .00043.

1.5   **a.** Solve for *n* in the equation $\dfrac{1}{\sqrt{n}} = .05$. Answer is *n* = 400 teenagers.

1.7   **c.** Randomized experiment because the researchers created the groups randomly and imposed the course method.
d. Observational study. The researchers only observed who smoked and who did not.

1.11   The placebo group estimates the baseline rate of heart attacks for men not taking aspirin. So, the estimated baseline rate of heart attacks is 189/11,034, which is about 17 heart attacks per 1,000 men (see Table 1.1 for the data).

1.15   **a.** The fastest speed was 150 miles per hour.
b. The slowest speed driven by a male was 55 miles per hour.
c. 1/4 of the females reported having driven at 95 miles per hour or faster. Notice that 95 mph is the *upper quartile* for females. By definition, about 1/4 of the values in a data set are greater than the upper quartile.
d. 1/2 of the females reported having driven 89 mph or faster. Notice that 89 mph is the *median* value.
e. 1/2 of 102 = 51 females have driven 89 mph or faster.

Technical issue: The proportion of the data values that lie at or above the median may not always be exactly half, due to ties. For this example there were no values equal to the median of 89, so exactly half of the responses were indeed at or above the median of 89 mph. However, 9 of the females' responses tied with the upper quartile of 95 (see the dotplot in Figure 1.1, or the data on page 2). Therefore, it would be incorrect to say that exactly 1/4 of the values were at or above 95. In fact, 32 out of 102 = .314 were at or above 95 mph.

1.19   Neither caution applies. The magnitude of the difference is given in Case Study 1.6, and considering the number of men between the ages of 40 and 84 in the United States population, the given difference has practical importance. Because men were randomly assigned to take aspirin (or not) we can conclude that the correct direction of the cause and effect is that taking aspirin caused the reduction in heart attacks

1.22   The base rate or baseline risk is missing from the report. You need to know the base rate of cancer of the rectum for men to decide if the increased risk from drinking beer is large or small.

1.26   **a.** For someone 18 to 29 years old, the risk of seeing a ghost is 212/1525 = .139.

b. The margin of error is about $\dfrac{1}{\sqrt{n}} = \dfrac{1}{\sqrt{1525}} = .026$.

c. The interval is *sample proportion ± margin of error,* which is 0.139 ± 0.026, or 0.113 to 0.165.
Interpretation: It is likely that the actual percent of all people in this age group that has seen a ghost is between 11.3% and 16.5%.

1.28   **a.** This is an example of a self-selected or volunteer sample. Magazine readers voluntarily responded to the survey, and were not randomly selected.
b. These results may not represent the opinions of all readers of the magazine. The people who responded probably did so because they feel stronger about the issues of violence on television and physical discipline than the readers who did not respond. So, they may be likely to have a generally different point of view than those who did not respond.

CHAPTER 2
SELECTED SOLUTIONS

2.1   **a.** 4
b. A state in the United States.
c. $n = 50$.

2.3   **a.** Whole population.
b. Sample

2.5   **a.** Population parameter.
b. Sample statistic.
c. Sample statistic.

2.11   **a.** Categorical.
b. Quantitative.
c. Quantitative.
d. Categorical

2.12   **a.** Not ordinal. It's categorical.
b. Ordinal

2.14   **a.** Not continuous. For instance, a student could not miss 4.631 classes.

2.15   **a.** Explanatory variable is amount person walks or runs per day; response variable is the performance on the lung test.

2.16   **a.** Whether a person supports the smoking ban or not is a categorical variable.
b. Gains on verbal and math SATs are quantitative variables.
c. Smoker or not and Alzheimer sufferer or not are both categorical.

2.17   **a.** Gender and pulse rate.

2.19   This will differ for each student. One example where numerical summaries would make sense for an ordinal variable is the response to the question "What grade do you expect in this class? 4 = A, 3 = B, 2 = C, 1 = D, 0 = F." The mean numerical response is an expected class GPA.

2.22   **a.** $1427/2530 = .564$, or 56.4%.
b. $1 - (1427/2530) = .436$, or 43.6%.

2.23   **a.** $1700/2470 = .688$, or 68.8%.
b. $1056/1700 = .621$, or 62.1%.

2.24   **c.** Feeling overweight: $38/143 = .266$, or 26.6%; right weight: $99/143 = .692$, or 69.2%;   underweight: $6/143 = .042$, or 4.2%.

2.26   **a.** Explanatory variable is whether a person smoked or not. Response variable is whether they developed Alzheimer's or not.
Interpretation: In general, the explanatory variable may not provide a *cause and effect* explanation of the differences in the response variable. The idea is that knowing someone's value (or category) for the explanatory variable may provide some information about that individual's value (or category) for the response variable.

2.30   The pie chart may more effectively show that there are three age groups with large percentages, and it might be faster to read these percentages than with the bar chart. One problem, however, is that the age groups are shown in a circular pattern. This is likely to be an unnatural way to view the age. The bar chart gives a better sense of the distribution of ages because the ages are shown along a more natural horizontal number line.

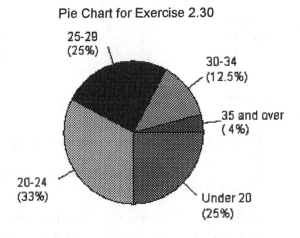

Pie Chart for Exercise 2.30

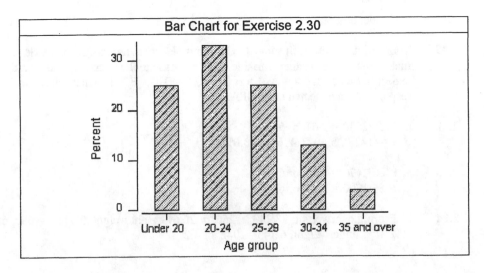

4

2.33   **a.** The fastest speed was 150 miles per hour.
b. The slowest speed driven by a male was 55 miles per hour.
c. 1/4 of the females reported having driven at 95 miles per hour or faster. Notice that 95 mph is the *upper quartile* for females. By definition, about 1/4 of the values in a data set are greater than the upper quartile.
d. About 1/2 of the females reported having driven 89 mph or faster. Notice that 89 mph is the *median* value.
e. About 1/2 of 102 = 51 females have driven 89 mph or faster.

2.34   **a.** The median value is 110 mph for males, compared to 89 mph for females.
b. The spread is about the same for the two sexes. The spread of the extremes is 150–55 = 95 mph for the males, compared to 130 – 30 = 100 mph for the females. The spread of the quartiles is slightly greater for males (120 – 95 = 25 for males, compared to 95-80 = 15 for females.)

2.37   **a.** The dataset is skewed to the right (it stretches in that direction).
b. 13 ear pierces looks to be an outlier because it is separate from the bulk of the data.
c. 2 ear pierces was the most reported value. About 44 or so women said they had this many ear pierces.
d. About 32 or so women said they had 4 ear pierces.

2.39   **a.** The dataset looks approximately symmetric and bell-shaped.
b. The highest temperature is 92°F.
c. The lowest temperature is 64°F.
d. 5/20 = .25, which is 25%.

2.44   Yes, a stem-and-leaf plot provides sufficient information to determine whether a dataset contains an outlier. Because all individual values are shown, it is possible to see whether any values are inconsistent with the bulk of the data.

2.46   **a.** Histogram is better than a boxplot for evaluating shape.
b. A boxplot is useful for identifying outliers, evaluating spread, and for comparing groups.

2.48   Skewed to the left. Along a number line, values stretch more toward the left (small values).

2.50   **a.** Mean = 74.33; Median = 74. The sample size ($n = 6$) is even, so the median is the average of the middle two values (72 and 76).
b. Mean = 25; Median = 7.To find the median, write the data in order from smallest to largest. Ordered data = 2, 6, 7, 10, 100. The middle value = 7.

2.52   **a.** Range = Maximum – Minimum = 225 –123 = 102 lbs.
b. IQR = Q3 – Q1 = 190 –155 = 45 lbs.
c. About 50%.. The given interval is from Q1 to Q3. By definition, this interval describes the middle 50% of the data values.

2.53 **a.** 12 letters.

2.54 **d.** $1.5 \times IQR = 1.5 \times (Q_3 - Q_1) = 1.5 \times (129.5 - 114) = 15.5$. A number will be considered an outlier if it is either less than $114 - 23.25 = 90.75$ or greater than $129.5 + 23.25 = 152.75$. No values fit this criterion, so there are no outliers.

2.59 The median annual rainfall in Davis, CA is 16.72 inches and the mean is 18.62 inches. The data values vary from 6.14 inches (in 1965) to 37.42 inches (in 1982). Although not an extreme outlier, the 1982 value is separated somewhat from the other values. The 1982 value of 37.42 inches is about 6 inches more than the next highest total, which occurred in 1981. It is interesting to note that the two highest values were in consecutive years.

2.62 Although the raw data are not available, we can determine that the median is somewhere between 21 and 25 words. There are $n = 600$ sentences, so the median occurs between the 300th and 301st observations in the ordered data. The total number of sentences with 20 or fewer words is the sum of the frequencies for categories up to and including the 16 to 20 words category. This is $(3+27+71+113) = 224$ sentences. There are 107 sentences in the 21 to 25 words category, so there are $224+107 = 331$ sentences with 25 or fewer words, The 300th and 301st values must be somewhere between 21 and 25 words.
Each quartile is the average of the 150th and 151st value from the appropriate side of the ordered data. Using the same reasoning that we did for the median, the first quartile must be somewhere between 16 and 20 words, and the third quartile is somewhere between 31 and 35 words. As a result, the *IQR* might be as low as $31-20=11$ words or as high as $35-16= 19$ words.
The exact values of the minimum and maximum aren't given, but the minimum may be about 3 or so and the maximum might be about 57, the range is likely to be somewhere around $57-3=54$.

2.67 *Tip:* For guidance on creating the five-number summary, see Examples 2.14 and 2.15 on pages 43-45. One quick way to order the data (necessary for finding the five-number summary) is to first create a stem and leaf plot.

There were $n=60$ ages, so the lower quartile is the median of the 30 lowest ages and the upper quartile is the median of the 30 highest ages. The five-number is shown below.

	CEO ages (years)		
Median		50	
Quartiles	45.5		57
Extremes	32		74

The five-number summary shows that the median age of the 60 CEOs of small companies is 50 years. The middle ½ of the CEOs have ages between 45.5 and 57 years. The youngest CEO is 32 years old. The oldest CEO is 74 years old.

2.71   This will differ for each student. One example is that a person 80 years old would be an outlier at a traditional college, but would not be an outlier at a retirement home.

2.72   You can not say whether this value is an outlier. You need to know whether it is the right hand-span measurement of the male author or of the female author.

2.76   *Tip:* Use the empirical rule givn at the bottom of page 52.
a. Mean ± St. Dev is 7 ± 1.7, or 5.3 to 8.7.
b. Mean ± 2 St. Dev is 7 ± (2)(1.7), or 3.6 to 10.4.

2.78   **a.** $z = \dfrac{\text{Value - Mean}}{\text{std.dev.}} = \dfrac{200 - 170}{20} = 1.5.$
Interpretation: A weight of 200 pounds is 1.5 standard deviations above the mean weight.

2.79   **a.** Mean =20; Standard deviation = 1.581.
Calculation of the standard deviation is as follows:

$$s = \sqrt{\frac{(18-20)^2 + (19-20)^2 + (20-20)^2 + (21-20)^2 + (22-20)^2}{5-1}}$$
$$= \sqrt{\frac{10}{4}} = \sqrt{2.5}$$

2.80   **a.** Range = Maximum – Minimum = 98 – 41 = 57.
b. Standard deviation ≈ Range/6 = 57/6 = 9.5.

2.82   *Tip:* For guidance, see Example 2.19 on page 53 of the text.

The Empirical Rule says that 68% of values fall within 1 standard deviation of the mean, 95% fall within 2 standard deviations of the mean, and 99.7% fall within 3 standard deviations of the mean. Of the 103 hand-span measurements for women, 74 or 72% are within 1 standard deviation of the mean (18.2 to 21.8 cm). 100 of the 103 or 97% are within 2 standard deviations. 101 of the 103 or 98% are within 3 standard deviations. The data seem to fit pretty well with the Empirical Rule.

2.83   **a.** $\bar{x} = 123$
b. $s^2 = 208.857.$
Calculation is $s^2 = \dfrac{\sum (x_i - \bar{x})^2}{n-1} =$
$\dfrac{(110-113)^2 + (123-123)^2 + \ldots + (122-123)^2}{8-1} = \dfrac{1462}{7} = 208.857$

2.86 **a.** A 52-centimeter head circumference will not occur often, but it will occur. The value 52 is 2 standard deviations below the mean ($z = \dfrac{\text{value - mean}}{\text{s.d.}} = \dfrac{52 - 56}{2} = -2$). This is at the lower end of the interval that describes about 95% of the values. Thus only about 2.5% of male head circumferences are smaller.

2. 90 **a.** The First Ladies constitute a population rather than a sample. They lived in unique circumstances, so it is hard to view these women as a representative sample from any larger population. And, they can't be considered to be a sample from a larger population of First Ladies because future First Ladies will have different circumstances affecting life expectancy.

b. If the First Ladies are viewed as a population, the population standard deviation is $\sigma = 14.76$ years. In Excel, this can be found with the command "=STDEVP( )" and many calculators have a key for the population standard deviation. See the technical note on page 52 of the text for a discussion of the population standard deviation. (If the argument is made in part (a) that the First Ladies constitute a sample, the correct answer here is that the sample standard deviation is $s = 14.97$ years.)

2.94 **a.** If the two possible outliers are ignored, the data appear to be more or less bell-shaped so the Empirical Rule should hold.

b. *Tip:* For guidance, see the section titled "The Empirical Rule, the Standard Deviation, and the Range" on page 54.

The Empirical Rule implies that the range should span about 4 to 6 standard deviations. About 95% of the data will be within 2 standard deviations (plus or minus) of the mean and about 99.7% of a data set should be within 3 standard deviations (plus or minus) of the mean. Here, *range = maximum − minimum* = 23.25 − 12.5 = 10.75 cm. This span is equal to 10.75/1.8 = 5.97 standard deviations so it is consistent with the Empirical Rule.

2.98 **a.** $z = \dfrac{\text{value − mean}}{\text{standard deviation}} = \dfrac{450 - 500}{100} = -0.5$, and the proportion below is .3085.

Excel Tip: The Excel command is NORMDIST(450,500,100,1) to find the proportion directly. Or, you can find the z-score and use NORMSDIST(−0.5).

b. $z = \dfrac{\text{value − mean}}{\text{standard deviation}} = \dfrac{36.5 - 34}{1} = 2.5$, and the proportion below is .9938.

Excel Tip: The Excel command is NORMDIST(36.5,34,1,1) to find the proportion directly. Or, you can find the z-score and use NORMSDIST(2.5).

2.100 The only possible set of numbers is {50, 50, 50, 50, 50, 50, 50}. A standard deviation of 0 can only occur if there is no variability among the data values.

2.103   **a.** The mean is 51.47 years and the sample standard deviation is $s = 8.92$ years.

Note: If this batch of data is viewed as a population rather than a sample, the standard deviation is 8.85 years. See the technical note on page 52 of the text for an explanation of the difference between sample and population standard deviations.

b. Range = Maximum − Minimum = $74 - 32 = 42$ years. This is a span of $42 / 8.92 = 4.7$ standard deviations, so the stated relationship between range and standard deviation does hold for the data.

c. For the youngest CEO, $z = \dfrac{\text{observed value} - \text{mean}}{\text{standard deviaiton}} = \dfrac{32 - 51.47}{8.92} = -2.18$.

For the oldest CEO, $z = \dfrac{74 - 51.47}{8.92} = 2.53$.

Remember that a z-score measures the number of standard deviations a value is from the mean. These values are about what you would expect because the Empirical Rule states that about 95% of the values fall within 2 standard deviations of the mean, and 99.7% of the values fall within 3 standard deviations of the mean. So, z-scores for the lowest and highest values are often somewhere between 2 and 3 in absolute magnitude.

2.110   The answers will differ for each student.
a. Most may prefer the data value to be near the average. If the data value were an outlier, the number of children would be excessive, not something most would want (although some may prefer this).
b. An outlier on the high side seems preferable. Most would want to make more money than everyone else does.

2.111   **a.** Telephone exchange is a categorical variable. Even though it's a numerical value, the numbers have no meaning or natural ordering.
b. Number of telephones is a quantitative variable.

2.113   **a.** Yes, a variable can be both explanatory and categorical. The phrase "explanatory variable" means that the variable might influence a response variable, and there is no restriction concerning whether the explanatory variable is categorical or quantitative (or ordinal). For an example, consider Example 2.2 on page 20 of the text, in which type of nighttime lighting is both a categorical and an explanatory variable.
b. No, a variable cannot be both continuous and ordinal. The term "ordinal variable" is used when the raw data are ordered categories while "continuous" means that all values in an interval are possible. [A restriction of ordinal numbers is that all possible values can be counted. For a continuous variable, however, all possible values in an interval cannot be counted. There always are an infinite number of values between any two points in the interval so it's impossible to determine what "exact" value is second, third, and so on.]

2.117   **a.** The heights of all of the children in an elementary school will have a larger standard deviation because there will be a wide variety of different aged students included. This will lead to a wide variety of heights.
Tip: It may help to think about the range of the data rather than the standard deviation. In general, the larger the range, the larger the standard deviation, especially when the measurements are of the same type.

2.119   **a.** Blood pressure and amount of beer consumed per week must be measured for each person.

b. Whether or not the person has colon cancer and his or her average daily calories from protein must be recorded for each person.

2.122   Do the students who studied the most last week tend to be the students with the highest grade point averages?
Tip: To answer questions 2.121 to 2.124, first determine whether the variable(s) are categorical or quantitative, or one of each. That will narrow down the possibilities to one of two questions. Think about each of those two questions in the context given, and it should be clear which is more interesting. Then phrase the question to fit the context. For instance, in Exercise 2.122, both variables are quantitative a question about two quantitative variables would be correct..

CHAPTER 3
SELECTED SOLUTIONS

3.3   **a.** Yes. Women in the psychology class probably will have heights similar to the heights of other women at the college.
b. No. Parents of children in daycare are likely to have different opinions than other adults in the state.

3.4   **a.** Population of interest = all registered voters in the community.

3.9   *Tip:* See pages 74-75 for a discussion of the types of bias.
c. Nonresponse bias.

3.11 This answer will differ for each student. There are many situations in which the available resources would not permit a census, and also there are many situations in which the process of taking the necessary measurements damages the product so a census would not be done. For instance, a manufacturer of potato chips would not test the quality of its product by examining the contents of every bag it produced.

3.13 *Tip:* See pages 74-75 for a discussion of the three types of bias. The choices are *selection bias*, which has to do with *how* the sample is selected; *non-response bias*, which has to do with whether the entire sample is contacted and responds; and *response bias*, which has to do with whether the responses received are honest and unbiased.

   a. Selection bias would be introduced because the sample would not be representative of the population of interest. The sample would be representative of all registered automobile owners, not all homeowners.
   b. Non-response bias would be introduced because some people will not fill out and mail back the survey. This is a common problem with mail surveys.

3.15 **a.** No, the "Fundamental Rule for Using Data for Inference" does not hold. In professional basketball, women get paid much less than men. This is not representative of all careers is which men and women have equivalent jobs.
b. Yes, the "Fundamental Rule for Using Data for Inference" holds. The pulse rates of students in a statistics class at a large university are probably representative of the pulse rates of all college-age people.

3.17 No, this would not be a simple random sample because not all combinations of four songs are equally likely. For example, it would not be possible with this plan to listen to four songs that all were on the same CD. But, in a simple random sampling plan this is a possible sample (and would have the same chance to be the sample as any other group of four songs).

3.19   *Tip:* The margin of error formula is on page 76.

Margin of error $=\dfrac{1}{\sqrt{n}}=\dfrac{1}{\sqrt{5000}}=.014$. As a percent, $.014\times100\%=1.4\%$.

Interpretation: For a 95% of all random samples of size n = 5000, the sample percentage will be within 1.4% of the population percentage.

3.24   *Tip* For guidance on calculating and interpreting confidence intervals, study Examples 3.3, 3.4, and 3.5 on pages 77-78.

b. For the proportion, the confidence interval is $.40\pm\dfrac{1}{\sqrt{5000}}$, which is $.40\pm.032$.

For the percentage, the confidence interval **is** 40% ± 3.2%, or 36.8% to 43.2%.

3.28   *Tip:* For guidance on calculating and interpreting confidence intervals, study Examples 3.3, 3.4, and 3.5 on pages 77-78.

a. The sample proportion is .49 and the margin of error, expressed as a proportion, is .03. The interval, calculated as *sample proportion* ± *margin of error*, is .49 ± .03, which is .46 to .52.
b. The sample proportion is .47 and the margin of error, expressed as a proportion, is .03.The interval, calculated as *sample proportion* ± *margin of error*, is.47 ± .03 = .44 to .50.
c. No, we cannot conclude that a clear majority of the population has either opinion. Note that the intervals computed in the previous two parts both contain .50, so it's possible that about 50% of the population has each opinion

3.37   **a.** Answers will vary according to method. One possible answer is 15, 33, 10, 42, 41, 17. This comes from taking two digits at time and discarding numbers not between 01 and 49. Another possible answer is 15, 23, 20, 21, 29, 05. This comes from selecting two digits at a time, using 01 to 49 as is, subtracting 50 from numbers 51 to 99, and discarding 00 and 50.
b. It doesn't matter because every number (and every set of six numbers) has the same chance of occurring in each drawing.

3.40   Simple random sample. It is basically a lottery method.

3.43   **a.** Stratified sample: Use the 3 types of schools as strata. Create a list of all students for each of the 3 strata. Draw a simple random sample from each of the 3 lists.
b. Cluster sample: Use individual schools or individual classes as clusters. Take a random sample of clusters, measure all students in those clusters.
c. Simple random sample: Obtain a list of all students in the classes at all schools; take a simple random sample from that combined list.

3.46   Random digit dialing is more like a cluster sample because a sample of exchanges is found and then only numbers within those exchanges are sampled. It would be more like a stratified sample if numbers were sampled within every possible exchange.

3.48   **a.** All local taxpayers.
b. Parents of schoolchildren in the local schools.

3.52   **a.** The sampling frame is the collection of 60,000 dentists who subscribe to one or both of the two dental magazines. The subscription lists of these two magazines do not include all dentists in the population, and this could create a bias if the subscribers to the magazines are different than non-subscribers when it comes to using Bristol Myers products. This could be the situation, for instance, if Bristol Myers frequently advertises in the magazines.
b. Non-response is a serious problem here because only 1,983 dentists out of 10,000 selected responded.
c. They could have sent a reminder to those dentists who had not responded, reminding them to fill out the survey, or could have sent them another copy of the survey form. They could have phoned the dentists if their phone numbers were also available.

3.61   Anonymous testing. The test results are not linked to the person's name.

3.64   This will differ for each student. Any 2 questions in which one changes the way respondents would think about the other can be used. An example: "Are you aware that over 30% of homeless people in this city are mothers with children?" and "Do you think more public money should be used to help homeless people?"

3.66   Confidentiality and anonymity, and desire to please.

3.69   **a.** Open-form.
b. Answers may vary. The poll could be influenced by the timing because more people may have felt it was necessary to pay tribute to Elvis considering it was the 25th anniversary of his death. Because his name was probably in the media due to the anniversary, more people may have recalled his name.
c. Answers may vary. Probably lower considering the timing of the poll. Without all of the publicity, his name may not have had as many votes.

3.76   Answers may vary. Any ordering of these 10 two digit numbers will suffice: 00, 07, 15, 19, 24, 33, 44, 51, 65, and 99. These are the numbers corresponding to the numbered locations of the sample selected. One possible answer is 00071 51924 33445 16599.

3.79   This will differ for each student.
a. Self-selected sample: Put an ad in the local paper asking people to fill out the survey.
b. Deliberate bias: Send a questionnaire with wording such as "Don't you agree that there is too much trash in our streets and that more public trash containers are needed?"

3.85   a. The population of interest is the population of all students at the university.
b. The sampling frame is the collection of all students enrolled in statistics classes at the time of the survey.
c. The sample is the 500 students to whom the survey was mailed.

3.87   To determine if the increase observed in the samples represents a real increase in the population, sample size or margin of error must be provided for each survey. The 20% versus 25% may be within the margin of error for the surveys.

3.89   The "Quickie Poll" would probably be most representative and fastest.

3.91   Non-response bias was the most problematic in that survey. Only 34% of the scientists responded and the ones who did were typically white males over the age of 50. Other scientists who did not respond may feel differently about the topic.

3.92   b. Nonresponse bias: Send the survey to a legitimate random sample, but make the questions so outrageous that only those who support the position would respond; others would not take it seriously.

3.96   *Tip:* Remember that the Fundamental Rule for Using Data for Inference focuses on whether the sample is representative for the *question of interest*. In this case, the question of interest is what proportion of *those who vote in November* will vote for Senator Feinstein, so the sample should be representative of that population.

No, the opinions of the 642 voters considered likely to vote are probably more representative of the population of voters who will participate in the Nov. 7 election.

3.99   *Tip:* The margin of error formula is given on page 76. Table 3.1 on page 79 provides information about how margin of error is related to sample size.

For GOP voters within the sample, the margin of error would be larger because the sample size is smaller than for the entire sample.

3.101   a. The margin of error for arts and humanities is $\dfrac{1}{\sqrt{n}} = \dfrac{1}{\sqrt{166}} = .078$, or 7.8%.

The confidence interval is *Sample percentage* $\pm$ *Margin of error*, which is 66% $\pm$ 7.8% or 58.2% to 73.8%. Expressed as an interval for a population proportion, the answer is $.66 \pm .078$ or .582 to .738.

b. The margin of error for engineering and sciences is $\dfrac{1}{\sqrt{n}} = \dfrac{1}{\sqrt{229}} = .066$, or 6.6%.

The confidence interval is *Sample percentage* $\pm$ *Margin of error*, which is 38% $\pm$ 6.6% or 31.4% to 44.6%. Expressed as an interval for a population proportion, the answer is $.38 \pm .066$ or .314 to .446.

CHAPTER 4
SELECTED SOLUTIONS

4.3   **c.** Observational study because the students picked their won groups. The teacher did not assign students to groups.

4.4   **a.** Explanatory variable is the mother's height; response variable is daughter's height.

4.7   *Tip*: The differences between a randomized experiment and an observational study are described on page 118.

  a. Randomized experiment.
  b. Observational study.
  c. Randomized experiment.
  d. Observational study.

4.9   *Tip:* In general, a "unit" is the smallest entity that can either receive a separate treatment, or for which individual information is obtained. In this case, individual plants can be raised in sun or shade, but, for instance, individual tomatoes cannot.

  a. A randomized experiment is probably not possible here. Although it would be possible to randomly assign some people to long-term meditation, it would be hard to be sure that participants complied. Also, some assigned to the "no meditation" group may really want to meditate and would do so anyway. It would be much more practical to do an observational study in this situation.
  b. Yes, a randomized experiment could be done. People could be randomized to two groups—one that takes the special training program and one that does not. Afterward, the standardized test scores of the two groups could be compared.

4.10   **a.** The explanatory variable is whether or not a person participated in long-term meditation and the response variable is blood pressure.

4.11   **a.** This will differ for each student. Some possible answers: One possible confounding variable is diet. People who practice long-term meditation may be more likely to follow a vegetarian diet, and this may affect blood pressure.

4.20   **a.** Yes, because the sugar tablet is designed to look and taste like vitamin C.
  c. No, because the researchers know the treatment assignment for each participant.

4.25   This is a completely randomized design because each child was randomly assigned to a different gym group (treatment). There were no natural matches of children or treatments and no blocks were established for the children, such as age groups.

4.29   **a.** This experiment was single-blind because the technicians who read the meters did not know the rate plan for a particular customer. The customers did know which rate plan they had. It was on their bill.

Tip: An experiment is single-blind if either the participants or those who are taking the measurements, but not both, are unaware of who has which treatment.

4.30   **a.** This was a "matched pairs" design because the 100 customers who received the special rates were matched with 100 other customers with similar electrical use and household size.

4.31   **a.** The explanatory variable is whether or not special rates were offered and the response variable is electricity use during peak hours.

4.32   **a.** A control group was used. The researchers measured electrical use of 100 customers who did not receive the special rates.

4.38   **a.** Yes, because we are looking into the future of the different jobs economics majors had 10 years after graduation.
b. No, because the participants are not being asked to recall any past events.
c. No, because there is no control group (for instance, students without this degree).

4.42   **a.** This was an observational study because 50 couples who owned cats or dogs were compared with 50 couples who did not. Couples were not assigned to own a pet or not. It might be considered to be a case-control study, with pet owners as cases and non-owners as controls. However, typically a case-control study is one for which the case/control distinction is for the response variable and in this study pet ownership was the explanatory variable.
b. The explanatory variable was whether or not the couple owned a pet and the response variables were marriage satisfaction and stress levels.
c. This will differ for each student. The careers of the couple could be confounding variables. People who work long hours and are already very stressed from work may not have enough time to take care of a pet. Their stressful careers may also make them less likely to have a satisfying marriage.

4.46   *Tip:* Interacting variables are discussed on page 138.

a. Interacting variables. The amount of difference between the average grade point averages of males and females depends on their living situation.

4.49   Response variable is the amount of weight loss (or gain); explanatory variable is whether the medication is being taken or not; interacting variable is sex of individual.

4.53   **a.** Yes. The participants may not have good memories of lifelong exposure, and may be inclined to create memories of exposure if they have lung problems.
b. Yes. Because this is an observational study, confounding is always a concern. However, the most obvious cause for lung problems is controlled because none of the participants have ever smoked, so smoking is not a confounding variable.
c. No. The participants are not in an experiment so the problem so this won't be a problem.

4.57   **c.** Relying on memory is likely to be a problem. It would be hard for people to accurately remember the fat content of their childhood diet.
Confounding variables also are likely to be a problem. For instance, people who have high fat diets might exercise less than those with low fat diets. If so, it would be difficult to separate the effects on heart disease of diet and exercise.

4.60   This was an observational study because the women were asked about their use of hormone therapy, so the researchers only observed the already existing hormone therapy groups. If it had been a randomized experiment, the women would have been randomly assigned to take hormones or not.

4.63   The increased risks of 8% and 1% are from a comparison with the women who took no hormones.

4.67   This is an example of extending results inappropriately. If women today take lower levels of hormones than the women in the study, these results may not apply to women currently on hormone therapy.

4.72   This is an example of interacting variables. The effect on self-esteem of thinking about their bad hair is different for men than for women.

4.78   *Tip:* In general, a "unit" is the smallest entity that can either receive a separate treatment, or for which individual information is obtained. In this case, individual plants can be raised in sun or shade, but, for instance, individual tomatoes cannot.

a. The individual unit is a tomato plant. The two variables measured were the number of tomatoes produced and whether the tomato plant was raised in full sunlight or partial shade.

4.80   **a.** Yes, a placebo and a double-blind procedure can be present in the same study. An example is the testing of a new medication given in pill form. A placebo pill that looks like the (new) experimental pill could be used. If neither the patient nor the evaluator of the patient know which pill the patient is taking, the study is double-blind.

b. Yes. In a case-control study, which is basically a retrospective observational study, pairing can be done by matching each case with a similar control.

c. No, this is not possible. A case control study is a type of observational study, so by definition, treatments or conditions are not assigned by the researchers Random assignment of treatment is done in randomized experiments.

4.87   **a.** A random sample of the electric company's customers was used, so the results can be extended to all of the company's customers.

CHAPTER 5
SELECTED SOLUTIONS

5.1 **a.** Negative, because coordination will decrease when amount of alcohol consumed is increased.
b. No association would be expected between height and grade point average.

5.2 **a.** Negative association. As percentage taking the test increases, average math SAT decreases.
b. More or less linear. There could be a slight curvature but a straight line appears to be a suitable description of the pattern.
c. Highest math SAT was around 600; about 5%, perhaps fewer, took the test in that state.
d. Lowest math SAT was around 475; about 85% took the test in that state.

5.3 **a.** Appropriate because both variables are quantitative.

5.7 **a.** The speed of the car is the explanatory variable and stopping distance is the response variable.
b. There is a positive association that appears to be curvilinear.

Figure for Exercise 5.7b

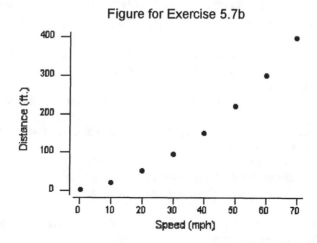

5.9 **a.** Average weight = −250 + 6(70) = −250 + 420 = 170 lbs.
b. Average weight increases 6 pounds for each 1-inch increase in height.
Tip: See the final bullet on page 160 for description of how to interpret the slope.

5.11   **b.** Average Math average $= 575 - 1.11(8) = 575 - 8.88 = 566.12$.

c. Residual $=$ Actual y – Predicted $y = y - \hat{y} = 573 - 566.12 = 6.88$.

5.12   This is a deterministic relationship because it holds exactly in all situations. There is never variation from the given equation.

5.14   **a.** For each one-centimeter increase in handspan, average height increases 0.7 inches.

b. $\hat{y} = 51.1 + 0.7(20) = 65.1 \, \text{in}$.

c. Residual $=$ Actual y – Predicted $y = y - \hat{y} = 66.5 - 65.1 = 1.4 \, \text{in}$.

5.19   *Tip:* Use Example 5.8 on page 164 of the text for guidance. To begin the calculations, find $\hat{y}$ at each value of x in the dataset. Do this for each line:

X	1	2	3	4
Y	4	10	14	16
$\hat{y}$ for Line 1 $= 3+3x$	6	9	12	15
$\hat{y}$ for Line 2 $= 1+4x$	5	9	13	17

a. Line 1, $SSE = (4-6)^2 + (10-9)^2 + (14-12)^2 + (16-15)^2 = 10$.

Line 2, $SSE = (4-5)^2 + (10-9)^2 + (14-13)^2 + (16-17)^2 = 4$.

b. Line 2 is better because it has a smaller sum of squared errors.

5.22   The two variables are not related. Assuming the relationship is not curvilinear, the pattern is that the average number picked is about the same regardless of response to fastest ever driven.

Tip: See Figure 5.13 on page 168 of the text for an example of this pattern.

5.23   **a.** As length increases, chest girth increases. The correlation value (r = 0.82) indicates a positive association.

b. The value 0.82 is indicates a strong association. The closer the correlation value is to 1 (in absolute value), the stronger the association.

c. *Tip:* See the third paragraph of Section 5.3 on pages 165-166.

The correlation would still be 0.82. The value of correlation is not changed if either or both variables are rescaled to different units.

5.26   *Tip:* See the third paragraph of Section 5.3 on pages 165-166.

The correlation would still be $r = 0.95$. A correlation value doesn't change when we change the measurement scale of one or both of the variables.

5.29   **a.** Graph 2 shows the strongest relationship while Graph 3 shows the weakest.

5.31   **b.** Positive because big cities will have many of each and small towns will have few of each.

    c. Negative because strength decreases as age increases.

5.40   **a.** The estimated distance is $-45 + 5.7(80) = 411\,\text{ft}$. This is only slightly more than the distance given for 70 mph, so it is probably too low.

    b. Extending the pattern of the scatterplot leads to an estimate of a little more than 500 feet.

    Tip: It is usually problematic to use a regression equation to make estimates or predictions beyond the range of the x values in the data used to create the equation. There is no guarantee that the same relationship will continue to hold beyond that range.

5.42   The negative correlation might occur due to inappropriately combining groups (males and females). Perhaps females, who are generally shorter than males, did better on the memorization test

    For the data in the following example sketch, the overall correlation is -0.685, but within each gender the correlation is close to 0.

Figure for Exercise 5.42

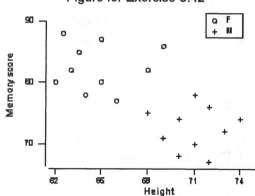

5.48   Sales of both will tend to be high in the colder months and low in the warmer months.

5.49   Sex of the respondent. Females generally have more ear pierces and tend to be shorter than females. So, over the whole dataset, it will appear that as height increases the number of ear pierces decreases.

    Note: With statistical software, it can be found that for males, the correlation between height and ear pierces is $r = -0.022$. For females, the correlation is $r = -0.014$. These values indicate that there is almost zero correlation between number of ear pierces and height within each gender.

5.68   **a.** For a woman who weighs 140 pounds, predicted ideal weight is
$\hat{y} = 44 + 0.6(140) = 128\,\text{lbs}$.

For a man who weighs 140 pounds, predicted ideal weight is
$\hat{y} = 53 + 0.7(140) = 151\,\text{lbs}$.

The predictions indicate that the average woman who weighs 140 lbs. would like to weigh 12 lbs. less, while the average man who weighs 140 lbs. would like to weigh 11 lbs. more.

b. No, the intercepts do not have logical physical interpretations in this example because people cannot weigh 0 pounds. Remember that an intercept gives the value of y when x=0.

c. Yes, the slopes have a logical interpretation. For each gender, the slope gives the average increase in reported ideal weight for each one pound increase in actual weight.

Interpretation: If two individuals differ by one pound, they are expected to differ by about 0.6 (for women) or 0.7 (for men) pounds in their reported ideal weight.

5.70   **b.** The correlation between price and pages is $r = -0.312$.

c. For hardcover books, the correlation is $r = 0.348$.
For softcover books, the correlation is $r = 0.637$.

5.72   **a.** The regression equation is $\hat{y} = 44.39 - 0.02095\,year$.

For 2010, the estimated value is $44.39 - 0.02095(2010) = 2.28$.

b. The slope is -0.02095, which means that every year the average persons per household decreases by 0.02095 on average, or by about 0.2 persons per 10 year census cycle.

5.80   **b.** The regression equation is $diff = -52.5 + 0.312\,Actual$.

For a 150-pound man (*actual = 150*), the predicted difference is
$diff\ {-}52.5 + 0.312(150) = -5.7\,\text{lbs}$.

On average, 150-pound men want to weight more than they do.

d. $r^2 = .353$, or 35.3%.

CHAPTER 6
SELECTED SOLUTIONS

6.1   **a.** $(1357 / 2057) \times 100\% = 64.3\%$. This is a row percentage. It is calculated as the percentage of the total number in a row of the table.
b. $(83 / 548) \times 100\% = 15.1\%$. This is a column percentage. It is calculated as the percentage of the total number in column of the table.
c. $(285 / 2858) \times 100\% = 10.0\%$

6.3   **b.** $(170/300) \times 100\% = 56.7\%$. This means that of the 300 females who auditioned, 56.7% were freshman.

6.5   *Tip:* A two-way table is only appropriate for summarizing two categorical or ordinal variables. With ordinal variables, sometimes a numerical summary may be preferable, but a two-way table is still appropriate.
a. Yes, both variables are categorical.
c. No, both variables are quantitative.

6.6   No, it is not sufficient. Totals are given for categories of each variable but counts for combinations are not provided. We do not know how many of the men were Democrats and how many were Republicans nor do we know how many women were Democrats and how many were Republicans

6.9   **a.**

	Heart disease	No heart disease	Total
No anger	8	191	199
Most anger	59	500	559
Total	67	691	758

b. Percentage with heart disease = $(8/199) \times 100\% = 4.0\%$ among men with no anger symptoms.
c. Percentage with heart disease = $(59/559) \times 100\% = 10.6\%$ among men with most anger symptoms.
Tip: Remember that it is best to put the explanatory variable as the row variable, and the response variable as the column variable. That makes it easier to find the percentages that are usually of interest, which are the percentages with a certain response, for each category of the explanatory variable. When the table is constructed as advised here, those percentages of interest are the row percentages, as they are in parts (b) and (c) of this problem.

6.12   **a.** 1.0. This occurs when the risk is the same in each category.
Tip: The formula for relative risk is given on page 198 of the text.

6.13 **a.** Risk = Number in category/Total number = 10/100 = .10, which also could be expressed as 10%.

6.14 **a.** Relative risk =Risk in drug group/Risk in placebo group = $\dfrac{10/100}{5/100} = 2$.

6.15 **a.** Odds ratio = $\dfrac{10/90}{5/95} = 2.11$.

Tip: See page 200 for an example of how to compute an odds ratio. Remember that odds involve a comparison of the chances of the two outcomes (side effect or not in this case

6.19 Relative risk = 1.4. To find this, start with the equation *Increase in risk* = (*Relative risk* – 1) × 100% , substitute 40% for *Increase in risk*, and solve for *Relative risk*.

6.22 **a.** Relative risk = $\dfrac{\text{Risk for "most anger" group}}{\text{Risk for "no anger" group}} = \dfrac{59/559}{8/199} = \dfrac{.106}{.04} = 2.65$

Equivalently, the percentages determined for Exercise 6.9 parts (b) and (c) can be used. If so, the calculation is 10.6% / 4% = 2.65.

b. Percentage increase in risk $= \dfrac{\text{Difference in risks}}{\text{Baseline risk}} \times 100\% = \dfrac{10.6 - 4}{4} \times 100\% = 165\%$.

Equivalently, percentage increase = (Relative risk–1)×100% = (2.65–1)×100% = 165%.

6.25 **a.** For age 18 to 29: (212/1525) × 100% = 13.9% report having seen a ghost.
For age 30 or over: (465/4377) × 100% = 10.6% report having seen a ghost.

b. Relative risk $= \dfrac{\text{Risk for age 18 to 29}}{\text{Risk for age 30 or more}} = \dfrac{.139}{.106} = 1.31$.

Adults under 30 years old are 1.31 times as likely to report having seen a ghost as adults 30 years old or older.
Tip: It is easier to interpret relative risks greater than 1.0, so it makes sense to put the category with the lower risk in the denominator when computing a relative risk. One exception is if one category serves as the "baseline risk" then it should generally be used in the denominator even if it results in relative risk < 1.

6.31 Probably not, although it's possible. For Simpson's Paradox to hold the relationship between blood pressure and religious activity would need to be reversed when separate categories of a third variable are considered.

6.33 Some possible "third variables" that could explain the difference are occupation, overall amount of long-distance driving, and amount of nighttime driving. These variables are also somewhat connected to each other. Men may be more likely to have jobs that require long-distance driving. In general, men probably do more long-distance driving (leading to drowsiness at the wheel), and men probably do more nighttime driving.

6.37   **a.** The response variable is outcome of treatment (successful or not).
    c. Separate the patients into severity of depression groups. Then, compare the treatments within each separate group.

6.38   **a.** Null: There is no relationship between gender and opinion on the death penalty.
       Alternative: There is a relationship between gender and opinion on the death penalty.
    b. Because the p-value is small (less than .05), we can conclude that in the larger population there is a relationship between gender and opinion on the death penalty.

6.39

Gender	Oppose	Favor	Total
Male	$\dfrac{631 \times 409}{1308} = 197.3$	$\dfrac{631 \times 899}{1308} = 433.7$	631
Female	$\dfrac{677 \times 409}{1308} = 211.7$	$\dfrac{677 \times 899}{1308} = 465.3$	677
Total	409	899	1308

6.43   *Tip:* See the two bullets under Steps 4 and 5 on pages 210-211 for guidance on making a decision between the hypotheses.

    b. Do not reject H_0. The p-value is not less than .05, the usual standard for rejecting the null hypothesis.
    f. Reject H_0 because the chi-square value is greater than 3.84.

6.46   **a.** Yes. By the luck of random sampling, the observed sample might show a relationship when none actually exists in the larger population. We will learn in Chapters 11 and 13 that this type of result is called a Type 1 error.
    b. Yes. By the luck of random sampling, the observed sample might not show a relationship when one actually exists in the larger population. We will learn in Chapters 12 and 13 that this type of result is called a Type 2 error, and the risk of such an error is influenced by the sample size.
    c. No. Presuming that calculations for a chi-square test are done correctly, the analysis of an observed sample in which there's no relationship will give the conclusion that the it is not a statistically significant relationship.

6.49   **a.** Null hypothesis: There is no relationship between gender and opinions about capital punishment.
       Alternative hypothesis: There is a relationship.
    b. The relationship is not statistically significant because p-value = .19 is greater than .05. The relationship in the sample did not provide enough evidence to conclude that there is a relationship in the population.

6.50   **a.** Chi-square statistic = 1.714.

The contingency table of *observed counts* is:

	Favor	Oppose	Total
Men	38	12	50
Women	32	18	50
Total	70	30	100

The table of expected counts is:

	Favor	Oppose	Total
Men	$\dfrac{50 \times 70}{100} = 35$	$50 - 35 = 15$	50
Women	$70 - 35 = 35$	$50 - 35 = 15$	50
Total	70	30	100

The chi-squared statistic =

$$\frac{(38-35)^2}{35} + \frac{(12-15)^2}{15} + \frac{(32-35)^2}{35} + \frac{(18-15)^2}{15} = .257 + .600 + .257 + .600 = 1.714$$

Tip: For a two-way table, the formula $\dfrac{\text{Row total} \times \text{Column total}}{\text{Total n}}$ only has to be used to determine the expected count for one cell. Other expected counts can be determined utilizing the fact that the row and column totals for the expected counts are the same as they are for the observed counts.

6.55   **a.** Yes, there appears to be a relationship. As the number of ear pierces increases, the percentage with a tattoo also increases.

Pierces	% with Tattoo
2 or less	7.4% (40/538)
3 or 4	13.4% (58/432)
5 or 6	27.6% (77/279)
7 or more	42.1% (53/126)

c. Among the 228 women with a tattoo, the number with 5 or more ear pierces is 77+53 = 130. The percentage is (120/228) × 100% = 57%.
Among the 1147 women who do not have a tattoo, the number with 5 or more ear pierces is 202+73 = 275 The percentage is (275/1147) × 100% = 24%.

d. Percentage with a tattoo = (228/1375) × 100% = 16.58%

e. Percentage with two or fewer pierces and no tattoo = (498/1375) × 100% = 36.22%.

26

6.57   **a.** *Tip:* Remember that it is best to put the explanatory variable as the row variable, and the response variable as the column variable.

	Lung cancer	Control	Total
Owned bird	98	101	199
Never owned bird	141	328	469
Total	239	429	668

b. Bird owners: 98/199 = .4925, or 49.25% have cancer.
   Never owned bird: 141/469 =.301, or 30.1% have cancer.

c. No, these risks cannot be used as baseline risks. This was a case control study in which the researchers purposely sampled more lung cancer patients than would naturally occur in a group of 668 people. The sample percentages falling into the cancer category are much higher than you would see in a random sample.

d. Relative risk $= \dfrac{\text{Risk for bird owners}}{\text{Risk for those who never owned bird}} = \dfrac{.4925}{.301} = 1.64$.

Tip: Remember that when there is a baseline risk, which in this example is the risk of lung cancer for those who never owned a bird, it should go in the denominator of the relative risk.

e. You would want to know "baseline" risk of lung cancer for people like yourself (similar age, smoking habits, etc.). That risk is probably small.

f. No, a causal connection cannot be established. This is an observational study so there may be confounding factors that explain the results. The "case control" sampling took age and sex into account, but did not take other variables, such as smoking habits, into account.

g. Compare the smoking habits of the bird owners and non-owners to see whether or not the bird owners generally smoke more.

6.61 Chi-square = 4.817 and p-value = .028. The relationship is statistically significant because the p-value is less than .05.

Minitab output is shown below (expected counts are shown below actual counts).

```
                    Minitab output for Exercise 6.61

               First      Two +      All

   Smoker         29         71        100
                38.74      61.26     100.00

   Nonsmoke      198        288        486
               188.26     297.74     486.00

   All           227        359        586
               227.00     359.00     586.00

   Chi-Square = 4.817, DF = 1, P-Value = 0.028

       Cell Contents --
                     Count
                     Exp Freq
```

The (almost) "by hand" calculation is as follows:

Step 1: Compute the expected counts:

	First cycle	2 or more cycles	Total
Smoker	$\dfrac{100 \times 227}{586} = 38.74$	$100 - 38.74 = 61.26$	100
Nonsmoker	$227 - 38.74 = 188.26$	$486 - 188.26 = 297.74$	486
Total	227	359	586

Notice that for a two-way table, the formula $\dfrac{\text{Row total} \times \text{Column total}}{\text{Total n}}$ only has to be used to determine the expected count for one cell. Other expected counts can be determined utilizing the fact that the row and column totals for the expected counts are the same as they are for the observed counts.

Step 2: Compute the chi-squared statistic:

$$= \frac{(29-38.74)^2}{38.74} + \frac{(71-61.26)^2}{61.26} + \frac{(198-188.26)^2}{188.26} + \frac{(288-297.74)^2}{297.74}$$
$$= 2.45 + 1.55 + 0.50 + 0.32 = 4.82$$

Step 3: Determine the p-value: In Excel, use CHIDIST(4.82,1), to find p-value = .028.

6.65 Using the approximate odds given in Exercise 6.64, the odds ratio is 24/8.5 = 2.82. The precise odds ratio is found as Odds ratio =

$$\frac{\text{odds for "no anger"}}{\text{odds for "most anger"}} = \frac{191/8}{500/597} = \frac{23.875}{8.475} = 2.817.$$

The odds of remaining free of heart disease versus getting heart disease for men with no anger are about 2.8 times the odds of those events for men with the most anger.

6.68 **a.** For men, the odds of being admitted to Program A are 400 to 250, or 1.6 to 1. (To get 1.6 to 1, divide both original counts by 250.)
For women applying to Program A, the odds are 50 to 25, or 2 to 1.
The odds ratio for women compared to men =2/1.6 = 1.25. The odds of being admitted for women are about 1.25 times what they are for men, so women have better odds.

b. For men, the odds of being admitted for the combined programs are 450 to 550, or about 0.8 to 1.
For women, the odds are 175 to 325, or about 0.54 to 1.
The odds ratio (women to men) is therefore about .54/.8 = .675. The odds of being admitted versus being denied admittance for women are about 2/3 of what they are for men, so women have worse odds of being admitted overall.

c. The last sentence of the part (a) solution makes it seem that the university favors women, while the last sentence of the part (b) solution makes it seem that the university favors males.

CHAPTER 7
SELECTED SOLUTIONS

7.1   <u>Random Circumstance:</u> Flight arrival time for a randomly selected flight on one of the top ten U.S. airlines during that time period.
  ➢   Flight arrives on time (or early) with probability .761
  ➢   Flight arrives late with probability .239

7.5   1000/125000 =1/125, or .008.

7.6   **c.** Yes. Valid probabilities are between 0 and 1 (including 0 and 1).
  d. No, because 1.25 > 1. Valid probabilities are between 0 and 1 (including 0 and 1).

7.9   **a.** The relative frequency interpretation of probability applies here. The probability was most likely determined by observing the number of Americans injured by lightning during a number of years and dividing this by the average population in those years.

  b. The personal interpretation of probability applies here. The probability was determined from the neighbor's previous experience with tomato plants and her knowledge of the soil, sunlight and other conditions where her plants are grown.

  Tip: When a random circumstance occurs only once, with unique conditions, associated probabilities are almost always personal probabilities. In part (b), if the neighbor routinely planted tomatoes of the same type, at the same time of year, in the same soil, and controlled other conditions as well, perhaps she would know the long run relative frequency of success and the stated probability would be a relative frequency one. But the way the question is worded implies that the situation is unique and not one that is being repeated frequently.

7.10   *Tip:* Notice that all three circumstances are repeatable situations, so the relative frequency interpretation of probability can be used to find the probabilities of the outcomes.

  For the first circumstance, Robin could repeatedly note whether or not her favorite song is playing when she first turns on the radio. The probability that her favorite song is playing is the number of times her favorite song is playing divided by the total number of days she did this.
  For the second circumstance, Robin could repeatedly note whether or not the traffic light was green when she arrived, and divide the number of times it was green by the total number of days she did this.
  For the third circumstance, Robin could repeatedly note whether or not she quickly found an empty parking spot in front of the building, and divide the number of times she found a good parking spot by the total number of times she did this.

7.12   An individual could determine his or her probability of winning this game by playing it a large number of times and recording how many games he or she won out of the total number of games played.

Tip: Remember that if a random circumstance is repeatable, a relative frequency probability of a particular outcome can be found by repeating the random circumstance and noting the long-run relative frequency of the outcome. In this problem, one important assumption is that the player's skill level does not change.

7.13   This will differ for each student. One possible example of a situation in which a probability statement makes sense, but for which the relative frequency interpretation could not apply is the event that the Yankees win the World Series. The probability that the Yankees win the World Series changes from year to year. The relative frequency method cannot be used to determine a probability that is always changing.

7.16   *Tip:* This is similar to the probability computation done in Example 7.6 on page 238.

Answer = .0988
Of the children who slept in darkness, the number with myopia or high myopia = 15 + 2 = 17. Thus the probability = 17/172 = .0988.

7.19   **a.** Yes, because they don't contain any of the same outcomes (simple events). Remember that A^c is the complement of A so it is the opposite of A.

b. No, they are dependent events. If A occurs then A^c has not. If A has not occurred, then A^c has.

7.22   **a.** Yes. The probability for each event is between 0 and 1, and over all possible outcomes, the sum of the probabilities equals 1.
b. No. The sum of the probabilities doesn't equal 1.
c. Yes (assuming that A, B, and C don't include all possible outcomes in the sample space). The sum of the probabilities is less than 1, and each individual probability is between 0 and 1. If it is assumed that A, B, and C cover the entire sample space, the answer is "No" because the sum of the three probabilities does not equal 1.

7.25   **a.** Yes, these are disjoint events because the red die cannot be a 3 and a 6 at the same time.
b. No, these are not disjoint events. The red die can be 3 in the same toss that the green die is a 6.

Tip: It is useful to specify the sample space, and then to determine what simple events are part of each event of interest. If there are any simple events in common, the two events are not disjoint. In this problem, the random circumstance involves tossing *both* dice, so each simple event in the sample space consists of a number for the red die and a number for the green die:

S = {11, 12, 13, 14, 15, 16, 21, 22, 23, etc.}. The simple events in parts (a) and (b) are then:

Part (a): A = red die is a 3 = {31, 32, 33, 34, 35, 36}
            B = red die is a 6 = {61, 62, 63, 64, 65, 66}
Notice that there are no simple events in common, so the two events are disjoint.
Part (b): A = red die is a 3 = {31, 32, 33, 34, 35, 36}
            B = green die is a 6 = {16, 26, 36, 46, 56, 66}
These two events have the simple event {36} in common, so they are *not* disjoint.

7.26 **a.** No, they are dependent. For instance, if the red die is known to be a 3, the red die cannot possibly be a 6.
b. Yes, they are independent. Knowing whether the red die is a 3 or not does not alter the probability the green die is a 6.

Tip #1: There are two methods you can use to decide whether two events are independent. Remember that they are independent if knowing whether one of them occurred (or will occur) does not change the probability of occurrence of the other. One way to determine this is through knowledge of the circumstances in space and time. For instance, if two unrelated women give birth, the probability that one of them has a male child is presumably not affected by whether the other one has a male child, so knowing the outcome for one will not change the probability for the other. The outcomes of their respective births are independent. The second method is to find P(B) and P(B|A) and see if they are numerically equal. If they are, then A and B are independent, because it means that knowing A occurred did not change P(B). (You can also compare P(A) and P(A|B).) In this problem, either method can be used. For instance, in Part (a) it is obvious that a die cannot land with both a 3 and a 6 as the face up at the same time, so the events are not independent. Numerically, P(B) = 1/6, but P(B|A) = 0 because once the red die is known to be a 3, the probability that it is a 6 is 0.

Tip #2: If two events are disjoint, they *cannot* also be independent (as long as neither event has probability of 0), because P(B|A) = 0 ≠ P(B). Therefore, in Part (a), because the two events are disjoint they cannot be independent. If two events are not disjoint, they may or may not be independent; in Part (b) the two events are not disjoint but they are independent. See "In Summary, Independent and Mutually Exclusive Events and Probability Rules" box on page 249 for more information about how these two concepts are related to probabilities involving events A and B.

7.29 Age and fertility status are not independent. The probability that a woman is fertile is related to her age.

Tip: See Tip #1 for the solution to exercise 7.26. According to the information in Exercise 7.27, if a woman's age group is known, the probability that she is fertile changes. So, the age group and fertility status are not independent.

7.32 **a.** A^C = flipping either 0, 1, or 2 heads in the 3 tosses of the coins. Put another way, it is the event that at least one tail occurs in the three flips.
b. 7/8. This can be found as 1− P(A) = 1− (1/8) = 7/8.

7.35   **a.** *Tip:* See Rule 3b on page 246.
No, they are not independent. P(A in both classes) does not equal P(A English)×P(A in history), as it would for independent events.
b. P(A in either English or history) = P(A in English) + P(A in history) − P(A in both classes) = .70 + .60 − .50 = .80.

7.38   **a.** Probability = 11/12 that the first stranger does not share your birth month.
b. Probability = 11/12 that the second stranger does not share your birth month.
c. Probability = (11/12)(11/12) = 121/144 = .84 that neither shares your birth month. Use the multiplication rule for two independent events (Rule 3b).
d. *P*(at least one) = 1−*P*(neither) = 1−.84 = .16, or 23/144.
The event that at least one of the two shares your birth month is the complement of the event that neither does.

Tip: When outcomes are of interest for two independent random circumstances, it is often helpful to create a table of possibilities. Then, probabilities for any combination of outcomes can be found easily. In this case, the two random circumstances are whether or not the first stranger shares your birth month and whether or not the second stranger shares your birth month. They are independent because knowing whether one shares it doesn't change the probability that the other one does. Here is a table of possibilities; probabilities for each outcome are found by multiplying the individual probabilities, using Rule 3b on page 246:

	Second stranger:	
First Stranger:	Shares birth month (1/12)	Doesn't share (11/12)
Shares birth month (1/12)	(1/12)(1/12)=1/144	(1/12)(11/12) = 11/144
Doesn't share (11/12)	(11/12)(1/12) = 11/144	(11/12)(11/12) = 121/144

The table shows the four disjoint combinations of outcomes, and you can check your answer about any particular combination or set of combinations using this table. For instance, the final probability of interest in part(d), that at least one shares your birth month, is a combination of the shaded cells, and their probabilities sum to 23/144.

7.41   **a.** These probabilities were determined by observing the relative frequency. The travel planner observed a large number of those specific flights and recorded the proportion of those flights that arrived on time for the ship.
b. Whether Harold's plane is on time is probably not independent of whether Maude's plane is on time. Bad weather conditions cause many flight delays. If there is bad weather and Harold's plane is delayed, there is probably a higher chance that Maude's plane will be delayed.
c. *P*(both arrive on time) = (.8)(.9) = .72
Use the multiplication rule for two independent events (Rule 3b).

7.41 continued:

d. Each of the pair can be on time or late, so there are four mutually exclusive options, listed with their probabilities in the table below. The outcomes that result in one of them cruising alone are in bold. The outcomes are disjoint, so P(one cruises alone) $= .18 + .08 = .26$.

	Maude is on time (.9)	Maude is late (.1)
Harold is on time (.8)	(.8)(.9) = .72	**(.8)(.1) = .08**
Harold is late (.2)	**(.2)(.9) = .18**	(.2)(.1) = .01

7.43   *Tip:* When sampling is done *with* replacement, the outcomes each time are independent. A table of probabilities similar to the one shown in the Tip for the solution to Exercise 7.38 may be useful. When sampling is done *without* replacement, the outcomes are not independent; probabilities for outcomes on the second draw are *conditional* on what happens in the first draw. In this case, a tree diagram is useful. See Example 7.25 on page 256 or the solution to Exercise 7.47 below for examples of how to draw a tree diagram.

a. P(both are friends of president) = (10/40)(10/40) = 1/16 = .0625.
The probability of picking a friend is the same for each draw because sampling is with replacement.
b. P(both are friends of president) = (10/40)(9/39) = .0577.
Note that the second probability (9/39) is the *conditional* probability of a friend *given* that the first selection was a friend.
c. P(neither are friends of president) = (30/40)(30/40) = .5626
The probability of not picking a friend is the same for each draw because sampling is with replacement.
d. P(neither are friends of president) = (30/40)(29/39) = .5577
Note that the second probability (29/39) is the *conditional* probability the second selection is not a friend *given* the first selection is not a friend.

7.44   **b.** P(includes international news | news magazine) = 20/30 = .67.
c. Answer is 25/50 = .50. There are 50 magazines, 20 include international news and 5 include international sports.

7.47   The tree diagram is below. The desired probability is the sum of the "final probabilities" for the two paths that end in "on sale."

P(on sale) = P(laptop on sale) + P(desktop on sale)

   = P(laptop) P(on sale | laptop) +P(desktop) P(on sale | desktop)

   = (.3)(.05) + (.7)(.1) = .015 + .070 = .085.

Figure for Exercise 7.47

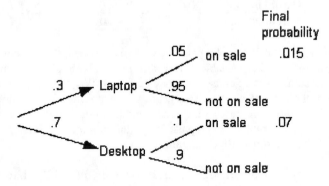

7.50   *Steps 1 to 3:*

Random Circumstance 1:

Possible Outcomes:

   A: happens if an ace is drawn.

   A^c: happens if a non-ace is drawn.

Probabilities:

   P(A) = 4/52 = 1/13.

   P(A^c) = 48/52 = 12/13.

Random Circumstance 2:

Possible Outcomes:

   B: happens if an ace is drawn.

   B^c: happens if a non-ace is drawn.

Probabilities:

   P(B |A) = 3/51.

   P(B^c|A) = 48/51.

   P(B |A^c) = 4/51.

   P(B^c|A^c) = 47/51.

Step 4: P(first card drawn is an ace and second card drawn is a non-ace).

Step 5: P(A)P(B^c|A) = (1/13)(48/51) = .0724.

7.53   A tree diagram is useful here. Make the first set of branches go to the two different
classes and the second of branches go to taking calculus or not in each class.

Figure for Exercise 7.53

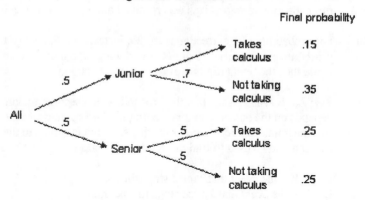

The desired conditional probability is P(junior | taking calculus).

$$P(\text{junior} \mid \text{taking calculus}) = \frac{P(\text{junior and taking calculus})}{P(\text{taking calculus})}.$$

This is Rule 4 for conditional probability.

A student taking calculus is either a junior or a senior, so (using Rule 2b):
$P(\text{taking calculus}) = P(\text{junior and taking calculus}) + P(\text{senior and taking calculus})$
Each element of the previous formula can be found using the multiplication rule (Rule
3a).
$P(\text{junior and taking calculus}) = P(\text{junior}) \times P(\text{taking calculus} \mid \text{junior}) = (.5)(.3) = .15$
$P(\text{senior and taking calculus}) = P(\text{senior}) \times P(\text{taking calculus} \mid \text{senior}) = (.5)(.5) = .25$

This leads to $P(\text{taking calculus}) = .15 + .25 = .40$.

So, $P(\text{junior} \mid \text{taking calculus}) = \dfrac{P(\text{junior and taking calculus})}{P(\text{taking calculus})} = \dfrac{.15}{.40} = .375$

7.56   number of occurrences / number of simulations = 45/10000 = .0045.

7.58   *Tip:* In problems involving simulation, the relative frequency interpretation of
probability is used to estimate probabilities of various outcomes. In this problem, each
probability is estimated by counting how many times the outcome of interest occurs,
and dividing by 50, the number of simulated attempts at buying six boxes of cereal.

a. Estimated probability = 8/50 = .16. There were 8 simulations in which prize 4 was
received 3 or more times.

b. Estimated probability = 7/31 = .2258. There were 31 simulations in which all four prizes were not received. Prize 4 was received 3 or more times in 7 of these 31 simulations.

c. Estimated probability is 1/50 = .02. There was only one simulation in which the full collection of four prizes was received and prize 4 was received at least 3 times.

7.60 For probability of a correct guess = .20, instead of .30, change the simulation procedure so that only two digits (8 and 9 for example) are counted as a correct guess while the other eight digits are counted as a wrong guess.

7.63 *Tip:* As soon as you see that the probability of a second random circumstance depends on the outcome of a preceding random circumstance, think about drawing a tree diagram. The tree diagram for this situation is shown in the solution to Part (b) and can also be used to find the solution to Part (a).

a. Let R = the event that Janice stops for the red light.
Let T = the event that Janice stops for the train.
$P(R \text{ and } T) = P(R) \times P(T \mid R) = (.3)(.4) = .12$.
This is an application of the multiplication rule (Rule 3a).

b. The desired conditional probability is $P(R \mid T)$, where R and T are defined in the solution to Part (a). A tree diagram is useful for displaying the possible outcomes of interest. Make the first set of branches represent stopping at the red light or not and the second set of branches represent stopping at the train or not within each red light category.

Figure for Exercise 7.63b

Final probability

Janice might have to stop at the train either if she stops at the red light or if she does not.
So (using Rule 2b): $P(T) = P(R \text{ and } T) + P(R^C \text{ and } T)$

7.63b continued:

Each element of the previous formula can be found using the multiplication rule (Rule 3a).

$P(\text{R and T}) = P(\text{R}) \times P(\text{T} \mid \text{R}) = (.3)(.4) = .12$ (as found in part (a))

$P(\text{R}^C \text{ and T}) = P(\text{R}^C) \times P(\text{T} \mid \text{R}^C) = (.7)(.2) = .14$

This leads to $P(\text{T}) = .12 + .14 = .26$.

$$P(\text{R} \mid \text{T}) = \frac{P(\text{R and T})}{P(\text{T})} = \frac{.12}{.26} = .4615$$

This is an application of Rule 4 for conditional probability.

7.66   All sequences are equally likely because P(Heads) = P(Tails) = .5. The probability for each sequence is $(1/2)^5 = 1/32$ by the multiplication rule for independent events.

7.70   **a.** Probability = 1/365 = .0027 that your teammate's mother would have the same birthday as you.

b. *Tip:* When you are asked to find the probability for "at least one" of a combination of outcomes, it is usually easiest to find the probability of "none" and then subtract that probability from 1.

The probability that none of the five family members has the same birthday as you =

$\left(\dfrac{364}{365}\right)^5 = .9864$ (using the multiplication rule along with the fact that the probability

is 364/365 that a single member does not match).

The desired probability is $1 - .9864 = .0136$.

c. No, it is not. While that specific event has low probability, it is quite possible that someone in the class would have a birthday matching a teammate's family member's birthday.

7.72   No, she is not correct. Assuming birth outcomes are independent, having 3 consecutive boys does not change the probability that the fourth child will be a boy. *Note:* Her misinterpretation is an example of the *gambler's fallacy*.

7.76   *Tip:* To find the probability of "at least one" of a combination of outcomes, it is usually easiest to find the probability of "none" and subtract that from 1.

   $P(\text{match on at least one topic}) =$

$$1 - P(\text{match on none of the topics}) = 1 - \left(\frac{49}{50}\right)^{10} = .1829.$$

Notice that the probability of no matches is calculated using the multiplication rule for independent events (Rule 3b extension).

It would not be a total surprise to match on at least one topic because at least one match will occur in about 18% of the occasions in which two strangers compare details for 10 topics.

7.79   **a.** For males,
    P(either Rationalist *or* Teacher) = P(Rationalist) + P(Teacher) = .15 + .12 = .27.
    b. For females, P(not Teacher) = 1–.14 = .86.
    c. For males, P(both roommates are Rationalists) = (.15)(.15) = .0225.
    d. For females, P(both roommates are Rationalists) = (.08)(.08) = .0064.
    e. If two roommates are both Rationalists, they could be *either* both males *or* both females. Thus,
    P(both Rationalists) = P(Males and Rationalists) + P(Females and Rationalists).
    The pieces of the equation just given are:
    P(Males and Rationalists) = P(Males)×P(Rationalists | Males) = (.5)(.0225) = .01125
    P(Females and Rationalists) =
                P(Females) × P(Rationalists | Females) = (.5)(.0064) = .0032
    Thus, P(both Rationalists) = .01125 + .0032 = .01445.

7.82   *Tip:* Draw a tree diagram where the first set of branches represent "regular attendance" or not, and the second set represent "get A in class" or not. Notice that the percents associated with the first set (attend regularly or not) are 70% and 30%, while the percents associated with the second set (get A or not) change; they are 40% and 60% for those who attend class regularly, and 10% and 90% for those who do not. It is easier to convert the percents to probabilities so they can be multiplied, then convert the answers back to percents.

   a. *P*(get A | regular attendance) = .40 or 40%.
   b. *P*(get A | not regular attendance) = .10 or 10%.
   c.   Students who get an A *either* regularly attend *or* do not.
        P(get A) = P(regularly attend *and* get A) + P(do not regularly attend *and* get A)

   The two components on the right side of the previous equation are:
   P(regularly attend and get A)
        = P(regularly attend) × P(get A | regularly attend)=(.7)(.4)=.28

   P(do not regularly attend and get A)
        = P(do not regularly attend) × P(get A | do not regularly attend) = (.3)(.1) = .03

   So, P(get A) = .28 + .03 = .31, which is 31%.

7.86   **a.** Probability = .5 that a randomly selected person is above the median. Recall that the median of a data set divides the ordered data into two equal halves.

   b. P(all 4 above median) = $\left(\dfrac{1}{2}\right)^4 = \dfrac{1}{16} = .0625$. The multiplication rule for

   independent events (Rule 3b extension) is used because we want to know the probability that the first *and* second *and* third *and* fourth students all are above the median.
   c. No, because the events are not independent. For example, the probability that the second person selected has a value below the median depends upon whether the first person selected had a value below the median or not.

7.89   **a.** P(both are) = P(first is)$\times P$(second is) = $(.35)(.35)$ = $.1225$.
This assumes independence, and the multiplication rule (Rule 3b) is used because we want the probability that the first *and* second person are both naturalized citizens.
b. If a married couple (both foreign-born) was selected, the citizenship status of the husband and wife almost certainly would not be independent. If one of these individuals decided to become a U.S. citizen, it most likely would affect the probability that the other decides this as well.
c. The probabilities reported by the Census Bureau are relative frequency probability. They observed a large number of foreign-born people in the U.S. in 1997 and noted what proportion of those were naturalized citizens.
d. The statement as written refers to the same person but uses the probabilities as if referring to two independent people. A correct version would be: "If a foreign-born person in the U.S. was randomly selected in 1970, the probability he or she was a naturalized citizen would have been.64. By 1997, if a foreign-born person in the U.S. was randomly selected the probability he or she would have been a naturalized citizen had dropped to .35.

7.92   Approximate probability = $485/1669$ = $.2906$ that a randomly selected person smokes.
Tip: This is a simple illustration of the 3rd bullet of "In Summary, Interpretations of Probability" on page 237.

7.94   Given the person has been divorced, approximate probability = $238/612$ = $.3889$ that he or she smokes.
This estimate is the proportion that smokes within the Divorced =Yes column of the table.

7.97   *Note:* The wording of this question may lead some students to misinterpret what is expected and answer the question as if the two people were randomly selected without replacement *from this sample* instead of from *the population* represented by the sample. If that is done, the answer is .4125. However, the question asks about the population, which is so large that sampling without replacement makes no difference and does not change the probabilities.

The probabilities that someone smokes or does not smoke must be estimated from the sample. There are two possible (mutually exclusive) sequences in which one person smokes and the other does not:

Sequence 1: first smokes, second does not ;   probability = $\left(\dfrac{485}{1669}\right)\left(\dfrac{1184}{1669}\right)$

Sequence 2: first does not smoke, second does ;   probability = $\left(\dfrac{1184}{1669}\right)\left(\dfrac{485}{1669}\right)$

The two possibilities have equal probability, so answer = $2\times\left(\dfrac{485}{1669}\right)\left(\dfrac{1184}{1669}\right)=.4123$.

Based on sample only, answer = .4125.

CHAPTER 8
SELECTED SOLUTIONS

8.2 *Tip:* A discrete random variable is one with a countable set of possible outcomes. For a continuous random variable, any value (to any degree of accuracy) within some interval is theoretically possible.
a. Discrete
b. Continuous because the actual time could be something like 15.2356 seconds even though we would round this to 15 seconds.
c. Discrete
d. Discrete

8.5 This will differ for each student. An example of another continuous random variable is the amount of rainfall (in inches) during the event time. Rainfall can be any number between 0 and some maximum value. One example of another discrete random variable is the number of police, ambulance, and fire vehicles driving by with sirens. The number of vehicles can be 0,1,2, …, and so on up to the logical maximum for the situation.

8.6 **a.** Answer = 3/6 = .5. This makes the probabilities add to 1.

8.9

k	0	1	2	3
P(X=k)	1/8	3/8	3/8	1/8

Possible numbers of heads are 0, 1, 2, 3. In the sample space, there is one simple event with no heads, three with one head, three with two heads, and one with three heads.

8.10 **a.** Answer = .80. Find this by adding the probabilities for $X = 0$, 1, and 2.
$(X \leq 2) = P(X=0) + P(X=1) + P(X=2) = .14 + .27 + .39 = .80$.

8.14 **a.** Simple events are {G, BG, BBG, BBBG, BBBB}

8.18 **a.** $30. This is the cost of the insurance.
b. X = $0 with probability .90 (the probability he doesn't need to be towed during a year). X = $100 with probability .10 (the probability he needs to be towed during a year).

8.20 The expected value is calculated as the sum of "value×probability."
$E(X) = (\$100)(.01) + (-\$5)(.99) = -\$3.95$.
Interpretation: If Mary plays the game many times, she should expect an average loss of about $3.95 per game played.

8.23   An intuitive solution (and a correct one) is that the expected value for the number of girls among three children is 3×.5 = 1.5 (because in the long run, 1/2 of the children will be girls).   A more elaborate solution is to determine the probability distribution for X =number of girls, and then use the formula for E(X). The distribution given in Example 8.6 on page 285 is:

k	0	1	2	3
P(X=k)	1/8=.125	3/8 =.375	3/8=.375	1/8=.125

The expected value is calculated as the sum of "value×probability."
$$E(X) = (0×.125) + (1×.375) + (2×.375) + (3×.125) = 1.5 \text{ girls.}$$

Interpretation: Note that it is impossible to actually have 1.5 girls in 3 children. The expected value gives the average number of girls over a population of families with 3 children.

8.26 $\sigma = \$29.67$. The standard deviation is calculated as $\sigma = \sqrt{\sum(x-\mu)^2 p(x)}$ where the sum is over all values of x. The expected value (mean) was found in Exercise 8.6 as μ = −\$0.35. The details for finding σ are:

X	\$4,999	\$49	\$4	\$0	−\$1
$x-\mu$	\$4,999.35	\$49.35	\$4.35	\$0.35	−\$0.65
p(x)	.000035	.00168	.0303	.242	.726

$$\sqrt{4999.35^2(.000035) + \$49.35^2(.00168) + \$4.35^2(.0303`) + \$0.35^2(.242) + \$0.65^2(.726)}$$
$$= \$29.67$$

8.29   The given information can be summarized as:

x = number of parents	0	1	2
p(x)=probability	.03	.22+.03 = .25	.72

(The probability for living with one parent is the sum of probabilities for mother only and father only.)

a. $\mu = E(X) = \sum xp(x) = (0×.03) + (1×.25) + (2×.72) = 1.69.$

b. The expected value is the average number of parents in the household over the population of all children. This value is not an "expected" value for an individual child because it is not possible to live with 1.69 parents. It is meaningful only as a long run or population average.

8.32   **a.** Yes. X is a binomial random variable with $n = 200$ and $p = .5$. *Tip:* The four conditions for a binomial experiment are given on page 294.
b. $E(X) = np = (200)(.5) = 100.$

8.34   **a.** $n = 30$ (number of rolls), and $p = 1/6$ (the probability of a "6" on any role).

8.35   *Tip:* See pages 298-299 for information about the mean of a binomial random variable.
$$\mu = E(X) = np = (30(1/6) = 5.$$

8.38   **a.** The probability of success does not remain the same from one trial (game) to the next. The probability of winning a game against a good team is not the same as the probability of winning a game against a poor team.
b. The number of trials is not specified in advance.
c. The probability of success does not remain the same from one trial to the next because whether or not the first card is an ace affects the probability that the next card is an ace, and so on. This also means that trials are not independent.

8.41   *Tip*: The answers for this exercise can be found using any of the methods discussed in Section 8.4, including the use of Minitab or Excel.

a. $P(X = 4) = .2051$.
Excel Tip: The Excel command is BINOMDIST(4,10,.5, FALSE).
b. $P(X \geq 4) = 1 - P(X \leq 3) = 1 - .6496 = .3504$.
Excel Tip: The Excel command is 1− BINOMDIST(3,10,.5,TRUE).

8.42   **b.** The desired probability is $P(X \geq 110)$, $n = 500$, and $p = .20$.
Tip: It's necessary to convert the given percent (20%) to a proportion (.20).

8.46   *Tip:* This exercise is similar in concept to Example 8.19 on page 301.
a. X is a uniform random variable (and it is continuous).
b. X ranges from 0 to 100 and the area under any density curve is 1, so $f(x) = 1/100 = .01$ for all x between 0 and 100. This creates a rectangle (with area=1) similar to Figure 8.5 in the text.
Note: $f(x) = 0$ for any x not between 0 and 100.
c. $P(X \leq 15$ seconds) is the area of the rectangle from 0 to 15 seconds. The interval width is 15 and the height is 1/100, so the answer is $(15)(1/100) = .15$.

8.49   **b.** $\dfrac{4-10}{6} = -1$.

8.53   **a.** $P(Z \leq -1.4) = .0808$.   Look for this value in the part of Table A.1 that is for negative values of z.

8.55   **a.** *Tip:* This is like Example 8.23 on p.306

For pulse = 71, $z = \dfrac{x - \mu}{\sigma} = \dfrac{71 - 75}{8} = -0.5$.

So, $P(X \leq 71) = P(Z \leq -0.5) = .3085$ (from Table A.1).

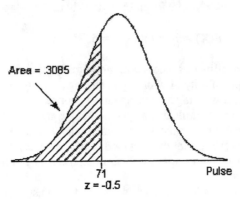

Figure for Exercise 8.55a

Area = .3085

71
z = -0.5

Pulse

8.57   a. $z^* = -1.96$. If using Table A.1, look for .025 within the interior part of the table.

8.59   a. *Tip:* This part of the exercise is like Example 8.27 on p.309.

For 65, $z = 0$ because 65 is the mean.

$$\text{For } 62, z = \frac{\text{Value} - \text{Mean}}{\text{Standard deviation}} = \frac{62 - 65}{2.7} = -1.11.$$

So, $P(62 \le X \le 65) = P(-1.11 \le Z \le 0) = P(Z \le 0) - P(Z \le -1.11) = .5 - .1335 = .3665$

8.60   *Tip:* This exercise is like Example 8.28 on page 310.
The following figure illustrates the problem.

Figure for Exercise 8.60

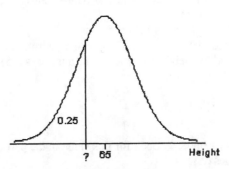

0.25

? 65

Height

The value of z^* for which $P(Z \le z^*) = .25$ is about -0.675.   To determine this, look for .25 as a cumulative probability within Table A.1.
This means the answer is 0.675 standard deviations below the mean. This height is
$(-0.675 \times 2.7) + 65 = 63.2$ inches.   A formula for this is $x = z^* \sigma + \mu$.
The percentile ranking for a height of 63.2 inches is .25 or 25%.

46

8.63   **a.** *Tip:* This part is like Example 8.23 on page 306.

For rainfall = 10, $z = \dfrac{10-18}{6} = -1.33$ so $P(X < 10) = P(Z < -1.33) = .0918$ (from

Table A.1).
The following figure illustrates the solution.

Figure for Exercise 8.63a

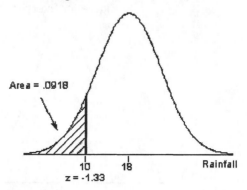

Area = .0918

10
z = -1.33

18

Rainfall

b. *Tip:* This part is similar to Example 8.25 on page.308.

For rainfall = 30, $z = \dfrac{30-18}{6} = 2$ so $P(X > 30) = P(Z > 2)$

$P(Z > 2) = 1 - P(Z \le 2) = 1 - .9772 = .0228.$ Equivalently, $P(Z > 2) = P(Z < -2)$
   $= .0228.$
The following figure illustrates the solution.

Figure for Exercise 8.63b

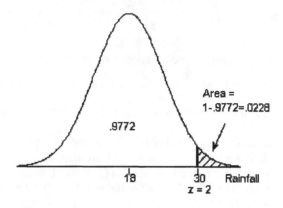

Area =
1-.9772=.0228

.9772

18

30
z = 2

Rainfall

c. *Tip:* This part is similar to Example 8.27 on p.309.

For rainfall $=21$, $z = \dfrac{21-18}{6} = 0.5$ while for rainfall $= 15$, $z = \dfrac{15-18}{6} = -0.5$.

So, $P(15 \leq X \leq 21) = P(-0.5 \leq Z \leq 0.5) = P(Z \leq 0.5) - P(Z \leq -0.5) = .6915 - .3085 = .3830$

The following figure illustrates the solution.

Figure for Exercise 8.63c

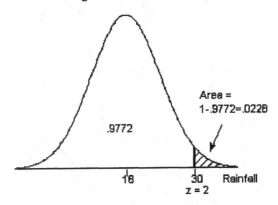

.9772

Area =
1-.9772=.0228

18   30   Rainfall
            z = 2

d. For 35, $z = \dfrac{35-18}{6} = 2.83$ so $P(X > 35) = P(Z > 2.83)$

$P(Z > 2.83) = 1 - P(Z \leq 2.83) = 1 - .9977 = .0023.$ Or, $P(Z > 2.83) = P(Z < -2.83)$
$= .0023.$

8.66   **a.** For a binomial random variable with $n = 50$ and $p = .512$:

$\mu = np = 50(.512) = 25.6$, and $\sigma = \sqrt{50(.512)(1-.512)} = 3.535$.

Thus, for X = 20, $z = \dfrac{20-25.6}{3.535} = -1.58$.

$P(X \leq 20) \approx P(Z \leq -1.58) = .0571.$
b. With the continuity correction, we find $P(X \leq 20.5)$.

For X = 20.5, $z = \dfrac{20.5-25.6}{3.535} = -1.44$.   So, $P(X \leq 20.5) = P(Z \leq -1.44) = .0749$.

Tip: See the **technical note** about the continuity correction on page 314.

8.70   **a.** The mean for the total of four individuals is the total of the means for individuals.
This is $100 + 100 + 100 + 100 = 400$ seconds.
b. The variance for an individual is $(10)^2 = 100$, so the variance for the total of four
independent individuals $= 100 + 100 + 100 + 100 = 400$. The standard deviation for the

total is $\sqrt{400} = 20$ seconds.

c. For $T = 20.5$, $z = \dfrac{360-400}{20} = -2$.   Thus, $P(T < 360) = P(Z < -2) = .0228$.

48

8.73　**b.** *Tip:* See "In Summary, Linear Combinations of Independent Normal Random Variables" on page 316.

For $X+Y$, the mean is $100+50 = 150$. This is the sum of the respective means for X. The variance is the sum of the variances for X and Y, which is $15^2+10^2=325$. The standard deviation is $\sqrt{\text{variance}} = \sqrt{325} = 18.028$.
The distribution of the sum is normal because X and Y both have normal distributions.

8.76　*Tip:* This exercise is like Example 8.33 on page 317.
Let X = train time and Y = bus time. If the train is faster than the bus, $X<Y$ which is equivalent to $X - Y < 0$.
The desired probability is $P(X-Y < 0)$.
For $X-Y$ (the difference in times):

Mean is 60 min.$-$50 min.$=$10 min.

Standard deviation is $\sqrt{\sigma_X^2 + \sigma_Y^2} = \sqrt{2^2 + 8^2} = 8.246$ min.

The distribution of the difference has a normal distribution.

For 0 min., $z = \dfrac{0-10}{8.246} = -1.21$ so $P(X-Y < 0) = P(Z< <-1.21)$

From Table A.1, $P(Z<-1.21) = .1131$.

8.78　*Tip:* This is similar to Example 8.25 on page 308.
The desired probability is $P(X>75)$ where X = vehicle speed..

For 75 mph, $z = \dfrac{x-\mu}{\sigma} = \dfrac{75-67}{6} = 1.33$ so $P(X>75) = P(Z>1.33)$

$P(Z>1.33) = 1- P(Z<1.33) = 1 - .9082 = .0918$.
Or, $P(Z>1.33) = P(Z<-1.33) = .0918$.
The following figure illustrates the solution.

Figure for Exercise 8.78

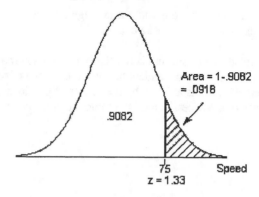

Area = 1-.9082
= .0918

.9082

75
z = 1.33

Speed

8.80   The histogram will probably not have a bell-shape because the different means for men and women may create a bimodal distribution (one with two peaks). The bimodal effect will not be as clear, however, as intuition might suggest. Taller than average women and shorter than average men combine to create frequent observations of heights between the two means. Here's what the theoretical population distribution looks like:

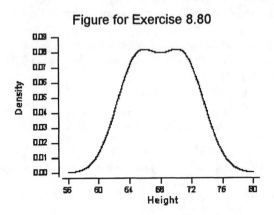

Figure for Exercise 8.80

8.83   **a.** There are 38 equally likely numbers, so the probability is 1/38 that the player picks the right number and wins $70.
The probability is 37/38 that the player picks the wrong number and loses $2.
A summary of the distribution of X = amount won or lost is:

k	$70	−$2
$P(X=k)$	1/38	37/38

b. Calculate the sum of "value×probability" over all values.
$E(X) = (\$70)(1/38) + (-\$2)(37/38) = -\$4/38 = -\$0.1053$.

Interpretation: In the long run, the average outcome will be that players lose about 10.5 cents to the casino per $2 bet.

8.86   **a.** The probability of success is not the same for each trial.
b. The trials are not independent because the chance of selecting a woman on a particular selection is affected by the results of previous selections. This also means the chance of a "success" is not the same on all trials.

8.89   **a.** If the children pick the books independently from each other, and if the length of the first book does not affect the reading pace for the second book, it's reasonable to assume independence.

b. *Tip:* The steps for this part are the same as those in Example 8.32 on page 317

Mean total time = sum of mean times for the two books = 5+5=10 minutes.

The variance of the total time is the sum of the two variances, which is $2^2 + 2^2 = 8$, so the standard deviation is $\sqrt{8} = 2.828$ min.

The distribution of the total is a normal distribution, so the remaining steps are done as a typical normal curve problem would be done.

For *Total*=15, $z = \dfrac{15-10}{2.828} = 1.77$ so $P(Total \geq 15) = P(Z \geq 1.77)$

$P(Z \geq 1.77) = 1 - P(Z \leq 1.77) = 1 - .9616 = .0384$.

Or, equivalently, $P(Z \geq 1.77) = P(Z \leq -1.77) = .0384$.

CHAPTER 9
SELECTED SOLUTIONS

9.1 **a.** Statistic because it is a sample value.
b. Parameter because it is a population value.
c. Statistic because it is a sample value
d. Parameter because it is a population value (errors in the entire manuscript).

9.4 The truth refers to the population parameter. The sample statistic is computer from the data, so we know its value. It is the population parameter we are trying to estimate.

9.7 **a.** Parameters. Here, the given means are population values.
Tip: Definitions for the terms statistic and parameter are given on pages 294 and 296.
b. Yes, because the population means are known exactly, the shareholders can be certain that the mean salary for men in the company is higher than the mean salary for women.

9.9 **a.** $\hat{p}$ because this is a sample proportion.
b. p because this is a population proportion.
c. $\hat{p}$ because this is a sample proportion.

9.11 *Tip*: This is an example of Situation 1 on page 336 of the text.
a. Research question: What proportion of parents in the school district support the new program?
b. Population parameter: p = proportion of all parents in the school district who support the new program
c. Sample estimate: $\hat{p} = \dfrac{104}{300} = .347$

9.16 This is an example of paired differences. Research question: What is the mean difference between hours spent studying and hours spent socializing for the population of students at the university?
Population parameter: μ_d = mean difference between hours spent studying and hours spent socializing for all students at the university.
Sample estimate: $\bar{d}$ = observed mean difference between hours spent studying and hours spent socializing for the sample of 100 students.

9.17 Paired data. Two different variables are measured for each individual and interest is in the amount of difference.

9.22 **a.** The population of interest is teens who go out on dates, and the parameter of interest is p = the proportion of that population who would say they had been out with someone of another race or ethnic group. The sample statistic is $\hat{p}$ = .57. (You could answer using percents instead.)

9.24 **a.** The mean of the sampling distribution of $\hat{p}$ is p.

b. One value from the sampling distribution of $\hat{p}$ is one sample proportion, denoted by $\hat{p}$.

9.27 **a.** The mean of the sampling distribution of the sample mean is μ = the population mean. Its value remains the same, regardless of the sample.

b. The sampling distribution of the sample mean remains approximately normal.

c. The standard deviation of the sampling distribution depends on the population standard deviation and the sample size, both of which remain the same, so it remains the same as well. In fact all features of the sampling distribution remain the same, because it depends on the population and the sample size, not on the sample itself.

9.29 **a.** Not likely. As shown in Figure 9.1 on page 346, the mean will almost surely be between 6.6 and 7.4 hours.

c. The distribution of original sleep hours is much more spread out than the sampling distribution shown in Figure 9.1, and an individual value between 8 and 9 hours would be quite likely. (Remember that the mean is 7.1 hours and the standard deviation is 2 hours.)

9.31 *Tip:* In each part, use the formulas for the mean and standard deviation given in the definition box on page 350.

a. Mean = p = .5; s.d. = $\sqrt{\dfrac{.5(1-.5)}{400}}$ = .025

b. Mean = p = .5; s.d. = $\sqrt{\dfrac{.5(1-.5)}{1600}}$ = .0125

9.33 *Tip:* See Example 9.9 on page 351 for guidance.

a. Mean = p = .55.

b. s.d. = $\sqrt{\dfrac{.55(1-.45)}{100}}$ = .0497 ≈ .05.

c. About .55 ± (3)(.05), or about .40 to .70. This is the interval Mean ± 3 s.d., which is the part of the Empirical Rule that says that about 99.7% of the values will be within three standard deviations of the mean.

9.35 **a.** $\hat{p}$ = 300/500 = .60.

b. $s.e.(\hat{p}) = \sqrt{\dfrac{\hat{p}(1-\hat{p})}{n}} = \sqrt{\dfrac{.60(1-.60)}{500}}$ = .022. *Tip:* The formula for standard error is on page 354.

9.39   *Tip*: Use the part of the Empirical Rule that says that about 95% of the values will be within two standard deviations of the mean. The sampling distribution of $\hat{p}$ is approximately a normal distribution, so about 95% of sample proportions will fall in the interval $p \pm 2\,s.d.(\hat{p})$.

Solution: In 9.19 part (b), it is found that the mean of the distribution of possible sample proportions is p = 0.05 and the standard deviation is

$$s.d.(\hat{p}) = \sqrt{\frac{p(1-p)}{n}} = \sqrt{\frac{.05(1-.05)}{400}} = .011$$

So, about 95% of all samples will have a sample proportion in the interval .05 ± (2)(.011), which is .028 to .072 (approximately .03 to .07).

9.42   **a.** p = .20 (20% expressed as a proportion).
All patients at the medical clinic constitute the population of interest.
b. $\hat{p} = 18/100 = .18$.
Notice how the notation is different for the sample than it is for the population.

$$\textbf{c. } s.e.(\hat{p}) = \sqrt{\frac{\hat{p}(1-\hat{p})}{n}} = \sqrt{\frac{.18(1-.18)}{100}} = .0384.$$

Notice that the standard error calculation uses the sample proportion $\hat{p}$.
Tip: The difference between the standard error of a sample proportion and the standard deviation of a proportion is explained on pages 353-354. The formulas are given there as well.
d. The mean of the sampling distribution of $\hat{p}$ equals the population proportion, which is .20.

$$\textbf{e. } s.d.(\hat{p}) = \sqrt{\frac{p(1-p)}{n}} = \sqrt{\frac{.20(1-.20)}{100}} = .04.$$

Notice that the standard deviation calculation uses the population proportion.

9.46   **a.** The mean is $p_1 - p_2 = .30 - .36 = -0.06$.

9.49   **c.** No, the sample sizes are not large enough. With only 10 observations for each method, it is impossible to have all of the quantities $n_1 p_1$, $n_1(1 - p_1)$, $n_2 p_2$, $n_2(1 - p_2)$ be at least 10.

9.52   **a.** The mean could be specified; it is $p_1 - p_2 = 0$.
b. Yes. The approximate shape could be specified because appropriate conditions are met for it to be approximately normal.
c. Yes. The standard deviation could be specified because the population proportions and the sample sizes are known.
d. No. The standard error could not be specified because it is calculated using the sample proportions, which would not be known before the samples are taken.

9.55   **a.** Yes, this falls into Situation 1.
   b. No, for a skewed population, this sample size is too small.
   c. Yes, this falls into Situation 2.

9.56   **a.** $s.d.(\bar{x}) = \dfrac{\sigma}{\sqrt{n}} = \dfrac{24}{\sqrt{16}} = 6$.

   b. $s.d.(\bar{x}) = \dfrac{\sigma}{\sqrt{n}} = \dfrac{24}{\sqrt{64}} = 3$.

   c. Increasing the sample size decreases the value of the standard deviation of the sampling distribution of the sample mean. . A fourfold increase in sample size cut the standard deviation in half.

9.58   **a.** $\bar{x}$ and s. These are sample statistics.

   b. $s.e.(\bar{x}) = \dfrac{s}{\sqrt{n}} = \dfrac{47.7}{\sqrt{28}} = 9.014$.

9.61   **b.** The sampling distribution of possible sample means for random samples of $n= 40$ is approximately a normal distribution. The mean is $\mu = 210$ pounds.
   The standard deviation of the sampling distribution

   is $s.d.(\bar{x}) = \dfrac{\sigma}{\sqrt{n}} = \dfrac{25}{\sqrt{40}} = 3.95$ pounds.

   d. If the total weight is 8800, the mean weight is 8800/40 = 220 pounds. The question asked is equivalent to asking, "What is the probability that the *mean* weight is greater than 220 pounds for 40 passengers?" Because the question is about a sample *mean*, use the sampling distribution described in part (b) to find the answer for $P(\bar{x} > 220)$.
   This can be done as a normal curve problem using the methods learned in Section 8.6.

   For $\bar{x}=220$ pounds, $z = \dfrac{220-210}{3.95} = 2.53$.

   Use Table A.1 to find that $P(Z \le 2.53) = .9943$.
   $P(\bar{x} > 220) = P(Z > 2.53) = 1 - P(Z \le 2.53) = 1 - .9943 = .0057$

   Notice that this probability is 57 in 10,000. In the long run, about 57 of every 10,000 sold-out flights will exceed the total weight limit. The figure below illustrates the solution.

Figure for Exercise 9.61d

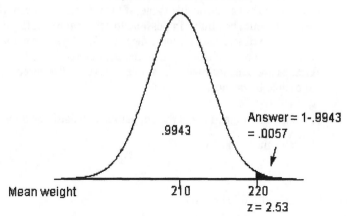

.9943

Answer = 1-.9943
= .0057

Mean weight   210   220

z = 2.53

9.62   The standard error of the sample mean is calculated using the standard deviation of the measurements in an observed sample, and it (the standard error) *estimates* the "true" standard deviation of the sampling distribution of the sample mean. The standard deviation is found using the known (or assumed to be known) value of the standard deviation of the population of measurements.

The formula for the standard error is $s.e.(\bar{x}) = \dfrac{s}{\sqrt{n}}$. (See page 361).

The formula for the standard deviation is $s.d.(\bar{x}) = \dfrac{\sigma}{\sqrt{n}}$. (See page 359).

In practice, the standard error will be used more often because the value of the population standard deviation usually will not be known.

9.65   **a.** Two independent samples. The dormitory students and the off-campus students constitute two distinct, unrelated samples.

9.68   **d.** The sampling distribution is approximately normal with mean 0 and standard deviation $5/\sqrt{12} = 1.44$.

9.71   **a.** The mean is $70 - 65 = 5$ inches.

b. The standard deviation is $\sqrt{\dfrac{3^2}{9} + \dfrac{2.5^2}{9}} = 1.30$

9.74 **a.** The mean is 0.

d. No. A sample difference of 3.6 days corresponds to a z-score of $(3.6 - 0)/0.514 = 7.00$, so it is not a reasonable value. If there is really no difference in the population means, it would be almost impossible to see a sample difference as large as 3.6 days.

e. No. If the difference in sample means is 3.6 days it is not reasonable to assume that the mean duration of symptoms in the population would be the same after taking placebos and zinc lozenges. A sample difference that large would be almost impossible by chance.

9.76 The population mean μ and the population standard deviation σ must also be known. The relevant formula is $z = \dfrac{\bar{x} - \mu}{\sigma/\sqrt{n}}$.

9.78 **b.** $(0.13 - 0)/.0707 = 1.84$

9.80 **b.** $(2 - 0)/0.775 = 2.58$.

9.83 **b.** A sample difference of 3.6 days corresponds to a z-score of $(3.6 - 0)/0.5137 = 7.01$.

9.85 *Tip*: See Example 9.15.

a. $z = \dfrac{\hat{p} - p}{s.d.(\hat{p})} = \dfrac{\hat{p} - p}{\sqrt{\dfrac{p(1-p)}{n}}} = \dfrac{.60 - .50}{\sqrt{\dfrac{.50(1-.50)}{100}}} = \dfrac{.10}{.05} = 2$.

b. $z = \dfrac{\hat{p} - p}{s.d.(\hat{p})} = \dfrac{\hat{p} - p}{\sqrt{\dfrac{p(1-p)}{n}}} = \dfrac{.60 - .50}{\sqrt{\dfrac{.50(1-.50)}{200}}} = \dfrac{.10}{.0354} = 2.828$.

9.88 **a.** *Tip*: See Example 9.15.

For $\hat{p} = .20$, $z = \dfrac{\hat{p} - p}{s.d.(\hat{p})} = \dfrac{\hat{p} - p}{\sqrt{\dfrac{p(1-p)}{n}}} = \dfrac{.20 - .25}{\sqrt{\dfrac{.25(1-.25)}{75}}} = \dfrac{-.05}{.05} = -1$.

For $\hat{p} = .33$, $z = \dfrac{\hat{p} - p}{s.d.(\hat{p})} = \dfrac{.33 - .25}{\sqrt{\dfrac{.25(1-.25)}{75}}} = \dfrac{.08}{.05} = 1.6$.

9.89 *Tip:* The formula for this exercise is given on page 370 of the text.

a. $z = \dfrac{\bar{x} - \mu}{s.d.(\bar{x})} = \dfrac{\bar{x} - \mu}{\dfrac{\sigma}{\sqrt{n}}} = \dfrac{74 - 72}{\dfrac{10}{\sqrt{25}}} = \dfrac{2}{2} = 1.$

b. $z = \dfrac{\bar{x} - \mu}{s.d.(\bar{x})} = \dfrac{\bar{x} - \mu}{\dfrac{\sigma}{\sqrt{n}}} = \dfrac{70 - 72}{\dfrac{10}{\sqrt{25}}} = \dfrac{-2}{2} = -1.$

9.92 a. *Tip:* See Example 9.16 on page 371.

$t = \dfrac{\bar{x} - \mu}{s.e.(\bar{x})} = \dfrac{\bar{x} - \mu}{\dfrac{s}{\sqrt{n}}} = \dfrac{5 - 10}{\dfrac{20}{\sqrt{16}}} = \dfrac{-5}{5} = -1;$ df $= n - 1 = 16 - 1 = 15.$

9.94 *Tip:* Whether the statistic is a t-statistic or a z-statistic is determined by whether the population standard deviation is known or whether the sample standard deviation is used instead. See the "in summary" box on page 371.

a. $t = \dfrac{\bar{x} - \mu}{s.e.(\bar{x})} = \dfrac{\bar{x} - \mu}{\dfrac{s}{\sqrt{n}}} = \dfrac{175 - 170}{\dfrac{24}{\sqrt{4}}} = \dfrac{5}{12} = 0.417;$ it's t because s is used instead of σ.

b. $z = \dfrac{\bar{x} - \mu}{s.e.(\bar{x})} = \dfrac{\bar{x} - \mu}{\dfrac{\sigma}{\sqrt{n}}} = \dfrac{175 - 170}{\dfrac{20}{\sqrt{4}}} = \dfrac{5}{10} = 0.5;$ it's z because σ is known.

c. $t = \dfrac{\bar{x} - \mu}{s.e.(\bar{x})} = \dfrac{\bar{x} - \mu}{\dfrac{s}{\sqrt{n}}} = \dfrac{161 - 170}{\dfrac{18}{\sqrt{36}}} = \dfrac{-9}{3} = -3;$ it's t because s is used instead of σ.

9.98 a. *t*-distribution with df $= 10$. Generally, a *t*-distribution is more spread out than a standard normal curve (although the difference is not great for larger values of degrees of freedom).
b. *t*-distribution with df $= 5$. Within the family of *t*-distributions, a *t*-distribution becomes less spread out as the degrees of freedom value increases.
c. Normal distribution with standard deviation $= 100$. A t-distribution is similar to a standard normal curve, which has standard deviation $= 1$.

9.99 a. *Tip*: See Example 9.16 on page 371.

$t = \dfrac{\bar{x} - \mu}{s.e.(\bar{x})} = \dfrac{\bar{x} - \mu}{\dfrac{s}{\sqrt{n}}} = \dfrac{105 - 100}{\dfrac{10}{\sqrt{25}}} = \dfrac{5}{2} = 2.5.$

Notice that the sample standard deviation is used so it is appropriate to use the symbol *t* to denote the standardized score.

9.105 **b.** 1/10 (only one way to have $R = 4$).
d. $R = 1$ is most likely; $R = 4$ is least likely.

9.107 **a.** For $T =$ total dogs in two households, possible values are 0, 1, 2, 3, and 4.

9.108 **a.** Probability = 1/2 that any particular line will be "broken." To verify this, list the eight possible outcomes for the three pennies, and notice that the number of heads is odd in one-half of the outcomes.
The possible outcomes are HHH, TTH, HTT, THT, HHT, HTH, THH, and TTT.
The outcomes with an odd number of heads are the first four sequences listed above.
b. B can be any of 0, 1, 2, 3, 4, 5, 6. Each one of the six lines can be broken or not.
c. *Tip*: Use the multiplication rule for independent events (Chapter 7, Rule 3).

$$P(B = 0) = \left(\frac{1}{2}\right)^6 = \frac{1}{64}.$$

d. The sampling distribution of B is a binomial distribution with $n = 6$ and $p = 1/2$. The six lines are like six trials of a binomial experiment. There are a fixed number o lines, there are two possible outcomes for each line (broken or not), the probability of being broken is 1/2 for each line, and lines are independent of one another.
The probabilities, which can be found using either the binomial formula (in Section 8.4) or software such as Minitab or Excel, are:
$P(B = 0) = \ \ 1/64 = .016$
$P(B = 1) = \ \ 6/64 = .094$
$P(B = 2) = 15/64 = .234$
$P(B = 3) = 20/64 = .312$
$P(B = 4) = 15/64 = .234$
$P(B = 5) = \ \ 6/64 = .094$
$P(B = 6) = \ \ 1/64 = .016$

9.110 **a.** The population of possible net gains is highly skewed (not bell-shaped), so this example does not fall into Situation 1 given on page 358. And, it does not fall into Situation 2 either because the sample size is small.
b. *Tip*: See the definition box at the top of page 375.

The mean of the sampling distribution of $\bar{x}$ is the population mean $\mu = -\$0.35$.

The standard deviation of $\bar{x}$ is $s.d.(\bar{x}) = \dfrac{\sigma}{\sqrt{n}} = \dfrac{\$29.67}{\sqrt{10}} = \$9.38$.

9.112 Because of the symmetry of the situation, the distribution of the lowest number should be a mirror image of the distribution given in Figure 9.12 for the highest number, so it should be highly skewed to the right. *Note*: The raw data are in the dataset **Cash5** on the data CD for the textbook, so this answer can be confirmed by drawing a histogram of the lowest numbers for the 1,560 plays.

9.115 **a.** X = number correct has a binomial distribution with $n = 10$ and $p = .5$. The number of trials ($n = 10$ questions) is fixed in advance, there are two possible outcomes for each trial, trials are independent, and the probability of success ($p = .5$) is the same for each trial.

b. $\mu = np = (10)(.5) = 5$ correct questions. Notice that this matches the intuitive solution, which is that if somebody guessed at 10 true-false question, they would get about five answers correct.

c. $\sigma = \sqrt{np(1-p)} = \sqrt{10(.5)(1-.5)} = 1.58$

Tip: For this part and for part (b), the relevant formulas are given in Section 8.4 on page 299.

9.122 The Rule for Sample Proportions applies because the three conditions given on page 350 are met. There is an actual population (the students at your college) and a fixed (although unknown) proportion of those students are left-handed. A random sample of 200 students at your college will be taken. The sample size, 200 is large enough so that both *np* and *n(1-p)* will be greater than 10.

9.125 **b.** Yes, a sample of 800 people from a population with a proportion of .50 would be unlikely to result in a sample proportion of .70. Nearly all sample proportions will be within 3 standard deviation of .50, which is .50± (3)(.0177) or .447 to .553.

9.129 *Tip:* See the definition box on page 359.
The distribution will be approximately a normal curve with mean 105 and standard deviation $s.d.(\bar{x}) = \dfrac{\sigma}{\sqrt{n}} = \dfrac{15}{\sqrt{100}} = 1.5$.

9.132 **a.** *Tip:* See Examples 9.9 and 9.10.

The distribution of possible sample proportions who watch the program is approximately a normal curve with a mean of .20 and a standard deviation of

$$\sqrt{\frac{p(1-p)}{n}} = \sqrt{\frac{.2(1-.2)}{2500}} = .008$$

b. If 20% of all viewers in the population watch this show, it is unlikely that a random sample of 2500 households would produce a sample percentage of less than 17%. We expect virtually all samples to have between 17.6% and 22.4% of viewers. This interval is determined as the *population percent ± 3×standard deviation.* Expressed as a percent, the standard deviation found in part (a) is 0.8%, and the "virtually all" interval is 20% ± (3×0.8%).

Alternatively, the z-score for 0.17 (which is 17%) is $\dfrac{.17 - .20}{.008} = -3.75$. The "In the extreme" part of Table A.1 indicates that the probability of a z-score this low or lower is only about .0001 (1 in 10,000).

9.135 **a.** No, the conditions are not met. The sample size is not large enough. If $p = .10$ and $n = 30$, then $np = 3$, which is less than 10.

b. Yes, assuming that the proportion of interest is a long-run relative frequency over all weekdays and seasons, and the days on which they do the survey is representative of all days and seasons. The fixed probability is that someone will be home during those hours at a randomly selected residence on a randomly selected day. The sample size is large enough. .

c. No, the conditions are not met. A random sample of days of the year was not taken, since the weather was recorded only for days in January and February. Clearly, snow or rain (depending on the area) will occur more frequently in those months than for the year as a whole.

d. Yes the conditions are met. The population consists of all employees of the company and a fixed proportion p of those employees is currently interested in on-site day care. A random sample was taken and the sample size of 100 is large enough unless p is very close to 0 or 1, which is not likely.

9.139 The phrase "almost sure" is vague but has been used in previous parts of the text to refer to the range covered by *mean* $\pm 3 \times s.d$ and will be interpreted that way for this exercise. The administration wants $3 \times s.d.(\bar{x}) = 1$ This means that

$$3 \frac{\sigma}{\sqrt{n}} = 3 \frac{5}{\sqrt{n}} = 1 \text{ which leads to } \sqrt{n} = 15 \text{ and } n = 225.$$

CHAPTER 10
SELECTED SOLUTIONS

10.1   **c.** This is a sample proportion. Actually, a sample percent is given in the problem. The corresponding proportion is .55.

10.4   **a.** ii. The number selecting the choice "more strict" could be 171 again.

10.7   **a.** *Tip:* See Example 10.1 on page 405.
The margin of error is given as 3.5%. Therefore, a 95% confidence interval is 36% ± 3.5% which is 32.5% to 39.5%. With 95% confidence, we can say that in the population of American adults, between 32.5% and 39.5% would say they don't get enough sleep each night.
b. No. Using the Fundamental Rule for Using Data for Inference, the sample could be used in this way only if American adults are representative of college students for this question. If college students generally differ from others on this question, which is highly likely, then this sample won't correctly estimate the percent for students.

10.9   About 190, which is 95% of the 200 computed intervals, should contain the population proportion and about 10 should not. Remember that the confidence level describes the confidence in the procedure and gives the percentage of all intervals that will contain the true value.

10.11   This sample should not be used to calculate a confidence interval because it is a self-selected volunteer sample and such samples are nearly always biased toward a certain viewpoint. In this case, it is possible that people who have been victims or know victims may be more likely to respond so the sample percentage will overestimate the population percentage. Therefore, the Fundamental Rule for Using Data for Inference doesn't hold.

10.12   100% − 95% = 5%. With a 95% confidence level, about 5% of all random samples from a population will provide a confidence interval that does not cover the population value.

10.14   **a.** p = the proportion of the population that suffers from allergies.

10.16   **a.** $s.e.(\hat{p}) = \sqrt{\dfrac{\hat{p}(1-\hat{p})}{n}} = \sqrt{\dfrac{.59(1-.59)}{1000}} = .016$
b. The 95% confidence interval is $\hat{p} \pm 2\, s.e.(\hat{p})$ which is $.59 \pm (2 \times .016)$ or .558 to .622.
With 95% confidence, we can say that between .558 and .622 of American adults think the world will come to an end.

10.19 **a.** The sample proportion is $\hat{p} = 166/200 = .83$.

b. The "formula" to use is *Sample estimate* $\pm$ *Multiplier* $\times$ *Standard error*. The sample estimate is $\hat{p} = .83$ and the standard error is

$$\sqrt{\frac{\hat{p}(1-\hat{p})}{n}} = \sqrt{\frac{.83(1-.83)}{200}} = .0266 .$$ For 95% confidence the multiplier is 1.96. The 95% confidence interval is $.83 \pm (1.96 \times .0266)$, which is .778 to .882.

Interpretation: With 95% confidence, we can say that if the whole population with this disease received this treatment, the proportion successfully treated would be between .778 and .882 (or 77.8% to 88.2%).

10.20 *Tip*: This exercise is similar to Example 10.3 on pages 412-13.

The "formula" to use is *Sample estimate* $\pm$ *Multiplier* $\times$ *Standard error*. The sample estimate is $\hat{p} = .83$ and the standard error is

$$s.e.(\hat{p}) = \sqrt{\frac{\hat{p}(1-\hat{p})}{n}} = \sqrt{\frac{.83(1-.83)}{200}} = .0266 .$$ For 98% confidence the multiplier

given in Table 10.1 is $z^* = 2.33$. The 98% confidence interval is $.83 \pm (2.33 \times .0266)$, which is $.83 \pm .062$ or .768 to .892. This interval is wider than the interval for the 95% confidence level given in part b of Exercise 10.19.
General Tip: In general, the higher the confidence level is, the wider the interval will be.

10.23 *Tip*: See Table 10.1 on page 412.

a. .90 or 90%
b. .95 or 95% (or 95.44%)
c. .98 or 98%
d. .99 or 99%

10.24 **a.** $\hat{p} = \dfrac{220}{400} = .55$.

b. $s.e.(\hat{p}) = \sqrt{\dfrac{\hat{p}(1-\hat{p})}{n}} = \sqrt{\dfrac{.55(1-.55)}{400}} = .025$

c. z* = 1.96, is the "exact" multiplier for 95% confidence (use Table 10.1 on p.412 to find this) The interval is $.55 \pm (1.96)(.025)$, which is $.55 \pm .049$, or .501 to .599. Approximately, this is .50 to .60.
d. z* = 2.33 is the multiplier for 99% confidence (use Table 10.1 on p.412 to find this). The interval is $.55 \pm (2.33)(.025)$, which is $.55 \pm .058$, or .492 to .608.

10.28   *Tip*: See Example 10.3 on pages 412-13.

The "formula" to use is *Sample estimate ± Multiplier × Standard error*.
The sample estimate is $\hat{p} = 57/300 = .19$ and the standard error is

$$s.e.(\hat{p}) = \sqrt{\frac{\hat{p}(1-\hat{p})}{n}} = \sqrt{\frac{.19(1-.19)}{300}} = .0226.$$ For 90% confidence the multiplier given in

Table 10.1 is $z^* = 1.645$. The 90% confidence interval is $.19 \pm (1.645 \times .0226)$, which
is $.19 \pm .037$ or .153 to .227. We are 90% confident that in the population of
employed Americans the proportion who would fire their boss if they could is
between .153 and .227.

10.29   *Tip*: See Example 10.4 on pages 413-14 for guidance.

$z* = 1.28$. To find this, use the standard normal curve to find the value $z*$ such that
the probability between $-z*$ and $+z*$ is .80.
If .80 is the probability between $-z*$ and $+z*$, then .10 is the probability to the left of
$-z*$. And, .90 is the probability to the left of $+z*$ (because .10 is to the right of this
value). In Table A.1, look either for .10 or for .90 where the probabilities are given,
and determine the corresponding z-value. The figure below illustrates the solution.

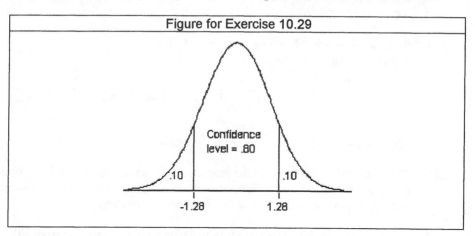

Figure for Exercise 10.29

10.32   **a.** 99% of the time.

10.34   *Tip*: See the two bulleted points in the middle of page 418.
The probability is .95 that the difference between the sample and population
proportions (or percentages) is less than the margin of error, so the probability that the
difference is greater than the margin of error (3% in this case) is $1 - .95 = .05$. The
long-run relative frequency interpretation of probability applies in this case, meaning
that in the long run, about .05 or 5% of samples will result in a difference greater than
the margin of error.

10.35 **a.** $2\sqrt{\dfrac{\hat{p}(1-\hat{p})}{n}} = 2\sqrt{\dfrac{.56(1-.56)}{100}} = .0993$.

b. $2\sqrt{\dfrac{\hat{p}(1-\hat{p})}{n}} = 2\sqrt{\dfrac{.56(1-.56)}{400}} = .0496$.

10.37 **a.** *Tip*: See Example 10.8 on page 422.

$\dfrac{1}{\sqrt{n}} = \dfrac{1}{\sqrt{501}} = .045$, or 4.5% which could be rounded up to 5%.

10.38 **a.** $s.e.(\hat{p}) = \sqrt{\dfrac{\hat{p}(1-\hat{p})}{n}} = \sqrt{\dfrac{.03(1-.03)}{883}} = .00574$

b. $2\,s.e.(\hat{p}) = 2(.00574) = .01148$, or 1.1%.

10.41 *Tip*: The necessary conditions for using the methods of Section 10.4 are given on pages 424-25.
a. Yes, there are two independent samples with sufficiently large sample sizes.
b. No, the sample sizes are too small.
c. No, The methods of Section 10.4 should not be used because the analysis involves means, not proportions.

10.45 **b.** Sample estimate $\pm$ Multiplier $\times$ Standard error
Sample estimate = $\hat{p}_1 - \hat{p}_2 = .466 - .380 = .086$
Standard error

$= s.e.(\hat{p}_1 - \hat{p}_2) = \sqrt{\dfrac{\hat{p}_1(1-\hat{p}_1)}{n_1} + \dfrac{\hat{p}_2(1-\hat{p}_2)}{n_2}} = \sqrt{\dfrac{.466(1-.466)}{4594} + \dfrac{.380(1-.380)}{7076}}$

Multiplier = $z^* \approx 2$ (or 1.96 would be more exact)

10.47 This is the difference between the proportions in two categories of a variable within the same single sample. The method in Section 10.4 is for the difference in the proportions with the same trait in two independent samples.

10.50 **a.** *Tip*: See the In Summary box on page 420 and Example 10.1 on page 405.
55% $\pm$ 3%, or 52% to 58%. This is calculated as *Sample estimate* $\pm$ *Margin of error*.

b. *Tip*: See Principle 1 on page 428.
Yes. All of the values in the 95% confidence interval are greater than 50%, so it's reasonable to infer that more than 50% of the population thinks their weight is about right.

10.51 *Tip*: See Principle 1 on page 428.
The claim of 28% is not reasonable because the value 28% not in the confidence interval.

10.54   **a.** *Tip*: See Principle 3 on page 428-29.
95% confidence intervals for the two years do not overlap. It's reasonable to conclude that the population percent is higher in 2002. The 95% confidence intervals can be computed as
Sample percent ± Margin of error. For 1999, the confidence interval is 46% ± 3%, or 43% to 49%. For 2002, the confidence interval is 55% ± 3%, or 52% to 58%.

10.56   **b.** While the sample is not a random sample, for the question of interest it may provide a suitable estimate of the proportion that is left-handed in the population. It doesn't seem that this sample of 400 students should be biased toward having a different proportion that's left-handed than in the population.

10.59   **a.** This is an observational study because the researchers simply observed the proportion with heart disease for both policemen and men of other occupations. The researchers did not assign certain men to be policemen. Instead, naturally occurring groups were compared.
b. We can not attribute the observed difference to job related factors since this is an observational study. The observed difference in heart disease percentages may be due to other confounding variables. For example, perhaps policemen smoked more than the other men or had worse dietary habits.

10.63   **c.** 71% ± 5% or 66% to 76%. We can be 95% confident that somewhere between 66% and 76% of all adult Americans would answer that they are for the death penalty when asked Question 1.
d. 56% ± 5% which is 51% to 61%. We can be 95% confident that between 51% and 61% of all adult Americans would respond "death penalty" when asked Question 2. Notice that all values in this interval are lower than all values in the interval of part (c). This is an example of how the wording of a question can affect how people respond.

10.66   **a.** The sample estimate is $\hat{p}_1 - \hat{p}_2 = .155 - .168 = -0.013$.

The standard error is $s.e.(\hat{p}_1 - \hat{p}_2) = \sqrt{\dfrac{.155(1-.155)}{207} + \dfrac{.168(1-.168)}{273}} = 0.034$.

For 90% confidence the multiplier is 1.645. Therefore, a 90% confidence interval for the difference in population proportions of women and men with tattoos is $-0.013 \pm 1.645(.034)$ or -0.013 ± 0.056 or -0.069 to $+0.043$ or about -0.07 to $+0.04$.
b. *Tip*: See Principle 2 on page 428.
The interval covers 0 so we cannot rule out the possibility that the population proportions are equal.

10.69   **a.** Approximate 95% confidence interval is .264 to .416, computed as $.34 \pm 2 \times .038$.
Parameter is $p_1 - p_2$ = difference in proportions of men (population 1) and women
(population 2) who have driven after having too much to drink
The interval is Sample estimate $\pm 2 \times$ Standard error, which is
$$\hat{p}_1 - \hat{p}_2 \pm 2 \times \text{s.e.} (\hat{p}_1 - \hat{p}_2)$$
Sample estimate $= \hat{p}_1 - \hat{p}_2 = .63 - .29 = .34$
Standard error $=$
$$\text{s.e.} (\hat{p}_1 - \hat{p}_2) = \sqrt{\frac{\hat{p}_1(1-\hat{p}_1)}{n_1} + \frac{\hat{p}_2(1-\hat{p}_2)}{n_2}} = \sqrt{\frac{.63(1-.63)}{300} + \frac{.29(1-.29)}{300}} = .038$$

10.72   **c.** A 99% confidence interval is about 0.090 to 0.302, computed as $0.1965 \pm$
$(2.576)(0.0412)$.
Parameter is $p_1 - p_2$ = the difference in proportions of men with a tattoo for
populations of Penn State men with an ear pierce (group 1) and without an ear pierce
(group 2).
For computing Sample estimate $\pm$ Multiplier $\times$ Standard error:
Sample estimate is $\hat{p}_1 - \hat{p}_2 = .2979 - .1014 = 0.1965$
$$\text{Standard error is s.e.} (\hat{p}_1 - \hat{p}_2) = \sqrt{\frac{.298(1-.298)}{141} + \frac{.101(1-.101)}{424}} = 0.0412$$
Multiplier $= z^* = 2.576$. Use Table 10.1 on page 412.
Check necessary conditions: The numbers in each category for each group are > 10.

Interpretation: We are 99% confident that in the population(s) of Penn State men
represented by the sample(s), the difference in the proportions with a tattoo for men
with an ear pierce versus men without an ear pierce is between 0.090 and 0.302. In
other words, the percentage with a tattoo among men with ear pierce is between 9%
and 30% above the percentage with a tattoo among men with no ear pierce.

CHAPTER 11
SELECTED SOLUTIONS

11.2 Are you asking a question about children in this school only, or using them to represent a larger population?

11.4 **b.** The difference in population means is estimated using the difference in sample means. So the sample estimate is $\bar{x}_1 - \bar{x}_2 = 22.5 - 16.3 = 6.2$ days.

11.7 *Tip*: See the discussion on pages 445-446.
a. Procedure for two independent samples.
b. Procedure for paired data.
c. Procedure for two independent samples.

11.10 **a.** Answers will differ for each student, but here is a possible answer. The two populations are women who got married in 1970 and women who got married in 2000. The response variable is the woman's age when she got married. The question of interest is whether the average age at marriage for women changed between 1970 and 2000. In general, the answer should include a categorical variable defining the two populations and a quantitative variable measured on each individual.

11.12 *Tip*: See Example 11.2 on page 448 and the discussion immediately following it.

$\text{s.e.}(\bar{x}) = \dfrac{s}{\sqrt{n}} = \dfrac{2}{\sqrt{64}} = 0.25$ cm. Over all possible samples of $n = 64$ from this population, the average difference between the sample mean and the population mean is about 0.25 cm.

11.14 *Tip*: See the discussion and formula for paired differences at the top of page 448.

This is paired data, so calculate the difference in pulse rates for each of the 50 people. Let s_d = standard deviation of the $n = 50$ *differences*.

Calculate the desired standard error of the mean as $\dfrac{s_d}{\sqrt{n}} = \dfrac{s_d}{\sqrt{50}}$.

11.16 Take a large enough sample or samples. One way to do this is to guess at what the standard deviation(s) will be and then figure out what size sample(s) are needed to produce a desired width for the confidence interval. For bell-shaped data, the standard deviation can be estimated if an approximate range is known. The Empirical Rule tells us that most of the data will fall within a range of 4 to 6 standard deviations, so if we know the approximate range, we can guess that the standard deviation will be about Range/6 to Range/4.

11.19   **a.** $t^* = 2.13$. *Tip*: Table A.2 or appropriate software can be used. In this case, use the row of Table A.2 for $df = 15$ and the column for confidence level of .95.

11.21   *Tip*: See Example 11.5 on pages 454-55.

     a. $76 \pm 2.31 \dfrac{6}{\sqrt{9}}$ or 71.38 to 80.62; $df = n - 1 = 9 - 1 = 8$ for t^*.

     e. $100 \pm 2.13 \dfrac{8}{\sqrt{16}}$ or 95.74 to 104.26, $df = n - 1 = 16 - 1 = 15$ for t^*.

11.23   **a.** 2.52; use the row of Table A.2 for $df = n - 1 = 22 - 1 = 21$ and the column for confidence level of .98.
     b. 2.13; use the row of Table A.2 for $df = n - 1 = 5 - 1 = 4$ and the column for confidence level of .90.

11.26   Compute interval as Sample estimate $\pm$ Multiplier $\times$ Standard error, which here is

     $\bar{x} \pm t^* \dfrac{s}{\sqrt{n}}$. The confidence interval is $8.1 \pm 2.82 \times \dfrac{1.8}{\sqrt{23}}$ or about 7.04 to 9.16 days.

     Sample estimate is $\bar{x} = 8.1$ days.   Standard error is s.e. $(\bar{x}) = \dfrac{s}{\sqrt{n}} = \dfrac{1.6}{\sqrt{25}} = 0.32$.

     Multiplier is $t^* = 2.82$. In Table A.2, use row for $df = n - 1 = 23 - 1 = 22$ and column for confidence level of .99.
     Compared to part (b) of the previous exercise, only the multiplier t^* changes.

11.28   For this answer, we'll round the mean and standard deviation to the nearest dollar. About 95% had textbook expenses in the interval $285 \pm (2)(\$96)$, which is \$93 to \$487. The calculation is $\bar{x} \pm 2 \times s$. Remember that the Empirical Rule tells us that approximately 95% of all values fall within 2 standard deviations of the mean.

11.31   **a.** *Tip*: See the standard error formula on page 448 and the approximate confidence interval definition on page 460.

     s.e. $(\bar{x}) = \dfrac{s}{\sqrt{n}} = \dfrac{2.7}{\sqrt{81}} = 0.3$ inch. Approximate 95% confidence interval is

     Sample estimate $\pm 2 \times$ *Standard error*, which is $64.2 \pm (2 \times 0.3)$, or 63.6 to 64.8 inches.

11.33   *Tip*: See the standard error formula on page 448 and the approximate confidence interval definition on page 460.

     s.e. $(\bar{x}) = \dfrac{s}{\sqrt{n}} = \dfrac{2}{\sqrt{64}} = 0.25$ cm.

     Calculate the interval as Sample estimate $\pm 2 \times$ Standard error, which here is $\bar{x} \pm 2 \times$ s.e.$(\bar{x})$. The interval is 27 to 28 cm, computed as $27.5 \pm 2 \times 0.25$.

     Interpretation: With approximate 95% confidence, we can say that in the population of men represented by this sample the mean foot length is between 27 and 28 cm.

11.34 Using the value of 2 as an approximation for the t^* multiplier will work well only if the t^* multiplier for 95% confidence is in fact close to 2. Examination of the values in Table A.2 reveals that this is the case for degrees of freedom higher than about 30 or 40, but not for smaller degrees of freedom. For instance, for 5 degrees of freedom the correct multiplier is $t^* = 2.57$, which is much larger than 2. The relationship df $= n - 1$ means that when n is very small, df will also be very small.

11.36 **a.** Using the information in Example 11.9 (page 463) for a 90% confidence interval, we need only change the multiplier to find a 95% confidence interval. The multiplier from Table A.2 with df $= 24$ and confidence level $= .95$ is $t^* = 2.06$. The 95% confidence interval is $5.36 \pm (2.06)(3.05)$, which is 5.36 ± 6.28 or -0.92 to 11.64.
b. *Tip*: See the discussion on page 464.
No. The interval covers 0, and any value in the interval is a plausible population mean difference.
c. Two different variables are measured for each individual.

11.38 *Tip*: See the discussion on page 464.
No. Any value in the interval is a plausible value for the difference in means. So the only way we could conclude that the two population means are identical is if the interval had no width, and 0 was the only value in it.

11.41 *Tip*: See the discussion at the bottom of page 470.
a. Conclude that there is a difference between the population means. The value 0 would occur if there was no difference between population means. The interval encompasses the plausible values for the population mean difference. So if the interval does not cover 0 it says that a mean difference of 0 is not plausible.
b. We cannot conclude that there is a difference between the population means. The value 0 would occur if there was no difference between population means. So, if the interval covers 0 we cannot reject a statement (hypothesis) of no difference. We can only conclude that the true difference is likely to be somewhere in the range covered by the interval.

11.42 **a.** Here, Sample estimate $\pm$ Multiplier $\times$ Standard error is $\bar{x}_1 - \bar{x}_2 \pm t^* \times \text{s.e.}(\bar{x}_1 - \bar{x}_2)$
$\bar{x}_1 - \bar{x}_2 = 11.6 - 10.7 = 0.9$

$$\text{s.e.}(\bar{x}_1 - \bar{x}_2) = \sqrt{\frac{s_1^2}{n_1} + \frac{s_2^2}{n_2}} = \sqrt{\frac{3.39^2}{16} + \frac{2.59^2}{10}} = 1.18 \text{ (unpooled)}$$

Multiplier is $t^* = 2.07$ (Use Table A.2 with df $= 22$)

11.45 *Tip*: See Example 11.3 on page 449 and Example 11.13 on page 472.

a. $\bar{x}_1 - \bar{x}_2 = 57.5 - 55.3 = 2.2$ cm.

b. $s.e.(\bar{x}_1 - \bar{x}_2) = \sqrt{\dfrac{s_1^2}{n_1} + \dfrac{s_2^2}{n_2}} = \sqrt{\dfrac{2.4^2}{36} + \dfrac{1.8^2}{36}} = 0.5$ cm.

c. Approximate 95% confidence interval for the difference in population means is *Sample estimate* $\pm 2\times$ *Standard error*, which is $2.2 \pm (2 \times 0.5)$, or 1.2 to 3.2 cm.

11.48 The variances (or, equivalently, the standard deviations) in the two populations are assumed to have the same value.

11.50 Confidence interval is about 2.62 to 4.58 days, computed as $3.6 \pm (2.01)(0.49)$. Parameter is $\mu_1 - \mu_2 =$ difference between mean days of symptoms in population of cold sufferers if taking placebo versus zinc lozenges.

Compute interval as Sample estimate $\pm$ Multiplier $\times$ Standard error:

Sample estimate is $\bar{x}_1 - \bar{x}_2 = 8.1 - 4.5 = 3.6$ days

Standard error (pooled) is $s.e.(\bar{x}_1 - \bar{x}_2) = \sqrt{\dfrac{s_p^2}{n_2} + \dfrac{s_p^2}{n_1}} = \sqrt{\dfrac{1.7^2}{23} + \dfrac{1.7^2}{25}} = 0.49$ days

where $s_p = \sqrt{\dfrac{(n_1-1)s_1^2 + (n_2-1)s_2^2}{n_2 + n_2 - 2}} = \sqrt{\dfrac{(25-1)\times 1.6^2 + (23-1)\times 1.8^2}{23 + 25 - 2}} = 1.7$ days.

Multiplier is $t^* \approx 2.01$.

For pooled procedure, df $= n_1 + n_2 - 2 = 23 + 25 - 2 = 46$. Table A.2 does not have an entry for df $= 46$. We've used the entry for df $= 50$, although a more conservative procedure is to use the entry for df $= 40$. Minitab, Excel, or a calculator with the relevant capability could be used to determine that $t^* = 2.013$ for df $= 46$.

11.52 **c.** Formula for approximate 95% confidence interval is $\bar{x} \pm 2\dfrac{s}{\sqrt{n}}$.

Calculation is $72.8 \pm 2 \times \dfrac{72.2}{\sqrt{204}}$, which is 72.8 ± 10.1 and this gives the desired result.

11.54 The two confidence intervals given do not cover 1.0, the value of a relative risk that occurs if the risks under two conditions are the same. So, it is reasonable to conclude that in the population(s) represented by the sample(s), the risk of death during a twelve-year period is higher for people with abnormal heart rate recovery after treadmill exercise than it is for people with normal heart rate recovery.

11.63   **a.** The interval will be wider for 95% than for 90% confidence.
b. The interval will be narrower if the sample size is doubled because the standard error will decrease.
c. Assuming the standard deviation stays the same, the width will remain the same if the sample size is the same. The observed value of a sample mean does not affect the width of the confidence interval.

11.66   **a.** *Tip*: See the two situations for which the methods apply described on page 454.

The last weight given for each team is an outlier. It is the weight of the coxswain, who gives instructions about the rowing cadence but does not row. A coxswain's weight is much less than the weights of the rowers, leading to the two substantial outliers. Because $n = 18$, the dataset doesn't qualify for either of the two situations on page 454.

11.69   *Tip*: See the summary box about paired data on page 446.
b. This is paired data. The differences between the ages of the husband and wife can be determined for each couple and are not independent.

11.71   **d.** *Tip*: See Example 11.3 on page 449 and Example 11.13 on page 472.

The formula for the difference between means for independent samples is used. The formula is $\bar{x}_1 - \bar{x}_2 \pm 2 \times \sqrt{\dfrac{s_1^2}{n_1} + \dfrac{s_2^2}{n_2}}$.

Substitution of relevant values gives $(2.37 - 1.95) \pm 2 \times \sqrt{\dfrac{1.87^2}{59} + \dfrac{1.51^2}{116}}$.

Note: Assignment of group numbers (1 or 2) to the specific groups is essentially arbitrary. We've designated the men as group 1 so that the difference in part (a) is positive.

11.73   **a.** A "success" for a researcher is that the computed interval covers the population mean.
b. The probability of a success is $p = .90$. This probability is the relative frequency of times over all possible random samples from the population that an interval covers the population mean.
e. Probability = $(.90)^{100} = .000027$ that all intervals cover the population mean. Use the extension of Rule 3b on p.246. It can also be calculated using Minitab or Excel to calculate $P(X = 100)$ in a binomial distribution with $n = 100$ and $p = .9$. For instance the Excel command BINOMDIST(100,100,0.90,FALSE) could be used.

CHAPTER 12
SELECTED SOLUTIONS

12.1   **a.** All babies.
b. p = proportion of babies in the population born during the 24-hour period surrounding a full moon.
c. H_0: $p = 1/29.53$

12.4   **a.** The populations of interest are all 21-year-old men and all 21-year-old women.
b. Researchers are interested in the hypothesis that the proportions of 21-year-old men and women who have high school diplomas are the same.

12.7   The answer will vary. An example is the hypothesis that equal proportions of mean and women are unemployed. The populations are men and women and the proportion of interest is the proportion unemployed.

12.10   **a.** No. A null hypothesis is a statement about a population value, not a sample value as in the statement for this exercise.
b. Yes. It's a statement of no difference and could be interpreted to apply to all newborns.
c. No. This statement would more appropriately be an alternative hypothesis (a statement of a difference).
The hypothesis test is two-sided. The alternative hypothesis does not give a specific direction for how the probability might differ from .5.

12.12   *Tip*: Null and alternative hypothesis are statements about populations. Always use notation for population values when writing hypotheses.

a. There are 5 choices so $p = 1/5 = .2$. Random selection means that each of the five choices is equally likely to be chosen.
b. H_0: $p = .2$ (random selection)
  H_a: $p < .2$ (less often than random selection would give)

12.14   The decision to use a one-sided or two-sided alternative hypothesis should be made before looking at the sample data. The alternative hypothesis usually expresses the research hypothesis, which in turn gives the reason for collecting the data. The reason for collecting the data should be defined before the data are collected.

Note: In Section 12.3 it will become clear that looking at the data first and making the alternative hypothesis consistent with it may distort the p-value, leading to the conclusion of statistical significance more often than is warranted.

12.16   **a.** Population is all school-aged children living in the state at the time of the study. Proportion of interest = proportion of them who live with one or more grandparents.

12.18   **b.** The null value is 32.

12.20   **a.** Cannot reject the null hypothesis. The *p*-value is not less than the level of significance.
b. Reject the null hypothesis. The *p*-value is less than the level of significance.
General Tip: Reject the null hypothesis when the *p*-value is less than or equal to the level of significance. If the *p*-value is greater than level of significance, you cannot reject the null hypothesis.

12.22   **a.** The *p*-value (.33) is not less than the level of significance (.05), so there is not enough evidence to conclude that smokers are more likely to get the disease.

12.26   *Tip*: See the discussion on page 503.
a. Cannot reject the null hypothesis. The *p*-value (.35) is greater than .05. The observed result is not statistically significant.
b. Reject the null hypothesis (or accept the alternative hypothesis). The *p*-value (.001) is less than .05. The observed result is statistically significant.
c. Reject the null hypothesis (or accept the alternative hypothesis). The *p*-value (.04) is less than .05. The observed result is statistically significant.

12.29   **a.** False. The *p*-value is the probability the test statistic would be as extreme as it is or more so, computed assuming the null is true.
b. True by definition.
c. False. A type 2 error can occur only when the alternative is true.
d. False. Type 1 and 2 errors are not complementary (opposite) events. A type 1 error can be made only when the null hypothesis is true and a type 2 error can be made only when the alternative hypothesis is true.

12.31   *Tip*: See the tree diagram on page 507.
a. The correct decision has been made. The null is true and it is not rejected.
b. A type 2 error has occurred. The alternative is true, but the null is not rejected.

12.34   In this situation, a type 1 error would occur if the patient is incorrectly diagnosed as having the disease. A type 2 error would occur if the patient was incorrectly believed to not have the disease.

a. The answer will vary. An example: A type 1 error would be more serious if the diagnosis of that the disease is present leads to a major surgery. For example, in certain elderly men prostate cancer grows very slowly and may never become life threatening, so a type 2 error may not be so serious. A type 1 error could lead to unnecessary surgery and would be more serious.

b. The answer will vary. An example: A type 2 error would be more serious for the diagnosis of an infection that could be cured by antibiotics but gets very serious if untreated (the consequence of a type 2 error). Although there is some concern about overusing antibiotics, it would not be particularly harmful for the patient to take them even though an infection is not present (the consequence of a type 1 error).

12.36   **c.** A type 1 error is probably more serious because this involves voting for the bill that implements substantial change, when a majority of the voters do not support it.
d. Type 1. The politician decided in favor of the alternative hypothesis, so the potential mistake is that he has incorrectly rejected the null hypothesis.

12.41   *Tip*: See Table 12.1 on page 517 as well as the three bullets above it.
a. *p*-value = .0358. This is the combined probability to the right of $z = 2.10$ and left of $z = -2.10$. Table A.1 can be used to find that $P(Z < -2.10) = .0179$. By symmetry, the area to the right of $z = 2.10$ is also .0179. So, the *p*-value = $2 \times .0179 = .0358$.

Figure for Exercise 12.41a

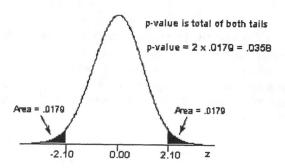

b.   *p*-value = .0228. This is the probability (area) to the left of $z = -2.00$. Table A.1 can be used to find $P(Z < -2) = .0228$.

Figure for Exercise 12.41b

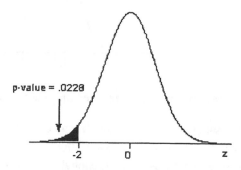

c. *p*-value = .1379. This is the probability (area) to the left of $z = -1.09$. Table A.1 can be used to find $P(Z < -1.09) = .1379$.

Figure for Exercise 12.41c

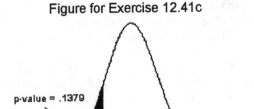

p-value = .1379

-1.09 0.00   z

d. *p*-value $\approx$.00001. This is the probability (area) to right of z = 4.25. By the symmetry of the normal curve, this probability equals the area to the left of z = −4.25. In Table A.1, use the "In the Extreme" section to estimate the probability. A probability (to the left) is given for z = −4.26, which is close enough for this exercise. Software or a calculator with the relevant capability could also be used to find this probability.

Figure for Exercise 12.41d

p-value = .00001
= area past 4.25

0.00   4.25   z

12.43   *Tip:* The necessary conditions are given on page 512 of the text.

a. Yes. The sample is a random sample, and the sample size is large enough because $np_0 = (20)(.50) = 10$, and $n(1-p_0) = (20)(1 - .50) = 10$.

b. No. The sample size is not large enough because $np_0 = (20)(.10) = 2$ is smaller than 10.

c. No. A test of hypothesis is not necessary because the all members of the population have been observed. In other words, this is not a random sample from a larger population.

d. No. This is not a random sample of all mall visitors, but instead is a somewhat haphazard convenience sample.

12.45   **b.** The test statistic is $z = \dfrac{\text{Sample estimate - Null value}}{\text{Null standard error}}$

$$\text{Null standard error} = \sqrt{\frac{p_0(1-p_0)}{n}} = \sqrt{\frac{.25(1-.25)}{60}} = .0559$$

$$z = \frac{\text{Sample estimate - Null value}}{\text{Null standard error}} = \frac{.10 - .25}{.0559} = \frac{-.15}{.0559} = -2.68$$

12.46   **b.** The *p*-value is 0.0037. It is the area under the standard normal curve to the left of (less than) −2.68 because the alternative hypothesis is a "less than" region. Using Table A.1, we see that $P(Z < -2.68) = .0037$.
Note: The figure given in the solution for exercise 12.41b illustrates the nature of the *p*-value region for this situation (although, of course, the values are different in that exercise).

12.47   The null standard error uses the hypothesized null value p_0, while the standard error uses the observed sample proportion $\hat{p}$.

$$\text{Null standard error} = \sqrt{\frac{p_0(1-p_0)}{n}} \quad \text{while standard error} = \sqrt{\frac{\hat{p}(1-\hat{p})}{n}}$$

12.49   **a.** We can't be certain that the conditions are met because we don't know whether the sample was selected randomly. We do know that the sample size is large enough. Both np_0 and $n(1-p_0)$ are greater than 10, as they should be to use a *z*-statistic. Here, $n = 180$ and $p_0 = .1$ (the proportion in the general population).

b. *Tip*: This is similar to Example 12.12 on pages 519-20.

<u>Step 1</u>: H$_0$: $p = .1$ (proportion left-handed same for artists as in general population)
        H$_a$: $p > .1$
<u>Step 2</u>: See part (a) for discussion of the necessary conditions.
The test statistic is $z = \dfrac{\text{Sample estimate - Null value}}{\text{Null standard error}}$
Sample estimate = $\hat{p} = 15/180 = .12$
Null value = $p_0 = .1$

$$\text{Null standard error} = \sqrt{\frac{p_0(1-p_0)}{n}} = \sqrt{\frac{.1(1-.1)}{150}} = .02449$$

$$z = \frac{\text{Sample estimate - Null value}}{\text{Null standard error}} = \frac{.12 - .10}{.0245} = \frac{.02}{.02449} = 0.82$$

<u>Step 3</u>: *p*-value ≈ .21. This is the probability that $z > 0.82$, which is illustrated in the following figure. By symmetry, $P(z > 0.82) = P(z < -0.82)$. Table A.1 gives $P(z < -0.82) = .2061$.

12.49 continued:

Figure for Exercise 12.49b

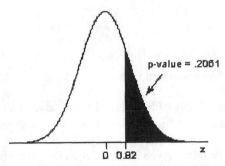

Note: An exact *p*-value can be found as the probability that $X \geq 18$ in a binomial distribution with $n = 150$ and $p=.10$. The exact *p*-value given by Minitab is .242.
Step 4: Cannot reject the null hypothesis. The result is not statistically significant because the *p*-value (.2061) is greater than .05.
Step 5: We cannot conclude that artists are more likely to be left-handed than people in the general population.
Note: Minitab can be used to find the *z*-statistic and corresponding *p*-value. See the Minitab Tip on page 526 for guidance. The output for this exercise is

Output for Exercise 12.49b					
Sample	X	N	Sample p	95.0% Lower Bound	Z-Value	P-Value
1	18	150	0.120000	0.076357	0.82	0.207

12.51 **a.** We cannot reject the null hypothesis because the *p*-value (.07) is greater than .05.
b. The *p*-value for the one-sided test is .07/2 = .035. We would be able to decide in favor of the alternative hypothesis because this *p*-value is smaller than .05 (the usual criterion for statistical significance).

Tip: In general, in the same situation, the *p*-value for a one-sided alternative hypothesis is one-half the p-value for a two-sided alternative. Consider the pictures and information given in Table 12.1 on page 517.

12.55 **a.** $P(X \geq 17)$ for a binomial random variable with $n = 50$ and $p = .25$. (See the table in the "in summary" box on page 522.)

12.58 *Tip*: See Step 3 on page 529 and Table 12.1 on page 517.
a. *p*-value = .0401. It is the area (probability) to the right of $z = 1.75$ under a standard normal curve. This can be found as $P(z > 1.75) = P(z \leq -1.75) = .0401$. Equivalently, $P(z > 1.75) = 1 - P(z \leq 1.75) = 1 - .9599 = .0401$.

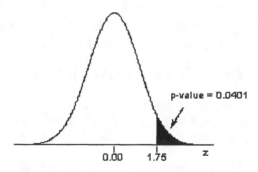

b. *p*-value = .9599. It is the area (probability) to the right of *z* = −1.75 under a standard normal curve. This can be found as $P(z > -1.75) = P(z \le 1.75) = .9599$. Equivalently, $P(z > -1.75) = 1 - P(z \le -1.75) = 1 - .0401 = .9599$.

Figure for Exercise 12.58b

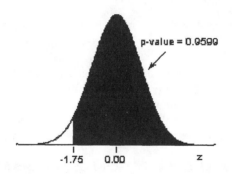

12.59 **a.** Reject the null hypothesis (accept the alternative); *p*-value = $P(z \le -1.99) = .0233$ is less than .05.
b. Reject the null hypothesis (accept the alternative); *p*-value = $P(z > 1.78) = P(z \le -1.78) = .0375$ is less than .05.

12.60 *Tip*: The rejection region rules are given on page 523 of the text.

c. Rejection region is $z < -1.645$.
Do not reject the null hypothesis. *z*-statistic = 0.33 is not less than −1.645.
d. Rejection region is $z > 1.645$.
Do not reject the null hypothesis. *z*-statistic = 0.33 is not greater than 1.645.

12.63 *Tip*: This is similar to Example 12.17 (continued) on pages 530-31.

Step 1: H₀: $p_1 - p_2 = 0$, or equivalently, $p_1 = p_2$ (no difference in proportions)

$\quad$ Hₐ: $p_1 - p_2 > 0$, or equivalently, $p_1 > p_2$ (proportion higher for women)

p_1 = proportion of women in the population who would claim they would return the money

p_2 = proportion of men in the population who would claim they would return the money

Step 2: There are two independent samples and the observed counts in both categories (yes and no) are greater than 10 for both males and females. We must assume the samples represent random samples from the population of all college students.

Test statistic is $z = \dfrac{\text{Sample statistic - Null value}}{\text{Null standard error}} = \dfrac{.1965 - 0}{.0602} = 3.26$. Details are:

Women, $\hat{p}_1 = \dfrac{84}{93} = .9032$; men, $\hat{p}_2 = \dfrac{53}{75} = .7067$; $\hat{p}_1 - \hat{p}_2 = .9032 - .7067 = .1965$

Combined $\hat{p} = \dfrac{84 + 53}{93 + 75} = .8155$

Null standard error =

$$\sqrt{\dfrac{\hat{p}(1 - \hat{p})}{n_1} + \dfrac{\hat{p}(1 - \hat{p})}{n_2}} = \sqrt{\dfrac{.8155(1 - .8155)}{93} + \dfrac{.8155(1 - .8155)}{75}} = .0602$$

Step 3: *p*-value = .0006 (or ≈.001). It is the area to the right of 3.26 under a standard normal curve. $P(z > 3.26) = P(z \le -3.26) = .0006$ (in Table A.1).

Steps 4 and 5: We can reject the null hypothesis. The conclusion is that in the population(s) represented by the sample(s) a higher proportion of women than men would claim they would return the money if they found a wallet on the street.

12.65 *Tip*: This is similar to Example 12.17 (continued) on pages 530-31.

Step 1: H₀: $p_1 - p_2 = 0$, or equivalently, $p_1 = p_2$ (no difference in proportions)

$\quad$ Hₐ: $p_1 - p_2 > 0$, or equivalently, $p_1 > p_2$ (proportion higher for women)

p_1 = proportion of women in the population who would say "more strict"

p_2 = proportion of men in the population who would say "more strict"

Step 2: There are two independent samples assumed to be randomly selected, and the observed counts in both categories (more strict or other answer) are greater than 10 for both groups (women and men).

Test statistic is $z = \dfrac{\text{Sample statistic - Null value}}{\text{Null standard error}} = \dfrac{.20 - 0}{.03193} = 6.26$. Details are:

Sample statistic = $\hat{p}_1 - \hat{p}_2 = .72 - .52 = .20$

Combined $\hat{p} = \dfrac{n_1 \hat{p}_1 + n_2 \hat{p}_2}{n_1 + n_2} = \dfrac{538(.72) + 493(.52)}{538 + 493} = .6244$

Null standard error

$$= \sqrt{\frac{\hat{p}(1-\hat{p})}{n_1} + \frac{\hat{p}(1-\hat{p})}{n_2}} = \sqrt{\frac{.6244(1-.6244)}{538} + \frac{.6244(1-.6244)}{493}} = .03193$$

Step 3: *p*-value < .000000001. It is the area to the right of 6.26 under a standard normal curve. $P(z > 6.26) = P(z \le -6.26)$. At the bottom of the left page in Table A.1, a cumulative probability is given for z = −6.00. The *p*-value must be less than that probability because −6.26 is more extreme than −6.00.

Steps 4 and 5: We can reject the null hypothesis. The conclusion is that in the population(s) represented by the sample(s) the proportion of women who would say there should be "more strict" laws covering the sale of firearms is higher than the proportion of men who would say this.

12.67   *Tip*: This is similar to Example 12.17 (continued) on pages 530-31.

Step 1: H_0: $p_1 - p_2 = 0$, or equivalently, $p_1 = p_2$ (no difference in proportions)

H_a: $p_1 - p_2 > 0$, or equivalently, $p_1 > p_2$ (proportion higher for women)

p_1 = proportion of women in the population who would say yes
p_2 = proportion of men in the population who would say yes

Step 2: There are two independent samples and the observed counts in both categories (yes or no) are greater than 10 for both groups (women and men). We must assume the samples represent random samples from the population of all college students.

Test statistic is $z = \dfrac{\text{Sample statistic - Null value}}{\text{Null standard error}} = \dfrac{.185 - 0}{.07708} = 2.40$.   Details are:

Sample statistic = $\hat{p}_1 - \hat{p}_2 = .611 - .426 = .185$

Combined $\hat{p} = \dfrac{n_1 \hat{p}_1 + n_2 \hat{p}_2}{n_1 + n_2} = \dfrac{131(.611) + 61(.426)}{131 + 61} = .552$

Null standard error = $\sqrt{\hat{p}(1-\hat{p})(\dfrac{1}{n_1} + \dfrac{1}{n_2})} = \sqrt{.552(1-.552)(\dfrac{1}{131} + \dfrac{1}{61})} = 0.07708$

Step 3: *p*-value = .0082. It is the area to the right of z = 2.40 under a standard normal curve.

$P(z > 2.40) = P(z \le -2.40) = .0082$. Equivalently, $P(z > 2.40) = 1 - P(z \le 2.40) = 1 - .9918 = .0082$.

Steps 4 and 5: We can reject the null hypothesis. The conclusion is that in the population(s) represented by the sample(s) a higher proportion of women than men would claim they would date someone with a great personality even if they did not find them physically attractive.

12.70   **a.** Null standard error = $\sqrt{\dfrac{p_0(1-p_0)}{n}} = \sqrt{\dfrac{.70(1-.70)}{40}} = .0725$.

d. Null standard error = $\sqrt{\dfrac{.70(1-.70)}{1000}} = .0145$.

Note: Notice that the (null) standard error decreases as the sample size increases.

12.72 *Tip*: See the cautions on page 533 and the discussion at the top of page 536.
Very large. A very large sample may provide enough evidence to detect small and possibly unimportant differences from the null value. This leads to a conclusion of statistical significance, even though the result may not have practical "real world" significance.

12.74 **a.** Assuming the true proportion actually is higher in the second group, $n = 1000$. The larger sample is more likely to provide a statistically significant result.
b. $p = .45$. The farther the true proportion is from the null value of .20 (as long as it's in the direction stated in the alternative hypothesis), the more likely it is that the sample p will be significantly greater than .20.
c. $\hat{p} = .45$. The value of the z-statistic will be greater because the difference between .45 and .20 (the null value) is greater than the difference between .25 and .20.

12.78 Probably the finding was that there was no *significant* difference, in the statistical meaning, not the ordinary language meaning. This finding could have occurred because there really is no difference, or because the sample was too small to detect it and a type 2 error was made.

12.80 **b.** No, this is not a contradiction. There is not much (if any) practical importance to the observed difference in incidence of drowsiness (6% versus 8%), but the large sample sizes led to a *statistically* significant difference.

12.84 *Tip*: This is similar to Example 12.13 on pages 520-21.
Step 1: H_0: $p = .1$ (proportion left-handed same as in national population)
 H_a: $p \neq .1$ (proportion left-handed not same as in national population.
Step 2: The necessary conditions for using the z-statistic are present. The sample is assumed to be representative of the larger population and the sample size is large enough so that both np_0 and $n(1 - p_0)$ are greater than 10. Here, $n = 240$ and $p_0 = .1$.

The test statistic is $z = \dfrac{\text{Sample estimate} - \text{Null value}}{\text{Null standard error}} = \dfrac{\hat{p} - p_0}{\sqrt{\dfrac{p_0(1 - p_0)}{n}}}$.

Sample estimate = $\hat{p} = 20/240 = .0833$

$z = \dfrac{\hat{p} - p_0}{\sqrt{\dfrac{p_0(1 - p_0)}{n}}} = \dfrac{.0833 - .1}{\sqrt{\dfrac{.1(1 - .1)}{240}}} = \dfrac{-.0167}{.01936} = -0.86$

Step 3: p-value $\approx .39$. This is the combined probability (area) to the left of $z = -0.86$ and to the right of $z = 0.86$. Table A.1 gives $P(z < -0.86) = .1949$. Because this is a two-sided test, p-value $= 2 \times .1949 = .3898$.
Note: An exact p-value based on the binomial distribution is given by Minitab as .395.
Step 4: Cannot reject the null hypothesis. The result is not statistically significant because the p-value is not smaller than .05, the usual standard for significance.

Step 5: We cannot conclude that the proportion of UCD students who are left-handed differs from the national proportion.

Minitab output for this exercise is shown below.

Output for Exercise 12.84

```
Test of p = 0.1 vs p not = 0.1

Sample  X    N    Sample p       95.0% CI          Z-Value  P-Value
1       20   240  0.083333   (0.048366, 0.118300)   -0.86    0.389
```

12.87 **a.** p = proportion of all people who suffer from this chronic pain that would experience temporary relief if taking the new medication.

$H_0: p = .7$ (new has same success rate as standard)
$H_a: p > .7$ (new has better success rate than standard)

The null hypothesis could also be written as $H_0: p \leq .7$.

12.89 *Tip*: See Table 12.1 on page 517 as well as the three bullets above it.
a. p-value = .1470. This is the combined probability to the right of $z = 1.45$ and left of $z = -1.45$. Table A.1 can be used to find that $P(Z < -1.45) = .0735$. By symmetry, the area to the right of $z = 1.45$ is also .0735. So, the p-value = $2 \times .0735 = .1470$.

Figure for Exercise 12.89a

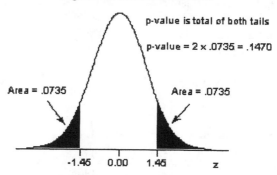

b. p-value = .0375. This is the probability (area) to the left of $z = -1.78$. Table A.1 can be used to find $P(Z < -1.78) = .0375$.

Figure for Exercise 12.89b

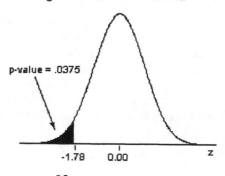

12.92 See the first row of Table 12.1, page 517 and the picture that accompanies it. Notice that the p-value will be greater than .5 for $z > 0$. Because the alternative hypothesis is $p < p_0$, the p-value is the probability (area) *to the left* of the z-statistic. This area is greater than .5 when the value of z is positive, as illustrated below.

Figure for Exercise 12.92

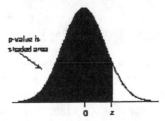

p-value is
shaded area

12.94 **b.** Population proportion. Only this class is of interest, and a census of all students in the class has been done.

12.97 *Tip*: This exercise is similar to Example 12.12 on pages 519-20.
Step 1: H_0: $p = .5$ (no preference for first drink)
        H_a: $p > .5$ (first drink is preferred)
p = proportion of population who would prefer first drink
Step 2: It seems reasonable to assume these students represent the larger population of UC Davis students for the question of interest, as was done in the previous exercise. The sample size is large enough so that both np_0 and $n(1 - p_0)$ are greater than 10.
Here, $n = 159$ and $p_0 = .5$.

The test statistic is $z = \dfrac{\text{Sample estimate - Null value}}{\text{Null standard error}} = \dfrac{\hat{p} - p_0}{\sqrt{\dfrac{p_0(1 - p_0)}{n}}}$.

Sample estimate = $\hat{p} = 86/159 = .541$.

$$z = \dfrac{\hat{p} - p_0}{\sqrt{\dfrac{p_0(1 - p_0)}{n}}} = \dfrac{.541 - .5}{\sqrt{\dfrac{.5(1 - .5)}{159}}} = \dfrac{.041}{.03965} = 1.03$$

Step 3: p-value $\approx .1515$. This is the probability that z is greater than 1.03. By symmetry,
$P(z > 1.03) = P(z < -1.03) = .1515$. Table A.1 can be used to find this.
Note: An exact p-value based on the binomial distribution is given as .171 by Minitab.
Step 4: Cannot reject the null hypothesis. The result is not statistically significant.
Step 5: Based on these data, we cannot conclude that more than one-half of the population would prefer the first drink presented to them.
Minitab can be used to find the z-statistic and corresponding p-value. See the Minitab Tip on page 526 of the text for guidance. The output for this exercise is as follows:

Output for Exercise 12.97					
Test of p = 0.5 vs p > 0.5					
Sample	X	N	Sample p	95.0% Lower Bound	Z-Value	P-Value
1	86	159	0.540881	0.475876	1.03	0.151

12.99 The researchers should be advised to use sample sizes larger than 500. Preferably, at least 3000 participants should be assigned to each condition. Assuming the true difference is similar to the previously observed difference, the probability is only .2768 that null hypothesis will be rejected with $n = 500$ per group. With $n = 1000$ per group, the power is only .4380 so with that sample size there's still less than a 50% chance that the new study will give a statistically significant result. With 3000 in each group, the probability of detecting a difference is .8250, so the research firm would have a relatively high chance of detecting the difference. If they want power even higher than .825, then they need to include even more than 3000 in each group.

12.100 b. Step 2: Sample sizes are sufficiently large so that observed counts in both categories (favored or not) are greater than 10 for both years. Assume that the samples represent random samples from the populations in the two years, and that the samples were independently selected.
Test statistic is given in the output as $z = 3.19$
Steps 3, 4, and 5: p-value = .001. Reject the null hypothesis. Conclude that the proportion of adult Canadians favoring marriages between people of the same sex was different in February 2000 than in April 1999.
Note: The reason this was of interest to researchers was provided in the article referenced in the problem. The article stated, "The Federal Liberals, the party currently in power in Canada, have recently proposed a bill to extend legal benefits and obligations of married couples to common law couples regardless of sexual orientation." The issue was whether the publicity generated by the bill had changed the proportion in favor, and the hypothesis test shows that it probably did so.

12.102 b. The consequence of a type 1 error would be that people would take aspirin although it doesn't help. The consequence of a type 2 error would be that people would not take aspirin and heart attacks that could be prevented would not be. Assuming that taking aspirin doesn't have serious side effects, a type 2 error is more serious in this situation.

12.104 *Tip*: This is similar to Example 12.12 on pages 519-20.
Step 1: H_0: $p \leq .50$ (not better than chance level)
        H_a: p >.50 (predict better than chance level)
p = proportion of population of pregnant women who can predict the sex of their babies
Step 2: We must assume the sample represents a random sample from the population of pregnant women. The sample size is sufficiently large so that $n\hat{p}$ and $n(1-\hat{p})$ are both greater than 10.

12.104 continued:

Sample proportion correct guesses is $\hat{p} = \dfrac{57}{104} = .548$

Test statistic is

$$z = \frac{\text{Sample statistic - Null value}}{\text{Null standard error}} = \frac{\hat{p} - p_0}{\sqrt{\dfrac{p_0(1-p_0)}{n}}} = \frac{.548 - .50}{\sqrt{\dfrac{.50(1-.50)}{104}}} = \frac{.048}{.049} = 0.98.$$

Step 3: p-value = .1635. It is the area (probability) to the right of $z = 0.98$.
$P(z > 0.98) = P(z \le -0.98) = .1635$. Equivalently, $P(z > 0.98) = 1 - P(z \le 0.98) = 1 - .8365 = .1635$.
Steps 4 and 5: We do not reject the null hypothesis for $\alpha = .05$. There is not enough evidence to conclude that in the population of pregnant women represented by the sample, the proportion able to predict the sex of their babies is higher than .50 (the chance level).
Note: Minitab could be used to do this exercise (see Minitab Tip on page 526). The program reports the exact p-value based on binomial distribution probabilities as .189.

12.107 **a.** *Tip*: This is similar to Example 12.12 on pages 519-20.
Step 1: H_0: $p \le .50$ (not a majority)
        H_a: $p > .50$ (a majority were dissatisfied)
p = proportion of U.S. adults dissatisfied with K-12 education in August 1999
Step 2: The sample was randomly selected from the population of U.S. adults and the sample size is sufficiently large so that np_0 and $n(1 - p_0)$ are both greater than 10 (and in fact are both the same at $1028/2 = 514$).

Sample proportion dissatisfied is $\hat{p} = \dfrac{524}{1028} = .5097$

Test statistic is

$$z = \frac{\text{Sample statistic - Null value}}{\text{Null standard error}} = \frac{\hat{p} - p_0}{\sqrt{\dfrac{p_0(1-p_0)}{n}}} = \frac{.5097 - .50}{\sqrt{\dfrac{.50(1-.50)}{1028}}} = \frac{.0097}{.0156} = 0.62$$

Step 3: p-value = .2676. It is the area (probability) to the right of $z = 0.62$.

This is found as $P(z > 0.62) = P(z \le -0.62) = .2676$. Equivalently, it is $P(z > 0.62) = 1 - P(z \le 0.62) = 1 - .7324 = .2676$. Minitab gives the p-value as .266. This minor difference occurs because Minitab keeps track of more decimal places in the z-statistic.
Steps 4 and 5: We do not reject H_0 for $\alpha = .05$. The conclusion concerning the population of U.S. adults in August 1999 is that we cannot say that a majority were dissatisfied with the quality of K-12 education.
Note: Minitab could be used to do this exercise (see Minitab Tip on page 526). The program reports the exact p-value based on binomial distribution probabilities as 0.277.

b. Step 1: H_0: $p_1 - p_2 = 0$, or equivalently, $p_1 = p_2$

H_a: $p_1 - p_2 \neq 0$, or equivalently, $p_1 \neq p_2$

p_1 = proportion of population of U.S. adults dissatisfied with K-12 education in August 2000

p_2 = proportion of population of U.S. adults dissatisfied with K-12 education in August 1999

Step 2: We assume two independent samples that represent the populations in the two different years. The observed counts in both categories (dissatisfied or otherwise) are greater than 10 for both years.

Test statistic is $z = \dfrac{\text{Sample statistic - Null value}}{\text{Null standard error}} = \dfrac{.1007 - 0}{.02192} = 4.59$. Details are:

August 2000, $\hat{p}_1 = \dfrac{622}{1019} = .6104$; August 1999, $\hat{p}_2 = \dfrac{524}{1028} = .5097$

Sample statistic = $\hat{p}_1 - \hat{p}_2 = .6104 - .5097 = .1007$

Combined $\hat{p} = \dfrac{622 + 524}{1019 + 1028} = \dfrac{1146}{2047} = .5598$

Null standard error

$$= \sqrt{\dfrac{\hat{p}(1 - \hat{p})}{n_1} + \dfrac{\hat{p}(1 - \hat{p})}{n_2}} = \sqrt{\dfrac{.5598(1 - .5598)}{1019} + \dfrac{.5598(1 - .5598)}{1028}} = .02192$$

Step 3: p-value ≈ 0. It is the combined area (probability) to the right of $z = 4.59$ and to the left of -4.59. With appropriate software or calculator, it can be determined as 2 $\times P(z < -4.59) =$
$2 \times .00002 = .00004$. Using Table A.1, the p-value would be estimated as p-value < (2 $\times .00001$), based on the cumulative probability given in Table A.1 for $z = -4.26$.

Steps 4 and 5: We can reject the null hypothesis. The conclusion is that the proportion of U.S. adults dissatisfied with the quality of K-12 education changed from August 1999 to August 2000.

12.110 Step 1: H_0: $p_1 - p_2 = 0$, or equivalently, $p_1 = p_2$

H_a: $p_1 - p_2 \neq 0$, or equivalently, $p_1 \neq p_2$

p_1 = proportion favoring legalization of marijuana in the U.S. population of men in 2002

p_2 = proportion favoring legalization of marijuana in the U.S. population of women in 2002

Step 2: The sample represents a random sample from the U.S. population and the sample size is sufficiently large so that observed counts in both categories (legal or not legal) are greater than 10 in both groups (males and females).

2.110 continued:

Minitab output is as follows.

Output for Exercise 12.110

```
Sample         X    N   Sample p
1 (male)     153  377   0.405836
2 (female)   153  474   0.322785


Difference = p (1) - p (2)
Estimate for difference:   0.0830507
95% CI for difference:   (0.0180230, 0.148078)
Test for difference = 0 (vs not = 0):   Z = 2.51   P-Value = 0.012
```

Step 2 continued and Steps 3, 4, and 5: The test statistic is $z = 2.51$ and the p-value is .012. Reject the null hypothesis and conclude that in the U.S. population in 2002, different proportions of males and females favored legalization of marijuana. Note that the observed proportion favoring legalization is higher for males ($\hat{p}_1 \approx .41$) than

for females ($\hat{p}_2 \approx .32$).

Note: One strategy for using Minitab is to first do a two-way table to find the relevant summary counts and to then enter these counts as "Summarized Data" in Minitab's test for 2 proportions (see the Minitab tip on page 532). This will allow you to choose the category "legal" as the category of interest, rather than letting Minitab choose which category to use.

CHAPTER 13
SELECTED SOLUTIONS

13.2   **a.** The difference between the means of two populations.

13.3   **a.** The parameter of interest is $\mu_1 - \mu_2$ where μ_1 = the mean height of the population of 25-year-old women and μ_2 = the mean height of the population of 45-year-old women.

13.4   Refer to the solution to 13.3a for the definitions of the parameter.
   a. H_0: $\mu_1 - \mu_2 = 0$

13.9   Yes, The hypotheses can (and should) be specified before collecting the data.

13.11   **a.** $t = \dfrac{\text{Sample mean} - \text{Null value}}{\text{Standard error}} = \dfrac{\bar{x} - \mu_0}{s/\sqrt{n}} = \dfrac{60 - 50}{90/\sqrt{100}} = \dfrac{10}{9} = 1.11$

13.13   *Tip*: See the appropriate steps on page 560 and examples in Table 13.2 on that page.
   a. Rejection region is $t \geq 1.72$; reject H_0. Use one-tailed $\alpha = .05$ column and df = 20 row.
   c. Rejection region is $|t| \geq 2.09$; reject H_0. Use two-tailed $\alpha = .05$ column and df = 20 row.
   g. Rejection region is $t \leq -1.83$; do not reject H_0. Use one-tailed $\alpha = .05$ column and df = 9 row.

13.16   *Tip:* Follow the steps in the "In Summary" box on pages 558-59.
   a. <u>Step 1</u>: H_0:$\mu = 72$ versus H_a:$\mu \neq 72$
   μ = mean pulse rate (beats per minute) for population of Penn State men
   <u>Step 2</u>: Sample size (57) is sufficiently large to proceed. We assume the sample represents a random sample of Penn State men.
   Test statistic is
   $$t = \frac{\text{Sample statistic} - \text{Null value}}{\text{Null standard error}} = \frac{\bar{x} - \mu_0}{\dfrac{s}{\sqrt{n}}} = \frac{70.42 - 72}{\dfrac{9.95}{\sqrt{57}}} = \frac{-1.58}{1.318} = -1.20$$

   <u>Steps 3,4, and 5</u>: df = $n - 1 = 57 - 1 = 56$. The *p*-value is $2 \times P(t < -1.20)$. Using Table A.3, *p*-value > 2(.103) = .206. We cannot reject the null hypothesis. Conclude that mean male pulse rate is not significantly different from 72. Using software like Excel or Minitab, or a suitable calculator, it can be determined that the *p*-value is 2(.1176) = .2352.

13.18 **a.** No. The mean is 8 minutes and the standard deviation is 10 minutes. Bell-shaped data would range from about three standard deviations below the mean to three standard deviations above the mean. In this case, even one standard deviation below the mean is negative, and it isn't possible to have calls of negative length.
b. Yes. The sample size is large (200) so it doesn't matter that the data are not bell-shaped.

13.21 *Tip*: See Example 13.1 (continued) starting on page 556.
Step 1: $H_0: \mu = 65$, $H_a: \mu < 65$, where μ = mean height (in inches) for the population of college women who prefer to sit in the front of the class.
Step 2: We will assume that the women in the sample are representative of all women in the population when it comes to height. The sample size (38) is large enough to continue, but a graph to check for skewness or outliers is a good idea for a moderate sample size. The histogram below shows that there are no extreme outliers or skewness.

Figure for Exercise 13.21

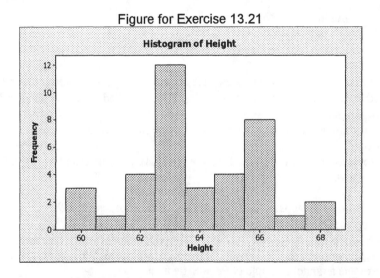

The summary statistics are $\bar{x} = 63.855$ inches and $s = 2.086$ inches. The test statistic is $t = \dfrac{\text{Sample statistic - Null value}}{\text{Null standard error}} = \dfrac{\bar{x} - \mu_0}{\dfrac{s}{\sqrt{n}}} = \dfrac{63.855 - 65}{\dfrac{2.086}{\sqrt{38}}} = \dfrac{-1.145}{0.3383} = -3.38$

Steps 3, 4, and 5: df = $n - 1 = 38 - 1 = 37$. The *p*-value is $P(t < -3.38)$. Using Table A.3, all we can say is that the *p*-value is less than .003, using the entry for df = 30 and the column for $t = 3.00$. Using Minitab the *p*-value is given as .001. Using the standard $\alpha = .05$, we can reject the null hypothesis and conclude that the mean height for women who prefer to sit in the front of the class is lower than it is for the population in general. In other words, women who prefer to sit in the front of the class are shorter on average than the general population.

13.24 *Tip*: See Continuing Step 2 and Step 3 on pages 555-56 and Table 13.1 on page 556.

b. $t = \dfrac{\text{Sample mean} - \text{Null value}}{\text{Standard error}} = \dfrac{\bar{x} - \mu_0}{s/\sqrt{n}} = \dfrac{-4 - 0}{15/\sqrt{50}} = \dfrac{-4}{2.12} = -1.89$.

df = 49, *p*-value is between 2 × .04 = .08 and 2 × .026 = .052, using Table A.3 with df = 40. Using df = 50, .05 < *p*-value < .078. Exact *p*-value (using software) is 2 × .032 = .064.

13.25 *Tip*: This exercise is similar to Example 13.2, which starts on page 562.

Step 1: H_0: $\mu_d = 0$

H_a: $\mu_d > 0$ (January weight is greater, on average)

μ_d = mean "January weight–November weight" difference for population represented by the sample.

Step 2: The sample size is sufficiently large to proceed. We must assume that the sample represents a random sample from a larger population.

Test statistic is $t = \dfrac{\text{Sample statistic} - \text{Null value}}{\text{Null standard error}} = \dfrac{0.37 - 0}{0.109} = 3.39$

Null standard error $= \dfrac{s_d}{\sqrt{n}} = \dfrac{1.52}{\sqrt{195}} = 0.109\,\text{kg}$.

Step 3: *p*-value ≈ 0. It is the area (probability) to the right of $t = 3.39$ in a *t*-distribution with df = $n-1$= 195−1 =194. With Table A.3, it can be estimated from the df = 100 row that the *p*-value is less than .002. With appropriate software of calculator, it can be found that $P(t > 3.39) = .0004$.

Steps 4 and 5: Reject the null hypothesis. The conclusion about the population is that the mean difference between January and November weights is greater than 0. In the sample, the observed magnitude of the difference was $\bar{d} = 0.37\,\text{kg} \approx 0.8$ pounds. (Note that this average gain of less than one pound may not have much *practical* importance.)

13.29 **c.** Test statistic is $t = \dfrac{\text{Sample statistic} - \text{Null value}}{\text{Null standard error}} = \dfrac{8 - 10}{\dfrac{4}{\sqrt{20}}} = -2.236$.

d. df = 20 − 1 = 19. The *p*-value is the area (probability) to the left of −2.236 in a *t*-distribution with df = 19. To use Table A.3, note that the absolute value of the observed *t* value is 2.236, which falls between 2.00 and 2.33. It's a one-tailed test, so the *p*-value can be read directly from the df = 19 row, and is between .015 and .030. Software or an appropriate calculator can be used to determine that the exact *p*-value is .0188.

13.32 *Tip*: See the pictures in Table 13.1 on page 556, which apply here as well, and compare them to the values in Table A.3, row for df = 8 and column for *t* = 2.33.

b. H_a: $\mu_1 - \mu_2 < 0$.

c. H_a: $\mu_1 - \mu_2 < 0$.

13.34   *Tip*: See the "In Summary" box on page 570.

    a. $t = \dfrac{(35-33)-0}{\sqrt{\dfrac{10^2}{100}+\dfrac{9^2}{81}}} = \dfrac{2}{\sqrt{2}} = 1.414$

13.36   *Tip*: This exercise is similar to Example 13.4, which begins on page 568, except that in this exercise graphical checks are required due to the small sample sizes.

<u>Step 1</u>: $H_0: \mu_1 - \mu_2 = 0$, or equivalently $\mu_1 = \mu_2$

        $H_a: \mu_1 - \mu_2 \neq 0$, or equivalently, $\mu_1 \neq \mu_2$

μ_1 = mean weight for population of Cambridge rowers

μ_2 = mean weight for population of Oxford rowers

<u>Step 2</u>: A dotplot (as well as a boxplot) shows that there are no outliers and the data are reasonably symmetric.

Figure for Exercise 13.36

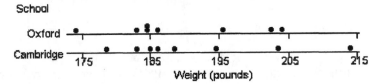

For the unpooled procedure, $t = 0.43$ (df ≈ 13, reported by Minitab).

Output for Exercise 13.36
Two-sample T for Cambridge vs Oxford

```
                N      Mean     StDev    SE Mean
cambridg        8     191.6     11.8       4.2
Oxford          8     189.3     10.4       3.7

Difference = mu Cambridge - mu Oxford
Estimate for difference:  2.38
95% CI for difference: (-9.67, 14.42)
T-Test of difference = 0 (vs not =): T-Value = 0.43  P-Value =
0.677  DF = 13
```

<u>Steps 3, 4, and 5</u>: *p*-value = .677 (from output). We do not reject the null hypotheses. There is not evidence to conclude that the populations of Cambridge and Oxford rowers differ with regard to mean weight.

Note: Because the sample sizes are equal the value of the test statistic for the pooled procedure is identical; see the bullet on page 571. The degrees of freedom would be slightly smaller but the conclusion would be the same. Either method is appropriate in this case.

13.39   **a.** <u>Step 1</u>: H_0: $\mu_1 - \mu_2 = 0$, or equivalently $\mu_1 = \mu_2$

              H_a: $\mu_1 - \mu_2 \neq 0$, or equivalently, $\mu_1 \neq \mu_2$

μ_1 = mean weight loss for population of sedentary men if they were to diet

μ_2 = mean weight loss for population of sedentary men if they were to exercise

<u>Step 2</u>: The sample sizes are sufficiently large to proceed. We must assume the samples represent random samples from larger populations of men who would either diet or exercise to lose weight.

For unpooled procedure,

Test statistic is $t = \dfrac{\text{Sample statistic - Null value}}{\text{Null standard error}} = \dfrac{3.2 - 0}{0.806} = 3.97$

Sample statistic is $\bar{x}_1 - \bar{x}_2 = 7.2 - 4.0 = 3.2$ kg.

Standard error is $\sqrt{\dfrac{s_1^2}{n_1} + \dfrac{s_2^2}{n_2}} = \sqrt{\dfrac{3.7^2}{42} + \dfrac{3.9^2}{47}} = \sqrt{0.6496} = 0.806$

For pooled procedure, $t = \dfrac{3.2 - 0}{0.808} = 3.96$.

$s_p = \sqrt{\dfrac{(42-1)3.7^2 + (47-1)3.9^2}{42+47-2}} = \sqrt{14.49} = 3.81$, and pooled standard error is

$s.e.(\bar{x}_1 - \bar{x}_2) = s_p \sqrt{\dfrac{1}{n_1} + \dfrac{1}{n_2}} = 3.81 \sqrt{\dfrac{1}{42} + \dfrac{1}{47}} = 0.808$

<u>Steps 3, 4, and 5</u>: p-value $\approx .0002$ for either procedure. It is calculated as $2 \times P(t > 3.97)$ for the unpooled procedure, and as $2 \times P(t > 3.96)$ for the pooled. For unpooled, df ≈ 41 (minimum of $n_1 - 1$ and $n_2 - 1$) and for pooled, df $= n_1 + n_2 - 2 = 42 + 47 - 2 = 85$. With Table A.3, the two-sided p-value would be estimated to be less than $2(.002) = .004$ for both procedures.

<u>Steps 4 and 5</u>: Reject the null hypothesis. We can conclude that the mean weight loss would be different for the population of sedentary men if they were to diet compared to if they were to exercise.

b. In this situation we can use the pooled procedure because the two groups have similar sample sizes and standard deviations. Either procedure would be acceptable.

13.42   **a.** <u>Step 1</u>: H_0: $\mu_1 - \mu_2 = 0$, or equivalently $\mu_1 = \mu_2$

              H_a: $\mu_1 - \mu_2 > 0$, or equivalently, $\mu_1 > \mu_2$ (mean speed higher with no seatbelt use)

μ_1 = mean speed under road conditions similar to those in the study for the population of drivers who don't wear seatbelts

μ_2 = mean speed under road conditions similar to those in the study for the population of drivers who do wear seatbelts

<u>Step 2</u>: We must assume the samples represent random samples from the larger populations of drivers. The sample sizes are small so plots should be used to determine if outliers or skewness are present.

13.42a continued:

The histograms below show the speeds for the drivers without and with seatbelts, and do not exhibit any problems with outliers or skewness.

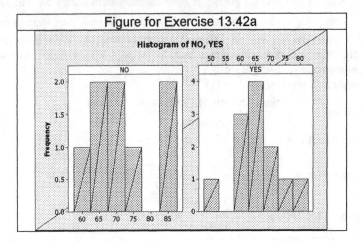

Using the unpooled procedure,

Test statistic is $t = \dfrac{\text{Sample statistic - Null value}}{\text{Null standard error}} = \dfrac{7.167 - 0}{3.795} = 1.89$. Details are:

Sample statistic is $\bar{x}_1 - \bar{x}_2 = 72.5 - 65.33 = 7.167$ mph.

Standard error $\sqrt{\dfrac{s_1^2}{n_1} + \dfrac{s_2^2}{n_2}} = \sqrt{\dfrac{8.82^2}{8} + \dfrac{7.49^2}{12}} = 3.795$

Step 3: From Minitab, df = 13 and p-value = .041. Using Table A.3 and the conservative df = smaller of sample sizes – 1, df = 8 – 1 = 7, p-value is between .047 and .053. Notice that this range differs from the p-value given by Minitab because the conservative degrees of freedom have been used.

Steps 4 and 5: Using the p-value of .041, the null hypothesis can be rejected. It can be concluded that the mean speed for the population of drivers who do not wear seatbelts is higher than the mean speed for those who do wear them.

b. Step 1 and the "checking the conditions" part of Step 2 are the same as in part (a).

For the pooled procedure, $t = \dfrac{7.167 - 0}{3.665} = 1.96$. Details are:

$$s_p = \sqrt{\dfrac{(8-1)8.82^2 + (12-1)7.49^2}{8 + 12 - 2}} = \sqrt{64.536} = 8.03 \text{, and pooled standard error is}$$

$$s.e.(\bar{x}_1 - \bar{x}_2) = s_p\sqrt{\dfrac{1}{n_1} + \dfrac{1}{n_2}} = 8.03\sqrt{\dfrac{1}{8} + \dfrac{1}{12}} = 3.665 \text{.}$$

Step 3: df = 8 + 12 – 2 = 18. From Minitab, p-value = .033. Using Table A.3 with df = 18, the p-value range is .044 to .030.

Steps 4 and 5: Reject the null hypothesis. Conclude that the mean speed for the population who do not wear seatbelts is higher than it is for the population of people who do wear them.

13.44 **a.** No. The null value is covered by the 95% confidence interval.
c. No. The null value is covered by the 90% confidence interval.
e. Yes. The entire 90% confidence interval falls above the null value, so it is likely that $\mu > 25$.

13.47 **a.** Reject H_0 for level of significance $\alpha = .05$. The null value (100) is not within the 95% confidence interval.
b. Do not reject H_0 for level of significance $\alpha = .025$. The entire interval falls into the null hypothesis region ($H_0: p \geq .10$). The *one-sided* level of significance corresponding to 95% confidence is $.05/2 = .025$.

13.49 **a.** Can't tell. The entire interval could be greater than 10 or it could include 10.

13.50 **a.** $\mu_1 - \mu_2$ where μ_1 and μ_2 are the mean running times for the 50-yard dash for the populations of first grade boys and girls, respectively.

13.53 **a.** It would be appropriate to estimate the difference in proportions of college men and women who would answer yes, $p_1 - p_2$, and test whether $p_1 - p_2 = 0$. You may also want to estimate p_1 and p_2 separately.

13.55 **a.** The mean is at 2; 68% of the differences fall in the range -2 to $+6$, 95% in the range -6 to $+10$ and 99.7% in the range -10 to $+14$. See the Figure for Exercise 13.55a (below).

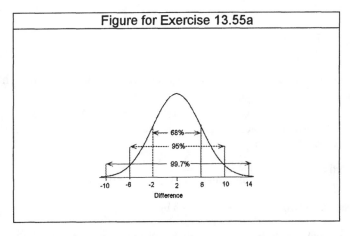

Figure for Exercise 13.55a

c. The power is .695, found from the row for $n = 20$ and the column for effect size of 0.5. The true effect size is found here as $d = \dfrac{\mu_1 - \mu_0}{\sigma} = \dfrac{2 - 0}{4} = 0.5$.

13.57 **a.** .6318; in Minitab, use **Stat** > **Power and sample size** > **1-sample t**. In the sample size box enter 45, in the "difference" box enter 0.3, use standard deviation =1 and use Options to change the alternative to "greater than."

13.60 **a.** The formula is given in Exercise 13.59; $\dfrac{p_1 - p_0}{\sqrt{p_0(1-p_0)}} = \dfrac{.35 - .25}{\sqrt{.25(1-.25)}} = 0.231$

d. No. In parts (a-c), $p_1 - p_0 = 0.1$, but the effect size changes.

13.62 Items 2, 4 and 5 should be of concern. As stated in item 2, with a large sample size a statistically significant result may not have practical significance. Item 4 is also concerned with this issue, and item 5 helps to resolve it because the magnitude of the effect can be used to determine practical significance.

13.65 **a.** All except item 5 rely on knowing the p-value. For item 1, the item itself explains why. For item 2, it would be useful to know if the result was just barely statistically significant, or if the p-value was extremely small. For item 3 when the null hypothesis is not rejected it would help to know if the p-value indicated a result that was close to statistically significant or not. For item 4 the same reasoning applies as in item 2. For item 6 it would be more convincing if the p-values for significant results were much less than 0.05.

b. Items 2, 3 and 4. For item 2, a confidence interval would allow us to see if the magnitude of the effect has real world importance. For item 3, it would be useful to know if the confidence interval is centered on the null value, or if it is mostly above or below it. For item 4 the reasoning is the same as for item 2.

13.66 **a.** Parameter = proportion of adult Americans between the ages of 18 and 30 who think the use of marijuana should be legalized. Null value = .5.

c. Parameter = difference in mean ages of death for left and right handed people. Null value = 0.

13.70 **a.** <u>Step 1</u>: $H_0: \mu_d = 0$

$\qquad\qquad H_a: \mu_d > 0$

μ_d = mean "husband age – wife age" difference in population of British married couples

<u>Step 2</u>: The sample size is sufficiently large to proceed. We must assume that the sample of married couples represents a random sample from the larger population of British married couples.

Test statistic is $t = \dfrac{\text{Sample statistic - Null value}}{\text{Null standard error}} = \dfrac{2.24 - 0}{0.3145} = 7.12$

Null standard error $= \dfrac{s_d}{\sqrt{n}} = \dfrac{4.1}{\sqrt{170}} = 0.3145\,\text{years}.$

<u>Step 3</u>: p-value ≈ 0. It is the area (probability) to the right of $t = 7.12$ in a t-distribution with df $= n-1 = 170-1 = 169$. With Table A.3, it can be estimated from the df $= 100$ row that the p-value is less than .002. Because a t-distribution with a large value for df is similar to a standard normal curve, Table A.1 could be used to estimate that $P(t > 7.12)$ is less than .000000001.

<u>Steps 4 and 5</u>: Reject the null hypothesis. The conclusion about the population of British married couples represented by the sample is that the mean difference between the ages of the husband and wife is greater than 0.

13.73   *Tip*: See the discussion and bullets on pages 575-76 and Example 13.8 on page 576.

Reject the null hypothesis (H_0: $\mu_1 - \mu_2 = 0$) using $\alpha = .025$. The confidence interval does not cover 0. Because the alternative hypothesis is one-sided, the significance level corresponding to 95% confidence is $(1 - .95)/2 = .025$.

13.77   **a.** The consequence of a type 1 error is that patients are retested without cause because the levels on days 2 and 4 are not actually different. The consequence of a type 2 error is that patients should be retested but they will not be, so the initial cholesterol readings may be too high.
b. Type 2 seems more serious because the most accurate data is not used to make medical decisions.

CHAPTER 14
SELECTED SOLUTIONS

14.1 **a.** Substitute $x = 40$ into the regression equation.
$\hat{y} = 119 - 1.64(40) = 119 - 65.6 = 53.4$ degrees Fahrenheit.
b. *Tip:* See Example 14.1 on page 602 for an example of calculating a residual.
$e_i = y_i - \hat{y}_i = 50 - 53.4 = -3.4$ degrees.
This is the difference between the actual and predicted April temperatures for Pittsburgh.

14.2 **a.** β_0 = intercept of the regression line in the population. β_1 = slope of regression line in the population and is the average increase in y per each one unit increase in x.

14.4 **a.** Slope = 0.9. Mean blood pressure increases 0.9 points per each 1-year increase in age.

14.6 **b.** Correct notation is b_1. This is a slope for a sample.

14.9 **a.** $R^2 = \dfrac{\text{SSTO} - \text{SSE}}{\text{SSTO}} = \dfrac{500 - 300}{500} = .40$, or 40% when converted to a percentage.

14.10 **a.** Substitute $x = 21$ into the regression equation.
$\hat{y}_i = 577 - 3.01(21) = 513.79$ feet (about 514 feet).
b. *Tip:* See Example 14.1 on page 602 for an example of calculating a residual..
$e_i = y_i - \hat{y}_i = 525 - 513.79 = 11.21$ feet. This is the difference between the actual and predicted distances for such an individual.
c. The approximate interval is $513.79 \pm (2 \times 50)$ which is 413.79 ft. to 613.79 ft. (about 414 to 614 ft.)

Tip: From the Empirical Rule (Chapter 2), we know that about 95% of individual values are within two standard deviations of the mean. In regression, $\hat{y}$ is an estimate of the mean for a specified value of x. Thus, the interval of values within two standard deviations of the mean is $\hat{y} \pm (2 \times s)$.
d. Yes. 650 feet is more than 2 standard deviations from the mean distance for drivers who are 21 years old, so it would be unusual. Notice that 650 feet is well outside the interval calculated in the previous part.

14.11 **a.** *Tip:* See the beginning of Section 14.2 on page 605 for guidance on interpreting this value.
$s = 2.837$. It is roughly, for any specific latitude, the average (absolute) difference between actual April temperatures and the predicted temperature for that latitude.

14.11 Continued:

b. *Tip:* See Example 14.4 on page 604 for an example of interpreting R^2.
Geographic latitude explains 91.7% of the variation among April temperatures for the cities in the sample.

14.13 *Tip*: The necessary equations are given on page 600.

b. $SSE = \sum e_i^2 = (-1)^2 + 1^2 + (-2)^2 + 2^2 + (-2)^2 + 2^2 = 18$

c. $s = \sqrt{\dfrac{SSE}{n-2}} = \sqrt{\dfrac{18}{6-2}} = 2.12$

14.14 **a.** No. The *p*-value is not less than .05, the usual standard for statistical significance.

b. *Tip:* See page 612 for a discussion of testing hypotheses about a population correlation.
The *p*-value will be .552, the same as it is for the test of whether the slope is 0.

14.17 **b.** *Tip:* See page 612 for a discussion of testing hypotheses about a population correlation.
The *p*-value will be the same as it is for part (a), so it is.165 (which means we cannot reject the null hypothesis.

14.18 **d.** The result may not have practical significance. The slope indicates only a small increase in television watching per 1-year increase in age, and $R^2 = 2.1\%$ so the relationship is weak.

14.20 **a.** $H_0: \rho = 0$ versus Ha: $\rho \neq 0$.
It may be that in reality the researchers' alternative hypothesis was $\rho > 0$, but computer software routinely provides a *p*-value for the two-sided alternative. There are two sets of hypotheses being tested. In the first set (with $p < .001$), ρ is the population correlation between weekly time spent watching music videos and concern about weight. In the second set (with $p < .05$), ρ is the population correlation between weekly time spent watching music videos and importance of appearance.

14.21 **a.** Prediction interval for a value of *y*, because the interest is in the GPA of one student.

b. Confidence interval for the mean because the interest is in the mean for a population with a certain high school GPA.

14.22 **a.** Grade point average of an individual student who typically misses two classes per week.
b. Mean grade point average for all students who typically miss two classes per month.
Tip: The prediction interval estimates the value for a single individual. Alternatively, it describes how individuals vary from each other. In contrast, the confidence interval estimates the <u>mean</u>, or average, value for a collection of similar individuals.

14.25 **a.** For $x = 40$, $\hat{y}_i = 3.59 + 0.967(40) = 42.27$ years old. The slight difference from the value on the output occurs because Minitab used more decimal places in the intercept and slope when doing its calculations.
d. The prediction interval is wide because there is variation among the individual ages of husbands married to women 40 years old. The confidence interval is narrow because, with $n = 170$ the regression line can be estimated with good precision.

14.26 The calculation is $42.258 \pm (2 \times 0.313)$, which gives approximately the interval provided by Minitab. The general format is *Estimate* $\pm$ *2× Standard error*. The *estimate* is the value under "Fit" and the relevant *Standard error* is value under "SE Fit".

A slight discrepancy occurs because Minitab used $t^* = 1.974$ as the "exact" multiplier (rather than 2). The degrees of freedom for the *t*-distribution used to determine the exact multiplier are df = $n-2$ = 170–2 = 168.

14.28 **a.** Conditions 2 and 4. A histogram of residuals can be used to determine if there are outliers and can be used to judge the shape of the distribution.
b. Conditions 1, 2 and 3. A scatterplot of residuals versus x can be used to judge whether the right form of regression equation was used, whether there are any outliers, and whether the standard deviation is abut the same for all values of x.
c. Condition 5.
d. Conditions 1, 2 and 3. A scatterplot of y versus x can be used to judge whether the right form of regression equation was used, whether there are any outliers, and whether the standard deviation is abut the same for all values of x.

14.30 There is an outlier (at about 14 as a value of the residual). Aside from the outlier, the distribution might be normal although it is difficult to judge.

14.33 **a.** Condition 2 is violated because there appears to be an outlier (the observation at *Neck girth* $\approx$ 10 with *Weight* $\approx$ 150).
Tip: For guidance, see Figure 14.11 on page 622 of the text.

14.34 **c.** The plot will have a U shape.
Tip: Remember that a residual is the difference between an actual value of y and the predicted value of y. Notice that all points between speeds of 20 and 50 mph are below the regression line. The residuals, calculated as *actual–predicted*, will be negative for these points. For speeds of 0 mph and 70 mph, the residuals will be positive. For speeds of 10 mph and 60 mph, the residuals will be near 0.

14.35   **a.** *Tip*: In general, the slope of a straight-line equation gives the change in y for each one-unit increase in the x-variable. In regression, the line describes the mean value of y so the slope of the regression line is the change in the mean y for each one-unit increase in the x-variable.

Answer: This is given by the sample slope $b_1 = -0.269$. (Or, with more decimal places, $b_1 = -0.26917$.) On average, hours of sleep decreases 0.269 hours per each one-hour increase in hours of studying.

b. *Tip:* This part is similar to Example 14.7 on page 611 of the text.

Interval is approximately $b_1 \pm 2\, s.e.\,(b_1)$.

This is $-0.26917 \pm (2 \times 0.6616)$ or about -0.401 to -0.137.

Interpretation: With 95% confidence, we can say that the slope of the regression line in the population is between -0.401 and -0.137.

The exact multiplier in this situation is $t^* = 1.981$ which can be found by using software like Minitab or Excel to find the value of t^* for which the probability is .95 in a t-distribution that has df $= n-2 = 116 - 2 = 114$.

c. H_0: $\beta_1 = 0$ versus H_a: $\beta_1 \neq 0$.

d. *Tip*: This part is similar to Example 14.6 on page 610 of the text..

$$t = \frac{\text{Sample statistic - Null value}}{\text{Standard error}} = \frac{b_1 - 0}{s.e.(b_1)} = \frac{-0.26917}{0.06616} = -4.07$$

df $= n - 2 = 116 - 2 = 114$.

e. The relationship is statistically significant. The p-value is .000, given in the output under "P" in the row labeled *Study*.

14.36   **a.** $s = 1.509$ hours. This is roughly the average deviation of individual y-values from the regression line. Equivalently, the standard deviation estimates, roughly, the average size of the residuals.

Tip: See the beginning of Section 14.2 on page 605 for guidance on interpreting this value.

14.37 $b_0 = 7.56$ hours. Yes, the intercept has a logical interpretation here. It is the estimated mean hours of sleep for students who studied 0 hours.

14.38   Conditions 1, 2 and 3 hold. The form of the equation is probably correct, there are no outliers, and the standard deviation is about the same for all values of x.

Tip: This exercise is similar to Example 14.9 on page 620.

14.39   The prediction interval is 3.746 to 9.750 hours of sleep. The two interpretations are:
(1) Of students in the population who studied 3 hours, about 95% slept between 3.746 and 9.75 hours.
(2) The probability is .95 that the hours of sleep will be between 3.746 and 9.75 hours for a student 0randomly selected from the population of students who studied 3 hours.

14.41 **b.** Minitab gives the following output:

Output for Exercise 14.41b				
The regression equation is				
Exam = 25.4 + 0.707 Quizzes				
Predictor	Coef	SE Coef	T	P
Constant	25.38	16.22	1.57	0.152
Quizzes	0.7069	0.2147	3.29	0.009

c. For quiz average equal to 75, $\hat{y} = 25.38 + 0.7069(75) = 78.4$

d. Minitab gives the 50% prediction interval as 72.97 to 83.83 (approximately 73 to 84). This interval estimates the central 50% of exam scores for students with a quiz average equal to 75.

14.43 **a.** *Tip:* See Example 14.4 on page 604 for an example of interpreting R^2. $R^2 = 44.7\%$. Father's height explains about 44.7% of the variation in son's height.

b. $r = \sqrt{0.447} = 0.67$. The correlation is the square root of R^2 (expressed as a decimal fraction). The sign of the correlation is the same as the sign of the slope, which is positive in this example.

14.49 **a.** There is a strong positive association between weight and chest girth for these bears. The two observations with the greatest chest girths could be outliers, or there may be a gently curving pattern.

Figure for Exercise 14.49a

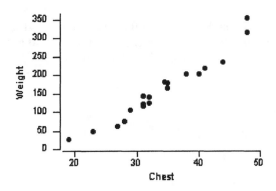

105

14.49 continued:

b. The regression equation is $\hat{y} = -206.9 + 10.76x$.

Minitab output (including results for the next four parts) is:

Output for Exercise 14.49
The regression equation is Weight = - 207 + 10.8 Chest

Predictor	Coef	SE Coef	T	P
Constant	-206.90	20.69	-10.00	0.000
Chest	10.7595	0.5937	18.12	0.000

S = 19.57   R-Sq = 95.1%   R-Sq(adj) = 94.8%

New Obs	Fit	SE Fit	95.0% CI	95.0% PI
1	223.48	5.72	(211.41, 235.55)	(180.47, 266.49)

c. $R^2 = 95.1\%$. The variable chest girth explains 95.1% of the observed variation in weight.

d. $\hat{y} = -206.9 + 10.76(40) = 223.5$ lbs. Notice that Minitab gives $\hat{y} = 223.48$. The software kept track of more decimal places than we did.

e. The 95% prediction interval is 180.47 lbs. to 266.49 lbs. About 95% of all bears with chest girth equal to 40 inches will weigh between 180.47 pounds and 266.49 pounds.

f. The 95% confidence interval for the mean is 211.41 lbs. to 235.55 lbs. We are 95% confident that for bears with a chest girth equal to 40 inches, the mean weight is between 211.41 pounds and 235.55 pounds.

CHAPTER 15
SELECTED SOLUTIONS

15.1 *Tip:* Both variables should be categorical.

a. Appropriate. Both variables are categorical.
b. Not appropriate. Both variables are quantitative.

15.4 *Tip:* See Examples 15.6 and 15.7 on page 643 of the text.

a. *p*-value = .05 In Table A.5, the value 3.84 is in the .05 column.
b. $.10 < p\text{-value} < .25$ (based on Table A.5). df = $(3 - 1)(3 - 1) = 4$. In the df = 4 row, the value 6.3 is between the values 5.39 (in .25 column) and 7.78 (in .10 column).
With Excel, *p*-value = CHIDIST(6.7,4) = .1526.

15.5 **b.** 16.81. df =(rows – 1)(columns – 1) = (3–1)(4–1) =6.
Look in the .05 column and df = 6 row of Table A.5.

15.7 *Tip:* In each part, the critical value will be in the .01 column of Table A.5.

a. No, $\chi^2 = 2.89$ is less than 6.63 (the critical value from Table A.5, df =1).

b. No, $\chi^2 = 5.00$ is less than 6.63 (the critical value from Table A.5, df =1).

c. Yes, $\chi^2 = 23.60$ is greater than 13.28 (the critical value from Table A.5, df = 4).

d. No, $\chi^2 = 23.60$ is less than 30.58 (the critical value from Table A.5, df = 15).

15.9 **a.** H_0: Gender and type of class are not related. [Or, distribution of males and females is the same for each class.]
H_a: Gender and type of class are related. [Or, distribution of males and females differs for the two classes.]
b. df = (2–1)(2–1) =1
c. $\chi^2 =$

$$\frac{(83 - 80.42)^2}{80.42} + \frac{(11 - 13.58)^2}{13.58} +$$
$$\frac{(65 - 67.58)^2}{67.58} + \frac{(14 - 11.42)^2}{11.42} = 1.258$$

d. Using Table A.5, p-value is between .25 and .50. The chi-square value of 1.258 is between the 0.45 (in .50 column) and 1.32 (in .25 column) of Table A.5. With statistical software or Excel, it can be found that p-value = .262.
e. Cannot reject the null hypothesis for α=.05 because the p-value is not less than .05. We cannot say there is a relationship between gender and type of class taken.

15.11 **c.** H_0: Opinion about death penalty and opinion about marijuana legalization are not related.

H_a : Opinion about death penalty and opinion about marijuana legalization are related.

d. Minitab output is given below (expected counts are beneath observed counts in each cell). $\chi^2 = 0.287$, df = 1, p-value = 0.592. If we use Table A.5, p-value >.50. We cannot reject the null hypothesis. We are *not* able to conclude that there is a relationship between opinion about the death penalty and opinion about marijuana legalization.

```
                         Output for Exercise 15.11d
                Legal   NotLegal    All
        Favor    191       341      532
                194.5     337.5    532.0

        Oppose   104       171      275
                100.5     174.5    275.0

        All      295       512      807
                295.0     512.0    807.0

        Cell Contents:      Count
                            Expected count

        Pearson Chi-Square = 0.287, DF = 1, P-Value = 0.592
```

15.12 For expected counts, proportion with no ear infection is .2195 within each treatment.

Placebo: 39.07/178 = .2195
Xylitol gum: 39.29/179 = .2195
Xylitol lozenge: 38.63/176 = .2195

15.15 **f.** We're not telling. Ask an engineer.

15.17 $\chi^2 = \dfrac{N(AD-BC)^2}{R_1 R_2 C_1 C_2} = \dfrac{807(191 \times 171 - 104 \times 341)^2}{532 \times 275 \times 295 \times 512} = 0.287$.

15.18 **a.** The researchers probably thought, in advance of collecting data, that short students would be more likely to be bullied. So, a one-sided alternative would be appropriate and a z-test for comparing two proportions should be used.

c. Step 1: H_0: $p_1 - p_2 = 0$ (or $p_1 = p_2$) versus Ha: $p_1 - p_2 > 0$ (or $p_1 > p_2$)

p_1 = proportion ever bullied in population of short students
p_2 = proportion ever bullied in population of students not short

Step 2: Sample sizes are sufficiently large and we assume the samples represent random samples.

The test statistic is $z = 3.02$. Output for comparing two proportions is given below. For "by hand" calculations, use the method described in Chapter 12. Alternatively, a chi-square test can be done and the relationship $z = \sqrt{\chi^2}$ used to determine the z-statistic.

Steps 3, 4, and 5: p-value = .001 (reported in output). Reject the null hypothesis, and conclude that a higher proportion of short students than non-short students have been bullied.

```
                    Output for Exercise 15.18

Sample      X      N  Sample p
1          42     92  0.456522  (short)
2          30    117  0.256410  (not short)

Estimate for p(1) - p(2):  0.200111
95% lower bound for p(1) - p(2):  0.0919200
Test for p(1) - p(2) = 0 (vs > 0):  Z = 3.02  P-Value = 0.001
```

15.21 Yes, because the alternative hypothesis is two-sided. The p-value and conclusion would be identical for the two different tests. *Tip:* Use Example 15.10 on page 648 for guidance.

15.24 *Tip:* See Example 15.12 and the discussion on page 650 of the text.
a. Given that 2 out of 10 participants have reduced pain, what is the probability that both would be in the magnet-treated group (of 5 individuals)?

15.26 **a.** Expected count = 100 in each of the three categories. The calculation is $np_i = 300(1/3) = 100$.

15.28 **a.** No. A chi-square statistic is a sum of non-negative numbers so it would have to be greater than or equal to 0.
b. Yes. This would happen if the observed count equaled the expected count in each cell of the table.
c. Yes. For example, see the solution given below for Exercise 15.32.
d. No. The observed counts will always be whole numbers.
e. No. The null hypothesis gives hypothesized probabilities for all possible categories, so the sum of these probabilities must be 1.
f. No. For a goodness of fit test, df = number of categories – 1.

15.30 **a.** H_0: $p_1 = .3$, $p_2 = .6$, $p_3 = .1$ where p_1, p_2, and p_3 are the proportions who drove, biked, and used another way that day, respectively.
c. $\chi^2 = \dfrac{(80 - 90)^2}{90} + \dfrac{(200 - 180)^2}{180} + \dfrac{(20 - 30)^2}{30} = 6.67$

15.32   *Tip:* For guidance, use Example 15.13 on page 654 of the text.

Step 1: H_0: $p_1 = .5$, $p_2 = .3$, $p_3 = .2$ (manufacturer's hypothesis)

H_a: not all p_i are as specified in H_0

Step 2: Expected counts: Silver, $111 \times .5 = 55.5$; Blue, $111 \times .3 = 33.3$; Green, $111 \times .2 = 22.2$.

All expected counts are greater than 5 so proceed with the chi-square test.

Test statistic is $\chi^2 = \dfrac{(59-55.5)^2}{55.5} + \dfrac{(27-33.3)^2}{33.3} + \dfrac{(25-22.2)^2}{22.2} = 1.766$; df = $k-1 = 3-1 = 2$

Steps 3, 4, and 5: $.25 < p\text{-value} < .50$ (based on Table A.5).

With Excel, p-value = CHIDIST(1.766,2) = .4135.

Do not reject the null hypothesis. Based on this sample, the manufacturer's hypothesis about color preferences is not rejected.

15.34   **a.** Possible sequences are HH, TH, HT, TT.

Probabilities are: $X = 0$, $p_0 = 1/4 = .25$; $X = 1$, $p_1 = 1/2 = .5$; $X = 2$, $p_2 = 1/4 = .25$

b. H_0: $p_0 = .25$, $p_1 = .50$, $p_2 = .25$

H_a: not all p_i are as specified in H_0

c. *Tip*: For guidance, use Example 15.13 on page 654 of the text.

Step 2: Expected counts: $X = 0$, $60 \times .25 = 15$; $X = 1$, $60 \times .5 = 30$; $X = 2$, $60 \times .25 = 15$.

All expected counts are greater than 5 so proceed with the chi-square test.

Test statistic is $\chi^2 = \dfrac{(8-15)^2}{15} + \dfrac{(40-30)^2}{30} + \dfrac{(12-15)^2}{15} = 7.2$; df = $k-1 = 3-1 = 2$.

Steps 3, 4, and 5: $.025 < p\text{-value} < .05$ (based in Table A.5). With Excel, p-value = CHIDIST(7.2,2) = .027.

Reject the null hypothesis. Conclude that observed student results are significantly different from expected results based on theory.

15.36   *Tip*: For guidance, use Example 15.13 on page 654 of the text.

Step 1: H_0: $p_1 = .3$, $p_2 = .2$, $p_3 = .2$, $p_4 = .1$, $p_5 = .1$, $p_6 = .1$ (manufacturer's claim)

H_a: not all p_i are as specified in H_0

Step 2: Expected counts are: Brown: $2081 \times .3 = 624.3$; Red and Yellow, $2081 \times .2 = 416.2$;

Blue, Orange and Green, $2081 \times .1 = 208.1$.

All expected counts are greater than 5, so proceed with the chi-square test.

$$\text{Test statistic is } \chi^2 = \frac{(602-624.3)^2}{624.3} + \frac{(396-416.2)^2}{416.2} + \frac{(379-416.2)^2}{416.2} +$$
$$\frac{(227-208.1)^2}{208.1} + \frac{(242-208.1)^2}{208.1} + \frac{(235-208.1)^2}{208.1}$$
$$= 15.8; \text{ df} = k-1 = 6-1 = 5.$$

Steps 3, 4, and 5 .005<p-value<.01; using Excel, CHIDIST(15.8,5) = .007. Reject the null hypothesis (because p-value is less than .05), and conclude that proportions are not as stated at M&M web site for the population from which these bags were drawn.

15.39 **b.** H$_0$: Number of ear pierces and having a tattoo (or not) are not related
H$_a$: Number of ear pierces and having a tattoo (or not) are related

c. Minitab output is given below (expected counts are beneath observed counts in each cell).

χ^2 = 119.279, df = 3, p-value =.000. If we use Table A.5, p-value <.001.

Reject the null hypothesis. Conclude that for the population of college women represented by the sample, there is a relationship between number of ear pierces and having a tattoo or not.

```
                        Output for Exercise 15.39c
              No      Yes    Total
    0-2      498       40     538
           448.79    89.21

    3-4      374       58     432
           360.37    71.63

    5-6      202       77     279
           232.74    46.26

    7+        73       53     126
           105.11    20.89

Total       1147      228    1375

Chi-Sq = 119.279, DF = 3, P-Value = 0.000
```

15.42 **a.** n = 10, p =.5.
c. Use the table in part b; combining 0 to 2 and 8 to 10. Expected counts are shown for use in Parts (d) and (e), and their calculation is explained in answers for those parts.

Number Correct	Sheep	Goats	Null probability	Expected (Sheep)	Expected (Goats)
≤ 2	6	5	0.054688	6.1251	4.3750
3	11	12	0.117188	13.1250	9.3750
4	16	15	0.205078	22.9688	16.4063
5	29	19	0.246094	27.5625	19.6875
6	28	16	0.205078	22.9688	16.4063
7	14	10	0.117188	13.1250	9.3750
≥ 8	8	3	0.054688	6.1251	4.3750

15.44   *Tip*: Use the chi-square test for a two-table (Section 15.1).

a. The conditions are met. In particular, only one of the expected counts for the twenty cells is less than 5. Expected counts are shown beneath observed counts in the output for part (b). Also, it is assumed the GSS sample represents a random sample from the population of U.S. adults.

b. Step 1: H_0: Religion and opinion about premarital sex are not related

   H_a: Religion and opinion about premarital sex are related

Step 2: $\chi^2 = 157$, df = $(5-1)(4-1) = 12$.

Steps 3,4, and 5: p-value ≈ 0. Reject the null hypothesis. Conclusion is that religion and opinion about premarital sex are related variables. Row percentages should be examined to determine how the religions differ.

Minitab output is as follows:

Output for Exercise 15.40b					
	Almost A	Always	Never	Sometime	All
Catholic	37	62	226	120	445
	42.97	106.14	195.14	100.74	445.00
Jewish	3	0	34	14	51
	4.93	12.16	22.36	11.55	51.00
None	13	20	147	45	225
	21.73	53.67	98.67	50.94	225.00
Other	13	15	40	23	91
	8.79	21.71	39.91	20.60	91.00
Protesta	117	355	384	227	1083
	104.59	258.32	474.92	245.18	1083.00
All	183	452	831	429	1895
	183.00	452.00	831.00	429.00	1895.00

Chi-Square = 157.017, DF = 12, P-Value = 0.000
1 cells with expected counts less than 5.0

15.47   **a.** Use the data in the first two columns, under "Identified Male Voice?"

The test statistic is $\chi^2 = .267$, df = $(2-1)(2-1) = 1$, p-value = .605.

With Table A.5, p-value > .50.

Do not reject the null hypothesis. There is not a statistically significant relationship between sex of listener and the ability to identify a male voice.

In the following output, expected counts are beneath observed counts.

```
                    Output for Exercise 15.44a
               Yes       No       All
    Male       145       207      352
               148.44    203.56

    Female     162       214      376
               158.56    217.44

    All        307       421      728

    Chi-Sq =  0.080 +  0.058 +
              0.075 +  0.054 = 0.267
    DF = 1,  P-Value = 0.605
```

b. Use the data in the last two columns, under "Identified Female Voice?"

The test statistic is $\chi^2 = 13.025$, df $= (2-1)(2-1) = 1$, p-value $= .000$.

With Table A.5, p-value $< .001$.
Reject the null hypothesis. Conclusion is that there is a statistically significant relationship between sex of listener and the ability to identify a female voice.

In the following output, expected counts are beneath observed counts.

```
                    Output for Exercise 15.47b
               Yes       No       All
    Male       132       220      352
               156.18    195.82

    Female     191       185      376
               166.82    209.18

    All        323       405      728

    Chi-Sq =  3.742 +  2.985 +
              3.504 +  2.794 = 13.025
    DF = 1,  P-Value = 0.000
```

c. For male listener use the counts under "Identified Male Voice?" (145 and 207).
For female listener use the counts under "Identified Female Voice?" (191 and 185).

The test statistic is $\chi^2 = 6.748$, df $= (2-1)(2-1) = 1$, p-value $= .009$.

With Table A.5, $.005 < p$-value $< .01$.
Reject the null hypothesis. Conclusion is that there is a statistically significant relationship between sex of listener and the ability to identify a voice of the same sex.

In the following output, expected counts are beneath observed counts.

Output for Exercise 15.47c			
	Yes	No	All
Male	145	207	352
	162.46	189.54	
Female	191	185	376
	173.54	202.46	
All	336	392	728
Chi-Sq =	1.877 +	1.609 +	
	1.757 +	1.506 = 6.748	
DF = 1, P-Value = 0.009			

d. For male listener use the counts under "Identified Female Voice?" (132 and 220).
For female listener use the counts under "Identified Male Voice?" (162 and 214).
The test statistic is $\chi^2 = 2.356$, df $= (2-1)(2-1) = 1$, p-value $= .125$.
With Table A.5, $.10 < p$-value $< .25$.

Do not reject the null hypothesis. There is not evidence of a relationship between sex of listener and the ability to identify a voice of the opposite sex.
In the following output, expected counts are beneath observed counts.

Output for Exercise 15.49d			
	Yes	No	All
Male	132	220	352
	142.15	209.85	
Female	162	214	376
	151.85	224.15	
All	294	424	728
Chi-Sq =	0.725 +	0.491 +	
	0.679 +	0.460 = 2.356	
DF = 1, P-Value = 0.125			

15.50 Between 0 and 5.99. In Table A.5, the value for df = 2 under column heading = .05 provides the answer. When the null hypothesis is true, 5% of the time the chi-square statistic will be ≥ 5.99. So, 95% of the time the statistic will be less than this value.

Tip: In general, when the null hypothesis is true, 5% of the time the chi-square statistic will be larger than the value in the .05 column of Table A.5.

15.52 **b.** Step 1: H_0: Own eye color and eye color attracted to are not related
$\qquad\qquad$ H_a: Own eye color and eye color attracted to are not related

Step 2: Test statistic is $\chi^2 = 15.5$, df = 4. Output is shown below, with expected counts beneath observed counts.

Steps 3, 4, and 5: *p*-value = .004. With Table A.5, .001< *p*-value < .005. Reject the null hypothesis. There is a statistically significant relationship between own eye color and eye color attracted to for the population of college students represented by this sample.

```
┌──────────────────────────────────────────────────────────────────┐
│                    Output for Exercise 15.52b                      │
│ Rows: Own        Columns: Attracted to                             │
│                                                                    │
│             Brown      Blue      HazGr        All                  │
│                                                                    │
│   Brown       30         22        19          71                  │
│             20.56      30.65     19.79       71.00                 │
│                                                                    │
│   Blue        15         37        14          66                  │
│             19.11      28.49     18.39       66.00                 │
│                                                                    │
│   HazGr        8         20        18          46                  │
│             13.32      19.86     12.82       46.00                 │
│                                                                    │
│   All         53         79        51         183                  │
│             53.00      79.00     51.00      183.00                 │
│              --         --         --          --                  │
│ Chi-Sq =   4.331 +    2.441 +   0.031 +                            │
│            0.886 +    2.541 +   1.049 +                            │
│            2.126 +    0.001 +   2.093 = 15.500                     │
│ DF = 4, P-Value = 0.004                                            │
└──────────────────────────────────────────────────────────────────┘
```

c. The "contributions" to the chi-square statistic are shown in the calculation of the statistic at the bottom of the output. The largest two contributions are brown attracted to brown (4.331) and blue attracted to blue (2.541). In both cases, the observed count is much higher than the expected count. People appear to be attracted to people with their own eye colors more often than would be expected if the two variables were not related.

15.54 *Tip:* Use the technical note on page 638 of the text for guidance.
a. Homogeneity. The issue is whether the distribution of responses for satisfaction is the same for the two years. The null and alternative hypotheses are:

$\quad$ H_0: Satisfaction with K-12 was the same for the populations of school parents in 1999 and 2000
$\quad$ H_a: Satisfaction with K-12 differed for the populations of school parents in 1999 and 2000

CHAPTER 16
SELECTED SOLUTIONS

16.1   *Tip*: One-way analysis of variance is appropriate when the response variable is quantitative and is measured for two or more independent groups, or when respondents can be categorized into two or more separate groups on the basis of another (categorical) variable. (The necessary data conditions given on page 673 must also be checked.) It is not appropriate if the same individuals are measured across categories, in which case a method called *repeated measures* analysis of variance is used.

a. Appropriate. The response variable is quantitative and this is a comparison of independent groups.
d. Not appropriate. It's not a comparison of independent groups. There was only one group and all individuals listened to all five songs.

16.2   **a.** *Tip*: The null and alternative hypotheses for comparing population means are discussed on pages 669-670.
The null hypothesis was that the mean body mass is the same for the three age group populations. Using symbols, this would be written as $H_0: \mu_1 = \mu_2 = \mu_3$
b. The *p*-value is small, below the usual .05 standard for significance, so it can be concluded that mean body mass is not the same for the three age group populations.

Tip: This is not the same as saying that the means for the three age groups all differ from each other.

16.5   **a.** *Tip:* Study Example 16.6 on pages 677-678 for guidance.

The interval for the difference in population mean heights in the two seat locations is 1.018 to 4.362. The interval does not include 0, so it is evidence that the population means are not the same.

16.6   **a.** *Tip:* The use of Table A.4 is discussed on page 675 of the text.
The critical value found in Table A.4 is 3.89. We can reject the null hypothesis because the *F*-statistic, 6.27, is greater than the critical value, 3.89.

16.8   *Tip:* This problem is similar to Example 16.6 on pages 677-678.
a. The population mean for the 60+ age group is different from the population means for the middle two age groups. (The confidence intervals for the differences do not include 0.) The population mean for the youngest age group is also different from the population means for the middle two age groups. We cannot conclude a difference between population means for the youngest and oldest age groups, and we cannot conclude a difference between the population means for the two middle age groups.

16.89 continued:

b. There is 95% confidence that all six intervals capture the corresponding population parameters. And, there is a 100%–95% = 5% chance that at least one of the six intervals does not capture the corresponding population parameter. (In this situation, a parameter is a difference in population means.)

16.9　**b.** The necessary conditions are present. Variation is about the same for each lab, there are no extreme outliers and there is not extreme skewness. (It may appear from the boxplots that data for labs 1, 3 and 5 are skewed, but remember that these plots are based on only 11 observations each.)

16.10　**a.** *Tip:* The null and alternative hypotheses for comparing population means are discussed on pages 669-670.
The null hypothesis is that the population mean is the same for all five labs. The population is the population of all measurements that might ever be made by these labs on this type of fabric. This is written using notation as
$$H_0: \mu_1 = \mu_2 = \mu_3 = \mu_4 = \mu_5.$$
The alternative hypothesis is that the population mean is not the same for all labs. This can be written as H_a: not all μ_i are the same.
b. Yes, there is a statistically significant difference. $F = 4.53$, p-value = .003. The difference is statistically significant because the p-value is less than .05.
c. Show the *p*-value as the area to the right of 4.53 under a skewed curve. The sketch should be similar to Figure 16.4 on page 676 of the text. Notice that the *p*-value is small, so the area to the right of $F = 4.53$ will be small.
d. The confidence interval for the mean for lab 4 does not overlap with those for labs 2 and 5. That information, combined with the fact that the null hypothesis of equal means was rejected, makes it reasonable to conclude that the mean for lab 4 is significantly lower than the means for labs 2 and 5. The other comparisons are more difficult to judge.

16.12　The completed table is:

Source	DF	SS	MS	F
Between groups	5	40	8	1.333
Error	10	60	6	
Total	15	100		

The general relationships used are: MS = SS/df, F = MS Between/MS Error, and the total *df* and total SS are the totals of the corresponding quantities for Between and Error

16.14　**c.** $MSE = \dfrac{SSE}{df} = \dfrac{1043}{150} = 6.953$; $s_p = \sqrt{MSE} = \sqrt{6.953} = 2.637$.

16.17 **a.** The completed table is:

Source	DF	SS	MS	F	P
Caffeine	2	61.40	30.70	6.18	.006
Error	27	134.10	4.97		
Total	29	195.50			

In the Caffeine row, df $= k-1 = 3-1 = 2$ and $MS = SS/df = 61.40/2 = 30.70$
In the Error row, df $= N-k = 30-3 = 27$ and $MS = SS/df = 134.10/27 = 4.97$.

Equivalently, the df and the SS can be determined by subtracting the df and SS for Caffeine from the corresponding values for Total.

Finally, $F = \dfrac{MS\,Caffeine}{MSE} = \dfrac{30.70}{4.97} = 6.18$

b. $s_p = \sqrt{MSE} = \sqrt{4.97} = 2.23$. This statistic estimates the population standard deviation of the response variable (for any of the caffeine amounts).

c. The p-value is small so we can conclude that the population mean finger taps are not the same for the three caffeine amounts.

Tip: Remember to state the conclusions so that they are about the populations (not the samples).

16.18 *Tip:* See the formula in the box on page 684 of the text. Example 16.10 on page 684 is similar to this exercise.

Each interval has the form $\bar{x}_i \pm t^* \dfrac{s_p}{\sqrt{n_i}}$ which in this case is $\bar{x}_i \pm 2.01 \dfrac{0.4058}{\sqrt{11}}$, or

$\bar{x}_i \pm 0.246$. Use Table A.2 to find the multiplier. The degrees of freedom are the Error df $= 50$.
The five intervals are: lab 1, 3.3364 ± 0.246; lab 2, 3.6 ± 0.246; lab 3, 3.3 ± 0.246; lab 4, 3.0 ± 0.246; lab 5, 3.6455 ± 0.246

16.19 *Tip:* For parts (b) and (c) see the formulas in the summary table on page 682.

b. $MS\,Groups = \dfrac{SS\,Groups}{k-1} = \dfrac{150}{4-1} = 50$ and $MSE = \dfrac{SSE}{N-k} = \dfrac{200}{24-4} = 10$.

So, $F = \dfrac{MS\,Groups}{MSE} = \dfrac{50}{10} = 5$.

c. df $= 3$ and 20. There are $k = 4$ groups and $N = 24$ total observations so the calculations are $k-1 = 4-1 = 3$ and $N-k = 24-4 = 20$.

16.21   *Tip:* See the summary table on page 682 for formulas. For part (d), note that you can find SSE by subtracting SS Groups from SSTO. This comes from the relationship SSTO = SS Groups + SSE.

  a. $\bar{x} = 8$, $\bar{x}_1 = 4$, $\bar{x}_2 = 11$, $\bar{x}_3 = 9$.

  b. $SS\ Groups = \sum n_i (\bar{x}_i - \bar{x})^2 = 3(4-8)^2 + 3(11-8)^2 + 3(9-8)^2 = 48 + 27 + 3 = 78$

  c. $SS\ Total = \sum (x_{ij} - \bar{x})^2 =$
  $(6-8)^2 + (4-8)^2 + (2-8)^2 + (10-8)^2 + (14-8)^2 + (9-8)^2 + (9-8)^2 + (12-8)^2 + (6-8)^2 = 118$

  d. $SSE = SS\ Total - SS\ Groups = 118 - 78 = 40$.

16.23   **a.** H_0: median ratings are the same for the four populations of hometown types
      H_a: population medians are not all the same
  Tip: See page 686 for a discussion of writing hypotheses about population medians..

16.25   **a.** Ordinal because an arbitrary rating scale was used.

16.27   *Tip:* This is similar to Examples 16.11 and 16.12 on pages 685 and 687 of the text.

  a. H_0: median testosterone levels are the same for the three populations of occupational groups
      H_a: population medians are not all the same
  b. Decide in favor of the alternative hypothesis (*p*-value = .002). The population median testosterone level differs for at least one of the occupational groups.

16.28   **a.** Gender and Greek membership (yes or no) are interacting variables. The size of the mean difference in mean hours spent studying for Greeks versus non-Greeks depends upon gender.

16.30   **a.** Males (described by the upper line in the graph).
  b. For both males and females, the mean rating is clearly lower for "Big city" than for the other three types of hometown.

  c. There probably is not a significant interaction (either statistically or in practical terms). The difference between males and females is about the same for each hometown type. Equivalently, the pattern of differences among the four hometown types is about the same for each sex.

16.33   *Tip:* There is interaction between two categorical variables if the differences in the mean responses across categories of one of them depend on the category of the other one. For an example, see the "Tip" given in the solution for Exercise 16.40.
  a. The amount of difference between mean GPA of men and women would depend upon seat location.
  b. The amount of difference between mean GPA of men and women would be the same in each seat location.

16.35 **b.** As the bacteria amount increases, the difference in mean rot for 10°C and 16°C increases as well. Notice in the plot that the line for high bacteria has a steeper slope than the line for low bacteria.

16.38 **a.** The null hypothesis is that the population mean violent behavior scores for students represented by the sample is the same for the five television watching groups. The alternative hypothesis is that the mean violent behavior scores are not the same for all five groups. These hypotheses are written as

H_0: $\mu_1 = \mu_2 = \mu_3 = \mu_4 = \mu_5$

H_a: not all μ_i are the same.

Tip: Remember to state hypotheses using the notation for population parameters, not the sample statistics. A discussion of hypotheses for comparing means is on pages 669-670.

b. The intended population is all school children of this age in the U.S although this could be questioned because the sample includes children only from Ohio.
c. Decide in favor of H_a because the p-value is less than .05..The conclusion is that not all the population means are the same.
d. The cause and effect might go in the other direction. Perhaps children prone to more violent behaviors also like to watch more television. This was an observational study, and there are many other possibilities for confounding variables, such as lack of parental attention.

16.40 There may be an interaction. The difference between boys and girls is largest in the <1 hour of television group and smallest in the 6+ hours of television group.

Tip: In this example, the difference in mean violent behavior scores between boys and girls depends on the category of "Hours of daily television watching" so there appears to be an interaction. There is interaction between two categorical variables if the differences in the mean responses across categories of one of them depend on the category of the other one.

16.43 *Tip:* On page, 681, you will see the relevant formulas.

$$SSE = \sum (n_i - 1)^2 \, s_i^2 = (162-1)(7.15)^2 + (67-1)(6.43)^2 + (105-1)(6.45)^2 \approx 15,286$$

$$MSE = \frac{SSE}{N-k} = \frac{15286}{334-3} = 46.18$$

$$s_p = \sqrt{MSE} = \sqrt{46.18} = 6.796$$

16.44 Regression methods could be used. Both variables are quantitative. An advantage would be that regression provides an estimate of the relationship between caffeine amount and mean tapping speed.

CHAPTER 17
SELECTED SOLUTIONS

17.1   **Study #1**: Explanatory variable is "treatment" (taking calcium or placebo) and the response variable is blood pressure.
Study #2: Explanatory variable is amount of walking per day and the response variable is mortality during 12 years (lived or died).
Study #3: Explanatory variable is daily tea consumption and the response variable is conception (conceived or not).

17.4   Study #3 apparently was an observational study. The article says that that the researchers asked the women to "record information concerning their daily dietary intake" so the investigators only observed tea consumption. The researchers did not assign amounts of tea drinking to the women. Because this is an observational study, the headline is not justified (see Rule for Concluding Cause and Effect on page 706). There may be confounding variables that contribute to the higher odds of conception for those who drank more tea.

17.6   *Tip:* Remember from Chapter 4 (page 120) that a confounding variable is one that both *affects the response variable* and also *is related to the explanatory variable*. In this example, a confounding variable is one that is related to whether or not someone drinks tea, and also affects the odds of conception.

The example given will differ for each student, but examples should fit the definition of a confounding variable, found on page 120. An example: Coffee drinking habits may be a confounding factor. People who don't drink coffee may be more likely to drink tea and may also be more likely to conceive for other reasons. Coffee drinking may be *related* to tea drinking and might also *affect* the odds of conception. Another example: Smoking or not may be a confounding factor. Perhaps tea drinkers are less likely to be smokers so the differences in odds of conception could be due to differences in smoking habits.

17.9   Yes, the results probably can be applied to a larger population. We are not told who was in the sample, but there is no indication that it was an unrepresentative group with regard to diet (and tea drinking) and conception. The Fundamental Rule for Using Data for Inference probably holds for the question of interest here.

Tip: Remember that the Fundamental Rule for Using Data for Inference requires that the sample be representative of a population *for the question of interest*. All we are told about the sample in this study is that the women were trying to conceive. Presumably there is nothing about this sample that would make them different from other women who are trying to conceive, so it is reasonable to conclude that the relationship between tea drinking and conception holds for the population of such women.

17.12　**a.** "Significance" most likely refers to statistical significance. The article described a research paper published in the American Journal of Public Health, and in that type of context the word "significance" usually has to do with the results of statistical significance tests.

The null hypothesis is that energy and fat intake are not related to tea consumption. A one-sided alternative hypothesis consistent with the research conclusion is that energy and fat intake increase as tea consumption increases. A two-sided alternative hypothesis is that energy and fat intake are related to tea consumption.

b. Energy and fat intake are confounding variables. (See the definition of confounding variables on page 120.) They are related to the explanatory variable (tea consumption) and may possibly affect the response variable (odds of conception).

Tip: An interacting variable would be one for which the relationship between tea drinking and conception differed depending on this additional variable, and we are not told that was the case for energy and fat intake. For instance, suppose that some women in both groups smoked, and that the relationship between tea drinking and conception was stronger for smokers than for non-smokers. Then smoking would be an interacting variable.

17.13　**a.** An association was observed in the sample, but it was not strong enough to be statistically significant for the sample size used.

17.15　**a.** Amount walked per day (less than one mile, between one and two miles, more than two miles) and whether the man died during the study (yes, no).

17.18　**a.** No, the entire population already has been measured.

b. Yes, if we assume that the mechanism causing geyser eruptions stays the same over time it would be reasonable to use data from these two weeks to represent the larger population of all eruptions (ever) of the Old Faithful geyser.

Tip: There are two reasons why a dataset may not be able to be extended to a larger population. One reason, as represented by part (a), is that the entire population of interest is *already* included in the dataset. In that case, statistical inference is not needed. The second reason is that the Fundamental Rule for Using Data for Inference may not hold. There may not be any larger group that is represented by the sample for the question of interest. An example of this is an Internet poll in which people who visit a certain website are asked to register their opinions on some issue. The only people represented by that sample are the people who responded.

SUPPLEMENTAL TOPIC 1
SELECTED SOLUTIONS

S1.2   Yes, X is a hypergeometric random variable with $N = 250$, $n = 5$, $a = 100$.

S1.5 $N = 100$, $n = 12$, $a = 40$.

S1.6 X is an integer between 0 and the smaller of (a, n), so in this case it's an integer between 0 and 12.

S1.9 X = number of winning numbers between 1 and 31; X is a hypergeometric random variable with $N = 51$, $n = 6$ and $a = 31$. The questions asks for $P(X = 6) =$

$$\frac{\dfrac{a!}{k!(a-k)!}\dfrac{b!}{(n-k)!(b-n+k)!}}{\dfrac{N!}{n!(N-n)!}} = \frac{\dfrac{31!}{6!(31-6)!}\dfrac{20!}{(6-6)!(20-6+6)!}}{\dfrac{51!}{6!(51-6)!}} = .0409$$

S1.13   **c.** X is a binomial random variable. $\mu = np = (200)(.20) = 40$ and $\sigma = \sqrt{np(1-p)} =$ $\sqrt{100(.2)(.8)} = 5.66$.

d. X is a hypergeometric random variable. $\mu = np = (100)(.2) = 20$ and $\sigma =$

$$\sqrt{np(1-p)\frac{(N-n)}{(N-1)}} = \sqrt{100(.2)(.8)\frac{(200-100)}{(200-1)}} = 2.836.$$

S1.16 $P(X=0) = \dfrac{\mu^k e^{-\mu}}{k!} = \dfrac{5^0 e^{-5}}{0!} = e^{-5} = .0067.$

S1.19 $P(X \ge 20) = 1 - P(X \le 19) = 1 - .9965 = .0035.$

S1.22   **a.** $\mu = 30 \times 2 = 60.$

S1.23   **a.** Mean = variance = 4, standard deviation = 2.

S1.24   **a.** $e^{-4} = .0183$.

S1.27   **a.** $n = 200, p = .01$.

b. X is approximately a Poisson random variable with $\mu = np = 2$, so the Poisson formula can be used to find probabilities related to X.

c. $P(X = 0) = (.99)^{200} = .1340$.

d. Approximate $P(X = 0) = e^{-2} = .1353$. The answers are very similar. There is about a 13.5% chance of no defective candies in a bag.

S1.31   Mean $= np_i = 30(1/6) = 5$, variance $= np_i(1 - p_i) = 30(1/6)(5/6) = 4.167$.

S1.34   Yes, this is a multinomial experiment. There are 1000 "trials" with 3 possible outcomes on each one and the outcomes are independent from one person to the next.

SUPPLEMENTAL TOPIC 2
SELECTED SOLUTIONS

S2.1 **a.** Yes, a sign test can be done. This is a question about the median of a single sample. H_0: median pulse = 72 (η = 72) versus H_a: median pulse greater than 72 (η > 72).

S2.4 **b.** Sample median = \$355. To find this "by hand," first write the data in order. The median is the mean of the 8th and 9th data values in the ordered sample.
c. S^+ = 4, S^- = 12, n_u = 16. **Tip:** S^+ is the number of data values greater than \$400, while S^- is the number of data values less than \$400.
d. Find $P(X \le 4)$ in a binomial distribution with n = 16 and p = .5.

Tip: We want to see how unusual it would be that S+ would be 4 or less. If the median really were less than \$400 (the alternative hypothesis), then we might see relatively few observations greater than \$400.

e. Exact p-value found using binomial is .0384. Reject the null hypothesis; conclude median amount was less than \$400. Excel, for instance, could be used to find this.

Using normal approximation, p-value = .0228. The z-statistic is $z = \dfrac{4 - (16/2)}{\sqrt{16/4}} = -2$.

If the continuity correction is used, z = −1.75 and the p-value is .0401.

S2.7 **a.** H_0: Distribution of pulse rates is same for populations of those who exercise and do not exercise
H_a: Pulse rates tend to be greater than for those who do not exercise (or lower for those who do)
b. W = 103.5 (sum of ranks for those who do not). Ranks in same order as data are:

Do not	14	19.5	11	14	5.5	19.5	17	3				
Exercise	5.5	14	3	7	16	9	3	1	9	18	12	9

c. $\mu_W = 8\dfrac{1+20}{2} = 84$, $\sigma_W = \sqrt{\dfrac{8(12)(8+12+1)}{12}} = 12.96$.

d. $z = \dfrac{103.5 - 84}{12.96} = 1.50$, p-value = $P(Z \ge 1.50)$ = .0668. With continuity correction, z = 1.466 and p-value = .0713.
e. Cannot reject the null hypothesis, so cannot say that those who do not exercise tend to have higher pulse rates.

S2.9 There's an obvious outlier in the diet plan group (value =35). With such a large outlier, procedures that analyze means aren't appropriate.

S2.14 **a.** $T^+ = 7.5 + 15 + 3 + 1 = 26.5$. Details are as follows.

x	250	450	300	279	360	300	670	50
+ or −	−	+	−	−	−	−	+	−
$\lvert x-400 \rvert$	150	50	100	121	40	100	270	350
Rank	13	7.5	9.5	11	5.5	9.5	15	7.5

x	430	350	220	420	375	275	360	365
+ or −	+	−	−	+	−	−	−	−
$\lvert x-400 \rvert$	30	50	180	20	25	125	40	35
Rank	3	7.5	14	1	2	12	5.5	4

b. $z = \dfrac{26.5-68}{19.339} = -2.12$ where $\mu_T = \dfrac{16(17)}{4} = 68$;

$\sigma_T = \sqrt{\dfrac{16(17)(2\times16+1)}{24}} = 19.339$.

c. p-value = $P(Z<-2.12) = .17$. Reject the null hypothesis. Conclude that median amount spent in population is less than \$400.

Tip: The p-value can be found using Table A.1 of the text.

S2.18   **c.** There are two issues. First, the sample size is not large so it's possible a type 2 error was made. Second, a conclusion that the median difference is 0 doesn't mean that the lengths are identical for all people. As a hypothetical example, suppose the forearm was 10 cm longer than the foot for one-half of the population and the foot was 10 cm longer than the forearm in the other half. The median difference would be 0, but the lengths would be unequal for all individuals.

S2.19   **a.** $\overline{R}_1 = 10, \overline{R}_2 = 12.8333, \overline{R}_3 = 5.6667$. Ranks are:

Method 1:	4	6.5	9.5	12	13	15
Method 2:	8	9.5	11	14	16.5	18
Method 3:	1	2	3	5	6.5	16.5

b. $H \approx 5.49$. Calculation is

$$\frac{12}{18(18+1)}\left[6(10-9.5)^2 + 6(12.8333-9.5)^2 + 6(5.6667-9.5)^2\right].$$

S2.21   **a.** H_0: Distribution of weekly times exercising is the same for each reason
H_a: Weekly times exercising tends to be larger for at least one reason than for other reasons.

SUPPLEMENTAL TOPIC 3
SELECTED SOLUTIONS

S3.4   The conditions appear to be met for these data. This is more or less a horizontal band of points with no obvious pattern, as it should be if the conditions are met. While there are one or two points that are separated from the others, they are not obviously outliers because the residuals for the points are not clearly greater than for other points.

S3.6   **a.** $\hat{y}_i = 20.8 - 0.415(49) + 1.24(56) = 69.905$.

            b. $e_i = y_i - \hat{y}_i = 64 - 69.905 = -5.905$.

S3.8   This coefficient corresponds to the average height of males students whose mothers and fathers have height = 0. These, of course, are impossible heights.

S3.9   0.539 inches (or 0.53897). This is the value of b_2. By holding mother's height constant, we are able to interpret the coefficient multiplying father's height as a slope. Remember that a slope tells us how much mean y changes when x changes by one unit.

S3.10   **a.** p-value = .031. This is less than .05, so with the .05 significance level, we can reject the null hypothesis. We can conclude that student height and mother's height are related variables.

            b. $t = \dfrac{0.19294}{0.08777} = 2.20$. This is calculated as t = sample coefficient / standard error.

S3.15   **a.** H_0: $\beta_1 = \beta_2 = 0$ versus H_a: At least one of β_1 and β_2 is $\neq 0$.

            b. Reject the null hypothesis ($F = 15.19$, p-value = .000). Conclude that left arm length is related to at least one of left foot length and right foot length.

S3.17   **a.** $s = 1.796$ cm. Roughly, the average absolute size of the deviations between actual and predicted arm lengths is about 1.796 cm.

            b. $R^2 = 36.9\%$. The two foot length variables explain 36.9% of the variation among arm lengths.

S3.18   **a.** $b_0 = 119.58$, $b_1 = 0.9636$, $b_2 = -1.0903$, $b_3 = 2.6295$, $b_4 = -1.2080$, $b_5 = -0.6413$

S3.21   **a.** $y_i = \beta_0 + \beta_1 x_{i1} + \beta_2 x_{i2} + \varepsilon_i$, where we assume that ε_i are normally distributed with mean 0 and standard deviation σ.

S3.23 **a.** The plots are shown below. There is an outlier in the plot of Weight versus Neck. Both plots have more or less a linear pattern.

Figure for Exercise S3.23a

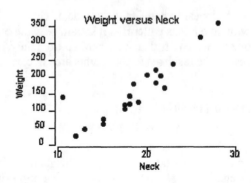

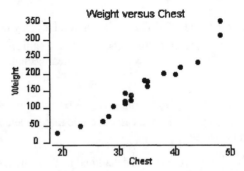

b. Regression equation is   Weight = − 226.07 + 8.758 Neck + 6.3386 Chest

c. Both explanatory variables are statistically significant predictors. For *Neck*, *p*-value = 0.034, and for *Chest*, *p*-value = 0.005. The Minitab output follows.

Output for Exercise S3.23c				
Predictor	Coef	SE Coef	T	P
Constant	-226.07	20.61	-10.97	0.000
Neck	8.758	3.745	2.34	0.034
Chest	6.386	1.949	3.28	0.005

d. R^2 = 96.4%. Neck and chest measurements explain 96.4 of the variation among weights.

SUPPLEMENTAL TOPIC 4
SELECTED SOLUTIONS

S4.1   **a.** Response variable is weight loss after two months. Factor A is whether the person smokes or not, $a = 2$. Factor B is the exercise program, $b = 3$.

S4.5   **a.** μ_{12} = mean for 18-21 non-coffee drinkers = 8.0 hours.
b. $\mu_{..}$ = mean for all groups = 28.4/4 = 7.1 hours.
c. $\mu_{1.}$ = mean for 18-21 year olds = 7.0 hours, $\mu_{2.}$ = mean for over 21 year olds = 7.2 hours
d. $\mu_{.1}$ = mean for coffee drinkers = 6.5 hours; $\mu_{.2}$ = mean for non-coffee drinkers = 7.7 hours

S4.8 $\mu_{11} = \mu_{..} + \alpha_1 + \beta_1 + \alpha\beta_{11} = 7.1 - 0.1 - 0.6 - 0.4 = 6.0$ hours, $\mu_{12} = \mu_{..} + \alpha_1 + \beta_2 + \alpha\beta_{12}$ $= 7.1 - 0.1 + 0.6 + 0.4 = 8.0$ hours, $\mu_{21} = \mu_{..} + \alpha_2 + \beta_1 + \alpha\beta_{21} = 7.1 + 0.1 - 0.6 + 0.4 =$ 7.0 hours, $\mu_{22} = \mu_{..} + \alpha_2 + \beta_2 + \alpha\beta_{22} = 7.1 + 0.1 + 0.6 - 0.4 = 7.4$ hours.

S4.10   **a.** Yes. Mean DDT appears to be much higher in the Arctic region than in the U.S. or Canada.

S4.11   **a.** H_0: The population mean DDT levels in falcons are the same in the Artic, the U.S. and Canada.
H_a: For at least one of the 3 sites the population mean DDT level is different.

S4.12   **a.** p-value = .000, reject the null hypothesis, conclude that mean DDT levels differ across sites.

S4.14   For Factor A, F = 8892.70/3.44 = 2585.1; for Factor B, F = 860.59/3.44 = 250.2, for the interaction, F = 4.43/3.44 = 1.29. Note that these differ slightly from the F values given by Minitab because the mean squares were rounded to 2 decimal places when they were printed, but were used with many more decimal places in the computer calculations of the F values.

S4.17   **c.** H_0: The difference in mean commute times for the three routes is the same across days.
H_a: The difference in mean commute times for the three routes depends on the day.

S4.18   **c.** $F = 8.40$, df = (4, 81). From Table A.4, p-value < .01 because 8.40 < 3.56. Reject H_0. Conclude that there is an interaction, so the difference in mean commute times for the routes depends on the day of the week category.

S4.22   **a.** 1, based on subtracting the given df values from the total value of 53.
b. 225, found as SS/df = 450/2.
c. 840 because df = 1.

S4.24 **a.** From knowing df = 2, a = 3.

S4.25 **c.** Degrees of freedom for groups = Total df – Error df = 53 – 48 = 5. Also, there are 6 groups so df = 6 – 1 = 5.
d. Degrees of freedom for error is the same, 48.

SUPPLEMENTAL TOPIC 5
SELECTED SOLUTIONS

S5.4 **a.** This would be a good idea. In cases where the response is ambiguous, Janet could frame the response to conform to her desired outcome based on which group she knew they had been in.

S5.7 Because the intervals overlap, it is not clear which component is better, so Marilyn should not report a firm conclusion. Notice that one of the intervals has a higher center but is more spread out than the other one. Assuming the same number of components was tested for each method, this would mean that one method may produce components that last slightly longer on average, but the other one has more consistent results. She might want to report this observation.

S5.10 This condition was not met. The 9-year-old girl was in immediate proximity with the practitioners, and she knew which hand she was hovering over with her hand.

S5.13 The main problem is that participants were deceived into thinking they were hurting others. But there would have been no way to conduct the experiment if they had been told the truth.

S5.17 The problem is that they chose the confidence level to present the outcome they desired. They should have reported the standard 95% confidence interval.

S5.19 The complaint raised by the letter is that the study was not measuring what it purported to measure.

Ship To:

Daniel Francoeur
80 Westmont St
West Hartford, CT 06117-2927 USA

Ship From:

TXTBOOKSNOW.COM-HALF
8950 W PALMER ST
RIVER GROVE, IL 60171

Date: 01/04/2011

SKU	Qty	Condition	Title
5196161U	1	Used	Mind on Statistics (SSM)
			3 9780495018070 Refund Eligible Through= 2/7/2011

Return Information (cut and attach to the outside of return shipment)

TXTBOOKSNOW.COM-HALF
8950 W PALMER ST
RIVER GROVE, IL 60171

(Attn: Returns)

Order #: 63137714101-34191945283

	Price	Total
	$ 23.44	$ 23.44

DF70805

Order #: 63137714101-34191945283

Sub Total	$	23.44
Shipping & Handling	$	3.49
Sales Tax	$	0.00
Order Total	**$**	**26.93**

Order #: 63137714101-34191945283

Refund Policy: All items must be returned within 30 days of receipt. Pack your book securely, so it will arrive back to us in its original condition. To avoid delays, please use the return section and label provided with your original packing slip to identify your return. Be sure to include a return reason. For your protection, we suggest using a traceable, insured shipping service (UPS or Insured Parcel Post). We are not responsible for lost or damaged returns. Item(s) returned must be received in the original condition as sold and including all additional materials such as CDs, workbooks, etc. We will initiate a refund of your purchase price including applicable taxes within 5 business days of receipt. Shipping charges will not be refunded unless we have committed an error with your order. If there is an error with your order or the item is not received in the condition as purchased, please contact us immediately for return assistance.

Reason for Refund/Return:
Condition   Incorrect Item Received   Incorrect Item Ordered   Dropped Class   Purchased Elsewhere   Other

Contact Us: For customer service, email us at customerservice@textbooksNow.com.

Page 1 of 1